jackie cassada

shadows on the hill

a
changeling: the dreaming
novel

White Wolf
Publishing

shadows on the hill	*jackie cassada*
cover illustration	*joshua gabriel timbrook*
book design & layout	*larry friedman*

White Wolf Publishing
780 Park North Boulevard
Suite 100
Clarkston, GA 30021

PRINTED IN CANADA

To the memory of Steve Glimpse

Special thanks to Ian Lemke, for his generous support and welcome advice; to Erin Kelly, for thinking of ways to make this a better story; to Nicky Rea and Carla Hollar, for their encourgement and friendship; to Steve and Billie Glimpse, for sharing their stories of Hawaii with me; and to my family, for believing in me.

> For a long time I lived in a cage;
> Now I have returned.
> For one must return
> To fulfill one's nature.
> —T'ao Ch'ien,
>
> "Once More Fields and Gardens"

> Between the idea
> And the reality
> Between the motion
> And the act
> Falls the Shadow
> —T. S. Eliot,
> "The Hollow Men"

part

o n e

4

prelude

"So far away," the dark-haired man murmured. His slender companion nodded knowingly.

"Until we are strong enough to make our move, such remoteness is necessary," she said.

He caught her hand in his and lifted it to his lips. Trapping her fingers, he increased the pressure of his grip until she winced with pain. His dark eyes glistened as he looked at her, head bowed over her pinioned hand.

"I think that you forget to whom you speak, *Lady* Glynnis," he said, continuing to squeeze her fingers until her knuckles became ghostly points of white against the reddened skin. "I have a title that has not been used in a very long time."

Lady Glynnis clenched her jaws, refusing to succumb to the tears that stung her eyes. For years, she had dedicated her every action to freeing this man from the timeless realm in which he had been imprisoned—a punishment for his acts of rebellion against the rulers of Arcadia. Now that he had escaped that prison of carefully wrought enchantments and walked freely in the mortal world, clothed in the body she had procured for him, she had hoped for something more than the subservient role into which he had cast her.

Her pride warred briefly with her patience, but the long period of preparation had schooled her to a discipline rarely found among the Unseelie fae. In familiarity with the ways of the mortal realm, she was his superior. Since his entry into the world, he had relied on her advice to ease his adjustment to the harshness of life outside the Dreaming. He had been long without courtiers or servants, she reminded herself. Later, after he had tired of testing and tormenting her with his newfound power, there would be time to wrest from him an acknowledgement of her own deserved position.

Allowing herself a gasp that signified her submission to him, she dropped to her knees and bowed her head.

"Forgive me, my Lord Prince," she whispered, pain inflecting her voice with urgency and sincerity. "I shall not fail again in my respect for you."

With agonizing slowness, Yrtalien, the Forsworn Prince of House Ailil, released his crushing grip on Glynnis' tortured fingers until he was once again merely clasping her hand in true courtly fashion.

She dared not rise without his permission, so she remained kneeling before him, her downcast eyes staring at the high polish of his leather boots. Finally he laughed softly and pulled her to her feet. Still holding her hand, Yrtalien drew her into an embrace that spoke of dominion more than affection. Pressed against his body, she steeled herself to motionlessness within the prison of his muscled arms. He brought his lips close to her ear.

"Let us always understand each other," he breathed. "I am your lord, your prince, and your master."

chapter

one

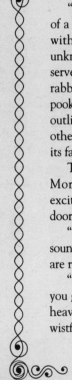

"So how could he just vanish without a trace?" Edmund wondered. The young redcap balanced precariously on his tipped-back chair, his heels resting on the round table near the rear of the Toybox Coffee Shop. Beside him, Valmont toyed with the remains of his cafe latte. The handsome eshu appeared to be lost in thought, his face an onyx mask.

"The fireworks that accompanied the opening of the gate left us little opportunity to observe the details of his entry," he murmured.

"Besides, we were expecting the sudden appearance of a visitor from beyond, so why would we even bother with little details like his hasty departure for parts unknown?" Rasputin sat atop the ornate toy chest that served as the centerpiece of the coffee shop. His velvety rabbitlike ears drooped nearly to his shoulders. The pooka's fingers nervously traced the chest's carved surface, outlining the myriad toy soldiers, carousel animals and other whimsical figures that gave the old steamer trunk its fanciful facade.

The door to the coffee shop opened, admitting Morgan, her face flushed with barely contained excitement. Behind her, his bulk momentarily filling the doorway, followed Tor.

"I've been Christmas shopping," Morgan said, sounding pleased with herself. "Only some of the presents are really Yuletide gifts."

"Like there's a difference," Edmund sneered. "I hope you got me something to eat," he said, hoping that the heavy layer of disdain in his voice would conceal the wistfulness of his words.

"What makes you think I'd get *you* anything?" Morgan retorted.

"That's right, Edmund," Rasputin said, sliding off the toy chest and crossing the room to join the others at the table. "Do you think that just because you are one of Baroness Morgania's oathmates, she should include you in her gift-giving?" The pooka pulled up a chair between Morgan and Valmont, forcing the childling to slide her own chair closer to Edmund's.

"I got something for everyone," Morgan admitted. She glared at Edmund.

"Well don't expect me to return the favor," the redcap said. "You need money to buy shit, and I don't have any."

"Lack of funds has never proven a serious barrier to anyone who's truly determined," Valmont observed quietly. "There are many kinds of gifts, and not all of them are purchased, though they all have their price."

"That's entirely too deep for me." The faces at the table turned to see the familiar form of Chip Fizzlewig, the proprietor of the Toybox. Small, plump and perpetually frazzled, the crusty boggan approached the group and deposited a platter of fresh-baked cinnamon and oatmeal muffins in the center of the table. Almost immediately, Edmund grabbed a handful.

"It's an old eshu saying," Valmont replied mildly, a slight upturning of the corners of his mouth the only hint that he might be speaking less than the truth.

"I'd heard that," Rasputin said, helping himself to a muffin.

"Where's Leigh?" Morgan asked suddenly, looking around the room. "I thought she'd be here by now. It's not like her to miss our weekly meetings."

"Maybe she had to pull a double shift," Tor said. "Waitressing doesn't exactly qualify as a nine-to-five job."

"This sure is some quest," Edmund mumbled, his mouth full of muffin. "All we've done is sit around on our butts and pat ourselves on the back 'cause we found a gateway to who-knows-where in Golden Gate Park and let some weird dude through who didn't even stop long enough to say 'thanks' before he disappeared." He swallowed audibly. "Oh, yeah," he continued. "And some of us went shopping."

Morgan turned her head to one side, ignoring Edmund's pointed reference.

As the afternoon turned into early evening, the coffee shop began to fill with members of San Francisco's changeling community. Many of the local Kithain stopped by the friends' table to chat for a few minutes before forming their own small groups either at Fizzlewig's polished mahogany bar or at one of the other tables and booths which filled the dining room.

"How come we're so popular all of a sudden?" Edmund had asked after his first experience with the parade of visitors to the group's table. "Most of those people never paid any attention to me before."

"You're a celebrity, now," Valmont had said. "Word spreads quickly in a community of Kithain, and our deeds have achieved a certain notoriety. We are touched by destiny, so they think, and proximity to us means that, in a way, they, too, are touched."

"I'll say we're touched," Edmund had replied. Now, after nearly four weeks, he had gotten used to the constant interruption.

A group of childlings clustered, as usual, near the toy chest. Now that the word had spread that the chest contained a legendary army of chimerical creatures, the carved chest elicited an even greater fascination for the young Kithain than it had previously. Many of them were present when the now-exiled satyr Malacar had used the Eye of Opening to solve the intricate puzzle lock on the chest's lid. They remembered the explosion of chimerical toys-come-to-life that burst from the chest and scattered throughout the city, and many of them hoped for a repeat performance.

"There she is!" Morgan's voice, a high-pitched childish soprano, pierced through the growing din of background conversations and clanking glasses. She pointed to the front of the coffee shop, where Leigh was making her way toward her friends, stopping now and then to speak to someone who caught her attention.

Valmont regarded her progress with open admiration. As one of the sidhe, Leigh moved with the natural grace of her noble kith. Tall and athletic, with short red hair framing an aristocratic face, she seemed unaware of her own beauty. As she neared their table, Valmont closed his eyes briefly. When he opened them again, his face wore its usual impassive expression.

"Sorry I'm late," Leigh said, seating herself next to Rasputin and giving the pooka a warm smile.

"Too bad you didn't dress for a formal meeting," the pooka muttered. Only then did the others at the table notice that in place of the usual casual attire favored by the patrons of the Toybox, Leigh wore a long gown of deep green watered silk. Like the other changelings, her clothing was chimerical, constructed from her own Glamour and visible only to other Kithain. Mortals would see only an attractive woman clad in an evening dress or a long coat, just as the unenchanted saw the facade of the Toybox as an abandoned building near the center of San Francisco's Haight-Ashbury.

"I just came from the duke's palace," Leigh said. "He wants to see all of us at our earliest convenience."

"Oh, well, then," said Rasputin. "We can certainly take our time."

the hill

"My car's outside," Valmont said. "Perhaps we shouldn't keep His Grace waiting."

Edmund was already on his feet. "At least it's something to do instead of just parking our butts," he said.

"How are your sword lessons coming, Edmund?" Leigh asked loudly enough for everyone in the group to hear.

The redcap's face grew ruddy. "Are we going or what?" he sounded belligerent.

"Sword lessons?" Morgan asked, suddenly looking at Edmund in a new light.

"So what if I'm taking some dumb lessons," Edmund said. "The duke gave me a real sword, so I figured I might as well learn how to use it. It's not like your stupid lady's dagger, which any turkeybrain can use."

Tor stopped long enough to pick up Morgan's shopping bags before he followed the others from the Toybox to Valmont's wine-colored convertible.

Morgan persuaded Valmont to stop at her parents' home in Pacific Heights so that she could drop off her afternoon's purchases.

"Hurry up," admonished Leigh as the childling climbed out of the car. "We shouldn't keep the duke waiting."

"I'll only be a few minutes," Morgan promised. "I just need to let Mother and Daddy know that I'll be out later than I expected."

Carrying the cumbersome bags, Tor accompanied his granddaughter to the door of the Daniels' house, a two-story Tudor building in one of the city's more upscale neighborhoods. Since Morgan had enchanted her parents so that they could see and accept the faerie world that made up such a big part of her life, they no longer argued about her erratic comings and goings.

Alicia Daniels greeted the pair at the door, embracing her father and inviting them in. She waved to the others who waited in Valmont's car. Morgan disappeared inside, while Tor, obviously declining the tendered invitation, stood uncomfortably outside the house. For years, Morgan's father had forbidden her to associate with Tor, seeing him as nothing more than a shiftless member of the city's homeless community who had forfeited all claims to the ties of family. Since his exposure to the truth, Gordon had changed his opinion of his father-in-law and the troll was once more welcome in the Daniels' home. Nevertheless, Tor felt uneasy around his son-in-law. Despite his efforts to comprehend the other reality which constituted the world of the Kithain, Gordon still sought logical explanations for his daughter's magical nature. Tor's fragile hold on his faerie nature, a product of his long life and his exposure to the Banality of modern war, made him reluctant to enter most mortal establishments. His shopping expedition with Morgan had been possible only because the childling radiated enough Glamour to keep both of them firmly grounded in the knowledge of who and what they were.

After a few minutes, Morgan rejoined her grandfather, and the two of them returned to the car.

"I told them not to wait up for me," Morgan said. "I didn't know how long we'd be at the palace."

Leigh smiled to herself as Valmont headed for Nob Hill and Duke Aeon's palace, the seat of the Duchy of Goldengate. She was grateful that Morgan no longer had to indulge in elaborate charades in order to visit her changeling companions or participate in the social life of the city's Kithain.

"I hope you realize how fortunate you are," Valmont said, voicing Leigh's thoughts. "Most childlings who live with their human families can't simply say, 'Bye, folks! I have to go visit the duke. Don't wait up for me.'"

Edmund snickered.

Valmont slowed his car as he approached the duke's estate. Concealed with enchantments that caused mortals to ignore its existence, the splendor of the palace was clearly visible to faerie sight. Leaving the convertible outside the palace grounds, the group made its way up the long sloping path that led to the duke's freehold.

Edmund made certain that he arrived at the door to the palace ahead of the others. He had to stand on tiptoe to reach the bronze, pelican-shaped knocker in the center of the door. Grasping the knocker tightly, he slammed it against the door, hearing a satisfying thud resound from the impact. A second pull and release was even louder. Valmont stopped him on his third try.

"I think the world knows we're here," the eshu said, looking down at Edmund with an amused smile on his face. "Now we wait."

Edmund turned to Leigh. "What's the duke want, anyway?" he asked.

"I doubt it's anything important," Rasputin said.

Before Leigh could reply to Edmund's question, the door opened. She turned instead to announce the group's presence to the palace attendant, but her words died in her throat as she stared at the figure who stood in the open doorway. Wearing a rich red velvet poet's shirt and black silk trousers, Duke Aeon held the door and motioned for the group to enter the palace.

"Thank you for answering my request so swiftly," the young sidhe lord said as the oathmates filed past him in stunned silence.

"This is by no means a formal audience," Aeon said as they all made themselves comfortable in the private library behind the throne room. The duke sat in an overstuffed chair in one corner of the room. Beside him, on a small marble-topped table, rested a large tome of iridescent leather.

"Are we in trouble?" Edmund asked. The redcap, taking the duke at his word, sprawled in a large cushioned armchair, his feet dangling over one of the arms. Leigh and Valmont shared a small sofa opposite the duke's chair. Tor stood beside the closed door, his posture suggesting that he had assigned himself a position of guardianship over the meeting.

"No," Aeon said, shaking his head gravely. "Not unless you have done something recently to endanger the Kithain of Goldengate."

"You mean like opening a gate and letting a freak from beyond into the world?" Edmund didn't bother to contain the sarcasm in his voice.

"Edmund, you forget where you are!" Leigh snapped, her green eyes growing dark with anger. She started to remind Edmund of the courtesies expected within the duke's palace, when Aeon held up a slender hand, motioning her to silence.

"The childling is right to voice his concern," the duke murmured softly. "His manner is blunt, but his words imply an understanding of the principles of cause and effect. I take no insult from his question."

From underneath his tangle of spiky dreadlocks, Edmund smiled triumphantly at Leigh.

"Besides," Aeon continued, "Edmund knows that should I wish it, I could compel both his obedience and his respect."

The redcap blanched, remembering how the force of Aeon's lordly presence, a power which enabled him to command the Kithain of Goldengate, had ruled over him before. The childling shifted in his seat, trying to look as if his decision to sit up straight in his chair was entirely unconscious.

"Yeah," he muttered. Seated next to the duke, in a velvet chair, Morgan beamed at Edmund, hiding her smugness with feigned congeniality.

"It is obvious to me why His Grace has called us here," Rasputin said from his place on a large brocaded ottoman near the foot of Edmund's chair. "It would be rude to wait to see what he has to say to us."

Aeon smiled at the pooka.

"I have come to believe that it was no wise decision to suggest your retirement as jester to this court," he said. "Both Lady Alyssa and I miss your insights, circuitous though they sometimes were."

"Your Grace's insult is most unkindly taken," Rasputin responded, bowing from his seat. Morgan giggled.

Leigh watched the exchange between Rasputin and the duke, trying to imagine the pooka as Aeon's court jester. According to Valmont, Rasputin's barbed humor had too often offended the sensitivities of members of the Seelie court.

"In truth," Aeon said, his tone implying that he had finished with pleasantries, "I requested your presence in response to a visit from an emissary from your lord." His final words were directed not at the group, but at Valmont. The eshu raised an eyebrow.

"Count Elias has some knowledge that concerns us?" he ventured. Although he lived in San Francisco, Valmont served as an adviser to Oakland's Count Elias, an eshu ennobled by Aeon after the Accordance Wars and granted the county of Oakhold as his fief.

"Perhaps," the duke said. "Late yesterday evening, a sluagh calling himself Runt delivered a message to me from Elias. According to the count, a group of Kithain have indicated that they possess information vital to the continuance of your quest."

"They know where Silver's Gate is?" Leigh asked, then bit her lip at her interruption of the duke.

Aeon shook his head. "I think no Kithain who currently walks the earth knows where that lost portal now lies. I believe, however, that this concerns the stone you have in your possession and its companion gems."

As if in response to an unasked question, Leigh reached for a small pouch she wore at her waist, withdrawing from it a translucent green gem the size of a large marble or a human eye. The duke nodded when she offered it to him but declined to take it. Instead, he placed his hand upon the book by his side.

"You may remember Lady Alyssa bringing this volume of the writings of True Thomas to our attention," he said.

"That was the night you charged us with finding and opening Silver's Gate," Morgan said, her eyes fixed on the book.

"Yes," the duke said. "Unfortunately, Thomas's accounting was incomplete, and his Geasa forbids him the luxury of speculation or educated guesses."

"Huh?" Edmund leaned forward in his seat. "What Geasa?"

"True Thomas," Valmont said, "was put under a Geasa long ago that prevents him from speaking and writing anything but the truth. No embellishments, no opinions, no pleasant glosses on the facts to make them palatable—or polite."

"A fate worse than death," Rasputin sighed.

"Gross," said Edmund. "What'd he do to deserve that?"

"There are many stories regarding how that state of affairs came to be," the eshu continued, "but none of them were written by Thomas himself, so none of them can be believed without proof."

"The point is," Aeon said, inclining his head apologetically to Valmont as if to ask forgiveness for his interruption, "that these Kithain may have some information which will help you in your quest."

"Why don't they just come here and tell us?" Edmund asked.

"According to the count's messenger, these folk insist on your coming to them."

"Where?" From his post by the door, Tor was the first to voice the question that was on the others' minds as well.

"You will need to travel north toward Point Reyes," Aeon said.

"How soon do we need to go there?" Leigh asked, "and where precisely do we need to go?"

Aeon's face grew serious. "I believe there is some urgency," he said, "although I do not think it will necessitate a precipitious flight from the freehold in the middle of the night."

A white swan pursued a black swan over the surface of a vast lake. The dark bird seemed to glide over the water, increasing its distance through no apparent effort of its own. From her place atop the swan's back, Morgan strained her eyes to keep the distant, fleeing figure in sight. Not swans, she realized, but boats, heading in a direction she somehow knew to be westward. She looked behind her, where her companions stood. Like her, they fixed their gaze upon the black swan ship, now only a mere speck above the horizon. "Faster," she urged, knowing even as she spoke it was in vain. As if in response to her command, the "ship" unfolded a pair of wide, pearlescent wings and made as if to soar in

*the air. Before the ship could rise, however, the waters below
them swelled upward, parting as they rose to reveal—*

"Morgan!" Tor's voice shattered the vision in her mind.
From his place by the door, the troll had seen his
granddaughter's face grow slack, her eyes glassy and
unseeing. He had intended only to watch her carefully,
but when her expression turned from puzzled reverie to
stark terror, he felt compelled to act.

Morgan blinked her eyes as the room around her
came back into view. Her grandfather knelt before her,
a large hand on either side of her head.

"Are you all right?" he asked.

Morgan nodded. "I'm fine," she said. "I was just
dreaming—" She glanced at her companions, all of
whom looked concerned—except for Edmund, who
regarded her with his usual disdainful smirk.

"What did you see in your dream?" Valmont asked,
remembering that often Morgan's sudden insights had
served to guide them toward their goal.

Aware that all eyes in the room were on her, Morgan
related what she had seen.

"So you hallucinated a pair of birds chasing each
other across the water. So what?" Edmund scoffed.

"So obviously it has nothing to do with us," said
Rasputin amiably. He stroked his long ears thoughtfully
as he spoke, however.

"I believe that Baroness Morgania's vision betokens
a need for reasonable haste," the duke said quietly.

"You think the black swan was the creature we
released in the Park?" Valmont asked, his voice carefully
devoid of any tinge of self-recrimination.

"His name," said Leigh, "is Yrtalien." There was an
edge of exasperation to her voice.

"You're so sure of that," Valmont replied. "Who is
he?"

Leigh looked toward Duke Aeon. The duke shook his head. "Since you mentioned the name to me when you first returned from opening the false gate, I have had my advisers make inquiries into the stranger's identity and his possible House. They have been able to turn up nothing, except—" he hesitated, as if unwilling to continue.

"Except?" Leigh prodded.

Aeon looked troubled. "According to Lady Alyssa, who is usually quite thorough in her research on my behalf, this Yrtalien belongs to none of the five Houses originally exiled here from Arcadia."

"Is that supposed to mean something special?" Edmund asked.

"It could," replied the duke. "There are other Houses in Arcadia who have never deigned to return from the Dreaming, except to send us their outcasts and renegades."

"So this Yrtalien is some sort of criminal?" Tor asked.

"Oh, undoubtedly," said Rasputin. "He's probably an Arcadian jewel thief or something."

"We can dispute who and what he is from now until the Long Winter," Valmont said, "but it seems our immediate course is to meet with these mysterious Kithain in Point Reyes. Shall we plan to go there tomorrow?"

"I'll have to tell my parents," Morgan said, "so they won't worry. And I'll have to pack."

"Pack?" Edmund said, his voice incredulous. "For a day trip up the coast?"

Morgan shook her head. "No, not for a day trip. Weren't you listening to anything? This isn't just a day trip. This is the beginning, the real beginning of our quest."

"Right!" The redcap didn't bother to disguise his skepticism.

"If Morgan is right," Valmont said, "then it might be more prudent to take most of tomorrow to make preparations for an extended journey."

"So we meet at the Toybox tomorrow afternoon," Leigh said. "That will give us most of the day to get ready."

The oathmates took their leave of the duke. As Valmont drove them back to the Toybox, Morgan began to go over all the things she would have to remember to do before their journey began. School was no longer a problem for her, since she had convinced her parents to enroll her in the local home-school program, but she would still have to reassure her mother and father that she would be safe traveling with her friends and her grandfather. A sudden thought occurred to her.

"I'm glad I've already done my Yuletide shopping," she said.

"Oh, don't worry," Rasputin said amiably. "We'll surely be back here before then."

chapter

two

Edmund stared in dismay at the pile of packages in the center of the table. He circled the display, eyeing the gaily wrapped parcels before he finally slipped some things from his pocket into the middle of the pile.

"I hope she's satisfied," the young redcap muttered to himself.

Overnight the Toybox had been transformed into a Yuletide feasting hall, its walls garlanded with boughs of California fir. Sprigs of holly intertwined with mistletoe decorated the tables, and the glow from the clusters of red, white and green candles spaced along the bar added a festive, flickering warmth to the room. The air was filled with the aroma of mulled cider and cinnamon.

Fizzlewig stood diffidently in his usual place behind the bar, a picture of studied nonchalance.

"This is beautiful," said Leigh, as she unpacked a large basket filled with warm pastries and sugared cookies, laying them on top of the bar, which was already loaded with fruit bars, mincemeat tarts, sugared dates, and a seemingly endless assortment of cheeses, breads and winter fruit.

The crusty boggan shrugged. "I heard you were going away," he said, "and it seemed the thing to do."

Leigh smiled and shook her head. "We only just found out yesterday," she replied. "We don't even know that this will be more than a day trip."

"That's not what Morgan implied when she told me you'd be heading out for parts unknown," Fizzlewig said. "Don't think this was my idea." The boggan's voice was gruff, but his prominent dark eyes sparkled with appreciation at Leigh's heartfelt compliment.

"I wouldn't dream of it," she said gravely, knowing that, as a boggan, Fizzlewig shared his kith's natural aversion to being thanked for their labors.

Aside from the six oathmates and Fizzlewig, there were only a few other patrons in the coffee shop. At one end of the bar, Georgia, the nocker cab driver who had acted as chauffeur for the companions during their previous escapades, nursed a mug of steaming mulled cider. In one of the booths that lined the wall opposite the toychest, a frail young woman sat surrounded by a shroud of self-imposed isolation, her large, dark eyes peering out from beneath a fall of limp, pale blond hair.

"Hey, Ellen!" Georgia called in a raspy voice that made the woman cringe as if in pain. "Why don't you join the party? Old Chip here," she indicated Fizzlewig as she spoke, "wouldn't have told you about it if you didn't belong." Without waiting for a reply, Georgia turned to Fizzlewig and whispered, "Why *is* she here anyway?"

"I know why," Morgan's voice broke in as the childling pulled herself onto a barstool. She placed a covered platter of butterscotch brownies on the bar. "I asked Mother to bake these," she said, looking at Leigh as she spoke. "I know they're probably nowhere near as good as the stuff you make."

Leigh smiled. "They smell wonderful," she said. "Just because I love to cook doesn't mean I'm the world's greatest chef. After all, I just wait tables for a living."

"So what's the scoop on Ellen?" Georgia asked Morgan.

"She was here when I went through my Chrysalis," Morgan said. "She brought me an embroidered pillow to make me more comfortable while the change happened."

"Huh," Edmund snorted, wandering up to the bar to assess the food. "Lucky you didn't just explode in the middle of the street or something."

"Luck played little part in Morgan's Chrysalis," Valmont said, coming to stand behind Edmund. "Tor had been keeping an eye on her ever since her birth, watching for signs that she might bear the blood of the fae." The eshu glanced toward Tor, seated in the back booth he favored, as he spoke.

"It wasn't easy, either," Tor rumbled. "Not with that son-in-law of mine trying to keep me as far away from her as possible."

"So how come she's not a troll like Tor?" Edmund asked.

Valmont shrugged. "The answer to that question lies somewhere beyond our ken," he said. "The forgetfulness imposed upon our faerie spirits at the time of our mortal births precludes our knowing what decisions went into the bodies we inhabit."

Edmund looked confused.

"What Valmont means," Rasputin said, joining the conversation, "is that obviously no thought was taken before Morgan was born as to who her mortal family would be. Her spirit was randomly tossed into her mother's womb without any consideration of the consequences."

Leigh nodded. "It could be that a decision was made to make sure Morgan grew up with Tor protecting her. Putting her spirit into his daughter's child would ensure that."

"Whose decision was it?" Edmund was fascinated. The logistics of changeling incarnation were not something that had ever been explained to him.

"It might have been her own choice," Leigh said. "Or someone else with the power to choose her destiny might have made the selection for her."

Awaiting her exile, Eleighanara listened in growing dismay as her parents, members of the royal family of House Fiona, discussed her fate.

"She will need to overcome her natural arrogance and willful disobedience," her mother said. "I propose a family with strong morals, one that can teach her the discipline she needs."

"It would be good if she were not overly burdened with the trappings of material wealth. Her life here has been far too easy," her father added. Beyond the crystal balcony on which they stood, the silvery light of the Arcadian moon glinted off the delicate spires and arches of the family's holding. "She should learn the value of what the mortal race calls honest work."

"You discuss my future exile as if it were a move in one of your elaborate games," Eleighanara said, her voice infused with outrage and barely controlled anger. "You are talking about my life!"

Her father regarded her with a faraway look in his pale eyes. "You are a move in perhaps the most elaborate pavane ever stepped this side of the Mists," he said. "And because of the importance of the role into which you have been cast, you have, perhaps, the least part in deciding where you must stand upon the stage."

"Edmund!" The crack of Fizzlewig's voice brought Leigh's reverie to an abrupt end. She looked about her quickly, trying to judge whether her friends had noticed her lapse of attention. Fizzlewig stood between Edmund and the food, a look of near-lordly wrath on his wrinkled face. Tor still sat in the corner of the coffee shop, quietly regarding the scene around him.

"First the giftings, then the food," the boggan admonished the childling.

Morgan was standing near the booth where the lonely sluagh sat, and Leigh could hear soft whispers

the hill

passing between the two. As she watched, Morgan held out her hand toward the mousy young woman. After a moment's hesitation, Ellen placed her hand in Morgan's and allowed the childling to lead her toward the group.

"This is Ellen," Morgan said. The young Kithain bowed her head, acknowledging her introduction and hiding her face with the same gesture. Leigh saw Ellen's lips move, but could make out only the barest whisper.

"She says she is pleased to have been included in this gathering," Morgan said. "Ellen has been keeping a journal of everything that's gone on since the toy chest was opened," the childling announced. "She knows a lot about what's been happening, but she didn't feel like it was her place to come forward."

The young woman raised her head enough for Leigh to see the look of painful shyness on her pale face.

"I—I hear things sometimes," she whispered, straining to push her voice into an audible range. "I know some people who think that the Shadow Court is out to stop you from finding—from finding what you're looking for. They work for him."

"Him?" Leigh echoed.

"The one who calls himself the Forsworn Prince," Ellen said. "Until a few days ago, he was staying with one of the sidhe of Oakhold—her name is Glynnis. They have been moving among the dissatisfied Kithain."

"Does Count Elias know this?" Valmont spoke up, his voice quietly urgent. Only then did Leigh realize that the eshu had silently been observing the exchange. Near him, Rasputin leaned against the bar, a thoughtful look on his face.

Ellen's head bobbed up and down almost vigorously. "I think so," she said. "I told Runt about it."

Valmont nodded. "If he knows, then Elias knows," the eshu remarked.

"I suppose you know where they are," Rasputin said.

The sluagh shook her head. "They left suddenly," she whispered. "But I don't think the danger to your quest left with them."

Valmont looked at Ellen intently. Although his face bore an inscrutable expression, Leigh saw the tension in his muscles.

"I appreciate your candor in bringing us this news," he said. "I know how highly your kith regards the possession of knowledge and how much it must have cost you to reveal what you know."

Ellen reached into the bag she clutched under one arm and withdrew a slim, leather-bound book. She thrust it toward Leigh.

"Here," she said. "Take this with you. You might find something helpful in its pages."

Leigh accepted the small volume and opened it at random. Its pages were filled with precise, handlettered print, the words crowded close together to take advantage of every available inch of paper.

"What is it?" she asked.

"It's the journal I've been keeping," Ellen said. "I think I meant to give it to you sometime, and now seems the best time to do it." She turned and fled back to her booth.

Leigh placed the book carefully on the table, next to the pile of presents.

"Thank you," she said, directing her words toward Ellen. "We shall certainly read it and take note of anything that seems relevant." She thought she saw Ellen nod slightly.

"I think it's time for the presents," Morgan announced.

the hill

Cyprian Ryder woke with a peculiar tingling in his left hand and a growing sense of urgency in his mind. He studied the bruise in the center of his left palm, a bluish circle about the size of a coin. Usually it merely throbbed, a constant but bearable annoyance. This feeling was different, an insistant twinge that was more like an itch, as if something inside his palm was worrying at the underside of his skin, trying to get out.

Ryder went through his morning rituals—thirty minutes of rigorous exercise followed by a shower and a shave—all the while trying to ignore the prickly sensation in his hand.

By the time he had dressed, it was seven in the morning, and from his apartment window overlooking Boston's Back Bay, he could see the predawn sky, full of the thick, fleecy clouds that signaled the probability of yet more snow. The streets below him were ugly, with dirty snow piled along the sidewalks and shiny patches of treacherous ice on the pavement. He pitied the people whose jobs called them out of their homes in the freezing weather.

He spent the early morning putting his small apartment in order, cleaning up after his light breakfast, making his bed, and removing any other evidence that anyone lived in the three rooms he called his own. As he reshelved a book on abnormal psychology, a standard text which he often used to lull himself to sleep with its monotonous litany of technical terms, his attention was drawn to a nearby book, its worn cover suggestive of multiple handlings. As he reached for it, his left hand convulsed as a knifelike stab of pain erupted in his palm. Gritting his teeth, Ryder grabbed the book with his right hand, clutching it in a deathlike grip until he felt the pain subside. Then he stared at the book's title: *Delusions of the Dream-World*. The author's name, Signe

Henderson, sounded familiar, and Ryder wondered if he might know her. He had been having severe memory problems for the last several weeks. He had no trouble remembering who he was, where he lived, or any of the mundane details of his life, but other things were blanked by a kind of mental fuzz.

He flipped through the pages of the book, scanning the text for something that might explain its sudden significance to him. The contents dealt with an observed phenomenon involving delusions shared by groups of individuals, each of whom contributed their own fantasies to the creation of an imaginary world in which each contributor assumed a highly defined persona. In places, the text became vague with esoteric terminology and Ryder's eyes blurred from trying to make sense of the incomprehensible language.

"This meant something to me once," he thought, as he finally closed the book, letting his hands linger over the worn binding. On impulse, he went to his small ecritoire and retrieved a black address book from its single drawer. He smiled as he turned to the page marked "H" and saw an entry for Henderson, S.

With a growing feeling that the clouds within his head were about to break apart, revealing something monumentally important, he picked up his phone and dialed the local number next to the name. After two rings, a woman's voice, clipped and precise, answered.

"My name is Cyprian Ryder," he began. "You may not know who I am—"

"Chevalier!" the voice on the other end sounded excited. "I've been hoping you would call."

Like the sudden illumination of a flash of lightning during a midnight storm, Cyprian Ryder, the apostate changeling, remembered everything.

The remains of shredded paper and ribbon cluttered the floor near the table where the oathmates sat opening their gifts.

"This is really beautiful," Morgan said, turning her wrist from one side to the other to admire the delicate silver and gold charm bracelet she now wore. "Thank you, Valmont."

The eshu smiled. "Each charm represents one of us," he said. "The rabbit is, of course, Rasputin."

Morgan nodded. "And the silver ax is Grandpa," she said. "I guess the tribal mask is supposed to represent you, isn't it?" she added. Valmont nodded.

"And the baseball cap is for Edmund," he said. At the sound of his name, Edmund looked up and scowled, reaching self-consciously to pull his cap down tighter over his dreadlocks. He had already stuffed his presents into his pockets and now fidgeted while the others seemed to take forever to finish unwrapping packages. He patted the pocket which held the small leather pouch from Morgan.

She couldn't have found out about Mr. Dumpy, he thought, trying to remember if any of his companions had ever seen the chimerical clown miniature he had snatched up from the toy chest when it was first opened and had kept hidden in his pocket ever since. The pouch was just the right size to hold the figurine.

Morgan looked at the two remaining charms. "Is one of these me?" she asked.

"The heart," said Valmont. "And the rose is for Leigh." The eshu's face bore a faint smile as he spoke.

Hearing Valmont's words, Leigh felt her cheeks grow warm. She fingered the silver chain she now wore around her neck, tracing the two crossed roses that formed its pendant.

"Do you like it?" Valmont asked her.

"It's lovely," she said, a knot forming in her throat along with the words. "I didn't expect anything this elaborate."

Valmont shrugged. "I had only a little time to choose presents," he said in a voice that sounded too casual. "Jewelry is something I am conversant with."

Leigh lowered her head quickly and concentrated on unwrapping her remaining present—a red velvet pouch with silk drawstrings from Morgan. *It's perfect for the Keystone*, she thought as she opened the plainer pouch at her side and transferred the emerald stone to its new container.

Tor placed the hand-tooled leather belt from Leigh on the table and picked up his present from Morgan, a slim maroon leather photo holder. He blinked hard as he looked at photos of Morgan as a baby in her mother's arms, Morgan on a tricycle in the front yard of the Daniels' home, Morgan and her parents posing for a studio shot, and other captured moments in the life of the family from which he had once been exiled. His friends' conversation faded into the background.

Rasputin finished packing his presents into his woven shoulder bag. He grimaced as he laid Edmund's present, a rabbit's foot on a leather thong, next to the wooden pennywhistle from Tor. Settling back in his chair, he adjusted Valmont's present, a silver chain bracelet, on his wrist. His own presents to his oathmates were not so elaborate—bead and knotwork rings for Leigh and Morgan, friendship bracelets for Edmund and Tor, and a handwoven belt for Valmont. *I wonder if any of them will realize that their presents are woven from strands of our hair*, the pooka thought.

t h ε   h i l l

Morgan watched anxiously as Valmont paged through the book of stories she had chosen for him. "The stories in it come from all over Africa," Morgan said, "and the illustrations are by African artists. I hope you don't already know all of them."

Valmont shook his head. "Even if the stories are familiar, the telling of them always varies from source to source."

Relieved, Morgan turned her attention to the rest of her presents. She obligingly sniffed the cheap rose-scented perfume from Edmund before setting the bottle on the table next to the carved wooden unicorn from her grandfather. The last present was from Leigh.

"I've never had a diary before," Morgan said, revealing a pocket-sized book covered with deep blue cloth imprinted with silver moons and stars.

"I had one when I was younger," Leigh said. "I thought you might enjoy keeping a record of our quest."

Morgan's face lit up. "That's perfect!" she said. "It can be a journal, like the one Ellen gave us. Only no one can read it unless I say so," she added, looking pointedly at Edmund.

"Huh," the redcap snorted. "Who'd want to read anything you wrote, anyway?"

"Now that you've opened all your gifts from each other, it's my turn." Georgia's raspy voice announced her presence. She went around the table, handing each of the six companions a bright purple and yellow button-sized disc. "These are lifetime passes good for free rides in my cab," the nocker said. "You can also use them to remember me while you're off looking for the gate."

"You never charged us before," Edmund said dubiously. Valmont frowned at the childling.

"I know," said Georgia. "I must have been feeling unusually generous to run you all around the city for free, even if you are my friends. Now I can't charge you even if I wanted to."

"We have something for you, too," Morgan said, reaching for an unopened package underneath her chair and handing it to Georgia.

"We do?" Edmund asked. Morgan glared at him.

"Open it," she said to Georgia. "And there's a package for Fizzlewig and one for Ellen, too." The childling rose from her chair and retrieved two more presents from beneath it. She walked over to the bar and deposited one of the packages in front of Fizzlewig, then crossed to the booth where Ellen sat quietly watching the festivities. She handed the last package to the sluagh.

"Awesome!" Georgia exclaimed, holding up a white silk aviator's scarf. She wrapped it around her neck and hurried over to the bar to admire herself in the mirror behind it. "I always wanted one of these things," the nocker added.

Fizzlewig unwrapped his present, a dragon-shaped pewter mug. "Not bad," he said, examining its workmanship before carefully placing it on a shelf behind the bar, alongside the rest of his collection of fanciful drinking vessels.

Morgan watched as Ellen opened her package, uncovering a black lace shawl. The sluagh fingered the delicate weblike weave in silence before giving Morgan a shy glance and mouthing her thanks. She handed the childling a small parcel, whispering words that only Morgan could hear.

Morgan returned to the table and placed Ellen's gift in front of Leigh.

"Ellen says that her presents to us are tokens which we can show to other sluagh wherever we go and they will know that we can be trusted. Her kith will honor the tokenbearers with help or knowledge if they can."

Leigh looked across the room at Ellen and nodded to her.

"I hope you conveyed our appreciation," she said to Morgan.

For a moment, the childling looked offended. She sighed heavily.

"Of course I did," she said.

"This is a gift of inestimable worth," said Valmont, "should we find ourselves in need of allies among strangers."

"Are we done now?" Edmund asked. "Can we eat?"

Valmont rose and led the others toward the bar and the waiting food. "We should keep in mind that we need to be on our way north before too long. It is already dark and we have some distance to travel."

"Oh, I don't think we need to be in any particular hurry," Rasputin said.

Glynnis sat at the feet of the Forsworn Prince, her head resting on his knee. "Do you think they will find us here?" she asked.

Yrtalien leaned back in his chair, a thronelike seat of native coral that formed the centerpiece of his private audience chamber. Soft chimerical globes of light bathed his angular features in a warm red glow. With one hand, he held up a dark, marble-sized gem, watching its opalescent colors reflect and refract the light. With his other hand, he absently stroked Glynnis' dark hair.

"Oh, I have no doubt that they will come eventually," he said, his low, melodic voice soft with anticipation. "And when they do, we shall welcome them and reveal to them the truth behind the lies they have been forced for so long to believe."

"If they follow the path we took," Glynnis reflected, "they will not get a warm reception from the natives." The dark-haired lady smiled enigmatically.

Yrtalien shook his head, his glossy black hair falling into his eyes. "No," he said, amusement lacing his voice. "And that is why, after all, they will have to come to us."

"Are you hoping to make them your allies in this?" Glynnis asked, sounding doubtful.

"If not more," he said, wistfulness softening his usual brittle speech. "If not much more."

"How far north do we need to go?" Leigh asked, as she settled into the front seat of Valmont's car, now headed northwest along the coastal highway.

"I don't know yet," the eshu replied. A fog clung to the road, decreasing visibility, particularly in the late afternoon darkness. Ahead, the car's headlights cast bright, diffracted beacons of light into the mist. They had left the city behind them. Now they had only the sea on their left and rising wooded hills on their right. They had passed Mount Tamalpais and Muir Woods and were headed in the direction of Point Reyes, a mist-bound peninsula jutting northward from the California coast.

"How do you do that, anyway?" Edmund asked from the back seat, where he sat on one side of Tor, his face pressed against the window of the wine-colored Cadillac.

Valmont chuckled softly.

"My kith is blessed—or cursed—with a knack for being where we need to be when we need to be there,"

the hill

he said. "I find it difficult to explain how it's done. How do you manage to digest some of the objects you put into your mouth?"

"Never mind that," Morgan said, her voice coming from Tor's other side. "How can you stand the taste of the stuff you eat?"

Edmund shrugged. "I'm just talented, I guess," he said.

"Does everybody in Goldengate know where we're going?" Rasputin asked, turning from his window seat beside Leigh in the front of the car to look over Morgan's head at the road behind them.

"Why?" asked Tor, not liking the tenor of Rasputin's question.

"Oh, nothing really," said the pooka. "I'm not terribly concerned about the car that's coming hard up on us."

Turning around in the back seat, Edmund scrambled to his knees to peer out the back window at the pair of blinding headlights that were approaching rapidly from out of the fog.

"Hit it, Valmont!" the redcap yelled. "He's gonna ram us!"

Valmont slammed his foot hard on the accelerator, trying to put some distance between them and the pursuer. As the car lurched forward, he caught a flash of movement to his left.

Next to him, Leigh saw headlights as a second car emerged from the fog before them, veering from its lane and heading straight into their path.

"Look out!" she called, and without waiting for Valmont's reaction she grabbed the wheel and jerked it to the right. The car veered off the road onto the shoulder with a hideous grinding sound, narrowly avoiding a collision.

"Brace yourselves," Tor warned, reaching for both Edmund and Morgan with his massive arms and pulling the childlings toward him. Leigh released her hold on the wheel and tried to shield her head with her arms. Beside her, Rasputin also brought his arms up in front of his face. Valmont gripped the steering wheel and grimly tried to keep control of the car as it bounced along the shoulder's uneven surface.

A sudden jolt from behind propelled the car forward and Valmont felt the right side of the car drop into a ditch. The car on his left swerved to block them, leaving him with no choice but to brake.

Morgan screamed, her cry muffled by Tor's bulk, as she felt herself flung forward. Tor grunted as he tightened his hold on his granddaughter and Edmund, letting his protecting arms absorb the shock.

Leigh felt herself thrown forward and just as suddenly jerked back as her seat belt pinned her to the seat. She bit her lip to keep from crying out. Valmont, attempting to avoid hitting the steering wheel, threw himself toward Leigh, while, on her other side, Rasputin gave a small whimper as he slammed into the door.

For a fraction of a second there was only silence.

"Is everyone hurt?" Rasputin asked, his voice trembling and faint. Morgan began to cry.

"Listen," Leigh said urgently. Morgan's sobs grew quieter. From outside, the oathmates could hear the sound of car doors opening, followed by the crunch of footsteps.

"Heads up!" Tor called out. "Out of the car before we're trapped. We've got company."

"Cool!" Edmund remarked, wriggling out from under Tor's arm and reaching for the door handle. "We're being ambushed!"

Rasputin tried his door, then muttered something that sounded like a curse.

"Hurry up," said Leigh, unfastening her seat belt.

"What's wrong?" she asked the pooka.

"Nothing," mumbled Rasputin. "The door's not jammed at all."

"Mine won't open either," said Morgan. "We're shoved up against the side of a ditch."

"This way," Valmont said, opening his door. "Watch out for the car in front of us."

Piling out, the companions found themselves standing in a pool of fog and headlights, unable to see more than a few feet beyond the glittering mist that surrounded them.

Tor shoved Morgan back into the car and placed his body in front of the open rear door, making himself a living shield between his granddaughter and any who would try to harm her. He reached for his ax just as a pair of figures emerged from behind the car, converging on him. In the beam of the headlights, the troll could see the glint of metal in their hands.

"They've got swords!" he called.

Valmont reached within him for the source of his faerie Glamour, letting his mortal self give way to his true nature. He reached for the chimerical scimitar at his waist. Beside him, he saw Leigh, now resplendent in her knight's armor, unsheath her sword, and turn to face the attackers approaching from the car in front.

"Move!" Edmund yelled at Tor, drawing his own short blade, a gift from the duke. The redcap scrambled around the troll's body and launched himself at one of Tor's opponents, a nocker armed with a knife in each hand.

"Step aside, Valmont," a familiar voice called from the fog. "We're not after you—just your Seelie friends."

Valmont's face hardened, recognizing Blade's arrogant stance. The mohawked eshu warrior carried himself with an assurance born of his martial skills. Before him, he held a dangerous-looking blade.

Like Valmont, Blade served as an adviser to Count Elias, the ennobled eshu who held the county of Oakhold for Duke Aeon. Although both were associated with the Unseelie faction, Valmont's affiliation with the Shadow Court of San Francisco was tenuous at best. Blade, however, controlled an increasingly vocal and violent group of Unseelie commoners who called themselves the Oakland People's Front. In order to maintain peace in his fief, Elias recognized the necessity of accepting their leader's counsel. For some time now, Blade had been pushing for the count to declare himself and his fief independent of the Seelie court of the Kingdom of Pacifica, a move Elias was unwilling to make.

"Does this mean that you have finally broken with your liege?" Valmont asked, stepping toward his rival, his own sword held at the ready.

Blade laughed. "What makes you think I am here without the count's knowledge?" the eshu scoffed. Behind him, other shapes, slim and graceful, began moving forward, forming a half-circle around Valmont and Leigh.

Valmont gestured with his head toward Blade's companions. "Those aren't your usual motley of street scum," he said, his voice soft with challenge.

His gaze still fixed on Valmont, Blade shook his head. "The Shadow Court has grown more powerful since you served as its prince," he said. "We are now a force to be reckoned with."

"Then reckon with this," Valmont said, lunging forward to attack.

"Valmont, no! Let them come to us!" Leigh cried, aware that her words were too late as the shadowy figures moved quickly to take advantage of the gap opened by Valmont's precipitous lunge. Bringing her sword into position, Leigh tried to calculate the odds she now faced alone. They weren't in her favor.

the hill

Inside the car, Morgan was fuming. She saw her grandfather locked in battle with another troll, while, beside him, Edmund waved his sword menacingly at a nocker armed with a pair of long knives. Once more, she tried to open the right-hand door.

"Don't you love feeling vital to the outcome of this battle?" a voice called from the front seat of the car.

"Rasputin!" Morgan said, surprised to find that she was not alone in the car.

"They really should let expert warriors like you and me take the brunt of the combat," the pooka said.

Morgan smiled ruefully at her companion. "I can't stand always being stuffed out of harm's way," she said.

"I couldn't agree with you more," Rasputin commiserated. "We're in no position to do anything subtle to help our friends," he said.

Morgan arched an eyebrow as the meaning of the pooka's statement crystalized in her mind.

"You're right!" she said, remembering another battle in which she and Rasputin had used their faerie magic to provide support from the sidelines for their companions.

"I'll cover Grandpa and Edmund," she said. "You help Leigh and Valmont."

Tor held his ax like a quarterstaff and rammed its polished handle under the chin of the young troll who faced him. The troll staggered backward.

"Get out of my face," Tor roared. "Go learn to fight somewhere else!"

Edmund felt a sting as one of the nocker's knives slipped inside his guard and slashed his sword arm.

"You cut me, you maggot-sucking piece of garbage," he snarled. The pain grew more intense, sending a cold wave of nausea through him. Edmund took a closer look at his opponent's weapons.

"No fair!" he cried. "That's iron! Hey, Valmont! These butt breaths are using iron!" Edmund blocked a thrust with the nocker's second knife, his lessons with Sir Cumulus in the practice room of the palace coming back to him as he realized that more than just his life was on the line. Cold iron, the ultimate symbol of Banality and the tool of the enemies of the fae, ate away at the essence of the faerie nature. Death from an iron weapon was true death to the faerie soul.

"If you're gonna play in the majors, junior, you're gonna have to take your cuts," the nocker leered as he readied himself for another dual thrust.

"Yeah?" Edmund said, his childish voice full of outrage. "Well you just made me mad," he said. He took a step backward, placing his back against the side of Valmont's car. Reaching across his body with his free hand, he drew his fingers along the shallow, bleeding cut on his arm.

"You drew blood," he said menacingly, wiping his red-stained fingers across his lips and licking the blood from them. He'd seen the gesture in a Bruce Lee film once, and had practiced it until he thought he had it down pat. His opponent stopped, watching him in puzzled fascination. *Hot spit*, Edmund thought, *it works!* Screaming, the redcap charged at his surprised enemy.

The nocker recovered quickly, bringing both knives up to intercept Edmund's attack. A sudden jerk on his arm, apparently from nowhere, caused him to lose his grip on one of his weapons. The knife dropped from his grasp, landing in the gravel at his feet.

"Yes!" Morgan whispered, her face plastered against the car window.

Leigh faced her three attackers with as much bravado as she could summon. Two of them were obviously sidhe, their elegantly handsome features marred only by the studied slovenliness of their dress. Like her, they wore chimerical armor, but theirs was dark and bore no house badge. The third was a female satyr clad in a spiked leather breastplate. The thick fur that covered her hooved legs served for armor.

Take out the weakest one first. The words in her head seemed to come from another time and place, one which until recently had been concealed by the mists of forgetfulness that plagued changelings in the mortal world. This was not the first time she had been outnumbered by enemies. She seemed to recall a battle in which she and a group of noble warriors—oathmates in Arcadia—fought against superior forces and overcame them.

She sized up the satyr, a strategy forming in her mind. Reaching within her for the Glamour that powered her faerie magics, she surrounded herself with an aura of splendor. Extending her sword upward in a gesture that implied an utter lack of concern for her own safety, she saluted her foe.

"I am a knight of House Fiona," she announced, channeling her power through her speech and stance. "Withdraw from this confrontation or know my grave displeasure."

As she spoke, her form undertook a subtle and terrifying change; a radiance poured forth from her, enhancing her visage so that she looked both beautiful and awe inspiring.

The satyr drew back, her eyes wide with fear. Leigh stepped forward, and the satyr bolted, fleeing into the foggy darkness.

"That may work on a commoner," a voice proclaimed as one of the sidhe warriors moved to take the place of the cowed satyr. "Now let us see what you can do against your equals."

"Or your betters." The second speaker was female, and as she stepped into Leigh's vision, Leigh had a clear view of the darkened blade in her hand. Adrenalin coursed through her as she realized that at least one of her opponents was armed with an iron weapon. Instinctively she raised her own sword to parry.

A few feet from her, Valmont and Blade circled each other warily, weapons extended. Blade had evaded Valmont's initial attack, and now seemed content to engage his rival in an elaborate dance, its rhythms dictated by the occasional clang of chimerical steel. Valmont's scimitar was in constant motion as he tried to defend himself and break through his opponent's guard simultaneously. In the back of his mind, he was aware of Leigh's struggle against a pair of expert combatants, but the demands of his duel with Blade forced him to block her from his attention.

"This is excellent," Rasputin murmured to himself, watching the conflict from his vantage point in the front seat of Valmont's car. "Leigh obviously needs no assistance." The pooka concentrated on the battle, wiggling his long ears and making outrageous faces at the nearer of Leigh's two attackers. The gesture focused his Glamour, allowing the power of his magic to manifest itself.

The ground beneath his target suddenly became a mire of slippery mud and gravel, and the sidhe warrior found himself struggling to keep his footing.

Tor's opponent had not given up. The young troll wielded a massive broadsword, and though Tor countered its sweeping strokes, the elder warrior could not match his opponent's speed in order to get in his own attacks with his ax.

Morgan watched her grandfather's battle in fascination, trying to gauge where best to use her Glamour to help him overcome his opponent. She knew that mortals would see two heavily muscled men locked in combat, the older one armed with an ax and the younger one apparently unarmed but making a show of wielding an invisible weapon. Only other

Kithain could see them for what they were—two massive trolls, one with a chimerical sword, the other with an enchanted ax.

"Grandpa's not trying to cut him," Morgan observed, noticing how Tor used the ax to block the younger troll's blows, then employed the ax's butt end to thrust at his opponent.

"Killing him would certainly seem the wisest course," said Rasputin.

"You're right," said Morgan. "It would be sort of hard to explain to the police, I guess."

"And, of course, your grandfather would certainly feel proud of himself for taking a life."

Morgan blushed. "That, too," she admitted. "But the other troll has a chimerical sword," she said. "That means that he can't hurt Grandpa's body."

"All he can do is drive his faerie nature from him," Rasputin said. "And that's not important at all."

Morgan's face registered her sudden concern. "I hadn't thought about that," she said. "If he takes too many blows, he might forget he's a troll and that we're on a quest—that's what they're trying to do!" Her voice was shrill as she abruptly realized the possible result of her companions' losing the battle.

"They're not attacking to kill," she said. "They want to drive us all the way into Banality so we won't remember our quest!"

"That never would have occurred to me," Rasputin said.

The young troll suddenly landed a lucky blow with his sword, catching Tor's right arm near the elbow. Tor felt his arm grow numb and his right hand fell away from his ax. He shook his head and looked about him, suddenly unsure of where he was. Lowering his weapon, still clutched in his left hand, he began to wander away from the battle.

Morgan saw her grandfather's faerie seeming fade away, leaving behind only his mortal guise—a tall, blond, heavy-set man in a worn-looking trench coat. She screamed. Grabbing for the door handle, she wrenched open the door, no longer blocked by Tor's bulk.

"Grandpa! Don't leave!" she cried as she hurled herself from the car and ran after Tor.

A massive hand seized her shoulder.

"I don't think you're going anywhere, pipsqueak," the young troll scowled.

Leigh, her male opponent now foundering in a stew of mud that sucked like living tendrils at his ankles, focused her concentration on her second attacker.

"Your choice of weapon indicates that you intend to do more than simply drive me from my faerie self," Leigh said, her words coming in staccato bursts of breath between feints and lunges.

Her opponent laughed.

"I might reconsider in return for that pouch at your belt," she said. "Give it to me and I'll call the others off." The sidhe warrior thrust suddenly at Leigh, who moved to dodge the blow only to find that her opponent had anticipated her, changing to a low sweeping cut that sliced into Leigh's thigh. She screamed with the cold pain that seared her upper leg.

"Give me the pouch," her attacker said, stepping out of range of Leigh's return thrust. Leigh tried to move forward, but her wounded leg gave way beneath her. She dropped to her knees.

"Morgan!" Rasputin called, as the childling struggled frantically with the troll who clutched her firmly by the shoulder.

Quickly, the pooka reached for the cloth bag that rested on the floor near his feet. He withdrew a pair of weighted juggling clubs. Opening the front door of Valmont's car, he stepped from the vehicle.

"Hey, nonny, nonny," he whispered softly, using his Glamour to create a bright pink rabbit face in the air in front of the troll. Taken by surprise, Morgan's captor jerked his head back. In that second, Rasputin let his club fly. It struck the troll solidly in the head.

Morgan reached for the small chimerical dagger she wore at her waist. She brought it up and stabbed it into the hand on her shoulder. Because it was created from the stuff of Dreaming and had no real physical substance, the dagger drew no blood, but the troll recoiled in pain as part of his faerie nature was ripped from him. He released his grip on Morgan.

The childling fled after her grandfather.

The young troll turned in the direction of the missile-thrower. Catching site of Rasputin, he howled and charged.

"Just what I had planned all along," the pooka muttered as three hundred pounds of what felt like solid rock plowed into him, driving the breath from his lungs.

Blade looked beyond Valmont and smiled.

"Your friends are losing," he said.

Valmont's eyes narrowed into dark slits. "That won't work," he said. "Cut the distractions." The handsome eshu lifted his scimitar above his head and brought it down, aiming at Blade's shoulder. His rival ducked and came up inside Valmont's reach, his own sword held vertically in front of him, its point pricking the underside of Valmont's chin.

"I've been studying blades the whole time you were running cons, my friend," Blade said harshly. "It shows, doesn't it? One move, and you'll be wandering around in the dark trying to remember why you ever left the city for a lonely drive along the beach."

Valmont froze.

Edmund felt his foot jerked out from under him as his opponent, now with only a single knife against the redcap's sword, abruptly changed his mode of attack. Edmund lost his balance and fell backward, landing heavily on the ground. His sword slipped from his hand and skittered out of his reach. Before he could regain his feet, the nocker threw himself on the childling and landed a fist in Edmund's face.

"Cheat!" Edmund yelled.

His opponent snorted and punched Edmund again. The redcap tried to get his hands up to return the blows, but the nocker now sat on his stomach, trapping his arms.

Tor found himself alone in the darkness. To his left, the sound of the ocean and the salty odor of sea air overwhelmed him. He stopped, trying to get his bearings. His body ached as if from some sudden exertion and he tried to remember what he had been doing last.

"Must've walked farther than I thought," he said to himself. Shoving his hands into his pockets, he headed toward the road which he knew must lie to his right.

"Grandpa?" Morgan, too, had run beyond the range of the cars' headlights and now foundered in the dark fog. Behind her, she could still hear the cries of her companions and the cacophony of battle. She stopped, torn between the need to go back and do what she could to assist her friends and her desire to follow her grandfather.

Suddenly she sensed movement on her left.

"Grandpa?" she called again, wondering if Tor had by some chance strayed away from the road and headed toward the sea.

A slender figure loomed out of the fog and a pair of moist hands clasped her gently on the shoulders. She tensed, ready to scream.

"Gently, little landfae," a silky voice said. "If you are one of the gateseekers, we mean you no harm."

the hill

Morgan peered in the darkness, trying to see who had spoken.

"Who are you?" she demanded, her voice tremulous as she strove to conceal her fear.

"Time for that later," the voice replied. "Right now, it seems you and your friends have need of our help."

"Our?" Morgan asked. "Where are the others?"

"Even now they are nearing the battle," the speaker said. Morgan's eyes were beginning to adjust to the darkness and she could just make out a young man with long brown hair that seemed to cling to his face as if he had just come out of the water. He let go of her shoulders and reached to take her hand.

"Let us find the one who has wandered away," he said. "Perhaps we can help him as well."

The soothing tone of his voice banished Morgan's anxiety and she allowed herself to be led into the foggy darkness.

Trapped under a barrage of constant pummeling, Edmund fought back with the only part of his body he could still move. Opening his mouth as wide as he could, he twisted his head to one side and bit down on the nocker's fist. With a shriek, his opponent tried to disengage his hand from the redcap's jawlock.

"'Et off of 'e or I'll 'wallow 'our 'and," Edmund threatened. The nocker's eyes bulged with pain and terror. Nodding furiously, he rolled off Edmund, taking care not to jostle his trapped hand.

"Let me go," he mumbled. "Just don't bite my hand off."

Releasing his jaws, Edmund scrambled to his feet and glared maliciously at the nocker. Taking a step back, the redcap opened his mouth.

"You look like a fish," he said. "Taste sort of like one, too."

Clutching his wounded hand to his chest, the

nocker fled into the darkness.

Rasputin tried to shove his opponent away from him, aware of the hopelessness of his situation as the troll continued to crush the hapless pooka against the side of the car. Suddenly the troll grunted in pain and tumbled away from Rasputin, landing on his side. The pooka stepped away from the car and looked at the chimerical weapon which had felled his attacker.

"A harpoon," he said. "I would have expected no less."

Valmont stared unblinking at Blade.

"I will grant your superiority with the sword," he said softly, letting his own weapon fall to the ground and watching his rival's face as he spoke. Blade's eyes softened at Valmont's unexpected concession, and he allowed himself the luxury of a sardonic grin. Valmont felt Blade's grip on his sword relax in that instant. Snapping his head back, Valmont thrust his arm upward, knocking his opponent's sword-arm to one side. At the same time, he landed a solid blow to Blade's jaw that sent him reeling back.

"But I am better at calculating the odds," he said, preparing to follow up before Blade had a chance to recover his balance. Just then, he heard a soft swishing of air as a rope of what looked like seaweed settled around Blade's head and tightened around his neck. Blade had just enough time to look surprised before he was jerked to the ground.

A slender figure stepped forward.

"I think he will trouble you no further," the stranger said quietly.

Valmont swore under his breath. Then he forced himself to smile at his unexpected ally.

"Thank you for your timely assistance," he muttered, hoping his voice did not betray his frustration.

Leigh looked up as her opponent prepared to move in for the kill. *Timing is everything*, she thought, as she watched the blade descend. Centering her focus on her good leg, Leigh thrust herself upward, her free arm outstretched to intercept the blow. Her momentum carried her forward, throwing her foe off-balance and onto the ground. Leigh allowed herself to fall, using her enemy's body to cushion the impact. She heard a soft "whoof" as the breath went out of her opponent and the iron blade slipped from her hand. Leigh struggled to her feet and stood to face the one remaining attacker, still mired in a morass of clinging mud. The helpless sidhe looked at Leigh and paled at her expression. Bringing his sword up to defend himself as Leigh advanced, he failed to hear Valmont's approach. The eshu rammed the hilt of his scimitar into the base of the sidhe warrior's skull. Unconscious, Leigh's last opponent slumped to the ground.

"What's going on?" Leigh asked, noticing that the sounds of battle had died away entirely.

"I think we won," Valmont replied. In a softer voice he added, "We seem to have company."

"You were told to expect us," a smooth female voice called out from the darkness. "Get in your car quickly, before they regain consciousness. Drive north for a quarter of a mile, then pull off the road. We will meet you there."

Leigh glanced quickly around her.

"We're missing Morgan and Tor," she said. "We can't leave without them."

"Don't worry about them," the voice reassured her. "We shall find them and bring them to the meeting point. For the sake of your quest, do as we ask."

"You heard the lady," Valmont said, coming up to stand beside Leigh. Rasputin and Edmund joined them, their expressions puzzled.

Valmont turned to look ruefully at his foundered vehicle. "We will be on our way as soon as we get my car out of the ditch and onto the road."

Leigh climbed into the car. "I'll take the wheel," she said. "You and Rasputin—and you, too, Edmund—can push. I don't think my leg can take the strain."

"Hey!" Edmund cried excitedly. "Did you know you're bleeding?"

The words were hardly out of the redcap's mouth when Rasputin appeared at Leigh's side, a scarf in his hand. The pooka knelt and firmly wrapped the gaily colored silk around Leigh's leg.

"This won't do any good," he said, admiring his handiwork.

A graceful, bright-eyed young woman approached Leigh and looked at the makeshift bandage. With a slender hand, she gingerly tested the tension of the wrapping. Leigh noted the weblike tissue between the woman's fingers and raised an eyebrow.

"There will be help for this, too, when we reach our destination," the woman said, looking up at Leigh and smiling.

A few minutes later, the companions were once again on the road heading north. Leigh kept her eye on the car's odometer.

"Here!" she called out, as the gauge indicated that the quarter mile mark had been reached.

Valmont pulled off the road.

"Now what?" he asked.

"Now we wait," Leigh said. "Our mysterious friends said they would meet us here."

"Who were they, anyway?" Edmund asked.

"Obviously not selkies," Rasputin muttered, his voice full of wonder.

the hill

chapter

three

Despite the reassurances of the guides who had met them at the designated rendezvous point, Valmont still worried about his car, parked inside a copse of trees by the roadside. *I hope I won't need it anytime soon*, he thought as he and his oathmates traversed a maze of narrow paths through the marshy landscape near Point Reyes, following the mysterious figures whose timely arrival had rescued them from a near disastrous battle.

"We're nearing the ocean," Leigh whispered to the others, as the roar of the sea reached her ears. She flexed her shoulders, trying to realign the straps of her backpack. On Morgan's insistence that their journey north was the first step in a longer voyage, she had packed a few essentials. The others, too, were burdened with backpacks and carryalls.

Morgan clutched Tor's hand, a little intimidated by the utter strangeness of the wilderness that surrounded her. Feeling the slight tremble in his granddaughter's hand, Tor tightened his grip around the tiny palm.

"It's okay," he muttered, his voice a bass rumble that mimicked the deep sound of the nearby water. Tor fought to keep his mind focused on his faerie seeming. The same people who had intervened in his companions' battle with their attackers had found him standing by the side of Highway 1. Surrounded by the Glamour of their natures, he had remembered who and what he was. Now he struggled to keep hold of that memory.

Rasputin's keen ears picked up the sounds of small creatures moving through the grass and the eerie calls of nocturnal birds. Used to the clamor of traffic that formed the constant background to life in the city, the pooka now reveled in the strange sensation of the absence of wailing sirens and screeching brakes.

"This place is creepy," Edmund said, trying not to seem obvious about staying as close to Valmont as possible. *Eshu always know where they're going*, he thought. Something rustled in the brush to his right and he started suddenly, bumping into Valmont.

"Watch where you're going," he snarled at the puzzled eshu.

"Mind your footing," their guide cautioned them as the group reached the end of the trail they had been following and began a winding descent down a rocky slope, assisted by their mysterious rescuers. The sound of the sea became louder until, when they finally reached level ground, the companions could see the expanse of the Pacific, visible beneath the mist that rose above the waters.

"Only a little farther," the strange Kithain said, turning northward along the beach.

"This place seems so isolated," Leigh remarked, looking to her right at the steep cliff which they had just traversed.

"Few people come here," their guide answered. "The tides are often treacherous to those who are not familiar with their ways."

"Great!" snorted Edmund. "I always wanted to be washed out to sea."

They reached what appeared to be the end of the beach, as an outcropping of rock from the cliff face blocked their northward path. Without hesitation, the woman who had been leading them began scaling the rock.

"There are hand and foot holds to make the climb easier," she called over her shoulder. "Take your time and you should have little trouble."

the hill

Leigh watched carefully for a few moments, straining in the dark to make out the small clefts in the rock.

"Do you want me to try it first?" Valmont asked, coming up behind her.

Leigh shook her head. "No," she said. "It looks fairly simple." Taking a deep breath, she reached for the first handhold and began to pull herself up the side of the rock, wincing from the pain in her wounded leg but determined not to give in to it. Moist hands grabbed hers as she neared the summit and helped her gain her footing atop the level rock plateau. Edmund was next. Gritting his teeth, the redcap scrambled up the rock to stand beside Leigh.

"Just like Spiderman!" he chortled. "C'mon Morgan," he called down. "Even you should be able to make a sissy climb like this."

Morgan was thankful that the darkness concealed the flush that rose to her cheeks at Edmund's words. She bit back the urge to respond and walked up to the rock, looking for a place to start her ascent.

"Here," Tor said, lifting her in his arms and helping her find her grip on the rock. "I'll be right behind you," the troll rumbled. Morgan started her climb, determined not to be outdone by Edmund. Tor watched his granddaughter maneuver her way upward until she was just beyond his reach, then he, too, started up the rock.

Halfway to the top, Morgan lost her footing and started to slide. She tried to remain calm and concentrate on regaining her hold on the rock, but the thought that Edmund was watching drove her to a state of near panic.

"Don't let go!" Tor called out. "Dig in with your hands and hold on." Grunting with the exertion, the troll heaved his bulk upward until Morgan's feet rested upon his shoulders.

Morgan gripped the handholds as tightly as she could, her fingers trying to dig into the unyielding surface of the cliff. She felt the solidity of Tor's body underneath her feet and knew he meant for her to use him as a makeshift foothold for her next upward movement. She tried to release her left hand to find the next indentation in the rock, but her fingers refused to obey her. *I must look like a fool,* she thought. *Edmund's probably laughing at me. He'll think I'm afraid of heights.* She felt her eyes grow watery with tears.

"I can't move!" she wailed, as fear and embarrassment combined to rob her of the ability to help herself to safety.

Edmund snorted in disgust. "I knew you were a wuss!" he called down to Morgan.

"Edmund's such a helpful lad," Rasputin murmured, standing with Valmont as the two waited their turn.

"That's enough, Edmund," Leigh snapped. She turned to her guide. "Can you do something?"

The woman nodded, and dropped to her knees atop the rock. Instead of lowering herself toward Morgan, she began murmuring, her face nearly touching the surface of the outcropping. A minute later, she rose again to her feet.

"The rock will not let you fall," she called down to Morgan. "Try again to climb."

Near her feet, Morgan felt part of the rock jut outward, forming a ledge just large enough for her to step onto. At the same time, the soothing tones of the woman's voice calmed the panic that gripped the childling. Tentatively, Morgan placed her foot on the steplike shelf. A second one appeared a little above the first. Above her, Morgan could see a series of deep depressions which she knew had not been visible before. Holding her breath, she reached up. The rock seemed to grab her and lift her as she steadily scaled the remaining distance. When she reached the top, Leigh put her arms around the shaken childling.

"It's all right," she murmured comfortingly. "You can't always be brave."

Morgan rested her head on Leigh's shoulder. The childling could see Edmund standing a little behind Leigh, a smug look on his face. *No, it's not all right*, she thought.

Freed from the need to support his granddaughter, Tor groped his way up the rockface. Seeing that Leigh was comforting Morgan, the troll stalked over to Edmund.

"I've had enough of your mouth," he growled down at the redcap.

Edmund stood his ground. "I was just trying to make her mad enough to forget she was a chicken," he said. "Honest," he added, blinking his eyes and trying to look as young and small as possible. Tor mumbled something unintelligible and turned away.

Unnoticed by the others, Valmont and Rasputin made their ascents with ease.

Morgan took a deep breath and gently extricated herself from Leigh's embrace.

"Thanks," she said to Leigh. Then she turned to the woman whose voice had coaxed her to safety. "I'm sorry I was so much trouble," she said. "Thank you for helping me."

The woman smiled. "When I was your age," she said, "I was not nearly so courageous."

"What did you do?" Leigh asked her.

"I spoke to the rock," she replied. "It was only too happy to help."

Valmont raised an eyebrow. "I knew that certain of our magics enabled us to converse with the inanimate," he said, "but I never would have thought to ask a stone to alter its shape."

The woman smiled. "This is more than just a stone," she replied. "This is the entry to our freehold."

"Where?" Edmund asked, seeing nothing around them but a wall of rock, and ahead of them, a dropoff to the sea.

"Look again." The words came from one of the other Kithain who had traveled with the oathmates to the rocky plateau.

"It's a cave!" cried Morgan, staring at the opening now visible in the cliff behind them.

"Enter and be welcome," the woman said, gesturing for the oathmates to step inside the cave. "The selkies of Rocky Shore have been awaiting your arrival."

Cyprian Ryder let his coffee cool as he related the events of the last few weeks to the dusky-skinned young woman who sat opposite him. They were in a small basement café on Newbery Street. Like him, Signe Henderson was one of the Dauntain, a changeling who had turned against her own kind and now hunted the Kithain, determined to eliminate the danger they posed to modern sensibilities.

"So you were in San Francisco when you were attacked by the demonspawn and your memories were driven from you?" she asked when he finally paused.

Ryder nodded. He retrieved a map of downtown San Francisco from the inside pocket of his greatcoat and spread it out on the table between them. The sheet was dotted with red and blue circles.

"I found this after I spoke with you," he said grimly. "It's marked with the results of my preliminary search for concentrations of Glamour. These are possible freeholds," he said, pointing to the small red dots within the larger blue circles. "The greatest concentration seems to be here," he pronounced, indicating one section of the map highlighted with a proliferation of red dots.

"Haight-Ashbury," Signe murmured. "It figures."

Ryder nodded his assent. "Even the normal residents—people who aren't infected by our curse—show some rather off-beat behavioral patterns. Either they're hooked on some new mystical hogwash or else they're borderline psychotics. I was stupid to go there by myself."

"I won't disagree," Signe said. She reached across the table and took hold of Ryder's left hand. Instinctively he tried to jerk it out of her grasp, but she held on, determined, giving him a small, deprecating smile. Finally, he relaxed.

Signe turned his hand over so that the palm was facing upward. With her other hand she traced the coin-sized bluish bruise that marked its center.

"Where the life and heart lines intersect," she murmured.

"What?" Ryder sounded dubious.

Signe laughed softly. "When I was a child, my parents took me to a carnival. There was an old woman telling fortunes by reading palms. I toyed with palmistry for a little while until I got bored with it."

Ryder's mouth curled into a half-sneering smile. "So what does it mean that this thing in my hand lies at the intersection of those two lines?" he asked.

"The heart line signifies the intensity of your passions," she said. "Yours is very pronounced—very deep. That shows your dedication to your goal."

Ryder shrugged. "I've been called a fanatic many times," he said. "By you, as a matter of fact."

"If I called you a kettle, then I'm a pot," Signe said.

"And the lifeline?" Ryder prompted.

Signe's face grew serious. "The lifeline supposedly indicates the length of your life—and its quality, to a certain extent. A faint line means illness or some other wasting condition." She released Ryder's hand abruptly and looked down, staring at the remains of her coffee and piroshky.

"So?"

Signe pursed her lips. She lifted her head, concern evident on her face.

"Your life line stops just beyond the blue mark," she said.

"I feel like I need to go back there," Ryder announced.

"To San Francisco?" Signe asked.

Ryder nodded. "Will you come with me?"

"I would have gone with you the last time," she replied. "What about the others? Shall I ask Vargas and Diana?"

The mention of those names brought to mind a wiry Puerto Rican man and a svelte blond woman. Together, the four of them had raided numerous changeling freeholds. Ryder considered them to be an unofficial SWAT team.

"Yes," he replied. "I'd like to leave as soon as possible."

In spite of the late-night December chill, the interior of the selkie freehold was comfortably warm. In the outer room, just inside the cavern entrance, Leigh and her friends sat on soft, plump cushions that appeared to be made from sea moss. Their hosts had brought out food and drink—small cakes that tasted of sea salt and pine nuts and elegant driftwood mugs filled with hot, berry-flavored tea.

The freehold's inhabitants filled in the spaces between the oathmates and soon the air was astir with animated chatter as names were exchanged and introductions made.

"I'll never remember everybody's names," Leigh said, shaking her head ruefully at the woman who had led the rescue team and who seemed to be in charge of the freehold. She had given her name as Ondine and now knelt at Leigh's side, examining the wound on her leg.

"I will," said Morgan cheerfully. "I'm writing them all down." The childling had rummaged in her backpack until she found the diary that Leigh had given her earlier in the day. Pulling out a pink ballpoint pen, she opened the small book and began listing as many names as she could recall.

"Pink!" Edmund sneered. "Gross." The redcap turned to the Kithain seated next to him, a lanky youth whose short brown curls clung to his head like a cap and whose bright green eyes regarded the redcap with mischief.

"So, uh, Drifter? Is that your name?" he asked.

The young selkie nodded.

"What do you do for fun around here?" Edmund surveyed the rock sculptures that decorated the freehold's interior. "Carve rock?"

"Some of us do," Drifter admitted. "Others comb the beaches." He held up a wrist to display an intricate bracelet of tiny shells. "I spend most of my time up where the surf's good."

"Killer!" said Edmund. "I always wanted to surf. Do you have a surfboard here?"

Drifter smiled. "I made it myself," he said proudly. "Want to see it?"

"Now?" Edmund thought of the crashing waves on the shore below the cliff.

"If you want," Drifter answered.

"Maybe later," Edmund said. *Way later*, he thought.

"Suit yourself," the selkie replied. "What do *you* do for fun?"

"I eat things," Edmund announced.

"This wound is going to need some serious tending," Ondine said to Leigh. Valmont, seated a few feet away and conversing with a pair of wilders who looked to be brother and sister, turned his attention to his oathmate.

"Do you want my help?" he asked. Leigh started to accept, remembering Valmont and Morgan had pooled their magic to heal first Rasputin and later the duke. Before she could speak, however, Ondine shook her head at the eshu.

"Rest and enjoy yourself," she said. "Let me care for her." She stood up and extended a hand to Leigh.

"Come with me where I can do a proper job on your leg," she said. Leigh clasped Ondine's hand and stood up, then followed the selkie into an inner room, deep inside the cliff.

Rasputin brought out his cloth juggling balls and began tossing them in the air, while a trio of selkie childlings watched in rapt fascination. Resting his bulk against a large pile of cushions, Tor allowed himself to doze, tired from the evening's exertion and his brush with Banality.

The selkie who had found Morgan wandering in the fog came up and offered her another helping of pine-nut cakes.

"What are you writing?" he asked.

Morgan looked up from her diary. "You're Simon, right?" she asked.

He smiled. "And you're Morgan."

"I'm keeping a diary," Morgan said. "I only started it just now. I thought that I ought to put down all your names so we won't forget them."

t h e   h i l l

He nodded gravely. "Perhaps one of your bards will write a song about us when your quest is done," he said.

"You seem to know an awful lot about our quest," Morgan said.

"Not so much as you think," Simon replied. "But what we do know is important for you to know as well. That's why we called you here."

Leigh returned with Ondine. Her wound had been cleaned, and she had changed from the jeans she wore beneath her chimerical armor into a pair of soft linen pants. She no longer limped and the pain was quickly receding.

"I'll mend the tear in your clothes later," Ondine said as the two women rejoined the group. "You'll all need to sleep here tonight. The Glamour within this freehold will help your healing more than anything else."

"You've been too good," Leigh said. "Without your help…" she let her words trail off.

Ondine held up a slender, webbed hand. "It is because of us that you came here at all," she responded quickly.

"And that is something I have been wanting to ask you about," Valmont said.

"Our people have heard that the first of the Eyestones has been found," Ondine announced.

Leigh looked startled. "The Eyestones?" she asked. "You know about them?"

Ondine inclined her head gracefully, her long hair clinging to her like a cloak. "We know about the Eyestones and about their origin, and this is why we requested that you come here."

"So why didn't you guys just hotfoot it to town instead of making us trek all the way up the coast?" asked Edmund.

"We have reasons for not wanting to stray too far from shore," Ondine replied.

"What, do you dry up and blow away?"

"That's rude, Edmund!" Morgan admonished, her voice indignant.

"Oh stuff it!" Edmund said.

"Hush, both of you," Tor interjected, starting from his nap as the tenor of the conversation around him changed.

"This is obviously not the time for us to keep silent and listen while our new friends impart some vital information," Rasputin said.

Ondine smiled at the pooka, her warmth almost a palpable caress.

"I have a story to tell, if you will hear it," she began, looking at Valmont. The eshu's eyes sparkled with interest.

"Our ignorance is your invitation to enlighten us," he said smoothly.

Ondine waited until everyone had formed a circle around her in the center of the freehold's main room. She stood, tall and graceful, dressed in a loose-fitting shift of sea-green gauze, her head thrown back as if she were listening for some distant cue to begin.

The room grew silent. Ondine opened her eyes and looked around at her expectant audience.

"This is a story from the time of the Shattering," she began. "It is a tale of pride and arrogance, of sibling rivalry." Her gaze strayed briefly to Morgan and Edmund before passing over their heads to settle on Valmont and Leigh. "Most of all, it is a tale of sacrifice and loss, yet it is not a tale without hope.

"When it finally became clear that the children of the Dreaming could no longer remain in the mortal world without sacrificing their faerie natures, the great exodus from this world to Arcadia began. It was not an orderly evacuation. Hordes of frightened fae scoured the lands, searching for the faerie trods and gateways that had so far withstood the onslaught of Banality.

"Many were too late, as gate upon gate crumbled into dust even as the desperate refugees sought to cross between the worlds.

"The lordly sidhe, they who felt most keenly the cold stabbing winds of the tides of disbelief and materialism, grew frantic. Many simply wrapped themselves in all the Glamour they could gather, often stooping to ravaging out of dire necessity, and hid themselves in faerie glens. Banality could not touch them in those sheltered spots of pristine beauty, but neither could they ever again touch the mortal world."

"Was that what we popped open?" Edmund whispered loudly to Valmont.

The eshu shook his head. "I don't think so," he said softly, frowning at Edmund and gesturing toward Ondine. "Listen," he mouthed.

"There were in those days twin brothers, Réamonn—whose name means mighty protector—and Rodhlann—which means fame of the land. Both were sidhe and both were lords of great power, but Réamonn followed the way of the Seelie while his brother traveled among the Unseelie court. From their earliest days, the two had been rivals, and as they grew older it became clear that they could not long dwell within the same holding. But though their temperaments were very different, their valor and fame were such that they each became lords of freeholds, with armies at their commands and loyal courtiers dependent on their leadership and protection.

"They, too, were caught up in the fierce competition for the dwindling gateways, and it was their folly that brought them both to grief."

Leigh's attention was distracted by a soft scratching sound. She followed the noise to where Morgan sat, her head bent over her diary, scribbling furiously, trying to keep pace with the speaker. Leigh smiled to herself and returned her gaze to Ondine.

"Only a few among the fae remember that Silver's Gate was the last to fall, and this, besides being the story of the two brothers, is the story of its falling. The knowledge of the gate's true location has been lost to the obscuring Mists that keep us from the Dreaming, but it is said that Silver's Gate once rested on a verdant isle and that its guardianship had long ago been given to the selkies and our distant cousins, the merfolk."

"Merfolk?" Morgan interrupted, looking up from her diary, delight evident on her face. Her expression changed suddenly into one of embarrassment. "Sorry," she whispered.

Ondine nodded, staring at Morgan. "Merfolk," she repeated. "They are somewhat like the sidhe, except they are even more impressed with their own grandeur."

Leigh felt her face grow hot as the rest of the group laughed softly. Words of self-defense rose to her lips, but even as she prepared to voice them, Leigh knew that the selkie's gentle gibe was not far off the mark. The sidhe were arrogant, and their assumption of power upon their return from Arcadia in 1969 had caused much strife among the changelings who had been forced by luck or circumstances to stay behind. She bit back the words she knew would only prove Ondine's statement, then noticed the selkie's warm look of approval.

"I see that the noble ones who sit among us are graceful enough to allow for one storyteller's opinion," she said. "I ask for your forgiveness as I continue my tale."

Without thinking, Morgan nodded her head, her pen poised over the pages of her book.

"Even as their dream-filled world was collapsing around them, the households of Réamonn and Rodhlann arrived on the shores of the Isle of Dreams, where Silver's Gate awaited them. Their chimerical ships, wondrous creations shaped like dragons and swans, began to shimmer and fade as the two households disembarked and streamed rapidly toward the gate."

Valmont heard Morgan's faint gasp at the mention of the swanlike ships. Remembering the childling's dream-vision, the eshu raised a wondering eyebrow.

"As luck would have it, both groups reached Silver's Gate at the same time. The massive portal already stood open, for the selkies and merfolk had thought to use it to take their leave of a world which no longer granted them the right to exist.

"Both brothers asserted their rights as sidhe to enter the gate before the seafolk. Determined not to give way to the latecomers, the merfolk rose from the waters to do battle before the gate. For the first time in their long lives, Réamonn and Rodhlann found themselves battlemates, and the two houses united long enough to drive the merfolk back into the sea.

"The selkies, though they, too, were drawn into the battle, were not so belligerent as their sea-kin. Moreover, they sensed the nearness of the Banal winds and knew that they were needed to keep Silver's Gate from closing as its Glamour began to fade. They withdrew to the sidelines and worked to shield the gate as Kithain fought Kithain over the right of precedence."

Valmont could not hold back a snort of contempt. He looked around him quickly to see if anyone had heard and saw Leigh staring at him, her green eyes sharp as daggers. The two Kithain had argued about the fairness of the sidhe, and though Valmont believed that Leigh was beginning to take her own kith with a grain of salt, she had yet to agree with him that the sidhe had usurped the rights of commoners. He met her gaze and shrugged apologetically.

Seated beside Valmont, Rasputin patted the eshu's knee consolingly.

"Why didn't the selkies just go through the gate while everyone else was fighting?" Edmund wanted to know. "That's what I would have done."

"That's 'cause you're just a redcap," Morgan said under her breath. As soon as she had mouthed the words, she felt ashamed. A quick glance told her that none of her oathmates had taken note of her words.

"Even if they had abandoned their duty to keep the gate open, the selkies could not have penetrated the frantic melee going on in front of the portal. Once the merfolk had been overcome, the brothers turned their hostility once more upon each other as each insisted that his own household should be the first to cross through the gate."

"Were these guys stupid or just jerks?" Edmund asked. A thump on the head from Tor silenced him, though the redcap took some satisfaction in the laughter that followed his impulsive comment.

"Aptly put, young babbler," Ondine said. This time Edmund scowled as a second round of mirth ensued at his expense.

"Finally, Merala, the queen of the selkies, interceded with the brothers. She pointed out that, even as they fought, Silver's Gate was beginning to weaken and that if they did not quickly reach some accord, none would be able to pass into the Dreaming.

"Thus the brothers ceased their battle and came to a compromise. The members of both households would enter the gate together, in small groups of equal numbers, until all the sidhe had passed into Arcadia."

"What about the selkies?" Morgan asked.

"Yeah!" echoed Edmund. For a moment the two childlings regarded each other in astonishment. Morgan quickly looked away and Edmund ducked his head, anticipating another warning tap from Tor. The troll's mouth hinted at a rare smile.

"If you had been one of the brothers," Ondine said to Morgan, "there would be no tale to tell, I believe. Your concern for us speaks well of a folk who have not always had our favor. Unfortunately, the brothers and their households used their powers of command to forbid any Kithain to pass through Silver's Gate until the sidhe had made their passage.

"The selkies, as I said, labored to hold open the fragile gate during the battle and now found themselves forced to wait as by twos and fours, the households of the brothers Réamonn and Rodhlann passed out of mortal ken and into the homeland of Arcadia. Because the brothers did not trust each other to hold to their pact, each took a position just inside the narrow gateway, halfway between the worlds. They added their own Glamour to bolster the diminishing power of Silver's Gate. It is said that some of the selkie who watched the dread parade saw the brothers age before their very eyes, as their essence was leeched away from them by the demands upon their magic. As each member of their household passed through, the brothers kept a tally, Réamonn counting those who wore his brother's badge and Rodhlann doing likewise for Réamonn's followers. Facing each other across the gate, they locked eyes in a battle of wills. Even as their bodies paid the toll of the Glamour they expended, the orbs in their faces grew harder and harder, until they glowed with malice like four cold, translucent gems."

Understanding dawned upon the faces of the companions almost simultaneously.

"Bitchin'!" breathed Edmund. Morgan stared, wide-eyed and speechless. Tor grunted. Leigh looked down at the pouch at her waist, shuddering at the thought of what she had been carrying. She recalled the circumstances under which she and her oathmates had gained possession of the Eye and grimaced. She brought to mind the vision of the satyr, acting as if under some compulsion, ripping the emerald gem from his own eyesocket and thrusting it in her direction. She fought against the impulse to cast the gem from her. *It's important to our quest,* she told herself firmly.

It was Valmont's turn to console Rasputin as the eshu noticed trails of moisture lining the pooka's cheeks.

"It is past and legend," Valmont whispered.

"Not future and destiny?" the pooka responded, his voice shaking.

"The procession continued until all from both households had traversed the gate save for the brothers themselves. Finally it was left for Réamonn and Rodhlann to pass through the gate. Unwilling to risk the ire of the sidhe lords, the selkies waited for one of the pair—or both—to make their move. They crowded nearer the gate, feeling the ground shudder beneath their feet as the onslaught of Banality eroded the protective barriers they had erected around the island. A few frantically tried to make their way through the gate, but the power of the brothers' stubborn pride acted as a barrier to prevent them from doing so.

"It was then that the selkies realized that they were doomed. In despair, Merala approached the brothers to plead for them to allow her folk to pass through before the rapidly diminishing gate disappeared completely. She knelt before them in supplication, her arms extended to both Réamonn and Rodhlann."

As she spoke, Ondine fell to her knees, mimicking the gesture of the legendary Merala, with her arms stretched to either side of her, the palms of her hands facing upward in expectation. Her gesture placed her on a level with the front row of her audience, her left hand almost touching Valmont, her right hand only inches away from Leigh.

the hill

"They did not respond," Ondine said, her voice hushed and icy. "So intent they were, so filled with hatred were their hearts, that each had forgotten everything but the need to prevail over the other. Realizing this, Merala grew even angrier. She felt the anxious gazes of her people, and saw that, even if the brothers allowed their passage, there would not be time enough for the selkies to pass through Silver's Gate.

"Then Merala pronounced her curse," Ondine's arms grew rigid and her webbed fingers curled like claws about her upraised palms.

"As your hatred has turned your hearts to stone, so let your outward forms reflect the hardness within. As you have kept us from returning to the Dreaming through this, the last gateway to Arcadia, so let this portal remain hidden from your kind and any Kithain who serve your kind until the inheritors of your legacies can face each other across its portals with love in their hearts."

Valmont groaned and shook his head.

"Because they had lost so much of their power, the brothers could not withstand the force of Merala's curse. Aghast at her hasty but impassioned words, Merala watched as her pronouncement, aided, perhaps, by their own hatred, transformed the brothers into statues of living stone." She paused and lowered her head.

No sound save the ceaseless crashing of the ocean surf broke the silence that engulfed the cavern. Slowly, Ondine raised her head and looked, first at her right hand, and then at her left. Finally, she regarded her spellbound audience.

"All except for their eyes," she whispered. "As Merala knelt before the petrified forms of the once proud sidhe lords, the gems that once had been the eyes of Réamonn and Rodhlann dropped from their stony faces and fell into her palms. In her right hand she held an emerald and a deep blue sapphire, which had once been part of Réamonn. In her left, she clutched a ruby and a translucent black opal, formerly Rodhlann's eyes. She gave a cry, realizing that the last of their Glamour had passed from them.

"Before she could rise to her feet, Silver's Gate slammed shut and disappeared from her sight. A great tremor rocked the island and Merala knew that only the greatest of her own magic could save even a few of her people and preserve the island which held the remnants of Silver's Gate.

"In haste, she distributed the four gems to four of her most loyal subjects, with instructions to take the powerful, but tainted, treasures to places of safety, if such could still be found. She pulled her own Glamour from her body to open up a pair of sea trods, through which her people could return to their freeholds along the shores of the world's continents and islands, hoping that there they could find safety, embracing mortal guises just as the eshu and the pookas and the redcaps and the trolls and the other Kithain had done."

Ondine rose from her knees and lowered her arms.

"Soon, only Merala and a few selkies who refused to leave her remained on the Isle of Dreams, which was rapidly breaking apart beneath their feet. It was then that the queen of the selkies found herself bound by her own curse. Feeling her doom upon her, she bowed beneath the weight of her words. Summoning the last of her power, Merala caused the Isle of Dreams to sink beneath the waves. Thus the last Arcadian gate and the queen of the selkies passed beyond the knowledge of the fae."

A reverent silence filled the room as Ondine bowed her head. A few of the younger listeners snuffled quietly. Leigh had to swallow to ease the pain in her throat.

"Isn't anybody going to clap?" Edmund asked.

Valmont rose to his feet, his dark eyes glistening with near rapture. Tor also stood, and nodded his head in approval for a story well told. One by one, the other oathmates and the rest of the audience stood and offered Ondine a silent ovation.

The graceful selkie blushed. "I have not done with my telling," she murmured, "though the drama is played out, there are still some few words to be said."

She waited for the rustling to stop as her listeners seated themselves again.

"This is kind of like an encore, isn't it?" Morgan asked, looking at Valmont.

The eshu nodded. "I suppose it is," he said.

"The four gems which were the brothers' eyes are the faerie treasures known as the Eyestones. You," she said to Leigh, "possess one of them, the one which has come to be called the Eye of Opening or the Keystone. The other three are still at large."

"So where are they?" asked Edmund.

Ondine hesitated before she answered him.

"When we heard that you had found the Keystone," she said, "those of us who have kept alive the tale of the selkie queen's curse came to believe that it was time for that curse to be lifted, if possible. You have been charged by your own duke to find and open Silver's Gate, but in order to do that, you must first find the other stones, for they are the means whereby the gate will open."

"Like I said," Edmund insisted, "where are the other three eyeballs?"

"Please stop exhibiting your patience," Rasputin said sharply. "None of us wants to know and I'm certain Ondine has no intention of telling us."

"I would that I had all the knowledge that you need," Ondine said ruefully. "Unfortunately, I can only set you on the path of one of the gems—the opal. It is called the Shadowstone, and although its powers are unknown

shadows on

to me, one of our legends tells of its whereabouts."

"Another story?" Morgan asked hopefully.

Ondine shook her head. "I'm afraid I have not the breath or the endurance to launch into another tale. Suffice it to say that we know that the Shadowstone resides with the menehune."

"The who-de-what-ni?" Edmund scoffed. "Is this a joke?"

"Edmund!" Morgan, Leigh, and Valmont exclaimed in chorus.

"The menehune," Ondine said gravely, "are not to be laughed at. They are one of the races of the Gallain, faeries who exist outside the rule of the sidhe. They hold to their own traditions and, some say, have developed their own methods of dealing with the world's Banality."

"Are they changelings like us?" Morgan asked.

Ondine shrugged. "Yes and no, I suppose," she said. "They are different."

"Like the nunnehi," Valmont observed. Seeing that his oathmates still looked puzzled, he added, "Faeries of the Native Americans. They, too, are somewhat different from the Kithain who serve as lackeys for the sidhe." He allowed an ironic smile to soften his words.

"Where can we find these men—men-e-hun-ee?" Leigh asked, stumbling over the unfamiliar syllables.

"Men-a-hoon-ay," Ondine corrected her. "Menehune." A brilliant smile transfigured her face. "They are the native faeries of Hawaii," she announced.

"Surf's up!" Edmund chortled.

Yrtalien surveyed the group of Kithain that had gathered about him. The assortment of disaffected

the hill

sidhe, angry redcaps, reckless eshu, lascivious satyri, and other commoners had responded to the sidhe lord's call. A light drizzle fell upon the deserted beach of black sand near the town of Koae, on the eastern tip of the island of Hawaii's Puna District.

To the clouded eyes of mortals, the people standing on the beach, heedless of the fine rain, appeared to be an odd assemblage of mismatched individuals except for the fact that most of them were young and all of them radiated an air of suppressed discontentment. More perceptive eyes would fasten on a trio of individuals standing a little apart from the main group, separated not only by a few feet of darkened sand but by an almost palpable aura that marked them as somehow different from the others.

"Are there none but these who will serve me?" Yrtalien demanded of the two Kithain who flanked him, one on either side.

On his left, Lady Glynnis labored to keep her face impassive. Experience had taught her that the Forsworn Prince was quick to perceive any exploitable weakness in his subjects. She steadied her voice and prayed that her liege would not blame the relative paucity of Kithain on her.

"I told Lord Devlin that you desired to meet with the most influential representatives among the Unseelie Kithain, my lord," she said, glancing at the tall, silver-haired sidhe who stood on Yrtalien's right.

Lord Devlin scowled and raised a hand to his cheek, affecting an air of nonchalance.

"Truly, Prince Yrtalien," he said, his voice flat and slightly nasal, "you will be better served by speaking to the few who are gathered here than attempting to address the entire Unseelie population of the islands. Besides," he added, "your consort gave me such minimal notice that it was impossible to pass along the news of this gathering to everyone."

Yrtalien closed his eyes and breathed deeply, filling his lungs with the salty smell of the ocean.

"I had hoped that both of you would be more responsive to my wishes," he said mildly, opening his eyes. "Still, if these are Kithain who can spread the news of my coming to others, perhaps my time will not be wasted in speaking to them."

The drizzle thinned to a barely perceptible mist, then stopped altogether.

The raven-haired sidhe prince raised one arm into the air as if reaching for an imaginary object from a shelf high above his head, using the gesture to focus his Glamour. Suddenly the area was bathed in a chimerical luminescence that created the illusion of moonglow despite the cloudcover overhead. The sudden brightening of the area brought the small crowd of Kithain to attention. When all eyes were turned to him, Yrtalien stepped forward into the middle of the circle of light.

"Children of the dark half of the year, our time is come round at last," he announced, his dulcet voice rich with overtones of authority and command. With those words, he invoked the majestic grandeur that was his kith's birthright. The beauty of his faerie seeming, already endowed with an unearthly and sinister attractiveness, became even more pronounced. Clad in a loose-fitting shirt of deepest purple velvet worn over black silk trousers, his long hair arranged in a stylishly disordered shag, Yrtalien projected an aura of natural arrogance and studied rebellion.

"Long ago when the faerie folk ruled as rightful lords over humankind, the Samhain Revels signaled the passing of the torch of rulership from the Court of Light to the Court of Shadows. From that night until the lighting of the Beltaine fires, the Unseelie exercised their rights of domain over all Kithain.

"Since the return of the sidhe, that oldest of traditions has been debased and degraded until it is now a mockery of an ancient and honorable sharing of power. It is time for the Shadow Court to become more than just a one night stand.

"My name is Yrtalien and I come to you from the Dreaming."

Not precisely true, but close enough, Glynnis thought to herself as she watched Yrtalien perform before an audience held captive by the power of his aura. The "prison" from which Yrtalien had been released by the power of the Eye of Opening had been located not in Arcadia but in a halfway realm somewhere between the faerie homeland and the mortal world. *Let them think that he is a messenger from Arcadia*, she mused. *It will lend strength to his image, and with this crowd he will need all the credibility he can muster.*

Shortly after his arrival in the physical realm, Yrtalien had commanded Glynnis to find a suitable location for him to establish his own Shadow Court within the boundaries of the Kingdom of Concordia, the name which the returning sidhe had given to the North American continent. Glynnis had made discreet inquiries through her network of Unseelie Kithain and had learned that the islands which made up the state of Hawaii housed a number of Unseelie changelings, drawn by the region's remoteness from the mainland of Concordia. Though the Kingdom of Pacifica laid nominal claim to Hawaii, distance made true governance of the area difficult. Queen Aeron had dispatched one of her nobles to the island of Oahu to act as Regent for the territory but otherwise took no notice of her westernmost province, involved as she was with Kithain politics closer to home.

Acting through Lord Devlin, whom she had lured to her side with flattery and promises of power, Glynnis had secured a small freehold in the city of Hilo, on the island of Hawaii—also known as the Big Island. From this base, Yrtalien could begin to realize the plan he had briefly outlined to her, a plan which he was even now describing in his stirring speech intended to enflame the spirits of his listeners.

"For twenty-five years, the Seelie fae have trampled upon our dual heritage," Yrtalien was saying. "It is time for that to change, and under the leadership which I offer, you will be the instruments of that change. Throughout Concordia, Shadow Courts are meeting in secret, constructing elaborate plots to snatch bits and pieces of power here and there. In Oakhold, the Unseelie are arming themselves with iron weapons against a time when they foresee war between themselves and the Seelie lords."

Glynnis smiled to herself as she heard those words. Arranging for the shipment to the Bay area of iron swords and daggers was one of her greatest triumphs, involving delicate negotiations with Unseelie enclaves along the west coast. It had originally been her dream to reenact the legendary Night of Iron Knives, this time with the leaders of the Seelie court as victims. That massacre of commoner leaders by iron-wielding sidhe nobles had been the first battle of the Accordance Wars. In that grand clash between the sidhe newly arrived from Arcadia and the commoners who had established themselves in the realm where the Shattering had trapped them, the sidhe, with their greater powers of leadership and their ability to exert control over other Kithain, had enjoyed an unfair advantage. Over the last quarter century, however, the number of Unseelie sidhe had grown as Arcadia continued to exile her outcasts and rebels to the mortal world. The odds were changing.

Yrtalien's coming had altered her plans. It was he who, in a dream, had contacted her from within his enchanted prison and—step by step—had directed her along the circuitous path that had culminated in his release. She had cultivated Malacar, then wizard to Duke Aeon's court, winning his allegiance and, through him, gaining access to the ducal library. A series of obscure references in arcane tomes housed within the duke's palace had led her to the discovery of the legend of the Eye of Opening, which Yrtalien had insisted was vital to his release. Although Glynnis had hoped that the Forsworn Prince would provide her fledgling Unseelie army with skilled leadership from beyond the mists, once Yrtalien had confided in her his own, greater scheme, she had come to share his audacious vision. Unlike most of the sidhe exiled from Arcadia, Yrtalien retained many of his memories of the fae homeland. And one of those memories would help him change the world, or so he claimed.

"Here, on this island where Pacifica has no real power," Yrtalien was saying, "we shall create a new vision of Kithain society, one governed not by outworn mores and rigid traditions but by the principle of change which is at the root of our undying spirit. We should, even now, be reveling in our abandon, taking the Glamour which is rightfully ours from those mortals whose destiny it is to supply us with the fruits of their labors."

His audience responded to those words with murmurs of approval. Glynnis knew that many of them preferred the easy method of ravaging, ripping Glamour from human sources, to the slow cultivation of human creativity encouraged by the Seelie rulers of the fae. By granting the ravagers his approval, Yrtalien had taken a crucial step toward winning their support.

"My new Shadow Court will provide a necessary distraction, keeping our adversaries occupied while you and I and a chosen few pursue my true objective," Yrtalien had told Glynnis when the pair first arrived on the Big Island. Since his entry into the mortal world, the Forsworn Prince had demonstrated an extraordinary ability to absorb a great deal of information about the current state of Kithain society. Despite his political acumen, however, his primary interest lay in pursuing his search for the legendary faerie gems known as the Eyestones. Those gems, he assured her, held the key to his goal.

Although he had not fully shared with her the nature of his mission, Glynnis knew that it involved acquiring the Eye of Opening and its companion gems. It had, in fact, been reports that one of those treasures lay "west of the Summer Lands' westernmost shores" which had led her to settle upon Hawaii as the best possible location for Yrtalien's freehold.

Acquiring the Shadowstone from the primitive Kithain on the island of Kauai had been their first priority, and, indeed, the faerie trod through which she and Yrtalien had traveled had led them into the arms of the guardians of that powerful treasure. Among the menehune, as they called themselves, Yrtalien had proven himself to be a master of lies and deceptions.

A second gem, the Eye of Opening, once in Malacar's possession, was now in the hands of the Seelie knight Eleighanara. When Glynnis had confessed to Yrtalien that she did not understand why he had compelled the satyr to surrender the gem to the sidhe maiden, the prince coldly informed her that it was not her business to question his dealings. She had suffered for her curiosity.

Focusing her attention once more on Yrtalien, Glynnis realized that he was approaching the end of his exhortation.

"When we are finally united, armed with weapons which will ensure our victory against the spineless rulers of the kingdoms of Concordia, we shall bring about a

the hill

revolution which will return to us the glory we deserve. And you will share with me the spoils of our conquest."

Enthusiastic cheers greeted the conclusion of Yrtalien's speech. The prince flashed a brilliant smile at his new followers. Turning, first to Devlin and then to Glynnis, he extended a hand to each of them.

"Shall we mingle with our subjects?" he murmured.

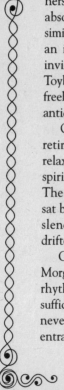

The companions spent the night in the freehold of Rocky Shore. At Ondine's insistence, Leigh made a bed for herself near the balefire, where she could more easily absorb the Glamour it radiated. She remembered a similar situation, when Valmont had taken a wound from an iron dagger. The eshu had accepted Fizzlewig's invitation to sleep in the boggan's apartment above the Toybox, so that he might take advantage of both the freehold's balefire and the Glamour residing inside the antique toy chest for which the coffee house was named.

Ondine also gave Leigh an herbal tea to drink before retiring for the night, or what was left of it. "This will relax you and help you sleep, so that your body and your spirit can concentrate on healing," the selkie told her. The decoction began its work almost instantly. Ondine sat beside Leigh, gently stroking her forehead with her slender webbed fingers until the exhausted knight drifted into slumber.

Curled up on her own bed of mossy cushions, Morgan fell asleep without any trouble, lulled by Tor's rhythmic breathing. Satisfied that the freehold was sufficiently protected without his assistance, the troll nevertheless arranged his bulk just inside the cavern's entrance. Rasputin found a small rocky nook not far from the room where Leigh slept. The pooka's rabbitlike ears draped softly around his face as he rested.

Edmund ventured outside the cavern entrance, maintaining that he wasn't sleepy and that he wanted to watch the surf. No one made a move to stop him, since the ledge outside the freehold was nearly as well protected as the freehold itself.

Once, during the night, Leigh awoke briefly to the sound of low conversation across the room, where Ondine had her bed. She recognized one of the voices as that of their selkie host. The other voice was Valmont's. Vaguely troubled, Leigh tried to push herself to full wakefulness in order to make out more than just the rise and fall of their words. It was a losing battle.

They were surrounded by a host of dark shapes that radiated a killing coldness. The sky overhead glowed with an unearthly red light, and sulfurous fumes filled the air around them. They were in the middle of a battle for their lives—and for their faerie souls—and they were losing that battle. One by one, they fell, overcome by foes who fought them with iron and Banality. Finally, they huddled together in defeat, bound with iron that rendered them helpless with its nauseating and numbing cold.

Five? There should be six, Morgan thought, as she struggled to retain her fragile hold on her faerie self. She tried to identify the faces of her companions, but their features were blurred by the thickening cloud of heavy smoke. It was vital for her to figure out which one of them was missing, for that one, she knew, had betrayed the rest.

With a sudden shock, she realized who among them had broken faith. She opened her mouth to speak the traitor's name—

—and woke with an incoherent sob lodged in her throat.

"Morgan?" Her grandfather's voice, still thick with sleep, rumbled in her ear. Alerted by his granddaughter's restless whimpers, Tor was at her side, groggy but awake. Morgan launched herself into the troll's arms and cried uncontrollably against his comforting bulk. After a few minutes, her tears were exhausted. Tor stroked her dark hair in an effort to soothe her.

"It's all right," he muttered softly, his lips pressed against her hair. "It was only a dream." Even as he spoke, Tor winced. Dreams were the stuff of Kithain magic, and Morgan's dreams often seemed to penetrate the mists to touch the Dreaming itself. Tor, who had lost the capacity to dream and who existed on Glamour borrowed from others, knew a moment of envy for the childling who dwelled so close to the realm he found so difficult to enter.

"It's *not* all right," Morgan whispered, her voice disconsolate. Her small chest heaved as she struggled to control the last remnants of the sobs that had wracked her body.

"It was an important dream," she said, raising her head to look at Tor with eyes that seemed far too old and too haunted for her eleven years. "We were fighting and there was smoke and—"

Even as she fought to retain the images that had been so vivid in her mind, the dream burst into fragments of mist and dissipated, leaving behind only an overwhelming sense of despair and loss.

"I can't remember it!" Morgan wailed, feeling a fresh spate of tears well up inside her.

Still holding on to her, Tor let his granddaughter cry herself to sleep.

Outside the freehold, Edmund had found a small shelf of rock a few feet down from the western slope of the stone plateau. He eased himself down until he rested on the smooth ledge, just big enough for two full-sized people to sit comfortably. The redcap childling's slight body barely covered a quarter of the surface and he was able to plant himself well away from the edge. Although it was too dark and misty to see more than a few feet ahead of him, Edmund could hear the pounding of the waves as they crashed against the jagged coastline below.

Certain that no one from inside the freehold could see him, Edmund reached for the new leather pouch that now rested snugly inside the righthand pocket of his jeans. Never mind that Morgan's gift to him had implied that she knew about his secret, the pouch *was* perfect for his own pilfered faerie treasure, stolen from the toy chest in the Toybox Coffee Shop on the night Malacar had released the chimerical toys from their long confinement. Carefully, Edmund withdrew the tiny painted clown miniature from the pouch and set it gently on the rock next to him.

Spitting into his hands, the redcap clapped his palms together three times, focusing his Glamour through the bizarre ritual and directing it toward the clown. The tiny figure began to shimmer softly as Edmund's Glamour invoked its magical change. In less time than it took to wipe the spit off on his jeans, a four-and-a-half foot tall, plump clown with a bulbous red nose, a lopsided grin, and spiky orange hair shared the ledge with Edmund. The redcap sighed in relief.

"I'll bet you're thinking that it's about time," Edmund addressed his chimerical companion. "How's it goin', Mr. Dumpy?" The redcap held out his hand, palm up. The clown cocked his head and brought his own white-gloved hand, palm down, to meet Edmund's.

Unlike most chimera, the creatures from the toy chest had a physical as well as a chimerical existence. In purely material form, they appeared as toys of various kinds. When touched by Glamour, however, they grew to life-sized versions of themselves.

At first, Edmund had been disappointed that the clown, whom he had named Mr. Dumpy, was unable to speak. Then the redcap realized that Mr. Dumpy's silence spoke volumes, and the clown's gestures usually telegraphed its "thoughts" clearly. Edmund was careful not to activate Mr. Dumpy too often, particularly when bringing the clown to life meant expending his own hoarded Glamour. Experiments had proven that Mr. Dumpy's magic could be triggered repeatedly, so long as the clown retained even a vestige of Glamour or remained in proximity to the stuff of faerie magic.

Mr. Dumpy plopped himself down beside Edmund on the ledge.

"Do you like your new traveling bag?" the redcap asked, indicating the leather pouch.

Mr. Dumpy nodded.

"Too bad it had to be a gift from Her Fussiness." Edmund sighed. "This would be a perfect adventure if it weren't for her. I really hate her sometimes," he said vehemently. "Most of the time," he amended. "Do you notice things when you're stuck in my pocket?"

The clown shrugged. Edmund thought he detected a slight nod.

"It's not fair," he announced. "I open my mouth and get stepped on or get my head thumped by some beefed-up, muscle-brained troll, but just let little Miss Perfection say something stupid and everybody falls all over themselves to tell her how smart she is."

The redcap noticed a pair of loose chunks of rock near the rim of the shelf. Picking them up, he stood up and hurled one as hard as he could toward the sound of the ocean. The move unbalanced him and he started to tumble forward. A chimerical hand locked firmly around his belt pulled him back.

"Thanks," Edmund said, resuming his seat on the ledge. He looked at the other piece of rock for a few

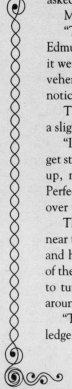

seconds, then shrugged and popped it into his mouth. For a moment he crunched away quietly, listening to the sea and enjoying Mr. Dumpy's silent sympathy.

"If I had some charcoal," he told the clown, "I would have written her name on that rock."

The sky was just beginning to turn from black to gray when Edmund finally yawned and turned to Mr. Dumpy, holding the pouch in his hand.

"I guess you'd better get small again," the redcap told his chimerical friend. "I need to sleep and you need to hide."

Mr. Dumpy looked sorrowfully from the pouch to Edmund's face.

The redcap reached out and patted the clown on the shoulder. "I know," he said. "It's harsh being forced to stay in a pocket, but if they found out I still had one of the toys from ole Fizzlewig's dumb chest, they'd probably make me FedEx you back to him."

Mr. Dumpy nodded. Waving his hand in a gesture halfway between a salute and a farewell, the chimera's aura began to fade. In seconds the clown once more lay on the ground at Edmund's feet, a tiny painted figurine. Edmund scooped the miniature up and placed it carefully inside the pouch, then returned the pouch to his pocket. He hoisted himself back onto the surface of the plateau and headed toward the selkie freehold.

chapter

four

At Signe's insistence, Ryder and his companions rented a car upon their arrival in San Francisco. Now the graceful, dark-skinned woman watched as Ryder and Vargas unloaded the group's luggage, including one long leather-covered, steel-reinforced carrying case labeled "Antique Weaponry" and stamped with various seals of authorization. Their fourth member, a tall, flaxen-haired Nordic beauty named Diana, stood next to Signe, looking around at the inside of the bleak parking building adjacent to their hotel.

"Are you sure this isn't the same place you stayed before?" Diana asked Ryder. The dark-haired, arrogantly attractive Dauntain shook his head.

"I'm positive," he said. "I found the hotel bill for my first night's stay."

"Good," said Signe. "We don't want to take any unnecessary chances until we know more about what we're up against."

"We're up against the minions of darkness," Vargas said, crossing himself as he came as close to naming their common enemy as he ever would. The wiry Latino had once studied to become a priest. Even as a boy, he firmly believed that malevolent spirits could take possession of luckless humans, and he dreamed of dedicating his life to driving out those unwelcome beings from their mortal hosts. Ryder had recruited him three years ago, when he first realized that a group of Dauntain acting together as a trained commando force could be more effective in rooting out the changeling menace than a single individual. His persuasive talents had so touched the young Puerto Rican that Vargas had abandoned his vocation in order to follow a path that promised more action in his chosen field and demanded less in the way of tedious rituals.

It had come as something of a shock to Vargas when Ryder confided that he was, himself, still struggling with infernal possession. In order to prove his claim, Ryder forced himself to use the residual Glamour that resided in the blue faerie gem embedded in his left palm to enchant Vargas long enough to allow him to glimpse the horror of Ryder's faerie seeming. One look at the towering figure in black chimerical armor, his dark brown hair swept back from a pair of slender pointed ears, was enough to convince Vargas that Ryder had intimate knowledge of the existence of the servants of the dark powers. Ryder then fell on his knees to beg forgiveness for so blatantly exposing his evil essence. In what was to be the first of many confessional sessions with the might-have-been priest, Ryder had convinced Vargas of his own dedication to locating and neutralizing others of his kind.

"If I am evil," the ex-sidhe lord once known as Chevalier had professed, "still I serve the cause of righteousness."

Both Signe and Diana were changelings who, like Ryder, had rejected their natures and embraced Banality. Diana was a troll, or giant, and sometimes Ryder could see a faint afterimage of the horridly grotesque faerie seeming she worked so hard to eradicate. Her human form reminded him of one of the Valkyrie, strikingly attractive with an imposing, almost masculine beauty.

Signe, whose heritage bore traces of African and gypsy blood, was an eshu. Members of her kith rarely turned against their faerie natures, but Signe was a special case. She was Ryder's protégé and his first true success. He had discovered her in Harvard Square, where she was hawking volumes of self-published poetry. On impulse, Ryder purchased one of her books and, upon reading it, recognized in her verses the telltale signs of changeling infestation. For weeks, he stalked her, determined to eradicate the threat posed by her existence. He even allowed himself to fall into his faerie seeming in order to reveal himself to her as a fellow changeling. As the brooding Lord Chevalier, Ryder won her trust. Flattered by his interest in her and in her poetry, Signe agreed to accompany her changeling companion on a weekend trip to New Hampshire's Berkshire Mountains, where Ryder had rented a cabin. In the isolated wilderness setting, "Chevalier" dropped his pose. Although he was prepared to kill her if necessary, Ryder gave the frightened eshu a choice—death or rehabilitation.

By the time the pair returned to Boston, Signe was firmly grounded in Banality, her faerie spirit dormant within her and her will broken. Over the years, she learned to appreciate the service Ryder had performed in freeing her soul of its tainted burden. Like him, she had become a staunch opponent of everything she once was. Now she was one of the few individuals whom Ryder allowed to address him by his faerie name, Chevalier, and it had become their private code word, used primarily to jog each others' memories when—as had so recently been the case with Ryder—one or the other of them chanced to fall afoul of the creatures they hunted.

"Is everything unloaded?" Signe now asked as the four Dauntain stared at the small pile of luggage at their feet.

Vargas nodded. Rather than trust their possessions to the hotel staff, the group had decided to carry their own bags from the parking building to their rooms. Once they were settled in the adjoining suites Diana had reserved for them, they would begin making serious plans to locate the changelings of San Francisco.

"This is our secret," Ondine said, her bright eyes gleaming with suppressed delight as she brought the oathmates to a sheltered cove a few minutes' walk from the selkie freehold. The climb down the rock cliff was, strangely enough, not as difficult as the ascent, and although the walk along the beach was strenuous, the exercise invigorated them. Leigh's wound had nearly healed and she was able to keep pace with the others, a slight limp the only reminder of her brush with cold iron.

The sidhe knight pushed herself to stay near the front of the group, just behind Ondine and Valmont, who walked together at the head of the small procession. Leigh could not help but notice that overnight, a bond had formed between the handsome eshu and the graceful selkie. Several times during their trek up the beach, Ondine reached for Valmont's hand, clasping it affectionately for a few steps before releasing her hold to maneuver over a tricky section of rock and sand. Leigh tried to ignore their easy familiarity and concentrated, instead, on not favoring her hurt leg.

"What's so secret about this place?" yawned Edmund. It had been nearly dawn when the young redcap had finally fallen asleep. He had not expected to be awakened soon after sunrise and was still struggling to stay conscious.

t h e   h i l l

"Watch," Ondine said, motioning to Drifter and Simon, who accompanied them. Approaching Ondine, they joined hands with her and formed a circle near the edge of the water. The three selkies began a stately dance, their feet moving in precisely measured paces to a beat set by the slap of waves upon the shore.

Valmont was the first to notice the change in the air where the trio danced.

"They are opening a trod," the eshu exclaimed, not bothering to hide the awe in his voice.

"A what?" Edmund asked sleepily.

"A faerie road, dummie," Morgan replied. The sidhe childling looked disgustingly rested, although Edmund thought her eyes seemed a little red. "They are pathways that connect freeholds and sometimes used to lead straight to Arcadia," Morgan informed Edmund.

"Huh," he snorted. "So if this is a road to Arcadia, how come we're looking for Silver's Gate?"

Morgan sighed in exasperation.

"I didn't say that *all* trods went there, only some of them, and the ones that do, don't anymore." She rolled her eyes upward.

"I suspect that we are all as familiar with the mechanics of fae travel as you, oh child of House Eiluned," Rasputin said mildly, waggling his ears at Morgan. The childling blushed.

"I thought everyone knew what a faerie road was," she said.

"Everyone but me, you mean," Edmund challenged. "You think I'm stupid, don't you, Miss Smartass?"

Morgan's eyes widened in shock.

"Will you two stop it!" Leigh snapped. "You're arguing like a pair of spoiled brats, and in the meantime, you're missing something few changelings will ever see."

"I am not a brat!" Edmund said hotly.

"I am not a brat!" Morgan echoed, only a beat behind Edmund's denial.

"Then behave yourselves and watch," Leigh said, pointing to Ondine and her companions.

As the selkies danced, the land around them underwent a steady transformation; a shimmering opening rent the fabric of reality. The air parted to reveal a sparkling waterway that stretched westward, the flow of its waters running counter to the mundane sea on either side.

Near the opening of the roadway, Morgan spied what looked like the head of a giant pearlescent swan, the rest of its body concealed by the framework of the portal.

"It's my boat!" the childling exclaimed. "Just like in my dream," she added in a whisper.

"Savage!" Edmund said, impressed in spite of himself.

The selkies moved apart from each other and stood at the edge of the entrance to the road. Ondine extended her arm in a gesture which invited the oathmates to step across the threshhold.

Valmont, his dark eyes glittering with anticipation, looked over his shoulder at Leigh. He crooked his arm and offered his elbow to her.

"Shall we?" he asked.

A gentle shove from Rasputin pushed Leigh forward. She stumbled a little and grabbed Valmont's proffered arm to steady herself.

"I really didn't need the urging," she said to the pooka.

"I know you didn't," Rasputin said.

Arm in arm, Leigh and Valmont stepped out of the world of mortals and stood at the edge of the faerie trod. Ondine motioned the others forward until everyone had entered the portal. They saw that they now stood on the edge of a pier that fronted on a rounded corridor of brilliant blue-green water capped with white seafoam.

the   hill

"It's like a big waterchute," said Edmund. The topography of the trod played havoc with his perceptions. Even with faerie sight, the redcap had to struggle to make sense of what he saw.

"More like a tunnel," Valmont suggested. "See how the edges curve in on themselves?" The eshu described an arc with his arms.

"I can't even begin to describe it," Leigh murmured, caught up in the mystery of standing in a place that had no coordinates in the mortal realm.

"The edges are fuzzy," Morgan said. "It's like traveling across the Bay Bridge on a foggy day when you can't see anything but the road in front of you."

"I'm utterly speechless," Rasputin added. Tor, who was the last of the oathmates to cross over, nodded agreement. The troll's faerie nature had responded to the Glamour that permeated the trod. Morgan gasped as she saw her grandfather's true self in clear detail.

"You look wonderful, Grandpa!" she exclaimed. Even in the Toybox or in the duke's palace, Tor's faerie seeming had never been so pronounced. "I can see your horns!"

Tor reached self-consciously for his forehead and touched the twin protruberances that typified his kith. He grunted with satisfaction, as the years seemed to drop away him. Unconsciously he drew himself up to his full height, nearly nine feet of troll warrior.

"Better enjoy it while it lasts," he muttered.

Morgan's attention turned next to the towering form of the graceful white swan ship, now clearly visible as it bobbed atop the waves.

"Is this for us?" she asked Ondine. The selkie nodded.

"With this ship, you can traverse the distance between here and your destination in a very short time," she said.

"That's strange," Drifter remarked, his voice registering a note of concern. "There should be a second boat."

Simon, who stood at the edge of the portal, stepped inside and looked around. "The black boat's missing," he said.

The three selkies traded worried looks.

"Could someone have breached the portal without our knowledge?" Ondine asked her kithmates.

"I wouldn't think so," Simon said hesitantly. "Not without a tremendous amount of power and some way of knowing the location of the trod."

Morgan gasped. At the same moment, Leigh shuddered.

"I know someone who could have done this," Leigh said slowly, looking at Morgan as she spoke. Morgan nodded gravely.

Belatedly, Leigh explained to the three selkies about their encounter with the sidhe lord whom they had freed from his enchanted prison. "He is called Yrtalien," Leigh said in conclusion. "And he is so recently come here that I fear his powers are much greater than our own faded enchantments."

Ondine listened carefully to Leigh's story, then gave the oathmates a rueful smile.

"What's done cannot be undone," she said, "and you are not responsible for the actions of your enemy."

"That's true," said Rasputin doubtfully.

"I think our best course of action would be to consider this water under the bridge," Valmont said wryly, "and be on our way with as much alacrity as we can manage."

"I agree," Ondine said, pointing to a ladder built into the side of the swan ship. Again, Valmont and Leigh led their companions as they boarded the ship.

"She will sail herself once she senses you are ready

to get underway," Ondine announced. "May your crossing be smooth, and may the guardian of the trod look favorably on your passage."

So effortlessly that the companions felt no sense of motion, the ship glided away from the pier and headed down the sea lane that stretched before it. Standing at the stern of the vessel, Edmund and Rasputin watched the figures of the three selkies dwindle rapidly in size.

"Guardian?" Edmund asked the pooka. "What did she mean, guardian?"

"Probably just a figure of speech," Rasputin replied, chewing thoughtfully on the tip of his left ear.

"You find our ways strange, don't you, Kanani?" Yrtalien asked. Kanani, the copper-skinned Kithain, sat uncomfortably on the edge of a delicately carved driftwood chair in the seaward room of Yrtalien's new palace. In the corner of the room, Lady Glynnis and Lord Devlin were engaged in a game of chess. A faint smile crossed the face of the prince as he contemplated his guest's unease with mild enjoyment.

"Too high," the girl said, her voice lingering over the syllables of the words as if savoring their strangeness on her tongue.

The girl is beautiful, Yrtalien thought, studying her dark, almond-shaped eyes, and the broad yet delicate features of her expressive face. Casually his fingers toyed with the tiny shell pendant that dangled from a thin silver chain about his neck.

"Your father gave me this so that I could speak your language," he said gently. "You need not struggle to speak an unfamiliar tongue." Yrtalien knew that so long as he touched the shell, Kanani would hear his words as if they were spoken in her own language. He himself could hear his words both as he formed them and, slightly out-of-phase, the translation of those words into the language spoken by the menehune, the native Kithain of the Pacific islands. "And you have a similar one so that you can speak mine," he added.

Kanani shook her head. "That is too easy," she said, forming the words slowly. "It is knowing without learning." Her hands remained folded in her lap as she spoke. "I came here as an offering of peace between our people and yours," she said, frowning slightly, as if unsure of the accuracy of her words. "Is that so?"

"The word you are looking for is ambassador, I believe," Yrtalien said, dropping his own hand from the shell and resting it on the arm of his chair.

"Ambassador," Kanani repeated, smiling. "It is a good word."

Yrtalien's freehold lay on the outskirts of Hilo, the largest city on the island of Hawaii. The two-story wood-and-frame house once belonged to one of the early missionaries to the island's native population; unlike others of its kind, which had been turned into museum pieces or were still inhabited by descendants of those evangelizers, this building had fallen into disrepair. Now faerie enchantments had transformed the rambling structure into an ethereal, airy palace of decadent opulence.

Since his arrival on the Big Island two weeks earlier, Yrtalien had gradually been making adjustments to the design of his freehold—his princely court-in-exile, as he privately dubbed it. Glynnis' contact in Hilo, Lord Devlin of the silver hair and the sniveling voice, had arranged for the acquisition of the house and had worked to imbue it with his own idea of a dwelling place for an

Arcadian prince. He had not quite succeeded, but Yrtalien had neither the time nor the will to make drastic alterations to what he perceived as only a temporary residence. Even as it was, it served adequately as the focus for his growing Shadow Court. In addition to Glynnis, Devlin and the original few Kithain who helped prepare for his coming, last evening's speech had succeeded in drawing other local changelings to the freehold to pay homage to a lord who promised them power and license. Soon, he would begin initiating them into the forgotten rituals of their Unseelie heritage.

He allowed himself an indulgent smile at the young menehune maiden now gracing his court with her presence. It had taken all his skill at manipulating people to win not only the Shadowstone but the daughter of Chief Makani. Kanani's presence was important to him for a number of reasons, one of them having to do with a tradition which, now abandoned by both Seelie and Unseelie courts in the mortal world, was once dear to the hearts of all fae nobles.

"Yes," he agreed. "Ambassador is a very good word." Yrtalien picked up a crystal goblet and languidly sipped its contents—a mixture of kiwi and lime juices. *Better than the word "sacrifice"*, he thought.

"Did anybody think to bring any food?" Edmund demanded. The redcap stood on the deck of the swanship, swinging his short sword at an imaginary foe.

"We ate this morning with the selkies," Morgan reminded him. From her place near the prow of the ship, the childling stared at the vista in front of her, all constantly shifting rainbow swirls except for the narrow ribbon of blue-green ocean that stretched ahead of the ship's course. Beside her, Leigh practiced a series of stretches, testing her hurt leg for signs of weakness.

"That wasn't real food," Edmund retorted. "I mean something that didn't come from a health food store or a weed-eater's backyard."

"Since you weren't going to bring it up," Rasputin muttered, leaving his post near the ship's midsection and approaching the redcap, "I had no intention of passing these around." Reaching into his woven shoulder bag, the pooka drew out a smaller sack and set it on the deck to display its contents. Inside were a dozen granola bars, six bars of semi-sweet chocolate, a half-dozen small packages of trail mix, a large box of raisins, and two packages of individually wrapped sticks of beef jerky. Edmund stared at the collection of food and grimaced.

"I guess the jerky's okay," he said, "but the rest is rabbit food."

Rasputin looked disappointed.

"Did *you* bring any food?" Valmont asked Edmund, a halfway accusing tone to his voice.

Edmund looked miffed. "I guess I can eat my clothes if I get hungry enough," he said.

"So you *didn't* bring anything," Morgan chortled. "I knew it."

Leigh paused in mid-stretch. "I think most of us dropped the ball on that one," she admitted. "I brought a small skillet and cookware; I just forgot to bring anything to cook."

"I should think that you, of all people, would have given some thought to our provisions," Valmont remarked.

Leigh flushed. "I may be an amateur chef," she said, "but I'm certainly no quartermaster."

"What's that?" Edmund asked.

t h e   h i l l

"Supply officer," said Tor. The troll stood, arms folded, in the center of the ship, where the mast would have been had one been needed. "In the army, there would have been one person responsible for seeing that a troop had the equipment it needed."

"It's not as if we'll be stuck in some wilderness where we have to hunt or forage for our own food," Rasputin said. "Surely there are restaurants and grocery stores where we're going."

"It won't matter if we starve before we get there," Edmund said dourly, picking up a piece of beef jerky and biting off a chunk experimentally. "Tastes like tires gone bad," he said.

"Yuck," said Morgan. She looked at Rasputin. "Can I have one of the granola bars?" she asked.

"Of course not," Rasputin said, handing her one and unwrapping another for himself.

"How long have we been traveling, anyway?" Leigh asked. "Surely it hasn't been more than an hour or so?"

Valmont shrugged. "Who knows? There are no accurate gauges for measuring the passage of time in a place between times." The eshu paused for a moment, his eyes closed as if listening for something. When he opened them, he had a wry smile on his handsome face. "Except for our internal processes," he murmured.

"Yeah," said Tor. "My stomach's rumbling, too."

"I think food is more important than that," Rasputin said suddenly, pointing straight ahead of the ship's course. His companions turned to look in the direction of the pooka's outstretched finger.

An enormous creature was rising in the water before them.

Morgan inhaled sharply, clapping both hands over her mouth to stifle a shriek.

Tor reached for the ax at his belt and moved to

interpose himself between his granddaughter and the emerging monster.

"What is it?" Leigh asked softly.

"It's not the guardian of the trod we were warned about," Rasputin said.

"Do we get to fight it or what?" Edmund asked, rushing toward the prow of the ship. Valmont clamped a hand on the redcap's shoulder. The ship itself showed no sign of slowing down as the creature, now visible as a towering sea-serpent formed from the stuff of the ocean itself, loomed larger and larger in their sight until it seemed to block the entirety of the trod.

Morgan remembered her dream.

"Maybe we can get the ship to fly over it!" she exclaimed.

"Like in your dream?" Leigh asked, unable to tear her eyes away from the awesome creature.

Morgan nodded, her eyes wide as she tried to peer around her grandfather to get another look at the guardian.

"That's cheating!" Edmund said, still struggling to free himself from Valmont's grip on his shoulder.

"You should know," said Morgan, then bit her lip, as she realized the cruelty of her automatic response.

"Do you know how to make this vessel take to the air?" Valmont asked the childling.

"It—it just—flew!" she said. "I didn't have anything to do with it." Her voice was almost a wail.

"Well if she's gonna fly," Tor said, "she'd better do it quick."

Ahead of them, the blue-green serpent filled their vision.

"It's like looking at a tidal wave," said Valmont, struggling against the fear that made his knees weak.

"It's too late," said Leigh, reaching for her sword, though she knew that the gesture was futile.

Suddenly, the companions felt the ship leave the surface of the sea as a pair of graceful pearly white wings extended from its sides. Birdlike, the vessel lifted into the air, its trajectory carrying it forward and upward.

Morgan clapped her hands in delighted surprise.

"It's happening!" she cried, then looked around anxiously at her companions, whose expressions did not mirror the relief she felt.

"Not high enough," murmured Leigh.

"Don't worry," Rasputin said in a shaky voice. "It's what they call a near miss."

"Hit the deck and hold your breath!" Tor called out. "We're goin' in!"

The swan ship's upward motion shifted as the port and starboard wings angled backward, sending the ship, beak first, into the center of the serpent's broad, foam-covered chest.

Leigh and her companions threw themselves onto the deck of the ship and braced for an impact that never came. Instead, there was a sensation of being immersed in warm liquid as the guardian's watery body engulfed the ship. Edmund, whose mouth was already open, struggled to breathe some substance that was more than air but less than water. One by one, the others gave way to the instinct that told them they could not hold their breath forever. Each felt a choking sensation, as if they were drowning.

Sleep, commanded a deep, liquid voice inside their heads. *And dream.*

"Help me, Edmund!" Morgan's voice sounded in the redcap's ear.

Edmund woke to find the sidhe childling struggling to escape a brawny, black-armored knight who clutched her firmly about the waist, holding her slight body against his

chest like a shield. Edmund looked around him. None of his other companions were in sight, not even Tor.

"Let her go," the redcap called halfheartedly to the strange knight.

"I only want to help her," the knight replied in a voice that Edmund thought he had heard before. He remembered his encounter with another faerie knight in dark armor. He had been on his way to the Toybox when he was accosted. Sensing the danger posed by the unknown warrior, Edmund attempted to use his Banality to drive the Kithain from him. Thinking about quiz shows and nuclear weapons had successfully eliminated the danger after a fashion, but it had also temporarily driven from his mind the memory of what he was. Later he had learned that the stranger was one of the Dauntain, the changeling traitors who hunted down other changelings to destroy their faerie selves.

"Where's Tor?" Edmund demanded, staring not at the knight, but at Morgan. He noticed that the childling's face seemed to be losing the delicate lines that emphasized her sidhe blood.

"He's gone," Morgan said, sobbing. "Help me, Edmund! It hurts!"

"What have you ever done for me?" the redcap demanded, remembering the hateful words that had passed between them. It seemed to him that he had always come out on the losing end of their arguments.

Morgan was crying too hard to answer his question.

"I can help you, too," the knight said. "Just surrender your pitiful weapon and I will show you the error of your ways."

Edmund looked at the sword in his hand. Briefly, he considered throwing it at the knight to distract him so that he could get a running start in the other direction. Then he heard Morgan's cries cease suddenly. He looked at her and saw nothing more than a little girl with straggly black curls and a sorrowful look on her face.

the hill

"*Coward,*" *she murmured, and slumped in the knight's arms.*

"*Surrender yourself, scumsucker!*" *Edmund called, holding his sword above his head and charging, full tilt, toward his enemy.* "*No one calls me coward,*" *he thought. As his sword came forward, the knight knelt, holding Morgan between himself and the gleaming blade. Edmund and his sword continued their forward lunge—*

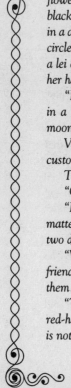

"It's not fair," Edmund screamed. "I only wanted a chance to use my sword!"

Clad in the finery of a dozen African tribes, Valmont sat upon a throne carved from mahogany and garlanded with flowering lianas. A beautiful young woman with hip-length black hair and skin like burnished copper stood before him in a dress made entirely of flowers. A wreath of tiny orchids circled her head like a bridal crown. Around her neck hung a lei of brilliant flowers Valmont had never seen before. In her hands she held a matching lei, which she offered him.

"Is this not better than your silly customs?" she asked in a lilting voice that reminded the eshu of birdsong and moonlight.

Valmont thought for a minute. "You mean Seelie customs, don't you?" he asked.

The maiden laughed. "I mean what I say," she said.

"Obviously you're no pooka," the eshu murmured.

"I am Kithain," the woman said. "That is all that should matter, unless what you profess and what you believe are two different things."

"What do you mean?" Valmont asked. "Where are my friends?" he added, realizing that he could locate none of them.

"They have already joined us," she said, "all but the red-haired knight who finds it impossible to accept that she is not our overlord."

"Who is us?" Valmont said, beginning to feel as if he no longer had any answers—only questions.

"We are the ones who will overthrow the tyranny of the European conquerors," she said. "We are the menehune and the nunnehi, the tengu and the gandharvas. We are all the children of the Dreaming whose lands have been dispossessed by those who impose unfamiliar customs upon our cultures, which were old before theirs had even begun."

"I cannot dispute your charge," Valmont said.

"I know," the dark-haired maiden replied, leaning forward to place the lei around Valmont's neck. "You will lead us into battle against the enemy," she said. "And I will fight alongside you as your consort and your queen."

"And who will lead the army of opposition?" Valmont asked, fearing that he already knew the answer.

"The woman with hair as fiery as her temperament," the woman replied. "The woman who betrayed you for a lover from her past."

"But our quest—" Valmont began. Her hand across his mouth stopped his words.

"—is over," she said. "Silver's Gate and Arcadia do not belong to us, but to her and her kind."

Valmont felt himself responding to the warmth of the woman standing so close to him that he could smell the fresh rainwater scent of her hair and the coconut fragrance of her skin. He thought of Leigh, whose beauty radiated light but no warmth, not unlike the balefires that burned without heat. If she had betrayed him, then she deserved the same from him.

Then he remembered. Standing up, he clasped the woman's wrist in one hand. With his other, he removed the lei from around his neck and placed it in her palm, curling her fingers around it. He released his hold on her arm and stepped away.

"Among my people," he said, "an oath is a serious matter. Whatever she has done, Leigh and I are oathbound. I will not be an oathbreaker."

t h e   h i l l

"Then you will die," the woman said, pulling from her waist a dagger carved from something that looked like volcanic glass. In one fluid motion, she plunged the dagger into Valmont's chest and a searing pain blossomed in his heart—

"Is it worth it?" Valmont wondered, as his consciousness faded once more into watery oblivion.

Morgan and her grandfather walked together in the misty twilight. Around her she could hear the footfalls and quiet murmurs of her companions, but they remained just outside her vision. Only Tor was real, his large hand firmly grasping her tiny one, his lengthy stride deliberately shortened to keep pace with her childish steps.

"I won't always be around to protect you," the troll said abruptly, breaking what had been a companionable silence with his gruff pronouncement.

Morgan felt her heart constrict with a momentary pang of fear.

"What do you mean?" she asked.

For a moment, her grandfather said nothing. Morgan could hear the labored sound of his breathing as they continued to walk over a ground that was steadily becoming more treacherous, with rocks and roots poking up out of the dirt beneath their feet in an almost deliberate effort to test their footing.

Tor sighed heavily. "Everyone gets old," he said. "I'm getting old. Soon—"

"Soon, what?" Morgan's voice shook. She wanted to retrace their steps, to return to a time before Tor had begun a conversation she had no desire to hear.

"I've forgotten too much," Tor said. "I have to keep reminding myself of too many things."

"I'll never let you forget," said Morgan.

Tor shook his head. "It's not enough," he muttered. "The truth is, I—I don't sleep well."

s h a d o w s   o n

"You sleep all the time." Morgan tried to make her voice sound light and cheerful, the way the ladies at the duke's court used their words to deflect unpleasant conversations onto a less treacherous path. "You always nap whenever nothing important's going on," she added.

"Not to dream," the troll murmured, his words almost lost in the low rumble of his voice.

"I have dreams enough for both of us. I'll dream for you," Morgan said.

Tor laughed once, a harsh snort that almost sounded like a sob to the childling.

"I wish you could," he said slowly. He stopped and knelt in the middle of the path, turning to grasp Morgan's other hand and drawing her around to face him. His broad, rocky face was close to hers and, even in the fog, Morgan could see that her grandfather looked more like an old man than the fearsome troll guardian she knew him to be.

"I'm a grump," he said. "Do you know what that means?"

Morgan nodded her head. "It means you're older than a childling or a wilder," she said.

"It means I'm losing my battle to stay a troll," he said. "The war between dreams and reality is one we all fight— and one we all lose."

"Don't say that!" Morgan said fiercely. "You swore an oath to guard me. I won't let you break it by growing too old to see me as myself!"

"There's nothing you can do to stop it," Tor said. "It happens to everyone. One day you'll be a grump, too, and all your dreams will start to fade."

"That's not true!" Morgan cried. "That's not true!"

Tor released Morgan's hands and stood up. Turning from her he strode away into the mists, his long legs carrying him quickly out of her sight.

"Grandpa!" she called after him. "Leigh? Valmont?" She heard no response from her companions. "Rasputin?

t h e   h i l l

Edmund? Grandpa's gone and we have to find him before it's too late!" She listened for their voices, but heard nothing.

Sobbing in earnest, Morgan plunged alone into the fog.

"Grandpa—"

"I'll never leave you," Morgan said, her voice quivering with desperate resolve.

The lanky brown hare stared in surprise at his oathmates, who stood in a circle around him. Beyond them stretched a forest full of strange trees and the sounds of unfamiliar birds.

"Rasputin, is that you?" Morgan asked.

"Of course it's not me," Rasputin said, not knowing or questioning how his rabbit form could still shape human words.

"This is not the best time to be a rabbit," Valmont chided. "You can be of little help to us as you are."

"Except as dinner," Edmund said, smacking his lips and grinning maliciously.

"If this is your idea of a joke," added Leigh, her brows furrowing in disapproval, "it's not very funny."

"Maybe he's not Rasputin," mumbled Tor. "Maybe it's just a rabbit."

"How many talking rabbits do you know?" Rasputin asked.

"He was only kidding," said Morgan. "Come on, change back so we can get on with our quest. We don't have much time."

Rasputin leaned back on his haunches and pondered his predicament. He could not remember what had driven him to assume the rabbit form which was his birthright as a pooka, but he knew that unless his companions gave him some privacy, he would be unable to resume his true shape.

"We're waiting," Leigh said. She sounded angry.

"Stay here," Rasputin said, expecting them to take the hint and leave him alone so that he could work his faerie magic and shed his rabbit guise.

"We have to hurry," Valmont said, his voice urgent. "We are being hunted even now and we have little time to dally waiting for you to finish with your joke."

A sudden wave of fear washed through Rasputin. He felt his jaws lock tight. "Don't go!" he pleaded.

"We're staying until you change back," Morgan said, tapping her foot in exasperation. "You know we won't leave you all alone."

Rasputin's ears drooped. Why are they so dense all of a sudden? he thought. At any other time, one or the other of his oathmates would have understood his contrary speech. Now they stood like statues, trapping him inside a shape that was useless to himself and to them.

From somewhere in the distance they heard the snap of branches and the crackling sound of footsteps approaching quickly, without stealth.

"There they are!" a man's harsh voice called out.

"Run!" cried Leigh. "Get under cover!"

The companions scattered. Rasputin started to follow, then realized that he had his few seconds of privacy and began to shift back into his human form. He heard the whistling of something moving rapidly through the air and then he felt a sudden pain as an iron-tipped arrow thudded into his back, just above the base of his spine.

He crumpled to the ground. For what seemed like hours, he drifted in and out of consciousness as he heard the sounds of struggle all around him. Finally, everything was quiet.

"He's hurt." Morgan's voice brought him to some small level of awareness. He opened his eyes.

"They're gone," Valmont said gently.

"I think he's dying," Edmund pronounced.

"Help me," Rasputin said, only he lacked the strength to speak the words aloud.

Leigh bent over him, her proud face worried. The weakening pooka summoned every ounce of will to speak.

the hill

"Don't touch me," he whispered. "I don't need any of you—"

"I can't help being what I am," Rasputin said, his eyes wet with tears.

Tor covered his ears to shut out the sound of screaming. Sharp bursts of gunfire peppered the air all around him. They had known the jungle was their enemy, but now its hatred burst upon them in violent and bloody frenzy. A few seconds ago they were patrolling an unfamiliar stretch of ground, eyes peeled for tripwires and deadfalls and the thousand other traps that lay in wait for them. One mistake was all it took, and now they lay on their bellies in the wet growth of the jungle floor, unable to move, targets for the picking.

Behind him he heard the frantic prayers of one of his platoon, while ahead and above all he could hear was the sharp retort of their invisible foe.

"For God's sake, do something!"

"We're gonna die!"

Something exploded not far from him, and Private Tor Larssen felt a hail of dirt and stones and bits of trees and other things, soft and wet, that he dared not try to put a name to.

With a savage cry of rage welling from deep inside him, Tor lurched to his feet, grabbing his rifle. Heedless of the spray of bullets in his path, he charged his unseen enemy—

—his battle ax bloody from the awful toll it had already taken. Close behind him, her own chimerical blade flashing in the sunlight, the dark-haired sidhe knight fought to stay within the shield of her guardian.

"Up ahead!" the knight called to her troll protector and battlemate. "The standard of my house—make for it and we shall win our safety and our lives."

"My life is yours," the troll responded, "so long as I

breathe you and all your blood are mine to guard—"

"Morgan!" Tor cried, startled into wakefulness and clutching desperately at the remnants of his dream.

Leigh walked with Yrtalien in a moonlit garden filled with fragrant flowers. Her hair had grown again until it touched the small of her back and fell in soft ringlets across her shoulders, forming a cape of flame against her iridescent gown. The prince wore black with traces of silver in the sash at his waist and in the clasp of his cloak.

"How can you ally yourself to them, Eleighanara?" he asked, his voice softly derisive. "All but one are commoners, little better than mortals."

"You speak of mortals so lightly," she said, ignoring the greater question posed by her companion.

He caught her hand and pressed it to his lips, then turned her to face him. Touched by the moon's white radiance, his face became a sculpture of light and shadow. Still holding her fingers lightly in his, he drew her to the center of the garden where a fountain rose from a small pool.

"Mortals are our food," he said. "We feed on their dreams. That is their purpose."

"They are more than that," she replied, thinking of her mortal family. "We are their dreams, their stories, their legends—"

"—and they hate us for it," Yrtalien finished. "As do your commoner friends."

"That's untrue!" she protested. "Valmont—"

"—is an eshu and he resents the sidhe, including you, for ranking his kith as something lower than nobility. He does not love you," the sidhe lord said.

"I don't love him either," Leigh retorted, "but that doesn't mean we hate each other. Valmont and I are friends. We don't have to agree on everything."

"The two of you rarely agree on anything." Yrtalien's

the hill

voice was mild. "And what of your redcap nemesis?"

Leigh bit back her first thought and tried to consider Edmund in a charitable light. "Edmund is a brat," she said. "He means well, but he doesn't know how to get what he wants."

"What he wants is power," Yrtalien said.

"What he wants is love," Leigh corrected him.

"Your delusions are as delightful as your presence," the prince said. "And I suppose Rasputin's frivolousness doesn't conceal some deep-seated resentment against the noble fae who dismiss the backward wisdom of his kith?"

"I don't think Rasputin knows how to hate," Leigh said.

"Then you know nothing of pookas," Yrtalien murmured.

"What do you make of Morgan, then?" Leigh asked. "You cannot label her a commoner."

Yrtalien's handsome face hardened into a sneer. "She wears our form, but she is so corrupted by her feelings for the peasants who raised her that she is more human than sidhe."

"She is the best of us all," Leigh said.

"You are more than all of them," Yrtalien responded, and his voice broke as if he were in pain. "I languished in my prison," he said, "but at least I was not subjected to the torments that were unleashed upon you." He pulled her hand toward him and gently traced the inside of her palm. "You should not have such callouses on your hands," he murmured.

Leigh jerked her hand from his grip and flexed her fingers. "Karate lessons," she said. "It's not as if I've spent my life laboring in the fields."

"And slaving as a waitress is not demeaning to one of your station?" he asked, pity still coloring his voice.

Leigh shook her head. "You don't understand," she replied. Then she realized that Yrtalien had omitted mention of one of her companions. "You haven't said anything about

Tor," she said. "He would give his life for any of us."

"He has little enough left to give," Yrtalien said. "He had best begin preparing for his own Long Winter."

"These are my oathmates," Leigh said. "Whatever you say about them, they are oathbound to me."

"You are my oathmate," Yrtalien whispered, his voice suddenly vehement. "Or have you forgotten that oath spoken in Arcadia? Will you break your oath to me?"

"You cannot ask me to choose between two oaths!" Leigh cried.

"You cannot make me choose," Leigh whispered, the Forsworn Prince's voice still echoing in her mind.

"Leigh? Are you awake?" Morgan's voice called out from somewhere nearby.

"Are we still alive?" Rasputin asked, sitting up on the deck of the swanship and feeling himself for telltale signs of their recent immersion.

Valmont stood up and looked around him. One by one the oathmates rose to stand with him along the prow of the ship. There was no sign of the creature, either in front of them or in their wake.

Tor placed a hand on Morgan's head. The childling looked up at him, concern in her eyes.

"Are you all right, Grandpa?" she asked. Tor nodded once, then looked away from his granddaughter.

"I just had a dream," he grunted.

"So what was that all about?" Edmund asked.

"We have been tested by the guardian," Valmont surmised.

"That was a test?" The redcap sounded incredulous. "So did we pass, or what?"

"I don't think it was a matter of passing or failing," Leigh said. "I think it just wanted to take our measure."

"I hope that's what it was," Morgan said quietly. "Otherwise, I would have failed."

the hill

Rasputin glanced around the deck, then bent over and picked up an object lying at his feet. Silently, he offered Morgan a foil-wrapped Granola bar.

Morgan shook her head. "No thanks," she said, "I'm not hungry."

"Hey! Neither am I!" Edmund exclaimed.

Valmont suddenly made a sharp hissing sound. "Look!" he said. "I think our voyage is at an end."

The companions clustered together and watched as the ship sailed through a slit in the sky just ahead of them.

"That's a waterfall!" Morgan exclaimed.

The swan ship glided to a graceful stop in the middle of a large rock-ringed pool at the base of a steep cataract of plummeting water.

"This is no beach," Leigh muttered, staring at the lush vegetation that surrounded them. "I expected we'd put in at some harbor—"

"I smell orchids!" Morgan said, taking a deep breath. "Does this mean we've reached Hawaii?"

"I think it does," Valmont said, chuckling softly. "The question is, where?"

"Actually," Rasputin said, "I wasn't going to suggest that a more appropriate question would be *Who are they?*"

The others looked in the direction indicated by the pooka and saw faces and forms emerge from the foliage that lined the pool. Faerie sight revealed them to be Kithain, but they were unlike any fae the oathmates had ever seen.

The strangers' skin was copper and golden and bronze, and their hair was dark and straight. They wore clothing made from leaves and flowers. Most of them carried spears or war clubs. They stood on the edge of the pool and gestured toward the boat.

"I think they want us to disembark," Leigh said, trying to interpret the gestures.

"What if they don't speak English?" Edmund asked suddenly.

"I didn't think of that!" Morgan exclaimed.

"Don't worry," Rasputin mumbled. "I think they're friendly."

the hill

part

two

prelude

Since their arrival with the humans who sailed from Polynesia to the shores of the islands that would later be known as Hawaii, the menehune had dwelled in their lush tropical paradise, untouched by time. They lived in harmony with the humans whose dreams gave them substance. Occasionally they lent their assistance to the works of these mortals who let the rhythms of nature pattern their lives, but for the most part they were content to remain on the fringes of human society, out of sight but sometimes heard or sensed.

As the growing tide of Banality began to sweep across the European continent, a few of the Kithain of the old world traveled the sea trods to the western lands, the Summer Lands of the Americas. An even smaller group sailed the magical paths through the Dreaming until they reached the islands that lay west of the western lands. The menehune hid themselves from these strange Kithain, watching as these faerie cousins built freeholds and staked their claim on the islands' abundance.

Selkies from other waters arrived, bringing tales of a great coldness that was sweeping the lands far to the east. These bright-eyed, webbed-fingered Kithain also brought a treasure to the menehune for safekeeping—a dark translucent stone in whose depths shone a spark of brilliant flame. *Pohaku aka,* they called it—the stone of shadow.

The coming of Captain Cook's ships in 1778, the harbingers of a steady trickle of European fortune seekers, adventurers, colonists and missionaries, heralded the end of innocence for the island's native populace. That same infusion of newcomers brought the first hint of Banality to a land previously untouched by the taint of disbelief.

Although the islands were among the last of the world's places to feel the Shattering, the children of the Dreaming were not immune to its ravages. As cities arose along the pristine beaches, as industrialists and entrepreneurs began to reap the rich harvest of exotic fruits and woods, as tourists flocked to a place advertised as a tropical paradise, and as missionaries brought their exclusionary faith to the native population, the menehune found their sanctuaries under assault, their sacred places violated.

Abandoning many of their favorite dwelling places, the menehune constructed enchanted grottos near towering waterfalls, and established their hidden villages in the islands' interior and on the slopes of the volcanic ridges that formed the backbone of the Hawaiian lands. There, far from the eyes of mortals, they tried to ignore the steady erosion of their dreams. Soon they were strangers in their own territories, unknown and unremembered save for a few surviving legends of the "little people," the secretive builders, of Hawaii.

The selkies and the merfolk sometimes visited the menehune, bringing news of the other Kithain who remained behind after the gateways to the Dreaming had fallen into ruin. More foreign changelings sought refuge in the islands, this time constructing their freeholds near centers of human population, feeding their Glamour with mortal dreams—although those dreams were fast diminishing.

The return of the sidhe in 1969 brought rumors of wars to the menehune, but the wars themselves did not touch the islands of Hawaii. When Queen Aeron sent a governor to Honolulu to claim the islands for the Kingdom of Pacifica, the menehune watched with amusement the strange rituals that seemed so important to their Kithain cousins. The governor paid no heed to the elusive and, when they so desired to be, invisible menehune. Instead, he made Oahu the center of Seelie activity in Hawaii and rarely ventured to the lesser-populated islands.

Then the menehune noticed another group of Kithain gathering on the island of Hawaii, near the town of Hilo. Unlike the fae who danced attendance upon Queen Aeron's governor, these Kithain stepped to a darker rhythm. A wildness and a freedom surrounded them, yet a secretiveness clung to them as well. Where they roamed, they stripped the Glamour from the mortals whose lives they touched. Unlike the Kithain of Honolulu, these did not shrink from contact with Banality. Rather, they dared to face the symbols and the trappings of the world of disbelief, and sometimes they emerged victorious from their confrontations. Fearing these reckless changelings, yet not knowing quite what it was they feared, the menehune left a few of their bravest warriors and *mana* weavers on the Big Island to watch them and withdrew to Kauai and the other islands.

In the shadows of sleeping Waialeale, the ancient volcano whose rise signaled Kauai's birth, the menehune built their greatest settlement, in a grotto where a secret waterfall cascaded into a miniature lake. Though not the only place where the native changelings made their homes, the Village of the Dream—*Moe'uhane*—became the center for the "little people," and its chief became the leader of a race whose numbers were daily growing smaller. To this hidden village, the menehune brought the Shadowstone, and the settlement became known as the Village of Hidden Treasures.

Then, one day, a trod within the center of the pool burst open, revealing an arcing ribbon of endless water atop which glided a boat shaped like a sleek black seabird. Stepping from the boat, appearing, with his black clothing, like a shadow cutting through the sun-speckled ferns and flowers that grew along the grotto's edge, an ebony-haired, pale-skinned Kithain approached the startled menehune. Surrounded by a glowing radiance that proclaimed him to be a leader among his own kind, the stranger made it known by gestures and by the majesty of his bearing that he had come to see the leaders of the menehune.

Yrtalien, the Forsworn Prince, had come to claim the Shadowstone.

the hill

chapter

five

"Say something!" Morgan whispered loudly to Leigh as she watched the steady approach of the menehune. The native changelings emerged from the cover of palms and lush ferns and began to walk slowly toward the companions, spears upraised and clubs pointed toward the ground.

"I don't know what to say," Leigh answered her. "I never considered that we might not speak the same language."

"Why don't you try?" said Valmont. "We're only assuming that they don't speak English."

"It's too bad none of us knows anything even remotely Hawaiian… like *aloha*," Rasputin said softly in Leigh's ear.

"Well, duh!" Edmund said. He squirmed past Tor's bulk, planted firmly next to Morgan, and stepped in front of Leigh.

"Aloha!" the redcap called out, bending his elbow to display his his right hand, palm facing outward in greeting. "How! We come in peace," he added as an afterthought.

Valmont groaned quietly.

"I can see seven of them," Leigh murmured. "I think the one wearing the feathered cloak must be their leader."

"It's the ones I don't see that worry me," Tor grunted, drawing Morgan closer as he watched for the menehunes' response to Edmund's greeting. The one whom Leigh had tagged as leader stopped suddenly and raised his spear. With his other hand he pointed toward the oathmates and uttered a string of unintelligible syllables to his companions. Three warriors, armed with spears, shifted their grips on their weapons, heaving them backward as if to launch them to the sky. The other three raised their clubs.

"Look!" Rasputin said. "They're coming to welcome us."

"Take cover!" yelled Tor, reaching for Morgan as he spoke.

"Where?" Edmund cried, then dove into the water of the pool.

"Scatter!" Leigh called out. "That way they can't get all of us at once." She drew her chimerical blade and ran forward through the shallow water at the pool's edge to meet the attackers. Behind her, scimitar in hand, Valmont selected another target and sped to join battle.

"Don't hurt them!" Morgan shrieked as Tor retreated, carrying her back toward the waterfall in the direction of the swan ship.

"You're loony," called Edmund from the middle of the pool. Near him, a spear plunked into the water. "Missed me, you stupid turds!" the redcap taunted.

A spear caught Tor square in the back. The troll grunted as the force of the stone spearhead battered into his chimerical armor. He stumbled to one knee, nearly dropping Morgan. The water of the pool lapped at his chest. Morgan screamed.

"Put me down!" she cried, seeing some of her grandfather's hard-won Glamour begin to fade from him. "You're hurt. Let me do something." She tried to pry herself loose from her grandfather's grip. At the same time she began humming a nursery rhyme to help focus her Glamour, hoping that the fickle magic of the fae wouldn't desert her when she needed it to undo the damage from the chimerical spear.

She felt a tingling sensation in her fingers and saw a faint, iridescent glow surround her hand. She touched

t h e   h i l l

Tor's shoulder and breathed a sigh of relief as she saw his troll-like features become more pronounced.

Rasputin found himself facing a young menehune with a war-club in one hand and a stone dagger in the other. The pooka leapt backward, dodging a jab from the dagger. The club caught him on the shoulder. Rasputin screamed as the blow ripped away a piece of his faerie nature.

"Just what I needed," he muttered, wincing with the pain. Although the weapon had no physical substance and would leave not so much as a bruise on his shoulder, it was capable of stripping Glamour from him, weakening his true form. Desperately, he looked around for something to use as a weapon or, preferably, a shield. Accustomed to standing on the sidelines of a battle and using his faerie magic to assist his friends, he panicked at the thought of being so close to his opponent. He had not even had time to retrieve his juggling clubs, useful when hurled at a target, from the cloth bag which still dangled from his shoulder.

"Here goes nothing," he said, unslinging the bag. Clutching it by the shoulder strap he swung it at his attacker, catching the menehune warrior in the face and sending him hurtling backward.

Tor stood up in the water, setting Morgan down behind him and placing himself as a shield between her and the menehune. The water came up to the childling's neck.

"It's not supposed to be like this," Morgan protested, near tears. "We're not supposed to fight them!"

"They didn't give us much choice," said Tor, grabbing his battle ax and holding it level in front of him as if it were a quarterstaff, one hand near the axblade, the other clamped firmly near the haft's end.

None of the companions noticed the feather-cloaked leader, who stood chanting on the edge of the battle, his own spear held crosswise above his head.

Valmont's chimerical scimitar sliced into his opponent's belly. The warrior screamed in pain and his fierce visage began to dim. Before the eshu's eyes, the young menehune seemed to grow smaller and duller, more human and less fae.

"Forgive me," the eshu whispered. "This is not my choice." He drew back for a second cut.

Leigh ducked beneath a wild swing of her attacker's club and brought her sword around for an upward slash at the arm that held the weapon.

The menehune in the feathered cloak ceased his chant and brought his spear down in front of him.

Suddenly, Leigh staggered as something caught at her feet, throwing her off balance. She glanced quickly at the ground and saw to her horror that the grass along the pool's edge, where she and her opponent struggled, was wrapping itself firmly around her ankles. To either side of her, long fern fronds were snaking out to grab her arms. A cry from Valmont told her that he was also in trouble.

Rasputin stumbled as a whiplike length of vine coiled around his calves, throwing him to his knees. The warrior he had been fighting recovered his own footing. Seeing the downed pooka, the menehune leaped forward to grasp Rasputin by his tender ears. He leveled his stone dagger at the pooka's chest.

Something yanked at Edmund's feet from beneath the water, pulling the redcap beneath the surface of the pool. Thrashing about as he struggled for a second time to keep from drowning, Edmund became entangled in a mesh net made of sturdy vines. *Caught in a fish trap*, he thought as his lungs gave up and he lost consciousness.

Tor watched helplessly as his companions were immobilized by the animated vines and ferns and long grasses of their tropical surroundings. From the forest

the hill

that encircled the pool, other figures now emerged and approached the helpless changelings, stone daggers gripped in their hands.

"Edmund's gone under!" Morgan cried, seeing the redcap disappear beneath the water. "Save him, Grandpa!" Before the troll could respond, a menehune warrior sprinted into the water where Edmund had fallen. Scooping up the netted redcap and tucking him under one arm, he stood facing Tor, a dagger held to the unconscious childling's throat.

From the shore, the feather-cloaked war-leader once again raised his spear, this time holding it high above his head with one hand.

"Sur-ren-der!" he called out.

"Like hell!" bellowed Tor, stepping toward the warrior who held Edmund. Morgan seized her chance and slipped out from behind the troll. Raising her hands, she walked toward the menehune.

"We surrender," she called, her childish voice ringing across the grotto.

"Morgan!" Tor cried in despair, as his granddaughter approached one of the warriors. The menehune clapped a hand firmly on her shoulder.

"It's the only way, Grandpa," she said, her voice solemn.

Seeing that Morgan had delivered herself into the hands of their attackers, Leigh stopped struggling and lowered her sword. Valmont did the same.

"Maybe *aloha* doesn't mean *hello*," Rasputin said disconsolately as he and his companions were herded away from the grotto and into the forest by their menehune captors.

"The Haight is crawling with them," Vargas said. His dark eyes glittered with an anticipatory fervor as he related his information to his companions.

The four Dauntain sat at a corner table in the rear of Marcotti's Pasta Parlor, a family-style Italian restaurant on the northern edge of the Haight, not far from Golden Gate Park.

"So far as I can tell," Diana said, pushing her plate of fettuccini and clam sauce aside and reaching for her wine glass, "the whole city is full of the creatures. At least the signs of their influence are all over the place."

Signe toyed with the last piece of veal on her plate. "I don't know," she said. "It's hard for me to tell the difference between normal human enterprise and fae-infested activities."

"It's a matter of degree," Ryder said. He had finished his meal before the others and now sat sipping his third cup of black coffee. "You expect to find artists and musicians in most cities. What you have to look for are the elements that we think—that we know—are connected to the Kithain."

"Art points in one of two directions," Diana said. "Either it draws you into a better understanding of the world or else it bypasses reality altogether and substitutes some other set of standards." The tall blonde paused to refill her wine glass from the bottle on the table. "Do we have time for this?" she asked, looking at Ryder.

The hawk-faced Dauntain checked his watch, then leaned back in his chair and nodded. "It's still early, not even nine o'clock," he said. "You've all done a yeoman's job of covering all the places I had marked on the map—and adding to them. We can afford to take the opportunity to relax, particularly when our cultural expert," he nodded in Diana's direction, "is willing to enlighten us."

Diana smiled faintly. Before she had become an active hunter of changelings, while she still held on to her Kithain form, Diana had taught anthropology at Boston University. Now she used her knowledge of human cultural and social development to trace the waxing and waning influence of the fae.

"Art and music and literature—anything, for that matter—that presupposes an extralogical view of the world is susceptible to changeling infestation."

"You mean things like pictures of unicorns and dragons...." Vargas interjected, his dark brows wrinkled in thought.

"Partly," Diana replied. "The interest in magical creatures expresses a desire to return to an age of darkness, where the world and the people in it were subject to the whims of mysterious, unknowable forces."

"What about astrology and crystals and magnet-therapy?" Signe asked.

Diana shook her head. "It's hard to tell the difference between passing superstitious fads and dangerous ideologies. My advice is to stay away from anything that even smacks of nonrational thought processes."

"How does religion fit in?" Vargas asked, his hand straying to the silver cross he wore at his throat, a relic from his seminary years.

"Religion—organized religion—is actually one of our strongest allies," Diana asserted. "For centuries it has opposed anything that posited an alternative to the reality of life followed by death followed by heaven or hell. There is. no other world, no faerie land full of immortal creatures."

"But they do exist," Vargas said, giving Ryder a sideways glance.

"They shouldn't exist," Diana responded quickly. "We," she lowered her voice, "shouldn't exist."

"I wouldn't go that far," Signe said. "We can't help what we are—what we were—any more than a bastard can help his illegitimacy." She folded her hands in front of her on the table. Recognizing that the conversation was beginning to upset her, Ryder placed a hand on her shoulder.

"No, we can't," he said. "But what we can do is fight to keep ourselves from giving in to what we are. We are carriers of a disease that has infected the human race for perhaps thousands of years, but the spread of that contamination is under our control so long as we have the will to keep ourselves in check."

"And we have the responsibility to stop others of your kind from harming the innocent," Vargas said.

Ryder nodded. "That is our prime justification for allowing ourselves limited contact with the source of our corruption."

"So where do we go from here?" Signe asked, visibly relieved that Diana's train of thought had been deflected from its logical path. She pitied her blond companion, whose self-hatred invariably led her to thoughts of self-destruction. More than any of them, Diana needed to be reminded constantly of the importance of their work.

"We have a list of probable places where our targets gather," Ryder said. "One of those places is a dive called Trickster's—a fairly rough crowd hangs out there."

"Redcaps?" Vargas asked, searching his mind for the bits and pieces of information on the Kithain that Ryder had supplied him with over the years of their association.

Ryder nodded. "And others. Mostly Unseelie."

"They're the worst of the offenders," Signe murmured. Diana nodded her agreement.

"The other place we're sure of," Ryder continued, "is a small coffee shop right in the center of the Haight.

It's hard to spot at first, but if you know what to look for, the place reeks of Glamour. It's called the Toybox."

Surrounded by their captors, Leigh and her companions picked their way carefully through the dense under-growth that lay beyond the grotto. The roar of the waterfall faded until it was lost in the other noises of the tropical forest. The menehune took little notice of their prisoners except to gesture with their spears in the direction of their journey. Carrying Morgan, Tor walked behind Leigh, his face set in grim determination as he tramped over the uneven, springy jungle surface, heedless of the roots and upthrust stones in his path. From the security of her grandfather's arms, Morgan studied the strange Kithain of Hawaii, her expression solemn and thoughtful. Edmund followed Tor, glaring at his captors even as he stumbled over the rough terrain. Behind the redcap, Valmont paced himself to avoid running into Edmund. The eshu appeared to be relaxed, although he constantly searched the trees above him and the thick foliage on either side of the narrow trail. Rasputin walked behind the rest of his companions, his head down in apparent dejection and his long rabbitlike ears draped back along the sides of his head. Behind him, a pair of menehune glided soundlessly over ground that proved no obstacle to their sure steps and fluid movements.

They traveled in silence, lost to their own contemplations and unwilling to voice their thoughts in the presence of the strange Kithain. For the most part, the rigorous trail kept them from speculating upon what awaited them at their destination.

Suddenly, the forest opened up, revealing a large clearing carpeted in thick grasses and brilliant red, yellow and purple flowers. Scattered about the encircled glen were at least a dozen buildings of a structure unlike anything the oathmates had ever seen. Constructed from stones that rose up from the ground to merge with dwarf trees that provided natural shelter, the graceful houses bespoke an artistry that blended the majestic forms of wood and rock into a wondrous symmetry of conscious design.

From these houses and from the giant tree ferns that lined the clearing's interior, figures began to emerge—women and children as slender and willowy as the island palms. The leader of the war party called out—again in a language that had no meaning to the ears of the companions but sounded like the splash of water upon rocks—and the villagers halted in their approach. Turning toward their prisoners, the feather-cloaked menehune gestured with his spear toward one of the smaller houses.

"I think he means for us to go inside," Leigh murmured softly to her companions. Valmont nodded, his dark face placid and unreadable.

"Then I suppose that we had better do so," the eshu responded.

"So is this jail, or what?" Edmund asked, as he and the others followed Leigh and Valmont between twin clumps of jagged ferns into the circular stone building. Once they were inside, the ferns bent inward, lacing their leaves together into a latticework screen that blocked their passage out of the structure.

"What do we do now?" asked Morgan, as Tor set her down on the floor of woven grass.

"We wait," the troll said, seating himself beside the doorway, his back against the stone. He leaned his head against the smooth rock and closed his eyes.

Ryder and his three teammates stopped in front of the Spark of Life health food store, two buildings away from the Toybox.

"That's the place," the tall sidhe Dauntain informed the others, jerking his chin in the direction of the coffee shop.

"That's just an abandoned building," Vargas muttered, squinting at the dusty store front as if trying to bring his vision into focus.

"You don't see it as we do," Diana said. "Here." The stately blonde handed her Latino companion a polished stone engraved with a Norse rune. Vargas stared at the offering and shook his head.

"Take it," Ryder snapped. "It's the only way you can see what we're seeing. You can lecture us later and we'll be grateful for it."

"Don't try to fight its power," cautioned Signe, "or your own disbelief will weaken its Glamour."

Vargas snatched the stone from Diana's outstretched palm, holding it gingerly between thumb and forefinger. He wrinkled his nose in obvious distaste, but forced himself to concentrate on the alien warmth that seemed to flow from his fingers through his arm, engulfing his entire body with a faint yearning for some unknown pleasure. Before his eyes, the dilapidated building with the faded sign and the dust-caked pane of glass in the upper half of the wooden door was transformed into a structure of sturdy, polished wood and dressed stone, its cheery sign brightly decorated with a picture of an ornately carved steamer trunk.

"*Madre*," he whispered, and moved to cross himself, as if for protection. Diana interrupted his gesture, grabbing his arm and forcing him to lower it.

"You don't need protection," she muttered fiercely. "They do," she said, nodding toward the Toybox.

"This is an unholy place," Vargas whispered, steeling himself to view the now obvious freehold with the borrowed Glamour of his enchantment. He suppressed a shudder as he caught sight of his companions, their dormant changeling forms now evident as they prepared to infiltrate the coffee shop. Clad in dark, glittering armor and wearing a heavy sword of chimerical steel in a scabbard at his waist, Ryder looked like the knight he once had been. His left hand glowed with a blue luminescence from the deep, sapphire-colored gem embedded in his palm. Next to him, Signe's eshu form challenged the sidhe lord's in height, although her slender mortal features were even more elongated. She looked at Vargas with dark, pupilless eyes full of compassion for his discomfort. Diana towered over the other two; her statuesque build now seemed to be carved from rock. A pair of stubby, hornlike knobs protruded from her forehead—a mark of her kith's damnation.

"Do we go in?" Diana asked. "Or do we wait for someone to come out?"

Soft lights, invisible to mortal eyes, shone through the frosted glass on the door. Their senses attuned to the Glamour that leaked from the building, the four hunters could hear the faint sounds of conversation and muted laughter from within. Outside the building, a garish yellow and purple cab pulled to a stop, and the driver, a punkish-looking woman in her thirties whose bony frame and spiky hair proclaimed her to be a nocker, the goblinesque race of Kithain, strode jauntily into the building.

"Signe and I will go in," Ryder said. "Vargas, you and Diana wait outside until we call you." The black-

t h e   h i l l

armored knight removed an iron dagger from his belt and put it into Vargas' hand. "Hold this," he said. "If I walk into their freehold carrying cold iron, they'll know something is wrong before we can do anything."

"What do you plan to do once we're inside?" Signe asked.

Ryder shrugged, his hawklike eyes gleaming with an inhumanly predatory excitement.

"If there aren't too many of them, we'll destroy the place." He looked at Vargas and Diana. "Come in fighting if you hear me give the word."

"And if the place is overrun with changelings?" Diana asked. "What then?"

"If there are too many of them for the four of us to take down," Ryder said, "we grab a hostage and retreat."

Leaving Vargas and Diana in front of the health food store, Ryder and Signe linked arms and walked together toward the door of the Toybox.

The ferns parted to admit a young female menehune dressed in a skirt of woven grass with necklaces of brilliant flowers draped around her neck. In one hand she held several thongs of braided twine. From each strand hung a tiny shell.

"Aloha," she said, smiling at the oathmates.

Tor grunted, startled from a fretful sleep.

"Aloha," Morgan replied, returning the Kithain's smile and curtseying as she spoke.

Edmund snickered.

"Are those for us?" Leigh asked, speaking slowly and using her hand to indicate the shell pendants.

The young menehune stretched out the hand

holding the thongs in Leigh's direction. Leigh looked at her companions. Valmont raised an eyebrow.

"They look relatively harmless," he said, his voice softly chiding. "You might as well accept them from her. It's the friendliest gesture they have made so far."

"Sparing our lives was certainly a hostile act," murmured Rasputin.

"You're no help," Leigh responded without rancor. She extended her own hand and took the thongs from the maiden, who then swept her arm in a gesture that included the others in the room.

"I think she wants you to give one of those to each of us," Morgan said, looking at the woman as she spoke.

"Duh," said Edmund. "Like that's not obvious," the redcap added.

Once Leigh had passed the shell pendants around, their visitor mimed the act of tying a thong around her neck, then extended her arms toward the oathmates.

"Oh, good," Rasputin said. "She wants us to choke ourselves and save them the trouble." The pooka smiled faintly as he took the ends of his thong and knotted them behind his neck. After a moment, his companions followed suit.

The young menehune clapped her hands and smiled broadly. She touched her hand to a similar shell she wore at her throat.

"Now you can understand the words I speak to you," she said in a clear, lilting voice. "If you touch your own shell, I will be able to understand your language."

"She said we can understand—" Morgan began.

"We heard," Edmund snapped. "You don't have to repeat it for us."

"We thank you for your consideration," Valmont said to the woman, one finger touching his shell. "Did you understand what I just said?"

the hill

The maiden nodded. "Your words come to me in the tongue of my people."

"I am Valmont," the eshu said, proceeding to introduce the others.

"And I am Lulani," the maiden said.

"So, are we still prisoners?" Edmund asked. Lulani looked at him questioningly, and tapped the shell at her throat.

"Yeah," the redcap said, grabbing the shell in his fist. He repeated his question.

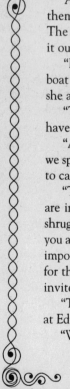

Lulani's face grew serious. "That is something I cannot tell you," she said. "My father, the chief of this village, must decide what to do with you now that you are here."

As Lulani spoke, the sounds she uttered shaped themselves into words that Leigh could understand. The word *chief* sounded like *alii*. Leigh tried to sound it out in her head so that she would remember it.

"Did we do wrong in coming here?" she asked. "The boat brought us to this place without our direction," she added.

"That is something that will be decided after you have spoken with my father," she said.

"Are there customs we should know about before we speak to the chief?" Valmont asked. "We don't want to cause offense because of our ignorance."

"There are many rules you must follow when you are in the presence of the *alii*," Lulani said. Then she shrugged. "But you will not remember all of them, for you are not accustomed to our ways. Only two are most important. Do not let your shadow fall upon the chief, for that will dishonor him, and do not speak unless he invites you to do so."

"That shouldn't be too hard," Rasputin said, looking at Edmund.

"When does your chief want to see us?" Tor asked.

"I have come here to take you to him," Lulani replied. "Your fate must be decided as quickly as possible."

"I've always been fond of quick fates," Rasputin murmured, neglecting to touch the shell as he spoke. Leigh shot him a sidelong glance. The pooka stared at his feet.

Lulani turned toward the doorway, where the ferns had closed again. She spoke a word softly, and the long fronds parted.

The companions followed the young menehune out of their house and across the clearing to a large, airy structure of open stonework and tall palms.

Seated on a low wooden bench covered with blankets of flowers in the center of what was obviously the chief's "palace," the menehune whom the companions recognized as the feathered-cloaked leader watched Lulani approach with her charges. Before she got to the doorway of the structure, she dropped to her hands and knees and began to crawl toward the chief.

"Do we have to do that?" Morgan whispered in a panicky voice.

"Custom would dictate that we follow the traditions of their kith," Valmont replied.

"You may approach me as if I were one of your own leaders," the chief said to them, his voice deep and mellow.

Leigh followed Lulani into the building, walking slowly and keeping her eyes fixed on the Kithain who would determine their future. She also tried to watch her shadow as she stepped closer. When she neared the throne, she dropped to one knee, as if she were paying homage to Duke Aeon in his audience chamber.

Morgan and Tor followed Leigh. Tor saluted the chief while Morgan curtseyed. Valmont knelt before the chief and gave him a formal salaam. Edmund and

Rasputin were the last to enter the palace. The pooka and the redcap stood uncertainly at the rear of the group. Finally, Rasputin bowed from the waist, doffing an imaginary cap. Edmund raised his hand in greeting and plopped himself down, cross-legged, on the woven mat of reeds that carpeted the palace floor.

"I, Makani, *Alii* of the people of the Village of Hidden Treasures, allow you to tell me what you are called and why you are here." Although he addressed the group, his eyes pinioned Leigh.

"I am Eleighanara, knight of Goldengate in the Kingdom of Pacifica," she said. She hesitated, and looked at her oathmates, uncertain as to whether she should introduce them as well.

"Your name in our tongue sounds like the word for light," the chief said before Leigh could continue. "Tell me, then, why you come to bring darkness upon our people?"

"We're off to a grand start," Rasputin mumbled, his voice barely audible.

As soon as Ryder entered the Toybox, crossing from the world of mortals into the enchanted atmosphere of the changeling freehold, he felt the power of its Glamour wash over his body, saturating his senses and awakening in him memories that he had long kept buried deep within. He gritted his teeth, fighting to keep from surrendering to the allure of his sidhe nature. He had faced this sort of threat to his sanity before, in other freeholds, and each time he experienced a moment in which he was tempted to give in to the madness of his fae essence.

He looked quickly at Signe and saw evidence that she, too, was experiencing the same overwhelming assault on her carefully erected barriers of Banality. He tightened his grip on her arm until he saw her wince. Catching her eye, he mouthed the words "Be strong," and was gratified to see her close her eyes and give a nod.

From behind the bar, Fizzlewig looked up as the door to the coffee shop opened to admit a pair of strange Kithain, one of them obviously a sidhe lord, the other a slender, hauntingly pretty eshu. *Visitors*, he thought, taking stock of the sidhe knight's ornate black chimerical armor and the eshu's colorful attire—a mixture of Arabian chic and African finery. Something about the knight tugged at his memory, and he watched them closely as they crossed the room to the bar. The knight's left hand, clenched in a tight fist, radiated with a soft blue glow.

The other patrons of the coffee shop paused in their conversations as the newcomers walked past them.

"Something wrong?" Georgia asked Fizzlewig. The nocker cabbie sat at the end of the bar, nursing a mug of mulled cider. "You look like you have a bug up your nose," she added.

Fizzlewig shook his head. "I feel like I ought to recognize him," the boggan muttered. "Her, I've never seen."

"Too bad none of Ragger's band is here," Georgia said, referring to the motley of childling rogues whose activities brought them into contact with most of the area's changeling community and who were among the best sources of local information. "Or Edmund," she remarked. The redcap childling had often boasted of his "connections" with the changeling underground.

"Edmund!" Fizzlewig said suddenly. The boggan remembered Edmund's description of his encounter with a knight that matched the description of the dark-armored sidhe. "Those are Dauntain," he whispered to Georgia. "We may have a fight on our hands."

Snatching up an empty tray, the boggan left his post behind the bar. "I'll pass the word," he said to Georgia. "Don't take your eyes off them." Georgia nodded, swiveling in her seat to face the front of the coffee shop. Quickly Fizzlewig began making the rounds of the tables and booths, picking up empty glasses and mugs and pausing for a few quick words with the Kithain he appeared to be serving.

As they passed near the carved steamer chest that stood against one wall of the coffee shop, a sharp stab of white-hot pain pierced Ryder's left hand. He stumbled, releasing his grip on Signe as the agony in his hand wrenched a ragged gasp of pain from his throat.

"What's going on?" a troll standing near the pair called out as Ryder doubled over.

Signe looked around her in panic; her leader was suddenly rendered helpless, his body wreathed in a brilliant sapphire-blue light. She started to reach for him when a hand seized her wrist. She turned her head and saw the nocker cabbie staring at her, a malicious grin on her face.

"I think you and your boyfriend had better leave," Georgia said.

"The toy chest is glowing!" a voice announced from somewhere near the front of the bar. Still holding onto the eshu's wrist, Georgia turned to look at the steamer trunk, which was surrounded by an iridescent glow.

Fizzlewig stopped his circuit of the room to stare at the toy chest, now beginning to pulse with a steady rhythm. He noticed that the blue glow from the sidhe knight's hand was shifting in intensity, matching the throbbing light from the toy chest. The boggan dropped his tray on the nearest table and hurried over to the fallen knight.

Kneeling at the sidhe's side, Fizzlewig reached for the glowing hand and pried open its fingers. A marble-sized blue gem, the source of the blinding, pulsating light, lay embedded in the knight's palm.

Ryder shrieked in pain and wrenched his hand from the boggan's grasp. Summoning all his will, he struggled to his feet.

"Abort!" he cried out to Signe. He stood shakily, his breath coming in ragged gasps as the pain from his hand tore through his body. Fizzlewig rose from his knees and planted himself squarely in the center of the room, arms folded across his chest.

"You and your kind are not welcome in this place," the boggan announced in his sternest voice.

"Let's get 'em!" a raucous voice called out from the back of the coffee shop.

Ryder looked around him and saw a group of Kithain slowly moving in his direction. A burly young troll pushed his way to the front of the crowd, brandishing a chair. Behind him a pair of satyrs, their eyes wild with gleeful menace, drew chimerical daggers from their belts.

Fizzlewig held up both hands, palms outward, his gesture halting the trio of hotheads in their tracks.

"As custodian of this freehold, I remind you of the ban against violence within these grounds," he said, his gruff voice filled with authority. Turning once more to face Ryder, the boggan angled his head in the direction of the door.

"Leave now and forget about coming here again, and this invasion of our territory ends here."

Over his shoulder, Ryder saw Signe being prodded unceremoniously toward the door. Stiffly, he nodded to the boggan.

"This is not over," he whispered, hardly able to form the words. Holding his glowing hand close to his chest, Ryder turned and staggered from the coffee shop.

Signe caught his arm as he emerged into the crisp December night. Once he was outside the confines of the freehold, the pain subsided with a suddenness that sapped Ryder's strength. He sagged against his companion.

"Help me!" Signe called to Vargas and Diana, who were already sprinting toward the coffee shop. Grabbing him by the wrist, Diana hoisted Ryder's arm over her shoulder. She leaned into him to support his weight.

"What went wrong?" Vargas asked as the four Dauntain began to walk away from the Toybox.

"I'm not sure," Signe said. "Let's go back to the hotel, where we can talk."

"I have a better idea," a voice called to them from the shadow of a side street.

"Who's there?" Vargas challenged.

A tall, mohawked eshu stepped into their path.

"Forget those nobodies," he said. "If you're hunting Kithain, I can put you on the track of bigger game."

"Why should you help us?" Signe asked. "You're one of them."

"Because of that," the eshu said, pointing to Ryder's hand, still faintly glowing with its strange blue light. "I've been watching you stalk the Toybox. I saw you check the gem in your hand as if it were some sort of homing beacon."

Ryder arched an eyebrow. "Obviously I wasn't as circumspect as I should have been," he muttered.

The tall Kithain laughed softly. "I'm just good at noticing things. And I happen to know of some Kithain who have another gem not unlike that one. Are you interested in hearing more?"

Ryder looked around at his companions. One by one, they nodded.

"It's your call," Diana said, the last of the three to give her consent.

"We're listening," he said.

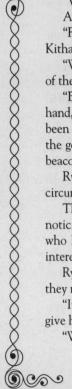

"Since you have asked for the story of our coming to this place," Leigh began, her eyes fixed on the stern face of Chief Makani, "I would request that you allow my companion and oath-brother Valmont, whose people are renowned storytellers, to speak for us." She turned her head slightly in Valmont's direction. The eshu regarded her with his usual impassivity, an arched eyebrow the only indication of his surprise.

"Over the years our people have been visited by members of your tribe," the *alii* said. "We have enjoyed the tales they have told us and from time to time we have shared our own stories with them. But there are two kinds of stories," Makani continued. "There are those stories which are meant to preserve the knowledge of what has gone before, and there are those stories which, though they may contain wisdom, are created from the dreams of the storyteller alone. Which kind of story will you tell me if I allow you to speak?"

Already on his knees from his greeting to the king, Valmont lifted his face and spread his arms in front of him, palms outward.

"I have been known to tell both kinds of stories," the eshu said. "I did not expect to be given the honor of recounting the history of our travels, but if you will listen to my words and judge their truth for yourself, you may determine which kind of story it is."

Makani nodded.

"That is an answer I would expect from one of your people. It is a fair bargain." The *alii* extended his arms toward the companions, spreading them out from his body in a gesture that encompassed all of them.

the hill

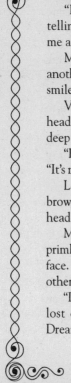

"You have shown me enough honor," he said. "Sit now and listen to the story."

Valmont waited for his companions to make themselves comfortable on the woven grass floor of the chief's palace. Lulani moved to join the circle of oathmates, seating herself next to Rasputin.

The chief motioned for Valmont to approach him. The eshu started to rise, then hesitated.

"The customs of the menehune are not yours," Makani replied.

Valmont nodded gratefully, and stood. Checking to make sure that his shadow remained behind him, the eshu walked toward Makani and stopped, halfway between his companions and the chief. He bowed low before the *alii*.

"If I may," he said, "it is my custom to stand when telling a story. I mean no disrespect if doing so places me above you."

Makani nodded. "While you tell your story, I am but another listener, although an important one." The chief smiled faintly as he spoke.

Valmont acknowledged this honor with a bow of his head. He drew himself up to his full height and took a deep breath.

"Relax, Valmont," the eshu heard Rasputin whisper. "It's not as if our lives depended on your next few words."

Leigh caught the pooka's eye. She furrowed her brows in silent admonishment. Rasputin lowered his head in mock apology.

Morgan sat between Leigh and Tor, her hands folded primly in her lap, a look of wistful solemnity on her small face. Edmund, looking bored and fidgety, sat on Tor's other side. The redcap picked at the grassweave carpet.

"Listen now to a tale that brings a group of Arcadia's lost children to the very edge of the world of the Dreaming," Valmont began.

Along with Makani, Lulani, and the other menehune who had gathered in the *alii*'s palace to view the newcomers, Leigh and her oathmates listened as Valmont first introduced his companions and then proceeded to tell the story of the discovery of the Eye of Opening. Leigh winced visibly when Valmont described how the oathmates were lured into believing that a gateway to Arcadia—perhaps the legendary Silver's Gate—lay in Golden Gate Park and that the emerald gemstone they had won from the satyr Malacar would enable them to open the gate. She saw Morgan shiver as the tale unfolded of how they were deceived into releasing a long-imprisoned prince of the sidhe and how that prince had stolen the body of an ensorcelled mortal before disappearing. Angry murmurs from the menehune accompanied that part of the tale.

Astonished that all of the menehune present seemed able to understand Valmont's words, Leigh stole a covert glance at the audience. She saw that a few of the listeners wore shell pendants like hers, and that these menehune had linked hands with others who did not wear the shells.

Valmont next spoke of the companions' encounter with the selkies. In words that closely mimicked those of Ondine, the eshu told the selkies' version of the fall of Silver's Gate. Finally, he described the opening of the seatrod and the voyage aboard the swan ship that brought the companions to the grotto.

"We have not come here with the intent to do harm," Valmont said as his story neared its end. "We were asked by our own *alii*, the duke of Goldengate, to gather together the four gems that were the eyes of the brothers whose war brought about the curse of the selkie queen. It is our hope that with those gems, we can find and open Silver's Gate so that the world of the

Dreaming may once more spread its Glamour to the parched lands of our exile."

At the end of his story, Valmont once again bowed low before Makani and resumed his seat beside Leigh.

The oathmates waited in silence, watching Makani carefully to determine whether or not he believed the eshu's story.

"That was a tale worthy of our own greatest tellers," Makani said. "Now that I have heard it, I will tell you that it is not exactly the same story that was told to me by another recent visitor to this place. It was he who warned us that you would probably come here looking for our treasure. I must consider both stories, one against the other, and I must decide which one of those stories contains the most truth."

Makani rose from his seat and extended his hands, palms down, over the oathmates. As he did so, the other menehune again prostrated themselves in the presence of their chief.

"Hear my words," Makani said. "Go from my presence and await my decision. You will remain in this village as the honored guests of my people. Your words have given me much to consider. Your actions in the time you spend here will give me more evidence of your intent. I will call for you again when I have more to say to you."

Lulani turned to the oathmates. "You have heard the words of the *alii*," she said in a voice barely above a whisper. "Do not turn your back to him as you leave his presence."

Walking slowly to be sure of their footing, the oathmates backed out of Makani's palace. When they were all standing in the clearing, Lulani touched her forehead to the carpet before her father and slowly crawled backward, on her hands and knees, until she reached Leigh and her companions. The graceful menehune maiden rose to her feet and smiled at the group.

"My father enjoyed your story," she said cheerfully to Valmont.

"Did he believe it?" Morgan asked anxiously.

Lulani's dark eyes sparkled as she looked at the childling. "If he did not believe at least part of the tale, he would not have given you the freedom of the village," she replied. "You are no longer our prisoners, but our guests."

Full night had fallen while Valmont regaled the menehune court with his story, and now the companions noticed that the village was lit by torches placed in baskets that hung from the branches of some of the trees. Soft halos of chimerical light glimmered from high atop other trees. Small fires burned in the open houses of the villagers, and a fragrant smoke filled the air. Near the center of the village a large bonfire blazed, and the companions could see several figures outlined against the flames.

"If we're not prisoners anymore, can we eat now?" Edmund asked plaintively.

Lulani laughed.

"Even if you were still prisoners, we would not let you starve," she said. "Come with me. We are preparing a luau—a feast—in your honor."

"Did you know that your father—I mean the *alii*—would accord us the status of guests?" Leigh asked.

Lulani shook her head. "Nothing was known before the alii heard your words," she said. "We would have honored you with a luau regardless of whether you were guests or prisoners. If you had been prisoners," she added, with a wry smile, "you would have deserved a final meal."

Tor grunted.

"You mean you would have killed us if the chief

the hill

hadn't believed Valmont's story?" Morgan asked, a horrified look on her face.

Lulani shrugged. "We would not have killed you," she said, "but we would have taken you to a place deep within the forests and left you there. The island itself would have decided your fate."

As they followed Lulani to the bonfire, where pungent cooking smells wafted through the air, reminding them of how long it had been since their last meal, Valmont caught Leigh's attention.

"It is one thing to tell a lie and get away with your deception," he said. "It is a different matter entirely to tell the truth and wonder if your words will be believed."

"None of us could have spoken as eloquently as you," replied Leigh.

"I haven't the faintest notion what you mean," added Rasputin.

the hill

chapter

SIX

"Are you certain we can believe him?" Vargas demanded of Ryder once the four Dauntain had reached the safety of their hotel. It was a few minutes past midnight when they parted company with their unexpected informer.

Still shaken by their encounter with the over-whelming Glamour of the Toybox and Ryder's unexpected collapse, Signe huddled in one corner of the sofa in their suite. Diana sat next to her. Vargas paced back and forth between the door of the suite and the window that looked out on the mist-covered city streets. Ryder sat in an armchair across from Diana and Signe. His left arm rested, palm upward, on the arm of the chair. The blue spot in the center of Ryder's palm, clearly visible as a large sapphire to the three apostate changelings and their still-enchanted mortal companion, glowed faintly.

"I'm certain of nothing," Ryder said bitterly, "except that if there are other gems like this in the hands of the Kithain, we owe it to the souls of those unfortunate individuals—and to ourselves as well—to find them."

"How did he know about you?" Diana asked.

"He said that he saw me snooping around the Toybox," Ryder said. "I thought I had been careful, but he may have seen me use the gem to test the area for the presence of Glamour."

"You have said that you used it as a homing beacon," said Vargas.

Ryder nodded. "It burns whenever it is near sources of Glamour—the stronger the Glamour, the more intense the heat."

"What happened in the Toybox?" Diana asked. "If we had known you were in trouble, if you had called to us—"

"There was nothing any of you could have done," Ryder said flatly. "The gem reacted to a powerful source of Glamour in the room."

"It came from that old steamer trunk," said Signe in a subdued voice. "It began to glow—it was so hard to fight it—"

Diana patted the eshu on the knee. "You did resist it," she said. "That is what's important."

"But I could do nothing to help Ryder," Signe said.

"So this eshu who accosted us on the street saw you using the gem to measure Glamour in the Haight," Vargas said, trying to bring the conversation around to its original subject.

Ryder nodded. "You heard his words as well as I did," he said. "He knows of a group of Kithain who possess a similar gem, and he told us where we would be likely to find them."

"Why would he give you that information?" Vargas asked. "I thought all of their kind protected one another."

"I don't know," Ryder said, shaking his head. "I can only assume that putting us on their trail serves some purpose that will benefit him. What that purpose is, is not really our concern." The hawk-faced Dauntain grimaced. "I believe I have already met one of the group he described."

"Which one?" Diana asked.

"The redcap childling," Ryder responded. "The one he called Edmund. I told you about meeting him not far from the Toybox on my last visit to San Francisco. I have reason to believe that he was the one who tipped off the Kithain who mugged me and destroyed my memory of what I had learned."

the hill

"Are you sure that this is not, then, a matter for personal revenge?" Vargas asked, his dark eyes fixed on Ryder with probing intensity.

Ryder was silent for a moment, considering his companion's question. "I cannot deny that there is an element of personal satisfaction involved in going after one of the Kithain who exposed me," he said slowly, "but I believe that even if the redcap were not included in this group, I would still feel obligated to seek them out."

Vargas continued searching Ryder's face, then nodded. "So long as you understand your motivations and do not hide them from yourself or from us, I can accept your decision."

"So our job here is done, then?" Diana asked.

"For the time being," Ryder said. "First thing in the morning, we call the airport and make plane reservations for Hawaii—the Hilo Airport. That's where he said they would most likely be headed."

Blade sat in the back corner booth of Trickster's, feeling pleased with his night's work. It was more than luck that had placed the group of Dauntain squarely in his path. His kith, the eshu, had a knack for being in the right place at the right time. That talent had not only led him to the changeling hunters just after their eviction from the Toybox; it had also enabled him to recall the earlier visit by their leader, the dark-armored sidhe knight who bore a blue, glowing gem in the palm of his left hand. The similarity between that stone, obviously a faerie treasure, and the green gem possessed by Valmont and his current companions had given

Blade the perfect opportunity to become the instrument of poetic justice.

There was a time, long ago, when he and Valmont had been friends as well as rivals, united by their common belief that the sidhe had no right to claim dominion over the other Kithain. Their differences hinged on method rather than principle. Over time, however, Blade had watched Valmont lose his sharp-edged criticism of the sidhe—particularly those who supported the Seelie court of Goldengate. Valmont's association with the Kithain who frequented the Toybox Coffee Shop was the first hint that his onetime friend was slowly abandoning the cause of freedom for all Kithain. His involvement in a quest for the duke of Goldengate and his oathbond with the Seelie knight Leigh and the childling Baroness Morgania was a sign to Blade that Valmont had broken faith with their common vision.

In a similar fashion, Lady Glynnis, for all her Unseelie convictions, had also betrayed Blade and his followers. He had believed, for a while, that Glynnis and her coterie of sidhe renegades would help bring about the promised overthrow of the Seelie rulers in Pacifica—beginning with the downfall of Duke Aeon. The sudden appearance of a mysterious sidhe who claimed to be an Arcadian prince had so dominated Glynnis' attention that she had apparently abandoned her previous plans for the Unseelie uprising, which Blade had counted on to bring himself and his group of followers to power. Glynnis' betrayal convinced Blade that the only path to achieving his goal lay in what he could do for himself.

He had found allies in some of Glynnis' former followers. Together with them, Blade had conceived of a plan to snatch the emerald gem that had once been Malacar's and was now in Leigh's possession. He had

been forced to act precipitously when word came to him through his connections with Count Elias' network of spies and informants—some of whom also worked for Blade—that Valmont and his friends were headed for a meeting with the selkies, who were rumored to guard one of the few navigable sea trods across the Pacific. That aborted attack had been a bad gamble. It had taken every ounce of subtlety and persuasion he possessed to ensure that Count Elias, his nominal liege, was unaware of his involvement in that fiasco.

When his information sources also leaked to him the news that Glynnis had taken her precious prince to Hawaii, it seemed to make sense that Valmont and his friends were likely to end up there as well. Until the arrival of the Dauntain, he had been afraid that both Glynnis and Valmont had slipped beyond his reach. The coming of the hunters had given him a second chance at revenge.

Although he knew he was treading on dangerous ground by associating with the Dauntain, particularly those who had spurned their faerie natures to join the ranks of those who persecuted the children of the Dreaming, Blade felt it was a risk worth taking. That, too, was part of his birthright as an eshu—the inability to resist a challenge, so long as the odds held out a reasonable chance for success. Trusting that the fates would look favorably on his gamble, he had brought the four Dauntain to Trickster's.

The bar, near the edge of the Haight, had the kind of reputation that attracted a varied assortment of bikers, hookers, and other nocturnal denizens of the city. It was also a favorite watering hole for many of the city's Unseelie Kithain. Although it was not a freehold, its surreal ambience served as a peculiar sort of barrier against the Banality of the outside world. Inside Trickster's, decadence and abandon ruled, and the Kithain who flaunted the Seelie conventions found the bar a congenial environment.

The hunters had been reluctant to enter the bar until Blade assured them that it was not a "Glamour-trap"—their words—like the Toybox. Once the eshu began to speak of the other gem and of the Kithain who now possessed it, the four Dauntain had lost their initial unease, their attention at once caught up by the prospects of a more significant target.

"Want some company?"

Blade looked up quickly, suppressing a sudden rush of adrenalin as he recognized the voice. A female redcap, dressed in tight black jeans and a sheer black lace blouse, knotted at the waist, slid into the booth opposite the mohawked eshu.

"Don't sneak up on me like that," Blade snapped, visibly relaxing hands that had been poised to lash out at a possible foe. "Hi Slique," he added as an afterthought.

"Who were those people who just left?" she asked abruptly. "I know three of them were Kithain, but one was just a regular guy."

Blade gave the redcap a hard smile. "Those people just made me very happy," he said quietly.

"Oh?" Slique raised a questioning eyebrow. "Anything to do with a certain rivalry between you and another of your kithmates?"

Blade shrugged. "Why should I tell you anything?" he asked, in a playfully mild voice.

Slique responded with a wicked grin. "Because I can make life very unpleasant for people who cross me," she said, matching the eshu's half-teasing tone.

Blade considered her response. "So I've heard," he answered. "If you really want to know, the people who were here with me were a group of hunters—"

"Dauntain?" Slique interrupted. "And you *talked* to them?"

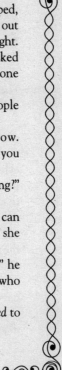

"I did more than just talk," Blade said. "I convinced them to leave town."

Slique gave him a dubious look. "I'm impressed," she remarked. "How did you work that little miracle?"

Blade leaned back in the booth, a look of satisfaction on his face.

"It wasn't hard," he said. "I set them on the trail of someone else."

"Valmont?"

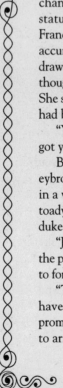

"Valmont isn't the only Kithain I have a problem with," Blade said enigmatically.

Slique looked thoughtful, digesting the eshu's words. Blade could almost see the redcap's thought processes at work. Slique operated on the fringes of the area's changeling community, and although her peripheral status left her open to being used by some of San Francisco's more ruthless Kithain, it also allowed her to accumulate a vast storehouse of information without drawing attention to herself. As he watched her, Blade thought that something must have clicked in her mind. She smiled, exposing a mouthful of grotesque teeth that had been filed to sharp points.

"You told him where to find that sidhe bitch who got you to do her dirty work," she said triumphantly.

Blade inclined his head toward her and arched an eybrow. "Lady Glynnis," he said, spitting out the name in a voice filled with venom. "She used Malacar as her toady, promising him that she could bring down the duke. She used me, too."

"Just like Malacar used me," Slique said, remembering the part that the satyr had paid her to play in his scheme to force open the steamer trunk in the Toybox.

"Then you should appreciate the irony of what I have just done," Blade said. "Glynnis made a lot of promises to a lot of Kithain. She brought iron weapons to arm us and told us we would be her vanguard in an uprising that would restore the Shadow Court to its true place in Kithain society." The eshu laughed bitterly. "We were all fooled into believing that she meant to do away with the distinction between commoners and nobles."

"Where is she now?" Slique asked. "I haven't seen her or any of her cronies for some time."

Blade snorted. "She took up with a sidhe noble who appeared from nowhere, claiming to be some sort of prince."

"Like calls to like," Slique murmured.

"It would seem that way," Blade said. "She dropped the rest of us to dance attendance on him."

"So you sent the Dauntain after her."

"I didn't say that."

"You didn't have to."

Abruptly, Blade got up from the booth. "It's been a long night," he said casually.

Slique looked rueful and stood up. "I can take a hint," she remarked. Blade walked with her to the door of Trickster's.

"I trust you won't share what I've told you with anyone else," Blade said. He had already told the redcap more than he had intended.

Slique narrowed her eyes. "I can keep secrets as well as anyone, for the right price," she said.

Blade nodded. "And what do you consider an appropriate fee?"

"You're still one of Elias's advisers, right?" the redcap inquired.

"With Valmont out of the picture, at least temporarily, I'm his chief adviser. Are you suggesting I use my clout to get you a position with the count?"

Slique smiled coquettishly. "I might be," she said.

"I'm going back to Oakland tonight," Blade said. "Shall we continue our discussion on the way?" He held

the hill

out an arm to her. If he handled her carefully, the redcap could prove to be another source of information, independent of Elias' network, about the underside of Kithain affairs in the Bay Area.

"I thought you'd never ask," Slique replied, linking arms with the muscular eshu.

"Do you eat like that all the time?" Edmund asked Lulani as the companions made their way back to their house—the stone building in which they had formerly been confined. Lulani had told them the secret phrase that would allow them to pass freely through the fern gateway, so they no longer thought of the house as a prison.

"We do not usually make one meal last from sundown until sunrise," Lulani said. All around them, the sky was beginning to lighten, and the air around the freehold seemed to be steeped in enchantment.

"I mean do you always bury a pig before you cook it?" the redcap asked.

Behind him, Leigh laughed. Despite the tenuousness of their position, the sidhe knight felt an almost giddy sense of freedom.

"The pig is buried because it's baked in an underground oven," she said. "It's called an *imu*," she added. "Is that right?" she asked Lulani.

The menehune nodded. "It is the traditional way of cooking the kalua pig, which is the main dish in our feast."

"I liked the dancing and the songs," Morgan said. The childling had watched in rapt fascination as the warriors of the tribe demonstrated their courage through elaborate dances with lit torches and spears. She had been even more impressed by the graceful steps and hand movements of the hula dancers.

"We have borrowed many customs from the mortals who came to these islands long ago," Lulani said.

"You speak as if you were already here when the islands were first settled," Valmont observed.

Lulani smiled. "Some of the elders of the village believe that," she said. "They say that we are the oldest of the *mana*-children."

"Is *mana* the same thing as Glamour?" Morgan asked. "That's the word I keep hearing in my head whenever you talk about *mana*."

"You will have to speak with our lorekeeper if you want to know such things," Lulani said. "He can tell you much more than I about how we came to be here."

"I feel so well versed in your culture, I'm sure there's nothing more I can learn," Rasputin said humbly.

Lulani looked at him, her face an open question.

"Don't mind him," Edmund said cheerfully, "he always talks like that."

"What do you mean?" Lulani asked.

"He lies," said Edmund.

"That's not true!" Morgan said. "Rasputin just says what he doesn't mean."

"That's what I said," Edmund retorted. "He's a liar."

"Careful," warned Valmont. "Not speaking the truth and lying are two very different things."

"Huh?" It was Edmund's turn to look perplexed.

"Rasputin belongs to a faerie race known as pookas," Valmont said. "All of his kith have an affinity with a particular animal. Rasputin's animal is the rabbit, as you might have noticed from his appearance."

Lulani looked sideways at Rasputin. "I have heard of those creatures," Lulani said, "though I have never seen one."

Valmont nodded. "The other characteristic of pookas is that they are unable to make statements that are completely true."

"Yeah, they lie," said Edmund.

"That's enough," said Tor, a warning implicit in his tone. Edmund glared at the troll, but said nothing.

"Some pookas exaggerate everything," Valmont continued. "Others, like Rasputin, simply say the opposite of what they mean."

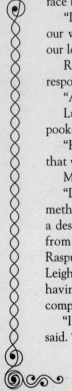

"So if you just turn his words inside out," Morgan said, "you can figure out exactly what he's saying. You just have to know how to translate his words. Rasputin may not speak the truth, but he never lies."

Lulani looked thoughtful. After a few seconds, her face broke into a smile. She turned to Rasputin.

"Did you mean to say that you feel so ignorant of our ways that you are sure you can learn much from our lorekeeper?"

Rasputin shook his head. "Absolutely not," he responded.

"And that means yes," Morgan announced.

Lulani pursed her lips. "I believe I understand this pooka-language," she said.

"Hey!" Edmund exclaimed. "Do you have a shell that will work on him?" he asked.

Morgan gave an exasperated sigh.

"Do you think I could learn some of your cooking methods?" Leigh asked, her question born in part from a desire to indulge her culinary interests, and in part from a need to shift the conversation away from Rasputin. In spite of the pooka's apparent insouciance, Leigh was certain that Rasputin could not possibly enjoy having his kith's inherent weakness dissected by his companions, however benign their intent.

"It would be an honor for us to teach you," Lulani said. "I will speak with some of my people."

Lulani left the oathmates at the door to their house.

"What time should we be up?" Morgan asked, looking around her dubiously at the clearing, which was growing brighter by the moment as dawn neared.

Lulani laughed. "Whenever your body tells you that you should be awake; you will know when it is time."

The menehune maiden embraced each of the companions in turn.

"Aloha," she said. "Sleep well."

"Aloha," Valmont replied.

"When's breakfast?" Edmund asked.

"I don't suppose you could have used the Eye of Opening to unlock the fern gate?" Rasputin quietly asked Leigh.

Leigh felt her face grow warm with embarrassment.

"It didn't even occur to me to use it," she whispered to the pooka.

Morgan stepped up to the ferns that barred the door to the stone house. "*Aloha hale*," she said. At her words, the long spiked fronds parted, allowing the companions to enter the building.

Leigh and Rasputin were the last to go inside. "I'm sure it would have worked," Leigh said softly to Rasputin. "But I don't think I would have used it."

"I won't ask why," the pooka muttered.

Leigh smiled. "It would have been rude," she said.

"Of course," Rasputin agreed doubtfully, stepping aside and gesturing with a flourish for Leigh to precede him into the house.

Inside the hut, the companions found a pile of soft mats woven from pandanus, the leaves of the screw pine. There were also lengths of brightly dyed cloth, grass skirts in two sizes for Morgan and Leigh, several carved wooden bowls and a collection of ornaments made from bright colored feathers, pale seashells, and delicate flowers.

the hill

"What are these?" Edmund asked, walking around the pile. He picked up what looked like a wristlet made from flowers and shells. "Looks good enough to eat," he said, grinning impishly.

"Don't!" Morgan cried. She grabbed the wristlet and tried to jerk it from Edmund's hands. The twine broke, scattering shells and blossoms all over the floor.

"You broke it!" Morgan wailed, dropping to her knees and attempting to gather up the pieces.

"You grabbed it from my hand," Edmund retorted. "I was just holding the stupid thing."

"That's enough!" Tor roared, startling both Morgan and Edmund into silence. The troll stalked over to the pair of childlings. "Some of us are tired," he said, his voice tapering to a low rumble. He held out a hand to Morgan. The childling looked questioningly at her grandfather, and then placed the flowers and shells she had collected into his open palm.

"Tomorrow you'll both go find the person who made this for us and apologize for breaking it. Then you'll ask if you can learn how to fix it. Understood?" He looked from one cowed childling to the other. Both Edmund and Morgan nodded their heads, Morgan's eyes wide with hurt and surprise.

Then Tor's face softened, and Morgan recognized in him the kindly protector she was accustomed to.

"Get some of those mats and make up beds for yourselves," the troll said gently. "Both of you are so tired you sound like a couple of grumps."

Leigh watched in amusement as Morgan and, more surprisingly, Edmund meekly obeyed the troll.

"Tor's advice might do well for all of us," Valmont said. Leigh nodded and began to select some mats from the pile. Before long, the companions each had a comfortable sleeping place along one of the walls of the house. Despite the brightness of the morning, the interior of the stone structure remained cool and dim. Soon both Morgan and Edmund were locked in slumber.

"Tor?" Leigh called quietly after she had settled herself for sleep.

"Uh!" Tor's response was a grunt that carried with it the weight of near-sleep.

"Thanks," she said.

"Don't mention it," said Tor, his words slurred.

"You've been so quiet since we got here," the sidhe continued, "that I was beginning to worry that something was wrong."

Tor snorted. "If there was something wrong," he said, "you'd know it. If there's nothing to say, I don't say it."

From his bed in the rear of the house, Rasputin made a noise that sounded like a quiet snort.

"That's easy for you to say," the pooka mumbled.

In the company of Glynnis, Devlin and a pair of ogrish-looking trolls named Argo and Mauler, Yrtalien strolled through the streets of downtown Hilo. The sidhe prince had abandoned his customary dark clothing for a flowing tunic of white woven napa and white linen trousers belted with a midnight-blue tasseled sash. His black hair, shagged in the front and trailing down to his waist in the back, was adorned with feathers woven into two braids on each side of his face, emphasizing the delicate points of his ears. About his neck hung a small velvet pouch strung on a silver chain. Inside the pouch were both the menehune seashell and the Shadowstone.

Walking beside Yrtalien, one hand hooked in his elbow, Glynnis ignored the admiring looks from

t h e   h i l l

passersby, keeping her eyes either on the ground in front of her or firmly fixed on the face of the prince. She did not feel like risking his ire by appearing to draw attention to herself. One of the first lessons she had learned when Yrtalien had come to the mortal world was that the Forsworn Prince was more than a little vain. Although surrounding himself with beautiful people and beautiful things was important to him, he insisted upon being the centerpiece of any gathering. Dressed in a simple, sleeveless sheath dress of pale lilac, a single black and purple orchid worn behind one ear, Glynnis felt plain in comparison to her lord; yet even this deliberate simplicity only emphasized her natural comeliness. Carefully, she glanced at Devlin, walking on Yrtalien's other side. She smiled to herself as she watched the silver-haired sidhe strut proudly in step with his new liege. In his turquoise linen shirt worn and close-fitting black trousers, with his long, silver hair draped like a cascade of water down his back, he looked like a peacock displaying his brilliant plumage. Hoping to deflect any potential competition, she had intimated to Devlin that the prince preferred ostentation in his close companions. The fool had taken the bait. Behind them, looking like the pair of bodyguards that they were, stalked the trolls, heavily clad in silver chains and black leather despite the humid air from the nearby ocean. Even in December, the weather was mild.

"Are we looking for anything specific?" Devlin asked after Yrtalien had poked his head into several tourist shops without giving any sign that he wanted to investigate them further.

Yrtalien sighed. He would have to enure himself to the appalling lack of civility among his courtiers, at least until he was in a position to enforce his own standards upon his new Shadow Court. In many ways, his memories of Arcadian life had ill-prepared him for coping with the egalitarianism so prevalent among the fae in exile. Here, Unseelie often meant undisciplined, and although freedom and the espousal of radical change were hallmarks of the Shadow Court, the prince was still used to at least some of the conventional distinctions that separated the ranks of the nobility from each other and from the commoners. Despite his foppish nature, Devlin was still the most knowledgeable and influential of Yrtalien's followers, and the prince could not afford to antagonize him.

"I will let you know when I find it," Yrtalien said, a peevish note creeping into his voice despite his efforts to mask his irritation. "Are there no establishments in this rural village that house the works of true craftsmen?"

Devlin snickered. "If you are looking for authentic Hawaiian artifacts," he said, "you are looking in the wrong place. Everything in these stores is geared for the tourist trade."

"Then take me somewhere else, if it isn't too much trouble," Yrtalien said mildly.

"My trouble is your pleasure," Devlin said blandly. Glynnis allowed herself a small smile of amusement as she realized that the sidhe noble was oblivious to the truth of his words.

Yrtalien followed Devlin's directions down a side street, away from the ocean. Here, the shops were less commercial in appearance and the sidhe prince could detect faint traces of Glamour wafting through the fragrant air. He paused before the door to a small shop that bore a simple sign reading *Nahele's Handmade Goods*.

"I will see what this place has to offer," Yrtalien said with barely disguised excitement. Nodding to Glynnis and Devlin to follow him inside, the prince entered the shop.

the hill

The interior of the shop was filled with exquisite carvings made from pieces of redwood, sandalwood, pandamus and other species of native trees. One wall displayed elegant leis made from tiny shells and dried flowers. A young Hawaiian sat behind a counter, putting the final touches on a carving of an orchid blossom.

"Aloha," the man greeted them. "May I help you?"

Yrtalien motioned for Glynnis and Devlin to look about the shop while he approached the shopowner.

"Are you Nahele?" he asked. The young man smiled and nodded.

"I am Nahele," he replied. As he spoke, he continued to trim the delicate piece of woodwork with a tiny knife.

Glynnis wandered around the shop, examining the items and listening as Yrtalien questioned Nahele about his work and complimented his skill. Her neck tingled as she sensed the prince weaving his enchantments upon the craftsman. She looked at Devlin, who stood impatiently near the door. The silver-haired sidhe shrugged and moved to join her.

"Has the prince decided to take up woodcarving?" he whispered softly.

Glynnis shook her head. "I believe he is making an investment," she murmured. She picked up a carving of a graceful double canoe, admiring the smoothness of the wood and the sleek lines of the design.

Soon Nahele was explaining to Yrtalien how he worked to capture the essence of the objects he carved. For him, the process of creating visual representations of a diminishing culture was a labor of love and a means of expressing his vision of beauty. Devlin, hearing the young man begin to open his heart to Yrtalien, arched his eyebrow and smiled faintly.

"Suddenly I understand," he said to Glynnis.

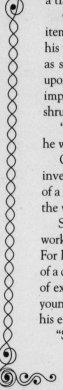

Finally, the prince purchased a small carving of a monk seal and turned to leave.

"I would like to return and speak with you further," Yrtalien said. "You have a rare talent and I am fascinated by the care you lavish upon your work."

"You are welcome anytime," Nahele said, pleased by his customer's interest. "Until we meet again, then, aloha."

"Aloha," Yrtalien replied. Glynnis and Devlin followed the prince out of the shop and back onto the street.

"In a few days, he should be ripe for the ravaging," Yrtalien said smoothly. "Let's see what other shops lie along this street. I wish to develop as broad a base of sources for my needs as possible."

Glynnis suppressed a sigh as Yrtalien began walking down the street. Another shop, this one displaying stone sculptures, caught his attention. As the trio entered the store, Glynnis touched Devlin's arm.

"This is going to be a long day, I fear," she said to her companion. Devlin nodded glumly.

chapter

seven

"We cannot afford to make a mistake," Ryder informed his companions as the four Dauntain settled into their rooms in the Seacrest Bed and Breakfast Hotel, overlooking the ocean just northeast of the city of Hilo. "We need to be as discreet as possible in our attempts to locate the centers of corruption in the city, and once we have pinpointed our targets, we must be certain that we are not discovered before we can act."

"I've got no quarrel with that," Diana said. The statuesque blonde drew back the curtains of the room she and Signe shared and stood for a moment admiring the view of clear blue water and white sand beach. "But we thought we were careful in San Francisco," she added.

Vargas unlocked the door which connected the two rooms the group had rented. "We were, perhaps, overly precipitious in our attempt to confront the creatures of infamy in their own lair," he observed.

"What should we do to make certain that we don't make the same mistakes we made in San Francisco?" Signe asked.

"I thought about that on the flight over," Ryder answered. "I'm not certain you will like what I am about to propose, but I believe it may be the only way we can proceed without showing our hand prematurely." He opened his hand and stared at the blue mark in the center of his palm.

Vargas looked questioningly at Ryder.

Ryder's hawkish features sharpened, so that no one could mistake him for anything but a predator.

"I intend to begin our investigations of the city, searching out places where the Kithain are likely to be. At the same time, we need to become familiar with Hilo so that we are not at a logistical disadvantage here." Ryder paused. With his right hand he massaged the palm of his left, which pulsed with a soft, steady reminder of the presence of the blue stone.

"We must avoid all direct contact with things or persons that radiate Glamour until we are confident that we have located our targets—the possessors of the stone that matches this one."

"Assuming that our informant didn't lie to us just to get us out of town," Diana muttered.

Ryder nodded. "I agree we may be following a false lead," he said. "But ever since we arrived here, I have felt a growing certainty that this is the course we must follow."

"What happens when we feel we are ready?" Signe asked quietly.

Ryder did not answer immediately. Instead, he rose from his seat and walked over to the window, where he stood gazing out toward the ocean. When he turned again to face his companions, his face had a faraway look.

"When we are ready, we will begin to insinuate ourselves into Kithain society," he answered, his voice devoid of all emotion.

"What do you mean?" Diana asked, her slate-blue eyes darkening with a sense of impending danger.

"I mean exactly what I say," Ryder said. "You and Signe and I will have to enter the realm of the Kithain."

Vargas' response was immediate and explosive. "This is insane," he said sharply. "You will be putting your very souls in mortal danger."

Ryder only nodded. "Where great rewards are to be had, great risks must be taken," he replied. "If we can locate and destroy—or render harmless—a source of

Glamour as powerful as this one," he said, holding up his left palm so that its blue center was visible to his three companions, "we will have won a major victory for our cause."

"Are you saying that you want us to revert to the madness which once consumed us?" Diana asked. Her speech was slow and deliberate, and Ryder could see her knuckles whiten as she clenched her fists in quiet distress.

"I am afraid that is exactly what I want," he said, almost gently. "We are all mature adults," he said. "We have faced danger before and survived with our bodies and our souls intact. We have experienced first-hand the evil against which we struggle."

"Why do you think this is necessary?" Signe asked.

"Because we must win their trust. Think about it," he said. "The Kithain we hunt are likely to be the leaders of the community—the bearers of the stone are apparently regarded as heroes in San Francisco, at least according to our information source. This means that we will have to be accepted members of their society before we can gain the trust of any of them."

"And what part am I to play in this?" Vargas asked. He was calmer now, his expression calculating.

Ryder allowed himself the barest of smiles.

"You, my friend," he said, "will be our lifeline to sanity."

Vargas stared at Ryder intently for a moment, then nodded, beginning to put the pieces of his leader's plan together in his head.

"Your part is perhaps the most difficult, and the most dangerous, of all," Ryder continued. "You will have to watch us from a distance while we succumb to our delusions and enter a world of lies, deceits, and impossibilities."

"I see more frustration and sadness than danger in

that role," the ex-seminarian said grimly. "To watch the three of you consort with the creatures of darkness will put me in fear for your souls, but I cannot see how it can pose a significant threat to me."

"The danger," Ryder said, "is that some of us may not be able to withstand the temptation of a life we once embraced and accepted as our heritage." He walked over to Vargas and put his hands on the wiry young Latino's shoulders. "The danger is that one of us may become so caught up in our madness that we betray you to the Kithain."

"It won't be me," Diana said harshly. "Just the thought of once again taking on the monstrous form I used to wear sickens me."

"And me," Signe said, though not quite as adamantly as her friend.

"We mustn't delude ourselves," Ryder said. "Any of us can fall prey to the seduction of a world in which dreams become reality."

"It is your soul for which I have the most concern," Vargas said, taking Ryder's hands from his shoulders and standing to face his friend. "You were once a lord among your kind," he said, "or so I understand."

Ryder nodded. "And I will have to become such once again," he said. "This is why I say that your part is as dangerous as ours. You must watch us and wait until we are ready for you to join us. We will find a way to keep in touch with you so that we do not forget our real purpose for being here and so that you, in turn, can monitor our progress. But you must keep in mind at all times that so long as we are consumed by our inner madness, you must not trust any of us."

Vargas' eyes were moist with tears as he nodded his understanding.

"What about the creature who recognized you?" asked Signe. "Won't he give you away?"

the hill

"The young redcap saw me as a fierce knight in dark armor," Ryder said. "I will not appear in so dramatic a fashion when next we meet." The severe features of the Dauntain's face grew softer, assuming a lordly, almost gentle mien. "He may not recognize a courtier in velvets and silks as the same person he met swathed in black chimerical metal."

"It is still risky," Vargas said. "You cannot be certain that he will miss the connection."

"Of course I can't be certain," Ryder snapped, "but I am more than a match for a redcap bratling. If he recognizes me, I will see that he tells no one about his discovery." The Dauntain's jaw hardened, and his cold eyes glinted like iron knives.

"You would kill him?" Vargas asked, concern written on his face. "A child?"

"There are other options," Ryder said. "If it is possible, I will simply drive him from his faerie nature into the real world, our world. I will force him to become sane, and with his sanity will come forgetfulness."

"What if something goes wrong?" Diana persisted.

Ryder shrugged. "I said it would be dangerous."

"We are not the only people of the dream who inhabit these islands," the lorekeeper began in a sing-song voice. He was shorter than most of the people of the village. He wore a loin-cloth of woven tapa and adorned himself with garlands of flowers and shells about his wrists, neck, and ankles. He wore a wreath of dried flowers around his head.

The companions sat on the floor of the lorekeeper's *hale*, the word they had come to recognize as meaning "house." They had just finished a meal of taro root, mangos and strips of broiled fish when Lulani informed them that if they wished to learn the answers to their earlier questions about the menehune, they could meet with the elder of the village who served as the keeper of the history of the tribe.

"Long ago, it is said, when these islands were still new to the world above the waters, there were mighty empires already spreading their knowledge and their ways throughout the world. Some of these people were great builders, although they were small of stature. Stories have been told of how these workers in stone and wood labored furiously to build an entire structure in one night, leaving forever unfinished anything that was not completed before dawn."

"So, were they vampire construction workers, or what?" Edmund asked.

The lorekeeper looked at the young redcap uncomprehendingly.

"I don't think the word means anything to them," Leigh whispered.

"The ancient builders, the original menehune, worked at night because they built with their dreams," the lorekeeper said. "And because it is hard to have the same dream two nights in a row, they were compelled to dream a work to its completion or leave it undone."

Morgan listened carefully to the lorekeeper's words. The sidhe childling had spent most of the day wandering around the village. The lei-weavers fascinated her and she'd tried her hand at stringing together the delicate mokihana berries. The fragrant aroma of the berries reminded her of licorice, and she now wore a string of them around her neck.

"Where are they now?" she asked the lorekeeper.

The old menehune shrugged and raised his hands. "There are many stories about that, too," he said. "When

t h e   h i l l

the mortals came from the islands to the west and south of here, they brought the children of their own dreams. They brought our people to this place which was all that was left of the great empires of the ocean."

"All that was left?" repeated Leigh.

The lorekeeper nodded. "A great catastrophe sank the island home of the original little builders, leaving only the tip of this island upon which we stand as a reminder of its former beauty and glory."

Valmont's face registered sudden enlightenment. "You are speaking of the legend of the lost continent of Mu," he said. When the others looked at the eshu question-ingly, Valmont turned his gaze to the lorekeeper.

"Forgive my interruption," he murmured.

The menehune elder nodded benignly. "There is no fault. I am the lorekeeper for this village," he said. "This means that I am also the lore collector. If you think you know a piece of the tale I am telling, please give me your words on it, that I may add them to my own. It will make my story richer in the next telling."

Valmont looked pleased. "Ancient legends tell of two great lands that once existed where the oceans are today. One of those was the continent of Atlantis, in the ocean which now bears its name. The other was known as Mu and was thought to lie in these Pacific waters. Atlantis also was said to have disappeared into the sea following a violent cataclysm."

The lorekeeper smiled.

"We were unlike anything the menehune had ever seen before," the lorekeeper went on. "The mortals brought new gods to the land and new legends."

"New dreams," Leigh muttered.

"Yes, new dreams—and we were those dreams," the lorekeeper said. "The king of the menehune feared that if our two peoples met, their own kind would suffer."

"Why?" Edmund asked.

"Because the builders were the last of their kind, with few, if any, mortals to sustain them. They believed that they would be assumed into a dream that was not of their own making. Their king ordered the builders to flee the island, telling them that if they were seen by the new mortals, they would be turned into stone."

"Would that really happen?" Morgan asked.

The lorekeeper shrugged. "No one knows," he said. "But there are many strange stone formations on this island, just as there are still remnants of the great works of the builders." He paused for a moment, as if gathering his thoughts.

"Most of the king's people took his word for truth and disappeared from this island, leaving it to the newcomers. Thus we inherited our home from the menehune."

"So you're not the menehune after all," Morgan said.

The lorekeeper shook his head. "We are not the original little people of the island," he answered. "But we are the menehune just the same. We are their heirs."

"You're not saying that menehune has become a general term for the changelings of Hawaii, are you?" Rasputin asked.

"That is exactly what I am saying," replied the lorekeeper. "It is believed that a few of the original builders refused to leave. They hid themselves in the most secret places of this island, wrapping themselves in deep enchantments so that they would not be found and destroyed—by the mortals who would shatter their dream souls, or by the new dream children—our people—who would change the nature of their dream and make them into something different."

"How could that be?" Valmont wondered, intrigued by the unfamiliar concept.

the hill

The lorekeeper smiled. "As I have said before, the people whose dreams gave life to the builders disappeared from the earth. The builders remained, although they no longer had dreamers to sustain them. They became exceedingly fragile, unable to withstand close contact with strangers of any kind, whether mortal or of the dreaming."

"Have you ever seen any of them?" Morgan asked.

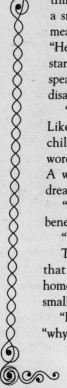

"Once," the lorekeeper said with a hint of sadness in his voice. "Once, long, long ago, when I was very young, I went on a vision quest that took me deep within the forests, almost to the top of the great volcano that sleeps in the center of the island. Just after sunset, I heard a soft movement behind me. I turned quickly, thinking to surprise whatever had made the noise. I saw a small person." The lorekeeper held his hand out, measuring a distance of about four feet from the ground. "He had a very red face and big bulging eyes. He was startled that I had seen him, and he fled before I could speak to him. I tried to follow, but it was as if he had disappeared into the ground itself."

"Where did they go?" Edmund wanted to know. Like all his companions except for Tor, the redcap childling had adopted the dress of the menehune. He wore a loincloth and a lei made of shells and feathers. A wreath of leaves was jammed over his spiked dreadlocks.

"Some say they found a way to their lost home beneath the waters," the lorekeeper said.

"You mean they drowned?" Edmund asked.

The lorekeeper laughed. "No," he replied. "I mean that they entered the dream-world in which their homeland still existed. Others may have traveled to the smaller islands nearby, where few mortals go."

"If they were the original menehune," Leigh asked, "why do you call yourselves by their name?"

"One legend of our people tells that before the king of the builders left this island forever, he took a great risk and asked for a meeting with the oldest of our people. Our *alii nui*, our great chief, cloaked herself with the softest of dreams and went forth to meet the leader of the builders. At that meeting, the leader of the menehune told our own chief that our people would inherit all the lands which once belonged to the builders. Along with that legacy, the menehune chief asked our *alii nui* to adopt the name of his tribe, so that it, at least, would not pass forever from memory."

"What about your own name?" Valmont asked. "What did you call yourselves before you became known as the menehune?"

The lorekeeper smiled. "That is a secret that we have sworn to keep to ourselves," he said. "It was our sacrifice to prove ourselves worthy of this paradise of dreams. We are the menehune," he said. "And that is the story I wished to tell you."

Valmont stood up and bowed before the lorekeeper. "We are honored by your gift of a part of the history of your people," the eshu said. The lorekeeper inclined his head in acknowledgment.

"I suppose we should stay here for awhile," said Rasputin, making as if to leave the lorekeeper's *hale*. The others stood and voiced their thanks before they left the menehune elder.

"Now what do we do?" Edmund asked.

"Whatever we want, apparently," Valmont said. "There doesn't seem to be an agenda we need to follow."

"I found the woman who made the bracelet you—I mean, we—broke," Morgan said to Edmund.

"So?" grumbled the redcap.

"So we promised Grandpa that we would apologize to her for breaking her gift and ask her to show us how to fix it," she reminded him.

t h e   h i l l

Edmund looked at Tor. The troll nodded.

"Great," the redcap said. "I can't wait to learn how to string together a bunch of shells and flowers."

"I'm sure you'll enjoy it immensely," Rasputin said.

Yrtalien stormed through the rooms of his palace, his eyes glittering with fury. He found Glynnis seated on a teakwood bench in the small back garden, plucking at the strings of a small ivory and jade lap harp. She looked up at the sound of his coming and had barely enough time to put the harp aside before the prince grabbed her hands and jerked her to her feet. Sensing the depth of his anger, she tried to pull away, but he held her fast, gripping her wrists so tightly that she winced in pain.

"How have you managed to saddle me with such fools?" Yrtalien demanded, his voice harsh with unveiled hostility.

Glynnis tried to meet the prince's eyes without blanching. "I don't know what you mean, my lord," she said, her voice shaking.

With a cry of exasperation, Yrtalien shoved Glynnis away from him. The raven-haired sidhe stumbled back, catching the bench with one hand to break her fall. She started to rise, but thought better of it. *Let him see me as no threat*, she thought as she looked up at the prince's stark face, its noble features accented even more by his fury.

"Your toady Devlin had the effrontery to caution me about wasting Glamour," Yrtalien said bitterly. Glynnis remained silent, knowing that until his anger passed, anything she said would only antagonize him further.

The prince stalked up to her and looked down upon his fallen consort.

"What is the point of all this," he said, waving an arm in a sweeping gesture that encompassed the garden and, by implication, the rest of the freehold, "if not to exercise the abilities that are part of our very essence? It is our right as sons and daughters of the Dreaming to take the creative impulses from whatever sources are available and use them to fuel our visions." As he spoke, Yrtalien's voice grew milder. Glynnis risked a second look at his face, and saw that his features had likewise begun to soften, a sign that his temper was diminishing.

"Perhaps Devlin only needs to understand what you envision," she said. "He and the others have been too long without a real leader to set an example for them to follow."

Yrtalien laughed scornfully. He stepped around Glynnis and took a seat on the bench. His hand rested briefly on the small harp. Picking it up, he studied the instrument carefully, his slender fingers caressing the harp's smooth finish and lingering over the inset pieces of jade along its frame. Glynnis started to rise, thinking to join her lord on the bench, but Yrtalien put a hand on her shoulder.

"Stay as you are," he said, handing the harp to her and settling himself comfortably on the bench's cushioned seat. "Play for me," he said.

Placing the harp on her lap, Glynnis began a soft, mournful melody of her own composition. The song had no words, but to its creator, its eerie cadences called to mind the constant longing for the return of the Dreaming.

Yrtalien sat brooding in silence as Glynnis's fingers moved across the strings of the instrument. When she had finished the tune, he sighed briefly.

the hill

"Another," he commanded. Glynnis chose a lighter tune, one made famous by the mortal harper O'Carolan, whose songs now graced the repertoire of most skilled traditional harpists.

"I do not mean to seem ungrateful," Yrtalien said, halfway through Glynnis' performance. Glynnis paused in her playing and tilted her head back to look up at the prince. He shook his head, and motioned for her to continue. "I realize that you have put forth a great deal of effort to find this sanctuary for me and to bring Devlin and other like-minded Kithain to my attention." Glynnis bowed her head, acknowledging Yrtalien's words as the closest thing to an apology that she was likely to get from him.

"I had hoped to find the Kithain of this realm more willing to accept the politics of change," Yrtalien said. "But I find them even more recalcitrant than their cousins beyond the Mists. Have they been so blinded by Seelie mores that they cannot see themselves for what they are?"

"That is not unlikely, my lord," Glynnis murmured.

"We are the lords of this world," Yrtalien said, more to himself than to Glynnis. "Because we were too weak-willed to assert our dominance over the mortals placed in this world to feed our souls, we allowed a race of lesser beings to gain the power to destroy us. Had we continued to harvest their dreams as we were born to do, the Sundering would never have occurred.

"Look at us," he continued. "We cower in freeholds enchanted to keep out the disbelieving world. Instead, men and women should be living in fear of arousing our displeasure. They should be lining up before us with offerings made of their dreams and hopes. This world was meant to supply our needs, not become our prison."

"They have not your eyes with which to see, my lord," Glynnis said. Her fingers were beginning to tire, but she gritted her teeth and segued into another O'Carolan air.

"The commoners are especially hard to convince," Yrtalien said.

"Their backs were broken by the Accordance Wars," Glynnis reminded him. "The sidhe who returned—and I believe my lord knows that I was among the original group of exiles—made it clear that the commoners could not hope to prevent the reinstatement of the nobility. They were also sensible enough to compromise on certain issues so that the commoners had no compelling grievances to fuel a concerted resistance—"

"I know," Yrtalien snapped. "You have taken great pains to inform me of the current state of affairs among the Kithain. What I need now is a way to rekindle that flame of resentment against the Seelie nobles."

"Or build up their own sense of themselves as a force to be reckoned with," Glynnis murmured. Belatedly, she added "My Lord," hoping that the prince would not notice her slip.

As if in response to her words, Yrtalien stood up suddenly, jarring Glynnis so that her fingers faltered in their rhythmic strumming.

"I've heard enough of your wispy music," he said, and although his words were cutting, his tone conveyed nothing more malicious than a lack of consideration. "Put that away and come with me," he commanded, extending a hand toward Glynnis and pulling her to her feet. She lowered the harp.

"Are we going out again, my Lord?" she asked.

Yrtalien nodded. "Find Lord Devlin and tell him I require his presence as well as his knowledge of the local night life," the prince said. "I want some real musicians installed in my freehold. In fact, it's time we started acquiring a suitable serving staff."

"Do you mean mortals, my Lord?" Glynnis asked.

"Of course," Yrtalien said. "The most effective way to convince others of one's beliefs is through proof—incontrovertible, tangible evidence. I have been maintaining that we are the rightful overlords of humanity. It is time to give some substance to my words."

"Aloha hale," Morgan whispered softly. She waited for the ferns to part before she crept out of the house where her companions slept. In the moonlight that bathed the clearing where the menehune village nestled, the sidhe childling could see the outline of the other houses. Most of them were dark, evidence that their occupants were sleeping like her oathmates—like she had been before her dreams had awakened her.

She had dreamed about the Eyestones, and although only vague memories of her dream still remained, she remembered seeing three of the four gems. In her dream, she saw the green stone, which she knew was called the Keystone or the Eye of Opening. Along with it were two others, a black opal and a blue sapphire. Leigh held the emerald in her dream, but the holders of the other gems were blurry figures, phantomlike. She was about to discover their identities when a voice had interrupted her with the words, "The last is yet to come."

She had awakened, and for a brief, panicky moment Morgan was sure that the speaker was standing in the house's single room. Then she heard a faint murmur in a voice she recognized as Rasputin's and realized that the pooka was talking in his sleep. She had lain awake after that, listening to the sounds of her sleeping

companions. Beside her, Leigh breathed deeply and
rhythmically. Near the door, Tor's heavy snore sounded
like rumbling thunder. Across the room, Edmund's
breath was interrupted by sudden snorts. She had to
listen carefully to hear Valmont.

I need to write this down, Morgan told herself,
realizing that she was too awake to go back to sleep.
She found her backpack in the dark and located her
diary before creeping across the room to the door. She
had been especially cautious not to awaken her
grandfather, and her stealth was rewarded as she
managed to pass by him without disturbing him.

Once outside, Morgan walked through the still
clearing until she found a small rock near the edge of
the village. She sat down with her back against the
smooth stone and placed her diary on her lap,
removing the pink ballpoint pen from the little leather
casing attached to the diary's cover. Realizing that she
couldn't see well enough to write, the sidhe childling
felt around her in the grass until she located a pair of
small twigs. Rubbing them together in what she
thought was a convincing imitation of the motions
necessary to build a fire, she imagined a softly glowing
lamp much like the cream-colored unicorn lamp on
her night-table back home.

Warmth spread through her body until it reached
the tips of her fingers. She put the sticks down and
waved her hands in the air, concentrating as hard as
she could on fashioning the Glamour she had awakened
into the shape of her imagining. Above her left
shoulder, a tiny, glowing creature that looked like a cross
between a unicorn and a pegasus hovered, shedding a
soft light onto her lap, illuminating the book.

She looked up at the little chimera and smiled with
delight. Then she picked up her pen and turned to a
clean page.

the hill

Dear Layla, she wrote, remembering the eshu childling who was her closest friend and coconspirator in San Francisco. Layla shared her kith's love of stories—as well as their affinity for risk-taking—and Morgan could think of no one better suited to be the imaginary recipient of her private correspondence.

We are in Hawaii as the guests of the menehune, she began. For a minute or two she looked at the words she had just written, admiring the neatness of her script and the bright pink ink against the paler pink page. *The changelings of Hawaii are very different from the rest of us. For one thing, they have a different way of gathering Glamour.* Morgan had wondered how the villagers kept themselves supplied with what they called *mana,* so she had asked Lulani. The chief's daughter had told her that the menehune no longer depended on the dreams of humans, but surrounded themselves with the magic that lived in the lush vegetation of the island. *My friend Lulani can't explain exactly how it's done, but she says that they listen to the dreams of the flowers and the trees, and those dreams keep them supplied with all the* mana *they need.*

She wondered if she should describe the crossing in the swan ship, but then decided it would be better to start with the present.

When we got here, she continued, *the menehune thought we were enemies and captured us. Then they decided to give us the chance to prove our good intentions. So now we are their guests and are trying very hard to make them like us. So far, I think we're doing okay.*

Leigh has been learning how to make all kinds of strange food, and some of it is really delicious. I don't think I like poi very much. It tastes like glue. Edmund loves it. Both Leigh and I have started wearing grass skirts and lots of flower necklaces. Leigh made some cloth halter tops for us, even though the menehune women don't wear anything like that.

We have only been here for a little over a day, but

Valmont has already spent a lot of time talking with the elders of the village and trading stories with them. The lorekeeper spoke to all of us after we got up this morning and told us a wonderful story about how the menehune came to exist. I think Valmont memorized it, so I won't write it down. I don't think I could remember all the details anyway.

Grandpa got challenged by some of the young warriors and hunters. They wanted to see how strong he was and if he could wrestle them to the ground. He kept trying to avoid it, but finally I asked him to do it. They are calling him the Rock that Walks, or something like that. I'm not sure how to spell the word.

The menehune speak a different language, sort of like Hawaiian, I guess, but maybe not exactly the same. They gave each of us an enchanted shell that can translate their words into English, but if you listen hard, you can also hear what they are really saying. I have learned a few words. Hale means house and mana means power or magic.

Rasputin is learning how to juggle lit torches like the tribe's dancers, and he is teaching them some of his own tricks. We had a hard time explaining to them that Rasputin always says the opposite of what he means, but now that they know how to interpret his words, they understand him almost as well as we do. They call him a kahuna, which is their word for priest. I guess it's because you always have to figure out what he's really saying.

I wish I could say something nice about how well Edmund is doing here, but I can't. I think Edmund is bored because it's hard for him to get into trouble. The menehune are fascinated with watching him eat, though, and I'm afraid he will get carried away and eat them out of house and home. That's a joke, only it's not funny when you think about it because he probably could if he tried. I know you like Edmund, so I won't tell you what I really think about him. He is my oathmate so I have to try to like him. I don't know what you see in him.

t h e   h i l l

I hope Chief Makani decides we can be trusted. I have a feeling that he wants to tell us something but is waiting until he makes up his mind about us. It's sort of scary to feel like everything you do is being judged by people who might not understand the reasons behind your actions. It's sort of like taking a test at school without knowing what the questions are and without knowing the answers either.

Has anyone at the palace told you about our quest to find the four gems that will open up Silver's Gate? I'm going to pretend that you do know so that I don't have to use up all my diary pages trying to explain it all to you. We already have one of the stones, the one that Leigh got from Malacar. But there are three others. I dreamed about two of them last night. One of them is a black opal, and it is called the Shadowstone. The menehune are supposed to have it, which is why we were brought here, I think, but so far I haven't seen it anywhere. The other one I dreamed about is a blue sapphire. I don't know where that one is. My dream didn't show me the last gem, the ruby one. I hope that doesn't mean that it has been destroyed. I'm having trouble remembering my dreams as well as I used to.

Morgan looked at those words in surprise, since until she wrote them down she hadn't realized their truth. She felt a small twinge of fear and thought about erasing the words from the page. Then she realized that they were written in ink and all she could do was draw a line through them. *That won't make them go away,* she thought, and sighed heavily, deciding reluctantly to accept what she had written and proceed with her "letter" to Layla.

I hope this doesn't mean that I'm becoming a wilder, because once I do, I'll become a grump like Grandpa and I don't think he dreams very often. Maybe if we spend a few more days and nights in the menehune village, where there is a lot of mana, I will start dreaming like I used to. That thought cheered Morgan.

Speaking of dreams, I'm beginning to get sleepy again, she wrote, *so I'll stop writing now and go back to bed. I wish you could be here to see how beautiful it is. I'll pick out the prettiest flowers I can find and make a lei just for you. Aloha.* Morgan smiled to herself as she wrote down the Hawaiian greeting. *From now on,* she thought, *I'll start and end all my diary entries like that.*

Morgan closed her diary and replaced the pen in its holder. She stood up and began retracing her steps across the clearing to her house, accompanied by the soft, glowing chimera. When she entered the house, she realized that the winged unicorn was bathing the room with its gentle light. She picked it up and tried to hide it in her arms, with only minimal success. Once she had tiptoed to her bed, she pushed it into her backpack, where it glimmered faintly, and then winked out. *I hope my toothpaste didn't kill it,* Morgan thought, feeling a small pang of guilt. By the time she had settled herself on her bed of woven mats, the childling felt her eyes grow heavy. A few minutes later, she was sleeping as soundly as her oathmates.

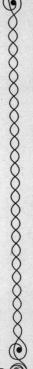

t h ε   h i l l

chapter

eight

Yrtalien's freehold glittered with tiny chimerical lights, limning the palace and its adjoining garden in glowing pinpoints of cobalt and pale blue, lavender, and deepest purple. Within the building, crystal-ball chandeliers fashioned from the prince's imaginings hung from the ceilings, bathing the rooms with strobing colors that played upon the faces of the courtiers who had come to attend the first official function of Yrtalien's Court of Shadows.

Heavy pulsating music dominated the palace's largest room, where a band of musicians clad in tattered velvet and silk finery churned out waves of throbbing sound that surrounded the Kithain who danced with careless abandon. Another room held a long table overflowing with food—carved pineapple, chunked coconut meat, glazed pork, broiled slivers of mahimahi, candied papaya strips and other succulent dishes. Bemused mortals, dressed in sheer garments of chimerical silk and gauze, circulated among the Kithain with trays of food and drink.

In the garden, small groups of guests wandered along the winding paths between the lush ferns and flowers, looking for the "monsters" that were supposed to be roaming the grounds, chimera created by the prince and Glynnis especially for the party. Now and then the sound of combat would rise up briefly from somewhere within the garden, signaling that one of the Kithain thrill-seekers had met and overcome some small manifest terror.

Yrtalien stood in the center of a small group of

Kithain, admiring the flow of gaiety and revelry around him. Next to him, Glynnis, radiant in a dark violet dress of layered silk and shredded gauze, tried to keep track of the comings and goings of the guests. Lord Devlin faced the prince, his posture unconsciously imitative of his host. A slender young satyr had attached herself to Devlin, clinging to his arm and idly fingering the sidhe noble's silver hair. A young woman, her long blond hair aglow with a chimerical crown of pink and gold plumeria blossoms, waited attendance, holding a silver tray containing tall crystal goblets of iced juices. She stared fixedly at the prince, her cornflower blue eyes soft with longing for the handsome figure who had swept her from the dullness of her everyday life and plunged her into a dream-realm filled with beautiful people and strange, inexplicable enchantments.

The prince lifted a goblet from the tray. Dressed in black silk, his black hair trimmed with side-braids of feathers and shells, Yrtalien radiated an aura of stark elegance and raw power. The sidhe lord sipped slowly from his glass before returning it to the tray. Casually, he reached out and, with one slender finger, traced the delicate features of the serving girl's face. He turned, smiling, to Lord Devlin.

"This," he said, indicating the girl, "is how it should be. We have lived for too long in fear of our own natures. Creatures like her are born to serve us, and we should do our utmost to help them fulfill their destinies. Don't you agree?"

Devlin selected a drink for himself before answering. The silver-haired noble was dressed in maroon and black, presenting a figure almost as compelling as the prince.

"How many mortals have you enchanted?" he asked, a faint note of disapproval in his voice.

Yrtalien laughed. "I'm afraid I lost count after awhile," he said. "After you found the band for me and assisted me in engaging their services on a long-term basis, Glynnis and I just walked around the city making our selections."

"Don't you think that's a little risky, plucking mortals off the streets?" Devlin persisted. "Aren't you worried that a rash of missing persons might attract unwanted attention from the police or something like that?"

The prince's face hardened into a stiff smile.

"I am not stupid," he said. "I made certain that the humans we enchanted were those whose absence would not be noticed. It's astonishing how quickly a stranger will confide in you that she has no living relatives, lives alone, and works for a temporary employment agency." He looked appraisingly at his blond attendant. "Is this not better than the life you were leading?" he asked her, his voice rich with condescension.

She nodded. "I am—"

Yrtalien broke in upon her words. "Your agreement was sufficient. I don't need to know what you are," he said curtly. "Your thoughts are not necessary right now, lovely one. Your careful attendance on me and my party is."

The woman blushed as Yrtalien stroked her hair before once again picking up his drink.

"This evening is the first of many such celebrations," Yrtalien said. "Unlike our Seelie cousins, who hesitate to make use of their powers except for certain designated festivals, this court will always be in session. There is Glamour enough for everyone on this island. Mortals come here to dream, and their dreams should feed us for quite some time."

"I thought you planned to strike a blow against the Seelie," Devlin began. "Somehow, throwing a party— even one that never ends—doesn't seem to me to present much of a threat to our opponents."

"Before the Shadow Court can take action against those who would deprive us of our rightful place, we must first *become* the Shadow Court," Yrtalien said, trying not to show his impatience at Devlin's lack of comprehension. "We are, at best, a gathering of poseurs and would-be rebels who have yet to learn the meaning of the word Unseelie. Do you even know what you are, Lord Devlin?"

Devlin looked offended. "Of course I do," he snapped.

"C'mon, Dev," the sidhe noble's companion cooed in his ear, "the prince is right. Sometimes you're just as stodgy as the Seelie prigs in Honolulu."

Yrtalien looked at the satyr, as if seeing her for the first time. "I don't believe we've met," he said mildly, replacing his drink on the waiting tray.

"I'm Siva," she said. "I heard your speech on the beach the other night and I liked what you said." She cocked her head coquettishly at the prince and smiled. "So how do I join?"

Yrtalien offered her a brilliant smile and extended a hand in her direction. Siva released Devlin's arm to clasp it, and Yrtalien drew her toward him. He bowed his head over the back of her hand, brushing it with his lips, then raised his head and released his hold.

"You have already joined my Shadow Court, Lady Siva," he said. Devlin raised an eyebrow and looked at the prince skeptically. Yrtalien shrugged.

"Have I not the right in my own court to bestow titles where I choose?" the prince asked, a warning implicit in the soft tone of his voice.

"You mean you just made me a noble?" Siva asked, a look of amazement on her face.

"Early enlistment has its rewards," the prince replied.

"I have no objections to your exercise of your princely rights," Devlin said nervously. "My only concern was that you and Siva—Lady Siva—have only just met." He paused, floundering in his thoughts.

"We have only just met," Yrtalien said, repeating Devlin's words, "and already I have determined that Lady Siva will be a worthy addition to our noble ranks by virtue of her comportment and her aesthetically pleasing presence."

"Are you saying you like the way I look?" Siva asked, tossing back her long red hair to expose her shapely figure. She wore a sheer blouse and a black lace vest atop a filmy skirt that did nothing to conceal the fine pelt of tawny fur that covered her thighs and slender legs.

The prince nodded approvingly. Then he turned once again to Devlin.

"One of the first lessons we must absorb," he said, "is that the definitions of nobility must change. The sidhe can learn much from the other Kithain, but only if we are willing to accord them the honor they deserve." It was evident to Glynnis that the prince's words were intended to be heard—and spread—by the newly titled Lady Siva.

"And now, if you will excuse me," Yrtalien said, extricating himself from the small gathering, "I believe I will see how the rest of the party is progressing."

Edmund sat alone in the stone *hale*. It was shortly after the midday meal, and his companions had once again scattered throughout the village, pursuing their own interests. Tor had accompanied a group of menehune warriors to the waterfall to check on the sea trod that had brought the oathmates to the hidden grotto.

Rasputin and Morgan were taking hula lessons in one of the long houses, while Valmont and Leigh had gone with Lulani to gather flowers for the lei-makers. The redcap had told his companions that he was feeling sleepy and that he would see them after he slept off his copious meal.

He reached for the small pouch in his pocket and withdrew the clown figurine. Setting it on the ground beside him, he scratched his head and patted his stomach, coaxing his faerie magic into the form he desired. Opening his mouth, he expelled a gargantuan burp. In seconds, the miniature clown's chimerical essence surrounded it and the comforting presence of Mr. Dumpy announced itself to the redcap with a sad smile and a tap on the childling's shoulder.

"Put 'er there!" Edmund exclaimed, holding out his right hand, palm flat and facing upward for the clown to slap with his own white-gloved palm. "I thought I'd never get any privacy around here," he muttered.

Mr. Dumpy shrugged his understanding.

"This place sucks, y'know," said Edmund. "There's nothing to do here but practice a bunch of crafts that shoulda died out years ago. Like I need to learn how to string shells and flowers!"

Mr. Dumpy pursed his bright red lips.

"Yeah, I know," the redcap said. "We gotta make nice with the natives so they'll let us leave with our skins. What I want to know is," he continued, "why did they bring us here in the first place?"

The clown held out his hands to either side, his elbows bent and his palms facing up.

"You don't know either, right?" asked Edmund. "According to the selkies, these guys were supposed to have one of the magic eyeballs, and we're supposed to get it from them. I guess that's why the boat brought us here. All I can say is they'd better hurry up and give it

t h ɛ   h i l l

to us, 'cause I don't want to be stuck here picking flowers and wearing diapers for the rest of my life."

Mr. Dumpy frowned.

"These many-hoonies or whatever they call themselves are way out of the loop," Edmund observed. "They think Rasputin's some kind of priest—a kahoona—because he lies. Maybe if I eat something really impressive in front of them, they'll think I'm a god." The redcap laughed at the thought of the menehune bowing before a wooden statue of himself. "That would be a hoot!"

Mr. Dumpy's shoulders shook in silent, companionable amusement.

"Wanna play cards?" Edmund asked, fishing in his back pocket and coming up with a crumpled deck of dirty playing cards. "I think most of 'em are still here," he said, sitting down and dealing out two hands. The clown plopped himself on the floor across from the redcap and picked up his cards, scratching his bald white head as he looked at them.

"You know how to play Crazy Eights?" asked Edmund. Even though the redcap had learned five different kinds of poker, the classic children's game was still his favorite. Mr. Dumpy nodded and watched as Edmund turned over the top card from the deck that sat between them. They played a few quick hands, complicated by the fact that Edmund's deck had seven eights and only thirty-four cards. The redcap won every hand.

"Guess you're just not a card shark, huh?" Edmund said, growing bored with both the deck's and Mr. Dumpy's limitations. He picked up the cards and returned them to his back pocket. Then he noticed Morgan's backpack.

"Do you ever wonder what some people keep stashed away?" Edmund asked the clown.

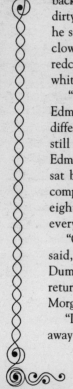

Mr. Dumpy wagged a finger reprovingly at Edmund.

"Yeah, it's bad," Edmund said. "That's why I'm gonna see what Baroness Baloney's got in her pack." The childling sidled over to Morgan's corner of the *hale* and knelt down beside her backpack. Quickly the redcap undid the buckles that held the pack closed and shoved his hand inside, feeling around for something interesting.

"Yowch!" he cried, withdrawing his hand and holding it up for inspection. "Something bit me!"

Mr. Dumpy, who had come up behind Edmund, suddenly tapped the childling on the shoulder. Edmund turned his head and saw the clown pointing toward the fern gateway of the house. The redcap listened and heard the sound of soft footsteps approaching.

"Quick, get small," he said to the clown. "See ya later, I hope," he added as Mr. Dumpy obediently shrank to his inanimate form, the Glamour within him dissipating as he did so. Edmund refastened the straps on Morgan's backpack and scooped up the miniature clown.

He had just enough time to place Mr. Dumpy back in the leather pouch and stuff the pouch into his pocket when the ferns parted and Morgan came in, clutching a string of brilliant flowers.

Edmund opened his mouth wide and yawned conspicuously as the sidhe childling crossed over to her backpack and knelt in front of it.

"I was just waking up," he announced.

Morgan opened her backpack and peered inside. A faint glimmer from near the bottom of the pack made her smile. "I'm glad you're still here," she whispered softly to her little chimerical creation.

"Did you say something?" Edmund asked diffidently.

"Yes," Morgan replied, "but it's none of your business."

"Suit yourself," Edmund retorted.

t h e   h i l l

Morgan coiled her new lei into a ball and carefully placed it in the backpack near the chimera. She hoped that it could feed off the creative energy that she had put into making the necklace of bright pink and purple blossoms.

"Wanna go play tag or throw stones or something?" Edmund asked, desperate to find something to amuse himself now that he'd had to cut short his conversation with Mr. Dumpy.

Morgan sniffed. "I wouldn't play with you if my life depended on it," she said haughtily. She picked up her backpack and hoisted it across her shoulders by one strap. "I'm going to participate in a cultural exchange," she said, brushing past Edmund and walking out of the *hale*.

"Like they have culture to exchange," the redcap muttered to himself after Morgan had left. The more he considered it, the more the thought of throwing stones appealed to him. Patting his pocket to reassure himself that the pouch containing Mr. Dumpy was safely tucked away, the redcap scrambled to his feet and sauntered from the house.

"Don't you like the party?" Yrtalien asked Kanani. He had found the menehune maiden sitting in the garden, near a shimmering pool of water. In her lap, a chimerical creature with bright blue scales and a knobby head lay on its back, its eyes closed in bliss as Kanani stroked its belly.

"It is a strange celebration," Kanani observed. "Some of your guests were trying to destroy this little one, but I removed it from danger."

Yrtalien chuckled. "That's one of the amusements I have provided for the evening," he said. "It is supposed to be destroyed."

"I don't understand," the menehune said, her brows wrinkling in distaste. "It is made of *mana* and so it should be taken care of."

"It's a party toy," replied Yrtalien. "There are some others wandering around which are quite dangerous. I thought they would provide a challenge for some of my more adventuresome guests."

"You created all of them?" Kanani's eyes widened in surprise.

The prince demurred. "Some of them were made under my supervision," he said. "Glynnis has quite a fertile imagination when she sets her mind to conjuring up nightmarish monsters. I think that one was an accident, though," Yrtalien said. "It doesn't look very prepossessing."

Kanani teased open one of the creature's six paws, exposing a set of four long claws. "I believe it is not entirely harmless," she said. She let go of the paw and the claws retracted. The creature shifted onto its side and nudged her hand with its head. She smiled and scratched it behind one of its ears.

"Would you like to keep it?" Yrtalien asked, a wry smile lending an endearing charm to his cold beauty.

"If it would not offend you," Kanani said.

The prince chuckled softly. "You could not possibly offend me," he replied gallantly. "Unless you refuse my hospitality by detaching yourself from tonight's festivities." He crooked his arm and bowed low enough for Kanani to grasp it.

Kanani looked at the creature snuggled in her lap and then turned her eyes toward Yrtalien.

"Take the little fellow with you," the prince said. "If nothing else, he can serve as a conversation starter."

Kanani accepted the prince's arm and rose to her feet, tucking the ugly little chimerical monster under one arm. Beaming at her, Yrtalien led Kanani from the garden toward the palace, where the party was beginning to grow livelier as his guests discovered that the prince's idea of acceptable behavior embraced a wide variety of activities.

"I want as many of my guests as possible to admire the native flora," he said to her.

"I am afraid I do not follow your words," Kanani murmured.

"I said that you are as fresh and lovely as the flowers that grace this garden," Yrtalien replied. "You are a rarity among the Kithain of this island, so I understand." He looked to Kanani for confirmation.

She nodded. "As I have told you, my people have retreated to some of the smaller islands. There may be some of us in the less traveled parts of this island, but I do not know of them."

"As the ambassador of your people," Yrtalien said, "it is important for you to be seen and admired. The honor of the menehune rests upon your lovely shoulders," he added.

Kanani looked solemn. "Then I shall do my best to be worthy of that burden," she said.

"I am sure you will," Yrtalien replied, escorting Kanani into the palace and steering her toward Devlin and the newly appointed Lady Siva. "Have you ever met a satyr?" he asked as Kanani's eyes registered her surprise at the unfamiliar Kithain. She shook her head.

Yrtalien decided that the next few hours should provide him with a great deal of private amusement. *Soon enough*, he thought as he prepared to begin the first of many introductions intended to allow the Kithain of his new court to view and savor the delicacy of the graceful daughter of the menehune chief, *she*

Tor was beginning to tire of all the attention. At Morgan's insistence, he had demonstrated his wrestling skills. Although he had tried to explain that his talent for physical combat came mostly from his size and corresponding strength, the young men of the village were still awed by his ability to overcome them. Now a group of warriors clustered about him, asking to see his battle ax.

"Is it better than our spears?" a young wilder named Kenu asked, his voice ingenuous, but his posture suggesting that he doubted the unfamiliar weapon's superiority.

"That depends on what you mean by better," Tor said. "Spears are thrusting weapons. This," he stepped backward and swung the ax in a lateral arc, "is for slashing open your enemy."

"A spear is meant to keep your foe at a distance," Kenu insisted. "How can you slash someone open when you cannot get close enough to touch them with your ax?"

Tor snorted. "That's where practice comes in. You have to get inside your enemy's guard."

Kenu looked at him skeptically. "Show me," he said.

"I need to wrap the blade first," Tor replied. "I don't want to take the chance that I might hurt you."

"I am not afraid," the wilder scoffed, looking around at his companions for approval and support.

"You may not be," said Tor, "but I am. If we're going to trade blows, I want to be sure that no blood is spilled."

One of the warriors handed Tor a length of heavy cloth and watched as the troll wound it carefully around the blade of his ax.

"Should I wrap the point of my spear?" Kenu asked.

Tor shook his head. "Why?" he countered. "You won't get it anywhere near me."

The menehune formed a circle around Tor and Kenu, who stood opposite each other, waiting for the signal to begin.

"Now!" one of the warriors called out. Kenu lunged toward Tor, his spear aimed directly at the troll's massive chest. At the last moment, Tor stepped aside and brought his ax around in the same sideways arc he had demonstrated earlier, catching the menehune solidly in his side. Tor pulled back as soon as he felt his weapon make contact, but the impact still sent the young menehune reeling.

Kenu recovered quickly, but found himself face to face with Tor, who had taken advantage of the warrior's momentary loss of balance to close the distance between them.

"If this were a real battle," Tor said, "it would be all over."

"I want to try again," Kenu said.

After his third defeat, the young warrior threw down his spear in disgust. "I will learn how to use your weapon," he said. "You will teach all of us how to fight like you do."

Tor stared for a moment at Kenu's eager face. *That was my face once*, Tor thought, *before I learned that there is no real joy in war.* He lowered his head and began to slowly unwrap his ax.

"You don't want to learn my methods of fighting," he said, replacing his weapon in the loop that hung from his belt. He turned his back on his audience and trudged toward the group's *hale*.

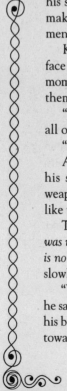

"Perhaps he does not want us to know his secrets," one of the warriors said as they watched Tor walk away.

"It is not that," Kenu replied thoughtfully, picking up his spear. "I saw his face. It was as if a great shadow had fallen across his spirit."

"I have found another hotel for the three of us who are going undercover," Ryder said to Vargas. He handed his Latino friend a slip of paper. "This is how you may get in touch with us anytime you feel the need."

Vargas looked at the address and phone number written on the paper. Later, when he had memorized the vital information, he would destroy the note.

"I am still concerned for your souls," he said, worry evident in his voice.

Ryder nodded his head once, curtly. "So am I," he replied.

"The temptations will be greater for some of us than for others," Diana said bitterly. Ryder used his faerie sight, which was usually dormant when he was not actively pursuing his changeling prey, to appraise the fae form of his troll companion. Diana towered above the other three Dauntain. She wore chimerical clothing that suggested supple leather and steel armor cut to emphasize her muscular arms and powerful thighs. Her blond hair was worn in a long, braided coil. Above her brow, a pair of horns protruded from her forehead.

Ryder shook his head sympathetically. "Yours is perhaps the most difficult transition," he said. "But even you cannot let your guard down for even a moment."

Diana nodded. "I swore an oath to you all as a mortal. I repeat it now in this form so that it may be

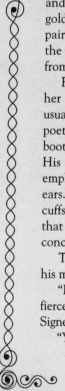

equally binding within the realm of madness." She extended her arm in front of her, hand closed in a fist and pointing downward. Ryder, Signe and, after a moment's hesitation, Vargas placed their hands on her fist.

"May my strength fail me and may my form be forever marked with the sign of my shame if any word or action of mine betrays our sacred purpose," she said. Vargas blanched.

"That is a very strong oath," he remarked.

"It is too late to retract it," Diana said. "I will stand or fall upon the truth of my words."

"I've never doubted you," Signe whispered. In her eshu form, Signe was tall and slim with ebony skin and elaborately corn-rowed hair. She wore a short golden vest held closed by links of silver chain and a pair of dark green, loose-fitting trousers gathered at the ankles. Silver and gold bangles adorned both arms from her wrists to her elbows.

Ryder fought back an urge to compliment her on her exotic beauty. He had worked hard to alter his usual Kithain form, substituting a simple loose-fitting poet's shirt worn over black silk pants and soft suede boots for his formidable suit of black chimerical armor. His long brown hair was swept back from his face, emphasizing his high forehead and his sharply pointed ears. At his wrists he wore a pair of matching gold cuffs. The hilt of a dagger emerged from the red sash that served as a belt. Black fingerless leather gloves concealed the palms of both his hands.

The former sidhe lord stepped forward and embraced his mortal friend.

"Pray for us until we meet again," he whispered fiercely into Vargas' ear. "As closely as you can, watch Signe for signs of recidivism."

"You watch her as well," Vargas whispered back.

"You will be better able to detect trouble in the bud than I."

Ryder nodded. He waited while Signe and Diana exchanged embraces with Vargas, then he signaled them with a sideways jerk of his head.

"We need to do this if it is to be done at all," he said.

Vargas watched his three Kithain compatriots as they turned from him and departed for their new accommodations. He had his instructions, and for the next few days—or however long it took for his friends to establish contact and join the city's Kithain society—all he could really do was attempt to keep track of their whereabouts and wait. Privately, he was not as convinced as Ryder about the wisdom of their plan. Last night, Vargas recalled with a shudder, Ryder had woken him from a deep sleep, his face taut with fear.

"The dreams have started," was all his friend would say when Vargas tried to elicit from Ryder the reason for his distress. "I had forgotten how real my dreams could be."

Once again, the companions received a summons from Chief Makani. This time, without hesitation, all of them except for Edmund dropped to their hands and knees, and, like Lulani, crawled into the chief's presence and prostrated themselves before him in homage.

"Edmund!" Tor growled, looking behind him at the redcap.

Gritting his teeth, the childling reluctantly joined his companions. "I feel like an ass," he muttered to himself.

"Rise and seat yourselves, my children," the chief said, beaming with pleasure.

Sitting in a half-circle below Makani's seat of office, the oathmates waited while villagers filed into the large *hale* and arranged themselves behind their guests.

"Hear my words of judgment," Makani announced. Leigh forced herself to continue breathing despite a sudden stab of fear. The chief's face broke into a smile.

"You came here as strangers," he began, "and as prisoners. We were warned by other visitors that you meant to do us harm. By your own actions, you have shown us that you are honest and willing to learn our ways. Because of this, it is a joy for me to grant you a sign of acceptance among our people."

The chief waved his hand toward Lulani, who knelt near her father, facing the oathmates. Picking up a bundle of garlands from in front of her, Lulani came to kneel before Leigh and the others. Reaching up, she placed a lei around each of their necks, kissing the cheeks of each of them in turn and whispering *"Aloha."* Leigh looked at Valmont and smiled faintly, recognizing the flowers she and the eshu had helped Lulani gather. Valmont offered her a small smile in return.

When Lulani had returned to her place, Makani stood.

"Now that you have proven yourselves to be our friends, I must speak of something which saddens me. It concerns the reason for your coming to us, and why I cannot give you what you seek."

Leigh looked around at her companions and saw surprised looks on all their faces.

"You seek the black stone of shadows, do you not?" Makani asked.

Beside her, Valmont nodded.

"I must tell you that the stone has been given into the hands of another, who claimed to be the one destined to receive it."

Leigh closed her eyes, realizing with a certainty who

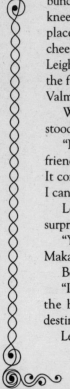

must now possess the Shadowstone. She heard Morgan gasp, followed by Rasputin's faint whisper.

"Surely not our creature from beyond the gate!" the pooka muttered to himself.

"He and his queen came in a big black boat to our grotto, where we welcomed them as the fulfillment of a prophecy that declared that the sunrise would bring children from a far land to claim their ancient birthright. We presented this stranger with one of our shells so that we could hear his words, and he told us that he had come to restore to our people our lost ties to the world of dreams. We did not test him as we have tested you, for we had no reason to think he spoke anything but the truth. When our people first agreed to undertake the guardianship of the stone, it was with the knowledge that one day it would be reclaimed by the heirs of those who once possessed it. We delivered the stone into his keeping and he departed from our island."

The menehune chief lowered himself to his knees before the oathmates and bowed to them. His abasement done, he stood once more.

"You have seen my shame," he said simply. "Now you must pass judgment upon me for my failure."

"You did nothing shameful," Leigh said without hesitation. "It was our own failure that brought this stranger into this world, and so it is fitting that we bear the burden of his schemes."

"Spoken like an eshu," Valmont whispered to her. Leigh felt herself flush with unexpected pride.

"Your words ease my heart," Makani said, "but they do not undo my hasty actions."

"If you know where he has gone," Leigh continued, "and would be willing to tell us, we will follow him and retrieve the stone that matches this one." She opened her pouch and displayed the Keystone to the chief.

"This is proof to me that we should have given our treasure to you and not to him," Makani remarked sadly. "We will take you ourselves to the place where we believe he has gone. There is one thing more, but I hesitate to ask it of you when our actions have already caused you so much trouble."

"If it's something we can do, we will try our best to help you," Morgan said.

"He requested that along with the stone I deliver into his care one of my people to act as a representative to the court of shadows he would be forming."

Valmont hissed audibly, but said nothing.

"I did as he asked," Makani replied. "To prove my trust in him, I sent my oldest daughter Kanani. He promised to place her under his protection and to treat her as if she were of his own household."

"Lulani's sister?" Valmont asked, his voice hard and flat.

Makani nodded. "She considered it a great honor, as did we. Now I am not so sure that she is safe with one who can twist his words so easily to mean something other than they seem."

"Do you want us to get her back for you?" Morgan asked, her voice rising with excitement.

Again the chief signaled his agreement.

"On behalf of all of us, I swear that we will do this for you," Leigh said.

Makani raised his head, his expression relieved. "Then you are truly my children," he replied. He sighed heavily and seated himself on his throne once again.

"Tonight we will feast in your honor," he announced. "Tomorrow, our boats will travel the hidden path to the Big Island where we hope you will be able to find the stone of shadows and my daughter Kanani."

The villagers who had gathered behind the companions cleared a path for them to leave the chief's

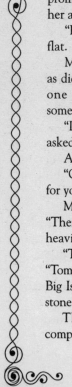

great *hale*. Once outside, Edmund stood up and dusted off his knees.

As the rest of the menehune streamed out into the clearing and headed for the feast that awaited them, Edmund looked up at Leigh with a disdainful expression.

"Am I way off base, or did we just agree to *another* quest?" the redcap asked.

Leigh gave him an amused look as she accepted a hand from Valmont and rose to her feet. Tor struggled to stand and took Morgan's hand. Rasputin helped himself up by way of a handstand. The pooka looked thoughtful.

"I believe we did," Leigh said.

"Crapola," Edmund remarked and ran off toward the smell of roasted pig.

chapter

nine

The sun was high in the sky before the companions awakened. Edmund groaned as he struggled to open his eyes.

"We're leaving today," Morgan announced. "I'm already packed."

"Oh, stuff it," Edmund muttered, rolling over onto his other side and screwing his eyes shut.

"Move it!" Tor bellowed in the redcap's ear. Behind her grandfather, Morgan giggled.

When Edmund finally dragged himself to his feet, rubbing his eyes and yawning, he noticed that his oathmates had already gathered up their belongings. They stood surrounded by a small pile of backpacks and shoulder bags, waiting for the redcap to join them.

"Fine," Edmund said. "I'm awake." As he glanced around the *hale*, making certain that he hadn't left anything behind that he could reasonably stuff into his pockets, he noticed that his oathmates looked different this morning.

"You're not wearing grass and leaves!" he announced. His companions had abandoned their grass skirts and loincloths for their own combination of real and chimerical clothing. To the redcap, the sight of Leigh in her tunic and trousers, Valmont in his Arabian pantaloons and short vest, Rasputin in his loose shirt and drawstring pants adorned with a colorful array of sashes and scarves, and Morgan in her belted tunic and tights was a comforting one. Tor, who had never adopted the native styles, still wore his sturdy armor and serviceable traveling clothes.

Leigh laughed congenially. "We're apparently headed for what the menehune call the Big Island," she began.

"Sounds like the name of a prison or something," Edmund interrupted. "Like the Big House."

"It's the popular name for the island of Hawaii," Valmont added. "And I believe that we will probably end up in Hilo, the largest city on the Big Island."

"I thought *this* was Hawaii," said Edmund.

"This is Kauai," Leigh said. "At least I think this is Kauai," she added. "The island chain is referred to as Hawaii, but so is the largest island."

"Hmph," Edmund snorted. "They musta been named by a pooka," he said.

"Undoubtedly," agreed Rasputin.

"In any case," said Valmont, "I suggest you change your clothes as well."

"Too bad," said Edmund. "I really liked wearing diapers and weeds."

"You sound like Rasputin," Morgan said, wrinkling her nose at the redcap. "Hurry up," she admonished. "Lulani said the *alii* himself is going to accompany us to the boat."

"Are we going to ride in the birdboat again?" Edmund asked.

"I'm not certain," Valmont replied. "Lulani just said that we would be returning to the grotto."

When the companions emerged from their *hale*, they found Lulani and Chief Makani waiting for them, along with a group of warriors.

"This looks like where we came in," Edmund said, noting the weapons in the warriors' hands and the chief's familiar feathered cloak.

Automatically, Leigh found herself checking the direction of the sun's rays and aligned herself so that her shadow fell away from the menehune chief. She beckoned her oathmates to stand near her as they received warm *alohas* from the chief and his daughter.

"Our hearts are saddened by your leaving," Chief Makani said as Lulani placed a lei made from the licorice-scented, green cube-shaped *mokihana* berries which grew near the village around the neck of each of the oathmates.

"And ours, too, feel great sorrow for leaving this place of welcomes," Leigh replied.

"Yeah, we're real torn up," Edmund said.

Rasputin looked at Morgan and winked. "You're right," the pooka muttered. When the *alii* and his daughter came to him, he lifted his rabbitlike ears to allow Lulani to settle the lei about his neck. "I will not begin to tell you how I feel," he murmured.

"We have learned that the word 'stranger' has no meaning among the children of the Dreaming," Valmont said. When Lulani placed her lei about Valmont's neck, the courtly eshu caught Lulani's hands in both of his and brought them gallantly to his lips. Watching, Leigh felt a sudden, sharp wave of resentment. *First Ondine, now Lulani*, she thought. *Does he collect them like he does stories?* She looked away quickly, feeling guilty for her thoughts.

"Thanks," Tor told the chief, leaning down for Lulani to reach him with her lei.

Morgan stood on tiptoe and kissed Makani's cheek. "What happens if someone's shadow falls on you?" she whispered.

"Morgan!" Leigh hissed, surprised by the uncharacteristic impertinence of Morgan's question.

Makani's face clouded.

"Was I not supposed to mention it?" Morgan asked, her eyes wide as Lulani placed her final lei around the sidhe childling's neck.

The chief smiled and shook his head. "You have followed our customs so well that I had forgotten that you do not always know the purpose behind them," he said gently. "The *alii* is not only the leader of the people, but the chief guardian of the *mana* of the village," Makani said, speaking so that everyone could hear. "The shadow of someone's mortal body will drain away the *alii's* store of *mana*. At least, so we believe."

"But our shadows fall across each other all the time," Morgan said. "And we don't lose any Glamour—or *mana*—because of it."

"Perhaps your shadows do not have the same power to steal *mana* as those of the menehune," Makani said.

"Maybe we use a different kind of shadow for that," Rasputin muttered softly to himself.

"I have never thought of Banality as a shadow before," Valmont said, glancing at Leigh as if he wanted to tell her something privately. Leigh nodded her head once.

"Are we gonna stand here and talk about shadows all day?" Edmund said. He opened his eyes wide, trying to mimic Morgan's tried-and-true expression of innocence. He didn't expect it to work. He shrugged as Tor glared at him.

"The child reminds us of why we have come here," Makani said sadly. "We must go to the boats."

Raising his arms wide above his head, Makani looked at the oathmates.

"When our people first saw you, you were *malihini*—strangers. You have become, in our eyes, *kamaaina*—children of the island." Lowering his arms, the chief turned his back on the group and walked to the edge of the clearing, followed by his escort of warriors. Lulani motioned for the oathmates to join the procession as it made its way from the Village of Hidden Treasures.

It was not difficult for Ryder to locate the Kithain of Hilo. Although his leather gloves concealed the gem in his palm, its painful throbbing pulled him in the direction of the Glamour that fueled the madness of the fae. Accompanied by Signe and Diana, Ryder combed the streets of the city, judging how near he came to his prey by the intensity of the ache in his hand.

A few times the pain caused him to wince visibly as he passed one of the wooden frame buildings along Kamehameha Avenue's east-west course.

"Freehold," he remarked on those occasions.

"So when are we going to make contact?" Diana asked. "Isn't that the point of what we're doing?" Her voice betrayed her distaste.

"We are looking for others of our kind," Ryder said, emphasizing the last two words and hoping that Diana would take it as a warning. The statuesque troll shrugged.

"I know it's hard," Signe said softly to her companion. She turned to Ryder and put a hand on his arm.

"Will we be introducing ourselves to our cousins in the city soon?" she asked, rephrasing Diana's question.

"Soon enough," said Ryder. "I want to get a feel for our surroundings first."

"We haven't actually seen any other Kithain on the streets," Signe remarked, worried. Her faerie sight should have been able to penetrate the mortal guises of any changelings she encountered.

"Maybe they're all somewhere else," Diana said.

Ryder considered this. "It is a little odd," he said after a moment. "We have passed at least four places I would label as freeholds of one sort or another just on this street. That indicates a fair concentration of Kithain throughout the city."

"This isn't a very large town," Signe said.

"No, it isn't," Ryder agreed. "I would hardly believe a place of this size capable of supporting the demands of a large number of Kithain." The Dauntain knew that a steady supply of Glamour was necessary to maintain the structure of the fantasy world in which the Kithain dwelled. Changelings fed on human dreams and inspiration, and neither commodity was easy to replenish.

"Maybe some of them are visitors, like we are," Diana said. "Maybe there are only a few long-time residents."

Ryder nodded. "That's certainly a possibility." They had come to the outskirts of Hilo, where the buildings had begun to give way to the lush rainforest that surrounded the city.

Signe gasped. "Look there," she said, pointing discreetly toward a large, two-story wood frame house that was visible ahead of them, though still some distance away.

Looking in the direction Signe had indicated, the three Dauntain saw a tall, silver-haired sidhe strolling toward them.

"I think he's seen us," Diana said, seized by a sudden desire to flee to the safety of Banality and cloak herself once more in her mortal guise. Ryder saw the troll's faerie essence begin to diminish and shook his head, his face stern.

"Stop that," he whispered. "Remember why we're here."

Summoning everything he could recall of the attitudes and posturings of his kith, Ryder straightened his shoulders and stepped boldly toward his kithmate. Signe and Diana followed a few steps behind him.

Ryder's palm pulsed furiously as he halted directly in the path of the silver-haired Kithain and waited, his face betraying nothing of his unease, for the stranger to speak.

"Well met, I hope," the obviously noble sidhe said in a slightly flat, nasal voice without discernable accent. "Have you come to pay your respects to the court?"

Ryder forced himself to smile. *You are one of the sidhe*, he told himself. *Until you know better, consider this creature to be your equal or less.*

He nodded once, in silent agreement. "I trust you will act as escort for myself and my companions?"

The silver-haired Kithain bridled faintly at Ryder's statement, but covered it with a smile.

"I would be only too happy to accompany you to the freehold of Prince Yrtalien and ease your introduction," he said smoothly. "The prince is most anxious to make the acquaintance of all newcomers to his realm."

"What realm is this?" Signe asked, her voice quiet. "And may we have your name so that we do not feel so much like the strangers that we are?"

Good for you, Ryder thought, admiring the eshu's skill with words. *She was a poet when I met her*, he reminded himself.

"This is the Twilight Realm of Yrtalien, lord of the Dreaming, and I am his minister, Lord Devlin," the sidhe noble said, speaking not to Signe, but to Ryder. Signe appeared not to notice.

"And I am Chevalier," Ryder said, using the name by which he was once known as a paladin in the service of the court of the Kingdom of Grass.

"Chevalier—doesn't the word mean knight in French?" Lord Devlin's words held only the barest derogatory tone. "Should I call you Sir Chevalier?"

He means to provoke me, Ryder thought. *I wonder if he already perceives me as a threat to his position.* He offered the sidhe lord a stiff smile. "I see no reason to separate my title from my name," he said.

"We are most anxious to meet Prince Yrtalien," Signe said, bowing gracefully to Lord Devlin. "I am called Signe, and my companion is Diana. Your kindness says much about the hospitality of your liege."

Diana steeled herself and nodded her head in the direction of the silver-haired noble.

Devlin looked again at Signe and, this time, appeared to notice her winsome appeal. The eshu's words seemed to mollify him, for he rewarded her with a gracious smile.

"Let us not waste time, then," he said. "The prince's palace lies there, atop the small rise." He indicated the house that the Dauntain had noticed earlier. Turning abruptly, he began to retrace his steps, not bothering to see if the others were following.

Ryder glanced at his two companions.

"A real gentleman," Diana remarked caustically.

"His attitude is quite typical for his kith," Ryder remarked.

"I can't imagine what his prince must be like," Signe said.

"Somehow, this seems a little too easy for my comfort," Ryder said. He glanced at his companions. Not bothering to disguise the sarcasm in his voice, he said, "Shall we follow our escort?"

Setting their own pace, the three Dauntain made their way toward the palace on the hill.

The swan ship was still waiting for the oathmates when they entered the hidden grotto.

the hill

"This place is saturated with Glamour," Morgan said. "I didn't notice it before."

"That's 'cause we were too busy trying to save our butts," Edmund remarked.

"Is this someone's freehold?" Leigh asked Lulani, looking around her for signs of habitation.

Lulani smiled and shook her head. "Once, perhaps, it belonged to the ones who preceded us," she said. "Now it belongs to itself."

"The enchantments are very strong here," Valmont said as he followed the warriors around the edge of the pool. A few of the menehune broke away from the main group and headed into the water in the direction of the waterfall.

"It is said that the builders knew how to weave *mana* into the rocks themselves," Lulani said. "Unless many, many people come to steal the power that is here, this will remain a place of dreams for a very long time."

"Steal the power?" Tor asked. "What do you mean?"

"With their black boxes and their hungry spirits," Lulani said, making a square with the fingers of both her hands and holding them up to her face.

"Tourists!" Morgan exclaimed. "With cameras!"

"I never would have guessed," Rasputin said. "I suppose this place is easy to find," he added.

"There are many beautiful waterfalls and grottos on this island," Lulani said. "But this is one which only exists to those with eyes to see it."

"What's that?" Edmund said, pointing toward the waterfall where the warriors were now emerging, guiding a bulky shape out from behind the cascade.

"It looks like a canoe," Valmont observed.

"It is called *wa'a kaulua*," Lulani said.

As the warriors cleared the waterfall's spray, the oathmates could see the vessel being coaxed into the deep water near the center of the pool. It was a double canoe, its twin hulls joined together by a wooden platform in the center.

"Are we gonna ride in it?" Edmund said.

"You will travel in your own vessel," Lulani said. "We will go with you part of the way to make sure you reach your destination."

"Wait," Leigh said. "Are you saying that there is another trod—dream road—besides the one that brought us here?"

"Oh, there are trods all over the place," Rasputin remarked diffidently.

Lulani nodded. "I told you the builders had very powerful *mana*," she said. "Long ago, they built roads through the water to connect the islands to one another so that they could travel back and forth without leaving the realm of dreams."

"Awesome!" Edmund said. "So where is it?" He looked around the grotto for signs of something that might be a faerie trod.

Lulani pointed to where her father stood atop a rock that jutted out over the pool. The menehune chief held his ceremonial spear with both hands above his head as he intoned a soft, toneless chant. "The *alii* will give some of his *mana* to the grotto and open the way for us to go," she said. "Our boat will lead the way, and you will follow in your own vessel. When we are sure that you are safely on course, we will turn aside so that you may continue on to the Big Island."

"I suppose we should stay where we are, then," said Rasputin.

"You're right," Leigh said. "We need to board our ship."

"Wait!" cried Morgan, slipping her backpack off her shoulders and rummaging around inside it.

"Great," moaned Edmund. "Isn't it a little too late to see if you left anything behind?"

"I *want* to leave this behind," the childling replied. She smiled in relief as she pulled her hand out of her backpack. Balanced on her palm was the small chimerical winged unicorn. Looking slightly the worse for wear, it radiated a dim light as Morgan held it out in front of her.

"Where did that come from?" Valmont asked.

"I made it one night when I couldn't sleep," Morgan said evasively. "I—I was outside at the time and when I went back inside our *hale*, it wouldn't stop glowing. I was afraid It would wake everyone so I put it in my backpack for safekeeping."

Edmund looked at his hand, remembering his attempt to rifle through Morgan's pack.

"How long has it been in your pack?" Leigh asked.

"I don't know," Morgan said. "A few days, I guess."

"A backpack is certainly a perfect habitat for something like that," Rasputin observed. "It looks really perky."

"I couldn't help it!" Morgan tried unsuccessfully to keep from sounding defensive. "I forgot about it," she confessed.

"You are very fortunate that it didn't fade away from lack of sustenance," Valmont said.

"I know," Morgan said in a small voice. "I thought that maybe I could leave it here," she said. "There's so much Glamour here that it ought to last a really long time. Look!" she cried. "It's glowing again, like it did when I first made it!"

She started to shoo the chimera into the air, and then stopped suddenly and looked at Lulani. "It's all right, isn't it?" she asked.

Lulani stared at the chimera in fascination. "I have never seen such a bird before," she said. "It is very pretty." The menehune maiden smiled at Morgan. "I think this place will make a good home for it," she said.

"When we come here, we will see it and remember our friends."

"Yeesh," Edmund muttered quietly.

Morgan watched as the chimera lifted its wings and fluttered into the air, heading for the edge of the pool.

"Thank you," she said to Lulani. "I'm ready to get on the boat now," the childling said, turning to Leigh.

"It's about damn time," said Edmund.

The oathmates boarded the swanship as Makani finished his preparations. Lulani joined the warriors who had seated themselves inside the canoe. The menehune began paddling toward their chief. As the twin-hulled canoe neared the rock upon which Makani stood, the air behind the *alii* shimmered and a rift appeared. Makani stepped from the rock to the platform in the center of the canoe as the vessel sailed into the opening where the rock had been.

Without any instructions from the companions, the swanship maneuvered itself into position behind the canoe and sailed onto the watery dream road. Ahead of them, the oathmates could see a vast expanse of ocean.

"How far is it to where we're going?" Leigh asked. In her mind, she tried to picture the islands that made up Hawaii and realized that she hadn't the faintest idea of Kauai's position relative to the Big Island.

Valmont shrugged. "I think actual distance is irrelevant," he said. "After all, we sailed from the mainland across half of the Pacific in what was probably less than a day."

For a time, the oathmates simply watched the changing waters beneath them and the menehune canoe in front of them, outlined against an iridescent sky. Without warning, the canoe turned aside suddenly, making a long, slow arc until it had reversed its direction. Atop the platform, Makani pointed behind him. Next to him, Lulani waved.

"*Aloha a hui hou!*" she called out. "Good-bye, until we meet again. May you find everything you seek and may you never walk in shadows."

As if driven by her words, the swan ship sped forward along the sea-trod.

"Why am I not comforted by her words?" Rasputin murmured to Tor. The troll shrugged.

"Is that land up ahead?" Edmund called out from the prow of the swanship. His companions joined him to stare into the distance.

"I believe you're right," Valmont said as the swanship rushed headlong toward a coastline that was looming nearer and nearer. Finally the ship began to slow, and coasted to a stop inside a tiny harbor surrounded by tall palm trees.

"Look!" Morgan cried. "The sand is black!"

"That's because of the volcano in the center of the island," Valmont said. "Mauna Loa, the most famous live volcano in the world."

"A volcano?" said Edmund. "Cool! Can we go see it?"

"I'd suggest that the first thing we do once we disembark is find out where we are," Leigh said. "Maybe later on we can go volcano hunting."

The companions stepped down from the swanship.

"Any sign of guys with spears?" Edmund asked, looking intently at the trees that framed the harbor.

Valmont laughed softly and shook his head. "I think if there were any of the menehune waiting for us, Makani would have warned us, so that we would be better prepared to meet them than we were to meet his people."

Leigh inhaled the scented air. "I love the way this place smells," she said.

"Is this another one of those hidden places?" Morgan asked.

s h a d o w s   o n

"No," said Rasputin. "I don't sense any Glamour at all in this harbor."

"Umm, I hate to bring this up," said Edmund, "but now that we're here, where are we supposed to go?"

Leigh looked at Valmont. The eshu smiled and tapped his head with a slender finger. "Give me a minute to concentrate," he said. The companions waited while Valmont closed his eyes and spun around in a circle three times. Opening his eyes, he began to walk toward the trees. "Our destination lies this way," he said.

"That's good enough for me," Leigh remarked, motioning for the rest of the companions to follow the eshu's keen sense of direction.

Inside Yrtalien's palace, the prince sat with Kanani in one of the upper rooms. Glynnis stood behind Yrtalien, gazing out the window overlooking the back garden. Downstairs and in the garden, the party which had begun days ago still continued, though its initial frenetic gaiety had subsided into a perpetual search for amusement by the guests who wandered at will throughout the freehold.

Yrtalien held the Shadowstone in his hand, staring at the pinpoint of red fire that burned within its dark, semitranslucent depths.

"Do you know what this does?" the prince asked Kanani.

Kanani reached out to touch the gem.

"It is the stone of shadows," she said.

"So I have been told," Yrtalien replied, somewhat testily. "That does not tell me what its powers are."

"It is one of the great stones of power that were scattered throughout the world long ago," Kanani said. "This one was given to us to protect."

"And now it has been given to me," Yrtalien said. "By your father," he added.

Kanani nodded. "It has power over that for which it is named," she said. "While you have it, the shadows cannot harm you."

"The shadows?" Yrtalien asked. "What have I to fear from shadows?"

"Shadows leech away your *mana*," Kanani said. "This is what I tried to tell you when you and Lady Glynnis came to our village."

Yrtalien looked up at Glynnis. "Do you know what she means?" he asked.

Glynnis pursed her lips, trying to recall their brief visit with the chief of the menehune. So many of the customs of the primitive Kithain made little sense to her; she, as well as the prince, had forgotten most of them. Finally, she dredged up a vague recollection of something Kanani and her sister had told them.

"They believe that it is bad luck for someone's shadow to fall upon their chief," she said slowly, looking to Kanani for confirmation.

The menehune maiden smiled. "It drains *mana*," she said. "Just like too much exposure to things that are not made from dreams drains *mana*."

"Banality," Glynnis whispered. "She is talking about Banality when she says shadows."

Yrtalien looked thoughtful. "I wonder why the word doesn't translate through this, " he said, touching the shell pendant around his neck.

"Perhaps they are not quite the same," Glynnis replied.

"Is that all it does?" Yrtalien asked Kanani.

She shook her head. "No, it also allows you to move

s h a d o w s   o n

about unseen and unheard, using the shadows over which it has command."

"How do you make it work?" Yrtalien turned the gem in his hand.

"I have never tried to make it work," Kanani said. "I believe you only have to think of what you want."

Yrtalien and Glynnis exchanged speculative looks.

"That could lead to some interesting possibilities," the prince observed quietly. Glynnis nodded.

"My lord," she began, "if it does have the ability to protect against Banality..." she left her thought unfinished.

"It could be exactly what we are looking for," the prince replied. He turned his attention once more to Kanani. "You say there are other stones?"

Kanani nodded.

"Do you know of the others?" the prince aksed.

"We know of one other," added Glynnis. Yrtalien glared at her.

"We will speak of that privately," he said, a warning edge to his voice.

Before Kanani could answer, a soft tap on the door frame caught the prince's attention. He looked up to see one of the enchanted humans who now served as palace attendants standing silently in the doorway. It was the long-haired blonde.

"Well?" he asked, staring through her.

She bowed low.

"My Lord Prince," she said, "Lord Devlin has returned with visitors."

"Should that concern me?" the prince snapped. "I gave no orders that I was to be notified of every coming and going in this household."

The woman hesitated nervously. Yrtalien smiled, enjoying her distress.

"Lord Devlin told me to inform you, my Lord

Prince," she said.

"Tell Lord Devlin that I am duly informed," the sidhe prince snapped dismissively. "Now go!"

The young woman fled the prince's presence. Yrtalien laughed.

"How easily dismayed they are," he observed. "They make such wonderful toys."

Kanani glanced questioningly at the prince. "Is she not under your protection?"

Yrtalien leaned forward in his chair, his elbows on his knees, his chin resting on his clenched fists. He still had the Shadowstone. He studied Kanani thoughtfully before he answered.

"I do not consider mortals worthy of protection except as whimsy dictates," he said, gently. "We—our kind—are as different from the race whose bodies we wear as they are from the plants and animals they eat."

"We are different, yes," Kanani said. "We are their dreams. We owe our being to them."

Yrtalien sighed. "And they can as easily destroy us unless we remind them of their place."

"My people choose simply to avoid mortals, for the most part," Kanani said. She lowered her head. Glynnis saw the young maiden's lips shut tightly. *I wonder what she isn't telling us*, she thought. Yrtalien had commanded her to cultivate Kanani's friendship and gain her confidence. She would have ample time to coax from her any secrets she might have.

The prince heard heavy footsteps coming up the stairs. Without ceremony, Argo, the larger of Yrtalien's troll bodyguards, entered the room and stopped, arms folded across his chest, a few feet away from the prince.

"Now what?" Yrtalien asked the troll.

"Lord Devlin—"

"I should have known," Yrtalien interjected, cutting the troll off. Wearily, the prince rose to his feet. He replaced the Shadowstone in the pouch about his neck, and concealed the pouch beneath his shirt. Turning to Glynnis, the prince waved a hand in Kanani's direction.

"Why don't you and Kanani see how our perpetual party is doing while I attend to Devlin's latest emergency?" he said airily. Glynnis nodded her acquiescence and watched as the prince, accompanied by Argo, left the room. Then she turned to Kanani and displayed her sweetest smile to the young menehune.

"Shall we wander through the garden and gather some fresh flowers before the guests destroy them all?" she suggested.

"I'm sure Valmont knows where we're going," Rasputin announced as the oathmates stopped for a rest in a small clearing. All around them, strange, twisted trees rose up from a blanket of ferns. Leigh sat on a large boulder of shiny dark rock and massaged her feet.

"I feel like we've been wandering around for hours," Morgan said. She looked at Leigh and grimaced. "My feet hurt, too."

"It's almost dark," Tor said, noticing the fading light.

"Maybe we should return to the beach and start again," Leigh suggested, inwardly quailing at the thought of retracing their route over ground that seemed determined to make their journey difficult.

They had followed Valmont away from the beach where their ship had deposited them, forging into the thick vegetation that encircled the expanse of fine, black sand. The companions had been able to sense, as the air around them grew moister and heavier, that they were leaving a place of enchantment and reentering the mortal realm. When they looked behind them, they saw only jungle with no sign of ocean, beach or swanship. Valmont had assured them that his sense of direction would lead them where they needed to go.

"We're lost," Edmund said, cheerfully. "Hey, Valmont, you got us lost!"

Valmont turned and glared at the redcap. Leigh felt a momentary surge of pity for the eshu. *He's always been so proud of his ability to get from one place to another*, she thought. *He must be mortified.*

"I said I would take us where we needed to go," Valmont replied, his words clipped and precise. "I did not say the journey would be an easy one, nor did I say we would travel in a straight line from point A to point B."

"Why don't we eat something while we're resting?" Morgan suggested. It was clear to Leigh that the childling was trying to deflect criticism away from Valmont. "We have some food the menehune gave us," she said. "At least I have some breadfruit and a couple of mangos."

"Yumm, just what I always wanted," Edmund said. "Nourishing fruit!"

"Food would be a good idea," Leigh said, opening her own pack and withdrawing her small skillet and a parcel wrapped in pandamus leaves. Inside the package were individual leaf-wrapped packets containing sun-dried coconut meat, dried fish, joints of sugar cane, and pats of mashed sweet potatoes. "Why don't we pool our supplies, and I'll see if I can come up with something palatable," she suggested. "Do we have anything to drink?" she asked, realizing that in her own preoccupation with packing food in case it was needed, she had neglected to take any liquids—even water—with her.

"No," Rasputin said, handing her a string of stoppered gourds and a large uncracked coconut. Leigh accepted them gratefully, handing the coconut over to Tor.

"Can you bore a hole in this?" she asked the troll. "I want the milk inside it to use as a sauce."

"A sauce?" Edmund repeated, incredulous. "What is this, gourmet dining in the jungle?"

Leigh smiled. "As near as I can make it," she replied.

"Do you want me to make a fire?" Morgan asked, looking around her for some sticks that might serve her purpose. "We should have carried a live coal with us like Lulani said the natives used to do," she remarked. "The mortal ones, I mean."

"Great idea, Morgan!" Edmund said acidly. "You could carry it in your backpack. Real swift thinking."

Morgan glared at the redcap and continued her search.

Valmont bent down and offered the childling a gold lighter engraved with an ornate V.

"There's only a little fluid left in this," Valmont said, "but it should be enough to kindle a small flame."

Morgan took the lighter and turned it over in her hands.

"I didn't know you smoked," she said to Valmont, a shade of reproof in her voice.

The eshu shrugged. "I use this to light other people's cigarettes," he said. "Common courtesy sometimes calls for such old-fashioned gestures."

"I don't get it," Edmund said.

"You're still too young to get it," rumbled Tor. The troll handed the coconut back to Leigh. She looked at the jagged hole in its top.

"I won't ask," she said, smiling up at her companion. "Thank you."

Tor grunted his acknowledgment and wandered off to stand self-appointed guard duty near the edge of the small clearing. Rasputin headed toward the trees.

t h ε   h i l l

"Where are you going?" Edmund asked the pooka.

"I thought the forest would be the last place to go to find wood for the fire," the pooka said. "Don't worry, I don't want you to come with me."

Edmund got to his feet. "I'll come," he said. "It's more exciting than watching the Jungle Gourmet."

"I hope it's all right to light a fire," Morgan said. "It just occurred to me that there may be a law around here against burning stuff."

Valmont gave the childling an amused smile. "If there is and someone sees the fire and comes to tell us to put it out, we can always ask where we are," he said wryly.

Night had fallen when the companions finally shared a meal of broiled fish flavored with coconut sauce, fried sweet potato cakes garnished with shredded coconut, and a fruit salad served on a plate of pandamus leaves. They passed around gourds of papaya juice. When everyone was done, Leigh took a long stick and poked around in the ashes on the edge of the small cookfire, withdrawing some tightly-wrapped packets of leaves which had been baking in the cinders.

"What's that?" Edmund asked as Leigh gingerly began undoing the wrappings, seemingly oblivious to the heat.

"Dessert, I hope," she said, looking anxiously at the first of the open packets. "Here," she said, passing another packet to Edmund. "Bananas stuffed with sugar cane," she announced. "Or, bananas *glacé*, if you want a fancier name."

"What's that in the sky?" Morgan asked suddenly, looking up. The others followed her gaze and saw that, despite the darkness, the night sky was lit by an eerie, red glow in the distance.

Valmont stared intently in the direction of the glow. "That," he said, "is a volcano."

s h a d o w s   o n

"I hope that's where your direction sense was taking us," Rasputin said, licking the last bit of sugary glaze from his fingers.

"Sooner or later, every visitor to Hawaii comes to Pele's home," said a strange voice.

From the direction of the volcanic light, an old woman appeared in the clearing. Although she was bent with the obvious weight of her years, her long hair was a lustrous white shot with streaks of fiery red. A simple length of undyed cloth secured by a tuck at the breast hung nearly to her ankles, which were garlanded with anklets of dark flowers. She looked around, her bright, birdlike eyes alert and amused.

"Are you here to tell us to put out the fire?" Morgan asked.

The old woman chuckled. "I saw your fire and smelled your cooking."

"If you're hungry," Leigh said, "I think we still have some food left."

Masking his surprise, Valmont approached the old woman and, taking her gently by the elbow, escorted her to the center of the clearing. She sank to the ground in front of the fire.

"Let me be rude and greet you with an official *aloha*, Rasputin said, seating himself beside the ancient visitor and handing her one of his gourds. The woman tipped the vessel to her mouth and drank, then passed the gourd back to the pooka. "Aloha to you, too. You're a strange-looking young man," she said.

"I hope so," Rasputin answered.

"In fact," the old woman said, her gaze focusing on each member of the group in turn, "you're all rather unusual in appearance. How did you do that to your ears?" she asked Leigh.

Leigh touched the pointed tips of her ears self-consciously. "That's just how they are," she replied

t h e   h i l l

lamely, wondering what gift allowed the old woman to see through their mortal guises. Flustered, she surveyed the remains of dinner and, taking out an unused pandamus leaf, filled it with some fruit salad, a piece of fish and a sweet potato cake.

"Here," she said, handing the leaf-plate to the old woman. They sat in silence as the woman applied herself to the meal, smacking her lips and licking her fingers with gusto.

"*Mahalo*," the old woman said. "That was very tasty. Do you know what *mahalo* means?" she asked, looking around her.

Morgan nodded. "It means *thank you* in the language of the indigenous people," she replied.

"We call them Hawaiians," the old woman said conspiratorially, "but it never hurts to be politically correct." She cackled at her own humor. "So you speak a little Hawaiian?" she asked.

"No, we have these shells..." Edmund began. Valmont elbowed him to silence.

"We are spontaneous learners," Rasputin quipped.

"If I may be so bold as to ask, would you mind telling us where we are on the island?" Valmont asked.

"Lost, are you?" The old woman's question held a hint of gloating.

"I'm afraid so," said Leigh. "We were hiking through the forest—"

"It's a rainforest around here, you know," the old woman said. "Nearer the volcano, the land changes to a desert."

"— and we must have taken a wrong turn," Leigh finished.

"Yeah," Edmund chimed in. "Valmont swore he knew where he was going and we were dumb enough to believe him."

"That's enough," Tor admonished sharply.

"I didn't swear to anything," Valmont added quietly.

"Do you want to know where you are, or do you want to argue about who got you lost?" the old woman asked, sounding amused.

"We'd like to know where we are," said Morgan. "We can't help arguing, though."

"If you had a map," the old woman said, "I could probably point to the exact spot you're sitting in. Since you don't, I can only tell you approximately where you are. That way," she pointed to the red sky behind her, "is Kilauea."

"Is that the name of the volcano?" Leigh asked.

The old woman nodded.

"I thought you said it was Mauna Loa," Edmund said accusingly to Valmont.

"There are two active volcanos on the island," the old woman said. "Mauna Loa is further inland. Kilauea is Pele's home."

"Who's Pele?" Morgan asked.

"The goddess of fire," she answered. "The natives who sailed here from Tahiti worshipped Pele, along with some other gods, and they brought her with them to these islands."

"Why would anyone want to bring a volcano goddess along with them?" Edmund asked. "Isn't that like asking for trouble?"

The old woman shook her head. "In fact," she said, "some say that the first natives to arrive here forgot to invite Pele to travel with them and she punished them by sending a great flow of lava to drive them away. So they went back to their original home and retrieved her image."

"What does she look like?" Morgan wanted to know. "Her image, I mean. Was it a statue or something?"

The old woman picked up one of the dark rocks from the clearing. "She looks like this, sometimes."

t h e   h i l l

"Like a rock?" Edmund scoffed.

"This is lava," their guest replied. Edmund took the piece of lava from her hand and started to pocket it.

"It is bad luck to take away rocks from Pele's garden," the old woman warned.

"Huh?" Edmund asked.

"I'd put it back, if I were you," Valmont said to the redcap. "It would be wrong to transgress against local customs."

Edmund looked at the piece of lava. "How about if I eat it?"

"No!" Morgan cried.

Edmund sneered at the sidhe childling, then got up and made a show of returning the rock to the woman. "There," he said.

The old woman chuckled. "I'm sure you would not want to do anything to bring bad luck upon you and your friends."

"We were trying to find Hilo," Leigh said, effectively changing the subject. "How far away is it from where we are?"

The old woman looked thoughtful. "It's on this side of the island," she said after a minute's pause. "It could be worse. If you continue traveling in that direction," she pointed away from Kilauea's glow, "you should come to a road. From there, it's about twenty miles to Hilo."

"That's a long walk," Tor said. "We may have to stay here overnight and travel in the morning."

The old woman shook her head. "That wouldn't be a good idea. Sometimes the winds from Kilauea blow sulfur and ash for miles around. It's not the best material to breathe."

"Pliny the Elder died from volcanic fumes when Vesuvius erupted," Valmont observed.

"Who?" asked Edmund.

Valmont raised an eyebrow mockingly at the redcap. "He was a Roman historian and an early investigator of natural phenomena. His curiosity got the better of his wisdom when Mount Vesuvius erupted and buried Pompeii. Pliny wanted to observe the eruption from what he thought was a safe distance. He failed to notice the noxious fumes from the volcano until it was too late."

Morgan sniffed the air. "I don't smell anything funny," she said.

"Not yet," the old woman cautioned. "But if you stay here tonight, there's a good chance that the wind will shift, and that would be unfortunate for you."

"Then I suppose we'd better get started," said Leigh. She stood and began to gather the remains of their meal.

"When you get to the road," the old woman said, "you can probably flag down a ride. People are usually willing to give strangers a lift, particularly lovely young women with flaming red hair."

"What do you mean?" Leigh asked.

The old woman smiled. "The natives believe that Pele herself sometimes wanders the island in the form of a young maiden with fiery red hair."

"But does she travel with a retinue?" Valmont asked sarcastically.

The old woman narrowed her eyes. "You," she said, pointing to Edmund, "could easily be one of the menehune."

"You mean the builders?" Morgan asked.

The old woman nodded, looking a little surprised. "So you have heard the story," she said. "As for the rest of you…" she shrugged and fell silent.

Leigh moved to cover up the fire.

"Leave it," the old woman said. "I'll be here for a little while longer. I promise to put it out before I go."

the hill

"Should you be out here by yourself?" Valmont asked her with some concern.

"My home is not far from here," the old woman said.

"What about the poison winds?" asked Morgan.

"I'll be safely away when the winds change," the crone replied. Seeing that the childling still looked worried, she rose unsteadily to her feet and walked over to pat the chidling on the head. "You must trust that I wasn't born yesterday," she said gently. "I know this island like the back of my hand." She raised her gnarled hand and stared at it for a moment. "In fact, in some ways, the island looks like the back of my hand," she chuckled. "Now, off with you." She pointed once again in the direction of the road. "*Aloha a hui hou,*" she said.

"*Aloha mahalo,*" Leigh responded as she and her companions finished gathering their things and started off into the trees, following the old woman's outstretched hand.

After several minutes of hard walking, they stumbled upon the promised road.

"Which way?" Leigh asked Valmont.

"Are you sure you trust me to take us in the right direction?" the eshu asked. "After all, I was the one who got us lost."

Leigh smiled. "Everyone is entitled to at least one mistake," she said.

"I agree," said Rasputin. "Meeting that old woman was certainly a waste of time."

"I hear a car," Edmund said. Soon after, the others heard the rattle of an approaching vehicle.

When the headlights were still some distance off, Edmund ran into the center of the road and began to wave his hands frantically.

"It's a pick-up truck," Tor said as the vehicle screeched to a stop less than a foot away from the redcap.

"Hey, mister!" Edmund called. "Which way's Hilo?"

"I hope he realizes how harmless we are," muttered Rasputin.

"Let me handle it," Valmont said. The eshu approached the truck and spoke briefly with the driver.

"Can you tell what he's doing?" Morgan asked Leigh with a knowing smile.

Leigh hardly had to concentrate to sense the tingling flow of Glamour that radiated from the smooth-talking eshu. Wordlessly, she nodded to Morgan.

Not long afterward, from the back of the pick-up, the oathmates saw the lights of the city of Hilo blinking in the distance ahead of them.

Ryder and his companions waited impatiently in the anteroom of the house that served as the prince's palace. When they had entered the grounds of the freehold, Ryder had blanched at the lancing stab of pain in his hand. It showed no sign of subsiding, and so he attempted to ignore it, concentrating instead on suppressing his discomfort at being surrounded by so much evidence of faerie enchantment.

To his disapproving eyes, the palace was a cesspool of ostentatiously decadent display. The room in which the three Dauntain stood, along with Lord Devlin, was draped with tapestries depicting scenes of satyrs, nymphs and other grotesque creatures of the faerie realm involved in licentious activities. From further within the palace, he could hear the sounds of pulsating music and raucous laughter. Scantily clad human servants, the stink of enchantment heavy upon their souls, drifted past the waiting Kithain.

Ryder heard Diana's low growl of suppressed indignation at the travesty of mortal servitude. He looked at her sharply and shook his head, a small gesture which she saw and heeded. The growling stopped. Signe looked around her in awe. It was obvious to Ryder that the gentle eshu had never experienced first-hand the conspicuous bedlam of life in a noble's freehold. As he continued to examine his surroundings, however, Ryder concluded that even his own former intimacy with Kithain society had not prepared him for the callous debauchery that surrounded him.

Unseelie, he thought, suddenly making sense of what he saw. He experienced a touch of grim satisfaction. *It will be a pleasure to bring down these perverse abominations*, he told himself, struggling to keep his face from betraying his abhorrence.

"It seems your prince is not as anxious to meet us as you thought," he observed mildly to Lord Devlin.

The silver-haired noble shifted uneasily on his feet. "I have just sent his chief attendant to remind him of his duty," Devlin said, gesturing toward the broad spiral stairs where a gigantic troll, resembling an ogre more than anything else, was lumbering up to the second floor.

"Is there a party going on?" Signe asked as a pair of redcaps in loud Hawaiian shirts and leather pants wandered through the room, stopping only long enough to greet a dog-faced pooka wearing a spiked collar and a bright yellow frock coat.

Devlin nodded. "The prince has opened his freehold to all Kithain who acknowledge his sovereignty. Most of them have moved into the upper wings of the palace."

Signe looked puzzled. "Upstairs wings?" she asked. "How big is this place?"

Devlin laughed. "This is a freehold, my dear," he said. "It doesn't have to conform to the laws of the outside world."

"Bigger on the inside than on the outside," Diana said.

"Exactly."

The heavy clump of troll feet descending the stairs brought the desultory conversation to a halt. Argos halted at the bottom of the spiral staircase and stood, arms folded across his chest, looking back the way he had come.

Ryder followed the troll's gaze and saw a slender figure round the final turn of the stairs, one graceful hand poised for balance on the polished ebony railing. The prince's features bore the classic marks of high fae nobility: a delicately sculpted jaw, straight aquiline nose, finely pointed ears and almond-shaped eyes that glinted with canny intelligence. His long raven-dark hair hung nearly to his waist in back, while in front a pair of elaborate braids framed his face. He wore a loose gray shirt, its wide sleeves gathered at the wrists, over black velvet pants. A silvery sash encircled his waist, serving as a sheath for a slim dark-bladed sword with a jeweled hilt. Silver dangled from his ears. Once again, the full import of the resplendently inhuman splendor that surrounded the uncloaked essence of the sidhe struck the Dauntain with the force of a lightning bolt.

"I'm in love," Signe whispered, her voice almost inaudible. Her comment brought Ryder to his senses and he steeled himself to resist the urge to bend his knee to the prince. He tore his gaze away from Yrtalien's figure long enough to frown at his eshu companion. Signe caught his look and quickly lowered her eyes, albeit with great effort. "Sorry," she murmured.

From his vantage point on the stairs, Yrtalien studied the trio of Kithain standing with Lord Devlin in the middle of the anteroom. His gaze rested appreciatively on the willowy form of the attractive eshu, then evaluated the brawny female troll who obviously considered herself on permanent guard duty. *As do all those poor losers*, he thought. Finally, he allowed himself to study the third member of the group. As was typical, the sidhe noble carried himself proudly, his stance respectful but not deferential. Yrtalien admired the strong jawline and the hawklike features of the newcomer. *A predator's face*, he labeled it. *A warrior's face as well. I must have the loyalty of this one*, he mused.

Devlin bowed as Yrtalien finished his descent. "My lord prince," he said, "May I present the knight known as Chevalier and his companions." Next, Devlin turned to Ryder.

"Allow me to announce the arrival of his highness Prince Yrtalien of the Court of Shadows," he said, his nasal voice striving for a dignity it did not quite attain.

The three visitors bowed as Yrtalien approached them, one hand extended in greeting.

"Welcome to my not-so-humble freehold," the prince said, reaching out to clasp Ryder's hand in his.

At the prince's touch, Ryder felt an agonizing wave of searing pain engulf him. Yrtalien flinched as the pouch at his neck sent a sudden electric shock through his body, causing him to draw back just as Ryder screamed and doubled over.

The troll caught him before he hit the ground and hoisted him upright.

Yrtalien took another step back and regarded the fallen sidhe warily.

"He'll be all right," Diana mumbled. "He—" She stopped, unsure of what to say.

"Lord Chevalier has recently recovered from a grievous wound, your Highness," Signe said, smiling slyly at the prince and speaking in her mellowest voice.

Yrtalien signaled for Argo to come forward.

"Assist your kithmate in taking our guest to the east wing," the prince ordered. Argo moved to Ryder's other side and grasped him around his waist. Supported between Argo and Diana, Ryder forced himself to will back the almost overwhelming pain. He stood for a moment, gulping in great breaths of air, fighting the urge to shudder. Finally he felt he had enough control over himself to speak.

"Forgive my weakness, your Highness," he gasped, his voice barely audible over the constant background din inside the palace. Instinctively, he glanced at his left palm, reassuring himself that the gem's blue light could not be seen through the leather glove.

Yrtalien caught the motion of Chevalier's eyes and smiled to himself.

"I take it the injury was to your hand?" he inquired. "Shall I have it attended to?"

Ryder grimaced. "The wound cannot be healed, your highness," he said, a little too quickly. "I have sworn an oath to conceal the hideous remains of my hand from the sight of any eyes but mine." He stared at Yrtalien, willing the prince to believe his lie.

Yrtalien nodded. "I am a great respecter of oaths," he said quietly. "But I do not wish to detain you when you are in such obvious distress. We shall speak, at length, I hope, when you have recovered some of your fortitude."

The prince watched as the trolls bore his visitor up the stairs. Signe curtseyed to the prince before she, too, ascended the stairway.

"Sometimes, Lord Devlin," Yrtalien said to the silver-haired noble, "you remind me of my wisdom in allying myself with you." The prince's hand strayed to

t h ᴇ   h i l l

the pouch at his neck, where the Shadowstone still tingled faintly. *Only one thing could evoke such a response from this gem*, he thought.

Later that night, Yrtalien rose from his bed, startled out of a pleasant reverie by a faint pulse at his throat. He put his hand to where the Shadowstone rested in its pouch.

Eleighanara is near, he said to himself with the knowledge that he had been touched by the Dreaming itself. *Now there are three*.

the   hill

chapter

ten

Leigh stirred her cup of rich Kona coffee and eyed the selection of pastries and fruit on her plate. One by one, her companions joined her with plates of their own from the lavish breakfast buffet offered by the Seacrest Bed and Breakfast Hotel. Although she had gotten used to sleeping on the woven pandamus-leaf mats in the menehune village, she had been grateful last night for a real bed.

"This is more like it," Edmund said cheerfully, sitting down at the table and admiring the two platters he had heaped full of muffins and breads, gooey sweet buns and large chunks of fresh pineapple.

"Just don't eat the silverware," Leigh admonished, as she watched the redcap demonstrate his skill at his favorite pastime—shoving copious amounts of food into his oversized mouth.

"I don't think I could eat a thing," Rasputin said, taking a seat next to Edmund and proceeding to slather honey over a bowl of fresh melon. Morgan and Tor joined the group at the breakfast table.

"This is a really nice hotel," Morgan said. "It has bubble bath in the bathroom and everything."

"The beds are too short," Tor grumbled.

Valmont was the last to seat himself at the table.

"Hey!" Edmund cried. "Where'd you get the mai tai?" The redcap looked hopeful.

The eshu pointed with his head toward an archway off the dining room.

"From the bar," he said.

"Forget it," warned Tor. "Not even a taste."

"Rasputin could get one and say it was for him," Edmund said, looking at the pooka.

"Oh, I'd contribute to the delinquency of a minor in a heartbeat," Rasputin replied, sipping what looked like a coconut shake.

"Can I have the umbrella?" Edmund asked Valmont.

The eshu handed the paper umbrella, complete with its skewer of fruit, to the redcap. Edmund twirled the colorful decoration in his hands and then popped it into his mouth.

"Ugh," said Morgan, peeling the skin off a piece of kiwi fruit before taking a small bite out of it.

"We were lucky the truck driver knew of this hotel," Leigh remarked. "I was afraid that once we got to town we'd just have to wander around until we found a place to stay."

"The owner is the cousin of the man who drove us here," Valmont said. "You may call it luck if you wish."

"I hope you tipped him for giving us a lift." Leigh finished her coffee and looked around for a waiter.

The eshu nodded. "I hope a twenty was sufficient. A cab would have cost at least that much."

"How long are we gonna stay here?" Edmund asked.

"Until we find what we're looking for," said Leigh. She glanced at Valmont. "How did we pay for the rooms, anyway? I was too tired last night to pay any attention."

"American Express," Valmont replied.

"It figures," said Edmund.

"I thought to bring along a little money," Leigh said. "If you like, I can help foot the bill."

Valmont shrugged. "I don't foresee any immediate problems," the eshu said. "Besides, if we run out of money, there are always ways to get more. We have more resources to draw upon than most people do."

"Sure," Edmund said. "We could rob a bank!" The childling's eyes widened in excitement. "We really *could*

the hill

rob a bank," he said, looking at Leigh. "With that stone you have, it would be simple."

"Edmund!" Leigh's voice registered her amazement.

"What a lovely idea," Rasputin said enthusiastically. "I've always wanted to conduct a vitally important quest from the confines of a jail cell."

"It was just a thought," the redcap muttered.

"Are you enjoying your stay so far?" a voice from behind Leigh interrupted. She turned to see a young Hawaiian in a gaily patterned shirt and shorts. He was holding a pot of coffee in one hand. Leigh smiled and held her cup out for him to refill.

"We only got in late last night," she said. "But the rooms are comfortable and the breakfast is excellent."

"You're the ones my Uncle Akoni found wandering around near Kilauea," the waiter said. He walked around the table filling coffee cups and clearing away empty plates. When he picked up Edmund's plate, he examined it carefully.

"This has a chip in it," he observed, sounding concerned. "I hope you didn't swallow any glass."

"If I had, I think I woulda noticed it," the redcap replied cheerfully.

"Is your father the owner of this establishment?" Valmont asked him.

The waiter nodded. "I'm learning the ropes so I can take over for him when he retires."

"Where do people spend their retirement when they've lived in Hawaii?" Leigh mused.

The young Hawaiian laughed. "Dad says he's going to Florida," he replied. "Do you know how lucky you are?" he asked, suddenly serious.

"What do you mean?" Valmont asked.

"The old lady blew last night, apparently not long after you passed through the area."

"Old lady?" asked Morgan, looking puzzled.

The waiter nodded. "The volcano."

"Kilauea erupted?" Tor's question sent a sudden chill down Leigh's spine.

"I hope the old woman got home safely," she muttered. "Maybe we should have gone back for her."

"Old woman?" The waiter raised an eyebrow. "What old woman?"

"We met this decrepit old lady when we stopped to have some food," Edmund began.

"She wasn't decrepit," Morgan corrected him. "She was just old, and she was very nice. She was the one who gave us directions to the road and told us that the air might be poisonous if we spent the night in the open."

"Has anyone told you about the legends?" the waiter asked slowly, setting the dishes and his pot of coffee down on an empty table nearby and pulling a chair up to the table.

Leigh shook her head. "We only just got here yesterday afternoon," she replied softly. "This is our first trip to the Big Island."

The waiter let his breath out slowly. "There are stories that say that sometimes, just before an eruption, Pele herself—she's the volcano goddess—wanders around warning the natives so they can take shelter or leave the area."

"The old woman told us that," Morgan said. "She said Pele looks like a beautiful Hawaiian woman except that she has fiery red hair."

"That's her usual form," the waiter said, "but sometimes she has been known to don a different disguise."

"Not an old woman," Rasputin said.

The waiter smiled and nodded his head. "Sometimes Pele appears as an old woman seeking assistance."

"Way cool!" Edmund said. "We met a god!"

t h e   h i l l

"Goddess," Morgan corrected.

"Whatever," the redcap replied impatiently.

"It's just a legend," the waiter said, getting up from the table and retrieving his coffee pot.

"But we did meet an old woman," Leigh murmured.

"Are we gonna sit here all day?" Edmund demanded. "There's a beach just below the hotel. Can we go down there before we start looking for the what's-it stone?"

Leigh hesitated. "I don't know…"

Valmont stood up and brushed off his clothes. "I don't know about you," the eshu said, looking down at the khaki shirt and tailored pants that clothed his mortal body, "but I feel a serious need for some wardrobe adjustment."

"I disagree," Rasputin said. "We look fine overdressed as we are."

Leigh relented. "I suppose it wouldn't hurt to spend the rest of the morning just playing tourist," she said. "I might want to get a guidebook to the island."

"I brought my swim suit," Morgan announced happily.

As the companions left the hotel, the dark-haired man seated in one corner of the dining room eyed them closely. They matched the descriptions he and his allies had been given.

If he had waited a little while longer, Vargas thought, *Ryder would not have had to search for the Kithain of the city in order to find his quarry. They would have come to him.*

The wiry Latino rose from his table and located the hotel phone, which he used to leave a brief message at the number Ryder had given him before disappearing into the demimonde of Kithain society. When he had finished, he left the hotel and headed in the direction of the beach.

They should not be difficult to follow, he told himself.

Even as mortals, the six servants of delusion stood out from the crowd.

Ryder awoke with only a dull ache in his palm. He was lying in a king-size bed which took up the majority of a sumptuously furnished bedroom.

"How do you feel?" Diana's voice inquired solicitously.

The Dauntain groaned. "Did I embarrass myself in front of the prince?" he asked, sitting up and throwing back the gossamer-thin coverlet.

Diana shook her head. "I think the prince was impressed," she said. From the doorway, Signe nodded her agreement.

"Prince Yrtalien has been most concerned about your well-being," the eshu said. "He asked to be informed as soon as you awakened."

"Have you been watching me all night?" Ryder asked Diana, noticing the troll's haggard face.

"I slept a little," she replied evasively. "Signe spelled me for awhile."

"Our rooms are just down the hall from yours," Signe said.

"Are you going to be able to manage?" Diana asked, staring at Ryder's hand, still sheathed in its fingerless leather glove.

The Dauntain nodded. "I'm not certain what set it off," he said. "I was all right until the prince touched me."

"This reminds me of the Toybox," Signe remarked. "I told you I saw the old steamer trunk glow when you got near it. Maybe there's something here that's equally as potent."

the hill

Ryder considered the eshu's words. "You might be right," he said. "If so, then it's something the prince has with him."

"So don't let him put his hands on you," Diana said, her voice implacable.

Ryder grimaced. "That's the last thing on my mind," he said. He motioned for Signe to enter the room. "Shut the door behind you," he cautioned.

Signe settled herself on a gold brocade day bed that stood against one wall of the enormous room. Diana walked across the bedroom to take up guard just inside the door.

"We have to assume that no one is listening to our conversation," Ryder began. "Still, we should try to be as careful as possible about what we say to each other while we're the prince's guests."

"Are we going to stay here, then?" Diana asked, her voice heavy with disapproval.

"I believe that if the prince extends such hospitality to us, we have an obligation to remain in this center of Kithain activity," Ryder replied. "You do realize that the prince and his allies are members of the Unseelie Court," he said.

Signe nodded slowly. "I was never as familiar with political factions among the Kithain as you are," she said. "But from the little I do know, I am inclined to agree with you."

Diana was more direct. "I know Unseelie when I see it," she said. "And this place stinks of it."

Ryder gave her a look of warning. "Stinks is perhaps too dramatic a word," he said. "It is true, however, that the Unseelie are even more detrimental to the well-being of humankind than their Seelie brethren. We should keep that in mind and act accordingly."

"I don't understand," Signe said, her delicate face creased with concern.

Ryder's own features hardened. "I mean that we must attempt, as best we can, to assimilate ourselves into the prince's court."

"You want us to be Unseelie?" Diana said, her voice rising with indignation.

Ryder held up a hand to calm her. "I want us to be thought of as such," he amended. "I am not asking either of you to compromise your principles. Just try not to be too soft-hearted or too critical of what you might see in the palace."

"Have you seen the mortals they've enslaved to do their bidding?" Signe asked.

Ryder shook his head. "I wasn't really in a position to observe much of anything," he said ruefully. "But that doesn't surprise me."

"It's heinous," the eshu whispered, her dark eyes aflame with suppressed anger.

"I agree," said Ryder. "But for now, there's nothing we can do about their lot. In fact, we can't appear to be overly solicitous of the household's servants or else we might lose the prince's favor."

"Are you certain that this is where we need to be to find the group we're looking for?" Diana asked. "Maybe they won't come here."

"They'll be here," Ryder said in a voice that rang with certainty.

"How do you know that?" Signe asked.

Ryder looked down at the floor for a moment. When he raised his head, his expression was haunted.

"Because I dreamed it," he whispered. Abruptly he stood up and walked over to the window, pulling aside the heavy drapes that had shrouded the room in semi-darkness. Morning light flooded the bedroom. Looking out over the grounds below his window, Ryder saw a few dissolute Kithain sprawled on the lawns, apparently recovering from the revelry of the previous night. In the distance, the island's lush vegetation stretched for as far as he could see. He drank in the view as an antidote to the illusory luxury that surrounded him. *That,* he thought, *is reality. I need to keep that in mind.*

"Shall I tell the prince you're up and about?" Signe asked.

Ryder nodded. As the eshu rose to leave, he caught up with her and stopped her with a hand on her arm.

"Find a servant," he said, "and order him to inform the prince."

Signe closed her eyes for a moment, then opened them and nodded solemnly.

"I'll try to remember not to say please," she remarked, extricating herself from Ryder's hold and opening the door.

Leigh sat on a colorful blanket spread out on the white sands of the Onekahakaha Beach Park. Within the breakwater that provided a safe area for swimmers, Morgan and Edmund splashed back and forth through the water. Tor watched them from the shore. Farther up the beach, Rasputin and Valmont paced each other near the ocean's edge, occasionally bending over to retrieve something from the glistening sand. True to his word, the eshu now sported a pink, blue and yellow Hawaiian shirt—an expensive one—and white shorts. *He looks classy even in tourist garb,* Leigh thought. Rasputin had purchased a light-weight sleeveless shirt made of unbleached pima cotton and matching drawstring pants, claiming his legs were too elegant to insult by wearing shorts. Leigh had settled for a pale green blouse that tied just below her breasts and a pair of tan cut-offs. She carried the Keystone in the leather pouch strung through a belt loop.

Viewing them all from a distance, Leigh felt a rush of affection for her companions. Partly because of the oath they had all sworn and partly because of an indefinable essence that surrounded them, they had become like a second family to her. *Even Edmund*, she thought ruefully. She sighed as she thought about her mortal relations back in San Francisco. Her father's job as a policeman would never allow him to bring his large family to a place as elegant as Hawaii. She tried to imagine her rowdy brood of siblings capering on the sand and in the water like Morgan and Edmund, or her mother lounging on the beach. She shook her head, chasing away the idle reveries. *Actually*, she corrected herself, *these friends are a third family*. Her thoughts turned suddenly bitter as she recalled another set of parents, nobles of House Fiona in Arcadia, and the harshness of the exile they had imposed upon her.

I will not wallow in the shadows of the past. She reached for the books she had brought with her to occupy her time while the others played along the shore. The guidebook to the Hawaiian Islands, published locally, held her attention for a few minutes as she leafed through its glossy pages and studied the maps. Kauai, the island where the menehune still maintained their precarious freeholds, lay near the western end of the archipelago that spanned nearly 1,500 miles. Hawaii, their present location, was the easternmost island. Between the island chain and San Francisco stretched more than 2,000 miles of ocean. For the first time, Leigh felt the vast distance that separated her from her mortal home. She put the book down and turned instead to Ellen's journal. Several times during her stay with the menehune, Leigh had thought about

the hill

the sluagh's gift, but so far she had not had the chance to examine it closely. She opened the book and began to read. Many of the entries were nothing more than bits of second-hand gossip about the nobles of Pacifica. Leigh was amused by the intricacies and shifting alliances that made up the chief pastimes of the noble fae. She began skimming the pages, looking for names and places that might have relevance to the oathmates' quest. Midway through the book, the words *Silver's Gate* caught her eye.

"Eleighanara?" A soft masculine voice uttered her name as a shadow loomed over her from behind. She turned her head, startled. A sharp jolt from the pouch at her side propelled her to her feet. She stared at the dark-haired stranger who had crept up so silently that she had had no forewarning of his arrival. His mortal seeming was handsome enough, but it paled in comparison to the wild, abandoned beauty of the figure revealed to her faerie sight.

She looked around her, panicked at the realization that her companions were occupied with their own pursuits. She considered calling out to them, but her pride surfaced and she made the decision to confront the familiar stranger without the support of her oathmates.

"Yrtalien," she said, her voice carefully noncommittal. "I was wondering when we would finally meet." As she spoke, she carefully closed the journal and laid it on the blanket next to her travel book.

"I had no doubt of our meeting, Eleighanara," the sidhe noble replied. He caught hold of her hand and drew it to his lips for a brief kiss. Leigh allowed the gesture, but gently slipped her hand from his grasp as soon as she could without seeming ungracious.

"Walk with me," Yrtalien said, his voice at once commanding and warmly affectionate. "We have much to talk about."

Leigh inhaled deeply.

"We have grown rotten with stagnation," the raven-haired prince told the royal flame-haired daughter of House Fiona. "It is past time for the wheel of change to turn."

"You are speaking of rebellion, Yrtalien," Princess Eleighanara said.

"I am speaking of survival for our kind and for the Dreaming," Yrtalien responded.

"How do you know I will support you in this?" Eleighanara asked. "It comes very close to treason."

"You will join me out of love," Yrtalien said confidently. "Already the shadows lengthen, signaling the changing of the seasons in this changeless place, yet your father and mother show no sign of bowing to the natural succession of power."

"I cannot go against my family," the princess said, her voice, like her will, beginning to waver.

"You cannot go against your nature, Eleighanara," Yrtalien said. "It is your fate to see what must be done and bring that thing to its fruition."

She gazed around her at the crystal spires and glittering palaces that adorned the misty horizon in every direction. For as long as she could remember, no new structure had risen to alter the landscape of Arcadia's timeless realm. For a moment she had the sensation that nothing new would ever disturb the relentless, pristine serenity of the faerie homeland.

"I will do what I can," she said simply.

"We swore an oath to each other long ago," Yrtalien reminded her. "For the sake of that oath, and for the love that we bear each other, you must join me."

"This course of action may be our undoing," Eleighanara said, her voice quiet and resigned.

"It may also be our destiny," Yrtalien said.

the hill

"The years have changed both of us, I think," Leigh said to Yrtalien. "At least I feel that I am no longer the person you once knew."

The prince regarded her with a faint smile. "I am not afraid of change," he said. "It is the essence of our kind."

Yrtalien held out his arm. "There is a low hill that overlooks the ocean," he said, pointing with his other hand down the beach in a direction that would take her farther from her companions. As if he could read her thoughts, the prince laughed softly. "Don't worry, Eleighanara," he assured her, "I won't attempt to take you from your friends. We can keep an eye on them from the hilltop."

Abruptly, Leigh relented and accepted the proffered arm. Together they walked in silence to the place Yrtalien had selected. Seating themselves upon a smooth rock, they looked out over the sea for a few moments. Leigh turned her gaze to the shore, where her companions were tiny figures silhouetted against the brilliant blue sky. Yrtalien noted her gesture.

"They don't even realize you're gone," he told her, and then added, "Thank you for releasing me from my imprisonment."

Leigh felt her face redden. "It was not what we intended," she said. Hearing her words, she blushed even more deeply.

The prince laughed, a rich, full sound that brought back distant memories of other times when she had heard his merriment.

"I am sorry if I was not what you were seeking when you unlocked the door to my prison," he said. "But I am grateful nonetheless." His face grew serious. "Would you have done it had you known what lay beyond the gateway? Would you knowingly have brought me here?"

Leigh tore her gaze away from her distant companions and forced herself to meet Yrtalien's eyes.

"I was sent here in exile for what we did," she said slowly. "For a long time I could not remember even that much. Still," she paused, considering her next words carefully, "I would not exchange my punishment for the one meted out to you."

"Not even if my punishment was duly pronounced by the rightful rulers of the Dreaming?" Yrtalien's voice was so soft Leigh had to strain to hear his words.

"I tried to intercede," she said. "They would not listen."

Yrtalien nodded. "It is their doom never to hear the truth until it is too late," he said. "I take it that your answer indicates you would have freed me anyway." Although he spoke lightheartedly, Leigh noticed the hardness in the prince's eyes.

"I have made my feelings clear," she said.

"You possess a very powerful treasure of the sidhe," Yrtalien said, suddenly changing the subject. "I have one as well." He withdrew a small pouch from its hiding place beneath his shirt. Leigh felt the air around them become charged with preternatural brilliance as Yrtalien removed a dark-colored gem from the pouch and held it flat in his palm. Leigh felt a tremor course through her body as the emerald in her own pouch began to resonate.

"Is this why you came here?" he asked, his voice mild.

As if following some inner compulsion, Leigh withdrew the Keystone from the pouch at her side. For a moment, the two Kithain lost themselves in contemplation of the gems, now glowing in coupled radiance.

"You acquired that by false pretenses," she said.

"Did I?" Yrtalien looked offended. "And what of the gem you have?" His voice was laced with soft menace. "Was that not acquired by force from the creature who sacrificed his own mortal eye for something greater than the flesh? Be honest with yourself, Eleighanara," the prince said. "You are as much an opportunist as I am."

"I was acting on behalf of my liege," she retorted. "I deceived no one!" She bit her lip, afraid that she had said more than she intended.

Yrtalien shook his head sadly.

"So many years since we last fought on the same side against those who would calcify our dreams, and we are already arguing like a pair of long-lost lovers," he said. "Let us not polarize ourselves so quickly." Once more, the prince's voice took on a cajoling tenderness. "I did not come here seeking to bandy words with you, Eleighanara," he said. "I came to invite you—and your oathmates—to enjoy the hospitality of my freehold."

Leigh's eyes widened in surprise.

"Was that unexpected?" Yrtalien asked. "It is only my duty as prince of the Court of Shadows to ensure that all Kithain within my realm enjoy the benefits I have to offer."

"The Shadow Court," Leigh murmured. The term awoke in her a sudden desire to speak to Valmont about Chief Makani's allusion to the menehune's belief in the danger of shadows. "I thought that was a quaint reminder of an abandoned custom," she said.

Yrtalien nodded. "It has been relegated to that, as I understand," he responded. "But that which has been consigned to the shadows is not necessarily driven out of existence. The Shadow Court of Samhain revelry is but a parody of something which has never died."

"A shadow of a shadow," Leigh said. "So the Shadow Court is real and is more than we have been led to believe?"

"My Court of Shadows is quite real," Yrtalien said. "And it is in the name of that court and the dream it represents that I extend my invitation to you."

"And my oathmates," she reminded him.

"And your—oathmates," Yrtalien said.

Leigh replaced the Keystone in its pouch and stood up. Yrtalien also rose and looked at her questioningly.

"I will convey your offer of hospitality to my friends," she said. "We will think about it."

The prince nodded. "My freehold is on the other side of town," he said. "It stands on a hill within sight of the ocean and the forest. It's a two-story house that looks a little seedy until you get close enough to see it for what it has become. You can't miss it, especially with your emerald to guide you—not to mention your eshu."

"He's not my eshu," Leigh retorted before she could stop herself.

"Good," Yrtalien said. "I would hate to think that someone had replaced me in your heart. You have always remained in mine."

Leigh turned away and walked quickly down the hill. Yrtalien stood alone for a moment, watching her go. He smiled to himself.

"Glynnis will be so pleased to make your acquaintance," he muttered to himself.

Despite his avowed interest in speaking with Ryder, Yrtalien had spent only a few minutes with him before pleading prior commitments. The Dauntain had taken advantage of Yrtalien's abrupt departure from the freehold to slip away, returning to the hotel room he had rented after leaving Vargas at the Seacrest. Before he left, he made sure that Signe and Diana knew that they would be on their own for a time. "You might want to stay in your rooms," he said in a tone that made it clear that this was more than just a suggestion. The two women readily agreed.

"I have no desire to mingle with these folk any more than is absolutely necessary," Diana said flatly.

When he reached his hotel, there was a phone message waiting for him from his mortal friend.

"Our quarry has arrived," Vargas' voice said. "They are across the hall from me. Send further instructions."

Ryder swore softly at the irony that placed him and his Kithain compatriots in the heart of the Unseelie Court and deposited the group of changelings they sought on the doorstep of his mortal ally. Torn with indecision, he paced back and forth in the small room. Finally he picked up the phone and dialed the Seacrest, where he asked to be connected to Vargas' room. There was no answer, so he left a brief message giving Vargas the location of the prince's freehold and an order to keep the group in sight.

Leaving his hotel room, he stood on the street in front of the building, still uncertain as to his next course of action. A throbbing began in his palm and grew steadily more insistent. He looked at his gloved hand. "Fine," he said in exasperation. "You decide where I should go."

Surrendering to the pain, Ryder let the stone direct him. Ruefully, he saw that his steps were taking him back to the freehold of the Unseelie prince.

Vargas stood on the hillside overlooking the beach, his

eyes fixed on his quarry. He noticed that a strange man approached the red-haired female and, after a brief discussion, led her away from the other members of her group to a small hillock further up the beach. A few minutes later, the woman stood up and rejoined her companions, while the stranger watched her before departing in the direction of the town.

"This is going nowhere," he thought. "If they are staying at the hotel, they will have to return to their rooms eventually." He shrugged and made his way back to his room at the Seacrest, where the message light on his phone was blinking.

"He wants us to do *what*?" Edmund snorted when Leigh had called the companions together and informed them of her conversation with Yrtalien.

"You actually went off with him by yourself?" Valmont demanded, his voice colder than usual.

"I had to do something to occupy myself while the rest of you were playing tourist," Leigh responded heatedly. Instantly, she regretted her hasty words. "I'm sorry," she apologized. "That was uncalled for."

"Are we going to accept his offer?" Morgan asked. "He's not a nice person, you know."

Leigh smiled sadly. "I knew him a long time ago," she said. "He is not so easily judged."

"You said he showed you the stone," Tor said. Leigh nodded.

"For that reason alone, I think we need to take him up on his invitation," she said.

"I agree," Valmont chimed in. "He also apparently has the *alii's* daughter."

"That's right," said Leigh. "I had forgotten."

"So we definitely should stay in our hotel," Rasputin observed. "Let's take our time about getting our things."

"This is gonna be *sooo* cool," Edmund chortled as he raced ahead of the group toward their hotel.

Diana and Signe greeted Ryder anxiously when he returned from town.

"Has the prince returned?" Ryder inquired, seeing the troubled looks on their faces. He massaged his left hand as he spoke. It was throbbing with a steady intensity, but he found that his second visit to the prince's freehold was less traumatic than his first.

Perhaps continual exposure lessens the pain, he thought.

Signe nodded. "I believe he is back from wherever he went a few minutes ago."

Diana's voice was venom-coated. "I could hear him from the upper landing," she said. Ryder smiled to himself at the thought of the statuesque troll poised at the top of the stairs to overhear the prince's conversation. "He said something to that Devlin creature about preparing another suite of rooms as near to his as possible. Then he grabbed a couple of the servants and started upstairs."

"We've heard—sounds—coming from his room since then," Signe said, her voice nearly inaudible. "They stopped a few minutes ago."

"What kind of sounds?" Ryder asked.

"Screams," said Diana.

Ryder tensed. "Come with me," he said, a look of determination on his face.

"Where are we going?" Signe asked.

"This is a large place," the Dauntain informed her. "We're going to get ourselves lost."

Ryder led his companions down the long hallway past a series of elaborately carved doors. At the fourth such door, Diana pointed. Ryder nodded his understanding.

Grasping the knob, he pushed the door open.

The prince was seated on a large bed, its head- and footboards carved with elaborate gargoyles and dragons. A young, blond woman huddled near the foot of the bed. Another servant, a slender young man with an athletic build, sat cross-legged at the prince's feet, his face buried in his hands, his shoulders shaking with silent sobs.

Yrtalien glanced up as the door opened, the irritation quickly fading from his handsome face as he recognized the intruders. He smiled instead and got to his feet, nudging the male servant with the tip of his foot.

"Leave us," he ordered the young man. At the sound of his voice, the blonde looked at him. "You, too," the prince said. "I will send for you when I need you again." The humans fled Yrtalien's presence through a door in the side wall of the bedroom. Turning to Ryder, he inclined his head and motioned the three Kithain into the room.

"Please," he said, "come in. I have ignored my guests for too long."

Ryder led Signe and Diana into Yrtalien's chambers.

"Forgive my intrusion, your Highness," he said.

"Yrtalien—please—I am not yet *your* Highness," the prince said smoothly. Signe noticed that his face looked even more finely formed than it had the night before.

"We were trying to find our way back to our rooms," the eshu said. "I felt certain that we had come through this door—"

the hill

Yrtalien laughed. "So the vaunted eshu talent for travel is at least partially flawed," he said.

"Did we interrupt something?" Diana asked, her voice bluntly cutting off the prince's pleasantries.

The prince shook his head. "I had just finished amusing myself," he said. Ryder looked at him, a frown on his face. Yrtalien chuckled softly. "Mortals have such tawdry little dreams," Yrtalien said. "I enjoy provoking them to nightmares just to liven up their shabby minds. Have you ever drunk the wine of terror unmitigated by the comforting film of reality?" he asked.

Ryder hid his clenched fist behind his back as he shook his head.

"I can't say that I have ever developed such a rarefied taste," he said. Behind him, Signe lowered her head, remembering her own awakening into reality by the iron-willed Dauntain. *It was different*, she told herself sternly. *He was trying to help me.*

"I ran into an old, old friend earlier this morning," the prince said, enthusiasm evident in the warm cadences of his speech. "I have invited her and her friends to be my guests. Again, I apologize for my hastiness with you this morning. Sit down and we can speak now."

Ryder seated himself in a massive teakwood chair. Signe wandered to the window seat at the far end of the bedroom. Diana took up a position behind and to one side of Ryder's chair.

"You radiate a tremendous amount of Glamour," Yrtalien said abruptly. "I suspect that you are concealing something from me—" he paused as he saw Diana stiffen at his words, "—and as far as I am concerned, I need not know your innermost secrets." The troll relaxd slightly. "I do wish, however, to enlist your obvious power."

He knows, Ryder thought suddenly, seeing the prince staring intently at his left hand.

Ryder forced himself to shrug with feigned casualness. "I have not yet decided whether I wish to settle in Hawaii," he said.

Yrtalien gave the three Kithain an enigmatic smile that stopped at his lips. "I believe that when you meet my old *oathmate*," he said, "you will be much more inclined to remain here."

The prince withdrew the opal from the pouch at his neck. "This is known as the Shadowstone," he said. "My oathmate carries with her an emerald called the Keystone. What I want to know is this." Yrtalien paused, watching with amused interest Ryder's growing discomfort in the presence of the darkly glowing gem. "Which stone do you bear upon your person?"

Ryder considered his options and quickly made a choice he hoped he would not regret.

"Mine is a sapphire," he said quietly. Signe shifted uneasily in her seat. "It seems to have led me to you," he added.

Yrtalien nodded. "I would agree," he said. "It seems that these treasures have an affinity for each other in addition to their normal powers."

"I would just as soon the knowledge that I have it not spread beyond this room," Ryder said.

"Not even to my oathmate?" Yrtalien asked.

Ryder shook his head. "To no one," he emphasized.

Yrtalien smiled. "I have become very good at keeping secrets when it suits me," he replied. "And when the incentive to do so is strong enough."

Ryder leaned back in his chair, resignation clearly evident on his hawklike features. "I understand," he said. "I understand completely."

t h ε   h i l l

The companions found the prince's palace without any difficulty.

"Just like before, when it led us to the gate in Golden Gate Park," Morgan said as the glowing emerald Leigh carried led them across the town to the large wooden house on the hill.

"So what's the story?" Edmund said. "Are we gonna claim we're Unseelie like he is, or what?" The redcap cocked his head. "He *is* Unseelie, isn't he?"

"Oh, most definitely," Valmont said. Again Leigh remembered her need to speak privately with the eshu. Realizing that this might be their last opportunity for unguarded conversation, she turned to him, an urgent look in her eyes.

"Can we walk a little ahead and talk privately?" she asked the eshu.

Valmont raised an eyebrow. "Of course," he said. "I'm sure the others won't object."

"What do you mean, *claim* to be Unseelie?" Morgan said to Edmund. "You're the Unseeliest person I've ever met."

Rasputin shooed Valmont and Leigh ahead of him and stepped in front of Tor and the pair of childlings.

"An Unseelie pooka," Rasputin said, looking over his shoulder at Tor. "I've often wondered what that would be like."

"I'm sure you have," the troll said.

"You oughta try it sometime," Edmund informed Morgan. "Maybe you'd actually like letting your hair down for a change."

"I can't let my hair down," the sidhe childling replied, an icy ring to her high-pitched voice. "You

s h a d o w s   o n

made sure of that," she added.

The redcap almost felt guilty as he remembered his impulsive prank involving Morgan's once waist-length black curls and a stray bottle of superglue.

"You look better with short hair," he muttered, kicking at a stone in the street.

Valmont and Leigh moved away from the others.

"Do you remember Chief Makani's words about shadows?" Leigh asked Valmont.

The eshu nodded. "It did sound as if he were describing what we call Banality," he observed. "I assume you made the same additional connection between the menehune concept of shadows and a more familiar use of the term?"

"The Shadow Court," Leigh said.

Valmont sighed. "And the Unseelie in general," the eshu added. "I must admit that those of us who espouse a less rigid view of Kithain law have less trouble with Banality than those who insist on upholding the outmoded ways," he began, but Leigh cut him off.

"Don't talk propaganda, please," she begged. "Just talk."

Valmont chuckled. "I didn't mean to upset you," he said mildly. "What I said is true, however. I have less of a problem dealing with the everyday assaults of rationality and prosaic thought than you—at least before you acquired the Keystone."

Leigh thought about Valmont's words for a moment, then nodded. "You're right," she said. "Since I've been carrying the stone, I haven't lost touch with who I really am, even in the middle of a tourist mecca like Hilo."

"I hear it's worse in Honolulu," Valmont said jokingly. "Perhaps we can test it there someday."

"The stone's power seems to rub off on the others, too," Leigh observed. "Tor has been at least marginally with us all along. Morgan seems to generate Glamour all on her own," she added wistfully. "But then I think she is a special case."

Valmont nodded. "I've seen Rasputin's faerie nature come and go," he remarked. "But not since we've been in nearly constant proximity to you and the Keystone."

"That just leaves Edmund," Leigh said.

"Edmund has never seemed to have much of a problem with the outside world," Valmont replied.

"Edmund is as Unseelie as they come," Leigh said. Valmont chuckled.

"That he is," he agreed. "And that is precisely my point. The Unseelie, including the Shadow Court, do not hold Banality in such dreadful regard as do the rest of you. I am beginning to think that this is because they—and myself as well, to a certain extent—believe that we should stop hiding from our shadows, to use the *alii's* terminology."

"If only we could," Leigh said.

"Perhaps, with the Shadowstone, there is a way."

Leigh stared at him. "I wonder if that was what he meant," she said, more to herself than to her companion.

"Who? Yrtalien?" The eshu inquired testily.

Leigh ignored Valmont's tone and nodded. "He mentioned something about a dream of his—a vision."

"Perhaps we should find out just what his vision is," the eshu said.

The two oathmates fell silent, lost in their own thoughts. Gradually they slowed their steps to let their companions catch up with them.

"There she blows!" Edmund sang out, pointing ahead of them at a two-story house that sat, bathed in the shadows of the trees that surrounded it, on top of a gently sloping hill.

The bright gleam from the Keystone confirmed his

observation. Leigh took a deep breath and started up the slope.

"Into the belly of the beast," Valmont muttered softly as he followed.

Glynnis dug her fingernails deep into the flesh of her palms to keep from crying out as pain coursed through her body. Though she knew that this agony was merely a product of Yrtalien's angry imagination, that he was compelling her to believe that her flesh burned from the illusory flames that licked at her hands and feet, she was helpless to resist.

"Are you certain you know nothing of the other gems? How many more of them are there?" The prince repeated the questions he had been asking her for what seemed like eons. With one hand, he touched the pouch containing the Shadowstone, using the gem to focus and amplify his Glamour. Glynnis' reactions confirmed his theory that the stone was, among other things, a magnifier of fae magic.

Glynnis gasped and shook her head, unable to form the words of denial he refused to accept from her.

"Oh, go ahead and scream," Yrtalien said, stepping up the intensity of the pain with a flick of his wrist in her direction. He felt the stone pulse as it channeled his Glamour toward his helpless victim. "It seems to be a common occurrence around me these days."

Glynnis had no trouble complying. She cringed with shame at the sound of her own tortured cries. Bringing every ounce of her strength to bear, she forced herself to speak, powering the words with the breath of her screams.

the hill

"I know nothing," she sobbed. Already driven to her knees by the pain, she doubled over until her head nearly touched the floor of the tiny underground room, originally the house's hurricane cellar. She repeated the words over and over, like a litany.

Finally, suddenly, the pain stopped. Glynnis nearly fainted with relief.

"Get up," Yrtalien commanded. She struggled to her feet and carefully hazarded a look at the prince. Yrtalien seemed preoccupied, gazing up, his hand poised at his throat above the pouch containing the Shadowstone. After a moment, he turned his attention back to her.

"We have company," he said, his voice barely containing his excitement. "Pull yourself together. You look like shit. I don't want Eleighanara to think that I consort with scullery maids."

Stung by his words, Glynnis pulled a comb from a pocket of her long skirt and smoothed her disheveled, dark hair. Her movements were automatic, devoid of feeling. With some effort, she brought her expression under control, assuming once more the look of cold disdain she reserved for public appearances. *I will make him pay for this*, she thought. *When I no longer need the power he commands, I will make him suffer for what he has done to me.*

"Incidentally," Yrtalien said, his voice cool and condescending, "I believe you are as ignorant of the other stones as you claim to be." He smiled at her and extended his arm for her to take. "Shall we welcome our newest guests?" he asked, a rakish smile imbuing his face with heartbreaking splendor.

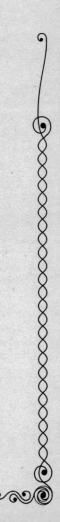

the   hill

chapter

eleven

Valmont walked with Kanani in the garden. It had taken him less than a day to locate Chief Makani's eldest daughter, apparently an honored guest of Prince Yrtalien. The menehune maiden was even lovelier than her sister, Lulani, although there was about her an intangible fragility. *Perhaps it is her exposure to this alien dream,* he thought. In her arms, Kanani cradled an ugly little chimerical monster that almost resembled a pug with six legs and a pair of bulbous eyes. The creature snuffled contentedly, occasionally snaking out a leathery black tongue to lick at his mistress' forearm.

"So my father sent you to inquire after my safety?" Kanani asked, flashing the eshu a look of undisguised admiration. "How is he? And my sister?"

"They are both well, although I believe they are saddened by your absence," Valmont said. He had not yet been able to broach the subject of Makani's concern, as Kanani seemed unaware of any danger.

"I am saddened as well," the menehune maiden replied. "This place is very beautiful in its own unusual way, but the customs here are very strange."

Valmont nodded. "They are, indeed," he said.

"Do you find them strange as well?" Kanani asked. "I thought these were your people." She looked perplexed.

"I am used to less opulence and more—gentility," Valmont said. "I found the customs of your people less incomprehensible the longer I stayed with them."

"While I seem to understand even less about the

ways of my host and his subjects than when I first arrived. They are always changing their minds."

Valmont nodded. "It is because they do not believe in the value of tradition," he said. "No, I misspoke," he corrected himself. "They do not believe in traditions that seem to have no value anymore. They are engaged in a constant search for new customs to replace the ones they have abandoned."

"Everyone here is very kind to me," Kanani observed. "I only have to express a desire for something and it is given to me."

"I am glad to hear that," the eshu said. "Your father was worried that you might be unhappy here among so many strangers."

"The prince has called me an ambassador," she said, "but I am honored as if I were a much greater personage."

"I have noticed that you spend most of your time here in the garden," Valmont said.

Kanani nodded. "It is quiet here, at least in this part of the garden," she said. "The prince's guests were told to stay away so that I might have a place of quiet. My people are very close to the world of growing things," she added, "and we begin to lose ourselves when we are too long apart from the life of the earth."

"I had gathered as much during my visit to your village," the eshu replied. "It was thoughtful of the prince to give you such a sanctuary."

Kanani laughed. "He calls it my temple, as if I were a *kahuna*. I feel more like a pig that is being fattened for a feast."

Valmont chuckled. "That image does not suit you at all," he said. A worrisome thought was beginning to gnaw at him as he considered her analogy.

"What are your duties as ambassador for your village?" he asked, trying to keep his tone light and conversational.

"Only to smile and enjoy myself, so the prince has told me," Kanani said. "I have asked him many times if I was serving my purpose as the representative of my people, and each time he assured me that I had no need for worry."

Valmont nodded, still trying to recall the thought that was playing hide and seek with his usually keen memory. Instead, he found himself preoccupied with watching Kanani's graceful movements and listening to the gentle warmth of her voice.

"He did say that on the eve of the longest night, I would be the guest of honor at a very special celebration," she said as an afterthought.

Valmont suddenly felt cold. He stared at the delicate figure of Kanani and fought to keep silent as the pieces of his mental puzzle assembled themselves to form a gruesome picture.

"You must be looking forward to that," he heard himself say, although his words belied the dread that numbed his senses.

"Oh I am," Kanani replied, her face alive with anticipation.

"Do you mind if I leave you here for a little while?" Valmont asked, feeling a sudden need to locate his companions and share his growing suspicion with them. *All except for Morgan and Edmund,* he thought. *They don't need to know until I'm certain.*

Kanani shook her head. "I am grateful for the time you have spent with me," she said. "If you desire to speak with me later, you will most likely find me not far from here."

As soon as he was out of her view, Valmont quickened his steps until he was nearly racing for the palace and his oathmates' suite of rooms.

Aloha, dear Layla, Morgan wrote in her diary. *We are still in Hawaii and we are still guests, but we are on the island of Hawaii instead of Kauai and we are the guests of the prince we accidentally freed instead of guests of the menehune.* The sidhe childling sat in a delicately carved chair made from dark *o'hi'a* wood in front of a matching desk. Prince Yrtalien had given each of the oathmates a suite of rooms all to themselves in the wing of the house where he had his own chambers. It was early evening, and downstairs Yrtalien was still holding his version of court. Morgan had claimed exhaustion and, although he had chided her gently for her lack of endurance, the prince had allowed her to retire for the night.

Morgan wasn't sleepy at all, just desperate to be alone long enough to compose another entry in her diary. She carefully turned back the covers of her four-poster bed and tossed and turned on the sheets to give them a rumpled, slept-in look. Then she clothed herself in a graceful, muu-muu style dark blue and gold nightdress. If anyone came in unexpectedly and found her still awake, she was prepared with an alibi that included nightmares and strange noises.

Keeping a diary is harder than I thought, she confided to Layla. She tried to imagine that her friend was sitting in the room listening intently as Morgan spoke the words she put down on the pale pink paper in her precise, girlish script. *Not the writing,* she added, *but finding the time to write when no one is around to peek over my shoulder.* She didn't want to admit to Layla that Edmund was the chief source of her worry, since the eshu childling had somehow developed a crush on the redcap. Idly, Morgan wondered what it would feel like to have a crush. The word sounded vaguely distasteful, though, so she decided that she would not actively seek someone to have a crush on.

I have been trying very hard to pretend that I am Unseelie, Morgan wrote. *I don't think I'm doing a very good job, though, because every time I try to sound like Edmund, I just get laughed at.* Morgan was very proud of herself for her honest self-evaluation and she stared at the sentence for a few minutes before she went on. *Edmund seems to be doing just fine, but then you know he's Unseelie to begin with. I'm worried about Grandpa, though, because he seems so out of sorts all the time. There is another troll here who seems to feel the way he does. At least I've never seen her smile. Her name is Diana and I'm wondering if I should introduce her to Grandpa or if he will find her on his own. I wonder if grumps can have crushes,* Morgan speculated.

Leigh's time is almost constantly taken up by the prince. They knew each other in Arcadia before Leigh got sent here and he got trapped in the gateway. He isn't at all like I thought he would be. He laughs a lot and is very polite to his guests. Valmont says that looks are deceiving. Valmont doesn't like him at all. Yesterday Valmont had a long, private talk with Leigh, Grandpa and Rasputin. When I asked him why Edmund and I couldn't be in on the conversation, he just said that it wasn't a matter for childlings and that if we needed to know, he would tell us later. I don't know what he said, but it really seemed to upset Leigh. She and Valmont haven't been talking since then. I guess it has something to do with the prince."

Lady Glynnis has sort of taken me under her wing. She has a wonderful collection of books of myths and legends and even one or two chimerical bestiaries with beautiful pictures, almost as nice as the ones my mother paints. She gets a little tiresome after awhile, though. All

*she ever wants to talk about is how important it is to study
the uses of Glamour.*

*Rasputin has been wandering around talking to a lot of
people. I don't think he's made any special friends yet.
Sometimes I think he's so friendly he doesn't know how to
be anything more. I don't know many pookas, so maybe
they're all like that. Valmont found the chief's daughter and
he has been spending most of his time with her. She is smaller
than Lulani and she has a really ugly chimera for a pet. I
always wondered why people like bulldogs and Boston
Terriers and persian cats. Maybe it's because they feel sorry
for something that ugly.* Morgan heard a noise outside her
door. Quickly she closed the diary and tiptoed over to
listen with her ear pressed against the space between
the door and the wall. She heard the sound of footsteps
nearing her room; they stopped just outside her door.
She jumped back, startled, at the sound of a sharp knock
on her door. Racing to her desk, she hid the diary in
the top drawer. She checked her bed to make certain it
still looked rumpled and then ran back to the door just
as her visitor knocked a second time.

Breathlessly, Morgan opened the door.

"I couldn't sleep after all," she panted as she looked
up at Lady Glynnis. The elegant noblewoman smiled
at Morgan.

"I thought you might be finding it difficult to sleep,"
she said. "May I come in?"

Morgan nodded. Glynnis entered the childling's
sitting room and took a seat on the dark blue velvet
sofa. Morgan sat at her desk, turning the chair to face
her visitor. She was careful not to let her eyes stray
toward the drawer which concealed her diary.

"Are you enjoying your stay with us?" Glynnis
asked Morgan. "I worry that the atmosphere in the
palace is not entertaining enough for you and your
friend Edmund."

Morgan gave a slight shrug. "It's very different here," she said, "and everyone has been very nice to me."

Glynnis's smile seemed amused. "That was cleverly spoken," she said. "If I had not already known, I would have concluded on the basis of your careful avoidance of my question that you bore the lineage of House Eiluned. That is my house as well," she added.

"Is that why you offered to teach me more about using magic?"

Glynnis nodded. "Some uses of Glamour come more easily than others, and only a few Kithain are able to comprehend all the ways in which to manipulate the power of dreams. I like to think that we of House Eiluned are among those few." Glynnis hesitated.

Morgan felt as if she were being graded by one of her teachers. Unconsciously the childling sat up straighter in her chair and arranged her face into a careful mask of polite attention.

"One of our greatest strengths as a House," Glynnis said in a smooth voice that indicated to Morgan that she had passed the test, "is our ability to direct the usually fickle streams of Glamour according to our desires."

Morgan smiled. "I know," she said, eager to impress her guest with her own famliarity with fae magic. "I can usually get things to work out the way I want them to." She hoped her voice didn't sound overly smug.

"It does not surprise me," Glynnis said. "There are ways, however, to increase the success and potency of our control over the uses of Glamour even beyond our natural affinities."

Morgan's brows wrinkled as she tried to follow the meaning of Glynnis' words. The dark-haired woman laughed. "I see I need to be a little more specific," she said.

For the first time in years, Morgan felt somewhat less than brilliant. She swallowed the nagging sense that she had just been mildly insulted and stared solemnly at Glynnis, determined to demonstrate her capacity for comprehension.

"Focusing Glamour through objects—faerie treasures—can often intensify the results of one's power," Glynnis said. "For example, the emerald stone your friend Eleighanara bears is an extraordinarily powerful collector of Glamour."

"I know that," Morgan concurred. "Leigh doesn't use it very often, though. She says that she doesn't want to depend on it for things she could do in other ways."

"An admirable sentiment for one of House Fiona," Glynnis said, a note of disparagement creeping into her voice. "Their skill with the arts of Glamour falls far short of their talent for other affairs." Morgan thought that Lady Glynnis placed a slightly disapproving emphasis on *affairs*.

"Why aren't you telling this to Leigh?" Morgan asked. "She's the one who claimed the stone."

"But is she the one to whom it rightfully belongs?" Lady Glynnis's question seemed more like a challenge than a simple query. Before Morgan had time to answer, Glynnis rose to her feet and walked across the room to where the childling sat. Gracefully dropping to her knees in front of Morgan's chair, Glynnis folded her hands in Morgan's lap and stared up into the childling's face. Her dark eyes burned with an almost unbearable intensity, but Morgan could not bring herself to look away from their hypnotic gaze.

"The stone should be under your command," Glynnis whispered, her voice a hot breath of passion. "You are of the house of secrets and sorcery. In your hands, the Keystone could be much, much more than just a handy lockpick. It could be the very key that will unlock for you the deepest secrets of the fae."

the hill

She stood in the place of honor before a throne of fire and rubies within a chamber of ice and gossamer. Around her, throngs of adoring people—some of them Kithain, others mortals cloaked in the enchantments of the Dreaming—paid homage to her. Her oathmates stood on a level just beneath her, lesser objects of adulation. A little behind her, wearing a black velvet robe embroidered with silver crescent moons and five-pointed silver stars, Lady Glynnis stood, a look of proud affection on her elegant face.

In her hand, Glynnis held a silver crown tipped with four glowing gems—an emerald, a ruby, a sapphire, and an opal—above Morgan's head. As she began to lower the crown onto Morgan's brow, a cheer rose up from the crowd. Above the din, Glynnis' voice rang out in triumph.

"Behold the High Queen of the joined worlds of Arcadia and—"

Morgan shook her head suddenly, her vision shattered by the simple fact that she was unable to put a name to the world of mortals. Glynnis had not moved, nor did her face indicate that any time had passed since the words that had sparked Morgan's waking dream and its abrupt dissolution. Morgan tried to remember what Glynnis had been saying. One word stuck in her mind.

"Secrets," she repeated.

Glynnis nodded. "You must borrow the stone from Eleighanara," she said. "If you can do that and bring it to me, I can show you how to release the fullness of your power."

"But what if she won't let me borrow it?" Morgan asked. "She's very protective of the emerald."

"Then you must try to acquire it without her knowledge," Glynnis replied.

"Steal it?" Morgan was aghast.

Glynnis shook her head quickly. "It is not theft if you intend to return the object you have taken," she said.

"Oh." Morgan sounded unconvinced. "I'll have to think about how to go about it," she said. "It may take a little while for me to come up with a plan."

"I hope it won't take too long," Glynnis said softly. "Eleighanara and the prince may have other plans that will interfere with your borrowing the stone. It would be best if you got the gem quickly so that we could experiment with it before your friend decides to make of it a gift to his Highness."

"Leigh would never give the stone to him," Morgan protested.

Glynnis made a small pitying sound deep in her throat. "You do not realize just how convincing Yrtalien can be," she said. "In fact, the more I think about it, the more important it seems that you acquire the stone from her for its own protection."

"Do you really think so?" Morgan asked, looking troubled.

"I really think so," Glynnis replied. She rose to her feet and kissed Morgan swiftly on the top of her head. "I shall leave you to your plans, child of Eiluned," she whispered. As quickly as she had come, Glynnis departed Morgan's chambers, shutting the door softly behind her.

Morgan ran to the door and listened until she could no longer hear Glynnis' footsteps. She counted to a hundred and then returned to her desk, retrieving her diary from the drawer.

I just had a visitor, she wrote, her hand shaking with excitement. *It was Lady Glynnis, who I thought was a good friend of the prince. Now I'm not so sure. She offered to help me learn how to use the Keystone, but to do that, I have to borrow or steal it from Leigh.*

Suddenly, the childling felt very tired. *I can't write any more right now,* she wrote. *I need to think about what I'm going to do. Remind me to tell you about the dream I had while Glynnis was talking to me. Edmund would say it was "way cool." Aloha, until my next chance to write to you.*

She carried the diary to bed with her, placing it beneath her pillows, and lay trying to sort through the thoughts that were jumbling around inside her head. Glynnis' words sounded convincing, especially when she talked about the prince's designs on Leigh's emerald. Morgan decided that Glynnis, like Valmont, must not like Yrtalien very much. Before she could come to a decision about whether to tell her oathmates of her conversation, she drifted into an uneasy sleep.

True to his word, Yrtalien kept Ryder's presence in his household a secret from the red-haired sidhe and her companions. By staying in the wing of the palace to which the prince had assigned them, the three Dauntain were able to avoid most contact with their quarry.

In the days since the arrival of the female called Eleighanara, the woman who carried the emerald gem, Ryder had received only a single visitor, the prince himself. Yrtalien insisted on seeing Ryder's own stone. At first, Ryder tried to fall back on his alleged oath, but Yrtalien persisted, reminding him of the terms of their bargain. Admitting that he had sworn no such oath, Ryder removed the glove in Yrtalien's presence.

Steeling himself against the pain which exploded within him, Ryder was unprepared for the prince's action. Yrtalien grabbed Ryder's wrist and touched the sapphire to the dark opal held between the prince's fingers. A blinding flash of light filled the room as the gems made contact. Then, suddenly, the pain vanished.

s h a d o w s   o n

Ryder could only stare at his palm in blank amazement. The gem was still there, glowing steadily, but the familiar throbbing ache had disappeared. In its place was a gentle, pulsing warmth.

"What have you done?" Ryder finally managed to ask. The prince laughed.

"It was a test," he said. Yrtalien's expression grew suddenly serious and he narrowed his eyes to stare at his guest.

"How did you know that it would ease the pain in my hand?"

"I have spent considerable time and effort trying to unlock the stone's secrets," the prince said. "I have discovered, among other things, that this stone has the ability to counteract many effects of the force we call Banality. I have perceived that a tremendous amount of Banality clings to you. That you—and all you come in contact with—do not suffer from it is due to the Glamour embedded in your flesh."

Ryder's troubled expression seemed to amuse Yrtalien. "The sapphire's own Glamour ensures that you never completely succumb to Banal influences, but the process of absorbing and transmuting so much mundanity is what causes you pain." The prince shook his head. "I don't quite understand all the fine details of the process," he admitted, "but the sapphire is the source of both your agony and your continued fae existence. Without it, you would be unable to sustain your disguise."

"What do you mean?" Ryder asked, although he could predict the answer.

"You may have once been the knight known as Chevalier," Yrtalien replied. "But you have abandoned your birthright and your title."

Ryder looked away from the prince, a strange feeling of shame flooding through him.

"You are one of the Dauntain, are you not?" Yrtalien asked, his voice gentle.

Ryder could only nod his agreement. He tensed, eyeing the slender sword at the prince's side and wondering if he could draw his own chimerical blade in time to fend off an attack.

"Rest easily," Yrtalien said. "Do we not have a bargain?"

Ryder stared at him, uncomprehending. Finally, he nodded his head. "My assistance for your silence," he said.

"Exactly," replied the prince. "And I have kept my silence. Now you must give me your assistance."

"Even though you know I have come here under false pretense?" Ryder asked.

"Precisely because you have come here in that fashion," the prince replied. "Think of what would happen if I announced to all my subjects—and my other guests—that a trio of Dauntain were in their midst. I'm afraid I could no longer vouch for your safety, or your much vaunted sanity."

"Your point is taken," Ryder admitted. "What do you want me to do?"

"For the moment, nothing," said Yrtalien "On the eve of the Winter Solstice, however, I shall need the resources of both you and your gem." In painstaking detail, the he outlined his intentions for the celebration that would take place during the longest night of the year. Ryder struggled to control his growing horror as he listened to Yrtalien.

"I cannot be a party to such a deed," the Dauntain said bluntly when Yrtalien had finished. "That is more than I had bargained for."

The prince nodded. "I agree," he said pleasantly. "Therefore, I am prepared to sweeten the pot." He leaned forward until his face was inches away from Ryder's. "You are a hunter of the Kithain," he said.

"Who is your chosen quarry?"

Ryder slowly began to understand what the prince was offering. "The Kithain who bears the stone like mine—and like yours," he said, realizing that the time for lying was past.

"I cannot give you Eleighanara," Yrtalien said, his voice quiet. "I am bound to her by an oath sworn long ago and I intend to keep my vow." His voice changed abruptly. "The others, however, hold no interest for me. If you agree to assist me, I will make certain that they are delivered into your hands."

Ryder closed his eyes. It galled him to have to deal with the Kithain under any circumstances, but the prince had—literally—forced his hand. *Partial success is better than no success at all*, he thought. At least he would have his revenge on the redcap brat.

He also had the prince's assurance that no harm would come to any mortals during the winter celebration. What Yrtalien planned would involve only the Kithain, and Ryder felt no responsibility for those who had willingly damned themselves.

"Your terms are acceptable," he informed the prince at last.

Yrtalien left Ryder's room shortly after they had sealed their pact. Before he departed, the prince paused inside the doorway and gave Ryder a brilliant smile.

"The relief from the pain is only temporary," he had informed the Dauntain. "It will return before too much longer. If it becomes unbearable, I will be only too happy to remove it again for another little while. Provided," he said softly, "you ask me to do so with the proper respect."

The pain returned in full force the next morning. Unable to stand the constant solicitousness of his companions, Ryder sent Diana and Signe out to discover as much as they could about Eleighanara's companions.

"They don't know who you are," he said. "I doubt any of them will suspect that you are anything other than what you seem to be."

From that time, Ryder closeted himself in his bedroom. Alone with his pain, too proud to beg the prince for relief, he counted off the days until the winter solstice.

Signe stood quietly on the edge of the crowd of Kithain that watched, with various degrees of interest, as the friendly faced, rabbit-eared pooka juggled a succession of balls, clubs, scarves and, finally, assorted items tossed to him from the audience. For a few minutes she lost herself in the artistry of the juggler, laughing at his mock misses—caught by his foot and kicked deftly into place in the endless loop-de-loop of circling objects.

This is one of the Kithain we have come to restore to sanity, she reminded herself as the pooka finished his performance with a flourish. The crowd drifted away to other pleasures, leaving only Signe and the juggler standing on the lawn in front of the palace. She watched as he began packing his juggling gear into the brightly colored cloth carryall he toted around. He looked up at her and flashed a winning smile in her direction.

"I love the aftermath of art," he remarked. "Picking up is half the fun, I always say."

"You're Rasputin," Signe said, moving forward to pick up a blue and yellow club that had landed not far from her feet during his finale.

"I am?" the pooka said. "Thank you for informing me of that. Otherwise I never would have known." His

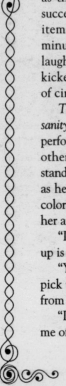

gentle voice betrayed no hint of sarcasm.

"My name is Signe," she offered.

The pooka stood up and held out a hand for her to shake.

"Appalled to meet you," he said as she clasped hands with him. "Now go away and leave me alone."

Signe looked at him with hurt surprise at his mild dismissal. Silently she turned and started to walk away.

"No!" he called after her. "That's not what I said!"

She paused and turned back to look at him. He was standing, forlornly outlined against the backdrop of the palace, his ears drooping down the sides of his face.

"Excuse me," the eshu said, "but you distinctly told me to go away. I don't mean to intrude on your wish to be alone."

"You have to intrude," Rasputin said. "I don't want you here."

Signe sighed. "Will you stop giving me mixed messages?" she asked. "Why don't you just say what you mean and stop playing games!"

"I am saying what I mean," the pooka responded heatedly. "Pookas always tell the truth!"

The eshu raised a hand to her forehead, lowered her head and slowly shook it back and forth. When she raised her head again to look at Rasputin, she was smiling.

"I think I understand," she said. "I'll stay for awhile if you want."

"That would be terrible," Rasputin said happily. He hoisted his bag onto his shoulder. "I hate walking," he said. "It's bad for the feet. Would you like to hate it with me?"

"I think a walk sounds good," Signe said. She looked around her at the palace grounds. "Is there someplace we can go where we won't be besieged by the party crowd?" she asked.

"There's a path on the other side of the hill that doesn't lead down to a private beach," Rasputin said.

"Won't it be crowded with revelers?" Signe was beginning to get the hang of deciphering the pooka's convoluted speech.

"Every time I've gone there, it's been packed," Rasputin said.

"We can only go there and see for ourselves," Signe stated. "If there are too many people, we can leave."

The "beach" was actually a thin strip of white sand, less than a hundred feet long, accessible only from the hill. Rocky cliffs rose up on either side just beyond the small expanse and the waves crashed against the jagged boulders that served as the cliff base. Signe understood why Rasputin had said—implied—that it was deserted.

"It looks like the tide has been chipping away at it for years," she said as she and the pooka stepped onto the sand.

"Perfect for sunbathing, swimming or surfing," Rasputin expounded. Signe laughed.

"I suppose you realize how funny you are," she told Rasputin. The pooka nodded his head.

"I know how funny I mean to be," he replied.

Signe thought about his statement, hearing a note of sadness in his voice. "Do you have a lot of friends?" she asked. "I would think that with your obvious talents and your expressive wit, you would be inundated with well-wishers and companions."

"I have more friends than I can count on one hand," the pooka said, holding out one of his hands for inspection.

His five companions, Signe thought. *Are they the only ones he counts as friends?*

"What brings you to Hawaii?" she asked, unwilling, at least for the moment, to pursue the subject of the pooka's social interactions.

"Nothing important," Rasputin said. He picked up a stone from the edge of the water and tossed it into the waves. Signe found a small clump of reedy grass and sat down.

"I love the light in these islands," she said. "It's not like anything I've ever seen."

"Ugly, isn't it?" Rasputin agreed, tossing a second stone and watching it arc high into the air before plummeting into the ocean.

Signe nodded. Looking out along the endless vista of sea and sky, she could understand why so many painters had spent their careers trying to capture the raw, ethereal quality of the light in the tropical islands. Gaugin, Chagall…

After a few minutes, Rasputin left his attempts at clearing the beachlet of rocks and joined Signe on her grassy blanket. The eshu found herself suddenly bereft of words. It had been a long time since she had been alone with one of the unrepentant Kithain. For a moment, she felt a little afraid. Perhaps she had given herself away and the pooka had lured her to this deserted place with the intent to harm her. She glanced sideways at Rasputin.

He sat, his knees drawn up to his chin, his arms locked about his legs, seemingly lost in his own thoughts. *He doesn't look dangerous*, she told herself. *I'm just letting my imagination run away with me*.

"What are your friends like?" she asked, hoping she sounded no more than casually interested.

Rasputin turned his head sideways, resting his cheek on his knees, to look at her.

"They're terrible people," he said. "I used to be ecstatically happy before I met them."

"I'm sorry," Signe replied. Thinking about the actual meaning of his words aroused in her a sense of profound pity.

"Please, feel free to wallow on my behalf," Rasputin said, winking at her from beneath one drooping ear. "I insist."

Signe smiled. *He's irrepressible*, she thought.

"You still haven't told me much about them, other than how terrible they are," she said, smiling. Ryder had asked her and Diana to attempt to find out more about their targets. She enjoyed the irony of getting her information from a pooka.

Rasputin sat up straight and stretched out his legs. "The childlings are the worst," he said. "I can't stand being around either of them for very long."

"Don't you sometimes wish you were a child again?" Signe asked a little wistfully. To her, Rasputin seemed like a child in the body of an adult. She tried to imagine him as a little boy.

"All the time," Rasputin said quickly. He turned his face away from her, but not before she could see his expression become grim.

Rafael's back was covered with blood before his father stopped. He had used the buckle end of the belt again, threatening to double the number of strokes if the child screamed. The boy's wrist bore deep imprints from where he had bitten it to stifle the sounds of his cries.

After his father was done, he made Rafael kiss his hands.

"Thank me," his father ordered him. "Tell me how glad you are that I have punished you for your constant lying."

The words came to the boy easily enough, for they were further from the truth than he could begin to imagine.

His father slapped him on the face when he had sobbed out his false thanks.

"You lie, of course," his father said, laughing without humor. "You always lie. Now you will lie in the dark on your back in the blood of your sins until I decide to let you try to clean yourself up."

The burly man jerked his son up by the shoulder and shoved him toward the small bedroom closet. He watched as Rafael tried to stretch out on the closet's rough wooden floor. He had to bend his knees to make himself fit. The raw wounds on his back burned against the unsanded, cracked boards. Rasputin whimpered.

"Shut up," his father said. "I do not want to hear any noises coming from this room. Your mother will not be back from work until late and I do not want your cries to disturb me."

His father slammed the door shut and turned the key in the lock, leaving the eight-year-old boy alone with the utter darkness and the agonizing pain.

"Rasputin?" Signe put a hand on the pooka's arm to get his attention. It was growing dark and she saw that the tide was beginning to inch its way up along the sand.

"Don't touch me!" Rasputin cried, his voice almost a scream. He jerked his head around, his face contorted in outrage. He pulled an arm back as if to lash out, but stopped himself as his eyes focused on Signe's face. He dropped his arm. Then he seemed to collapse in on himself, burying his face in his hands as shuddering, soundless sobs wracked his body. Signe again reached out as if to place a hand on him, but paused, her fingers hovering just above his shoulder.

That was a true statement, she said to herself. *He doesn't want to be touched, at least not now.*

"I didn't mean to say that," Rasputin whispered in between silent sobs. "I meant—I don't know what I meant."

"The light is going," Signe said. "We should go back to the palace before it gets too dark to find our way."

Rasputin's trembling gradually ceased. Without speaking, he rose to his feet, picked up his shoulder bag and held out a hand to the still-seated eshu.

t h ε   h i l l

"Are you sure it's all right?" Signe asked, looking at the pooka's outstretched hand.

Rasputin shook his head. "Please," he said quietly, "don't let me help you stand."

Signe grasped his wrist and allowed the pooka to pull her to her feet. As soon as she was standing, she released her hold.

"I'm sorry that what I said upset you," she said as they retraced their steps up the hill toward the palace.

"It's not all right," Rasputin said gently. "You're not forgiven." So softly that she almost failed to hear, he added, "I had an absolutely painless childhood."

"You look a little peaked," Lord Devlin observed as he stood with Tor watching a mock battle between a group of redcaps and an equally determined mixed group of nockers and pookas.

"Yeah," Tor grumbled, irritated by the pesky cheerfulness of the silver-haired sidhe noble who had apparently appointed himself the troll's official tour guide and host in Yrtalien's palace. "I'm not exactly in the best of moods."

Devlin had dragged him through the streets of Hilo in the morning, on what the sidhe lord had called his "rounds." Only after Tor began to feel an upsurge of Glamour within him did he realize what Devlin had been doing as he conversed in seeming idleness with the store owners, independent craftsmen and women. By the fifth or sixth stop, Devlin nearly crackled with Glamour. He patted the troll heartily on the back and Tor felt almost rejuvenated.

He finally collared the sidhe in a side street, away

from mortal eyes. "You were ravaging those people," he accused the startled noble.

"Take your hands off me," Devlin croaked. "You can't do that. I'm one of the sidhe."

"You're a piece of trash," Tor growled, releasing Devlin abruptly and stalking off in the direction of the palace.

Devlin caught up with him before Tor had traversed a full block.

"I didn't know it would offend you," the sidhe lord said, sounding annoyed rather than apologetic. "If I had, I would have left you to your own devices."

Tor shrugged.

"It's done," he said. "I can't undo what you did, so there's no point in dwelling on it. Just leave me out of your raids next time."

Devlin sulked all the way back to the palace, but refused to leave Tor's presence. Instead, he insisted that the troll accompany him to watch the rough-and-tumble free-for-all on the front lawn of the palace. Now a cluster of courtiers stood on the sidelines as the combatants bashed each other with wooden clubs, fists, and occasionally heads. Periodically, someone fell to the ground, unconscious, only to be dragged away by some of the spectators, where they would be revived and their dormant faerie natures reawakened with Glamour-infused pieces of rock and shell—the Dross which passed for currency among the Kithain. Destroying Dross released the Glamour it contained and was usually enough to arouse in a temporarily Banalized changeling the memory of his faerie nature.

The slapdash brouhaha had restored Devlin's temper to its normal state of insouciance. Tor, however, had become even more gloomy at the sight of the pointless exercise.

"'S'cuse me," he said, shoving himself past Devlin

and heading toward the palace, this time determined not to be pursued by the silver-haired lord. He nearly stumbled into another troll, a tall, handsomely statuesque blond female, who was not quick enough to move out of his way.

"Sorry," he apologized. "I don't believe we've met," he said, giving her what was for him a smile.

"We haven't," the troll replied. "And I don't think we need to, either, considering the habits of the company you've been keeping." She glared past Tor in Devlin's direction.

"He's no friend of mine," Tor growled.

"I never said you two were friends," she replied. "Just that you've been hanging around with him. Ravagers don't have friends."

She turned away from him with a flourish and strode off in the opposite direction.

Tor sought refuge in his room. He pulled the heavy curtains closed, plunging his bedroom into darkness, and slumped in the heavy reclining chair in one corner of the room. There he sought vainly for the solace of a slumber which was a long time in coming.

"I feel like I haven't had the opportunity to talk to you alone since you came here," Yrtalien said as he led Leigh into his private library.

"You haven't," Leigh responded, settling herself into the rattan chair Yrtalien pulled out for her. The prince seated himself opposite her on a large, black velvet ottoman. "You have squired me from place to place and introduced me to more Kithain than I can possibly remember, yet we've never really had the chance to be alone together."

"Until now," Yrtalien said. "Tell me, Eleighanara," he continued, "what do you think of my Court of Shadows?"

"Do you want an honest answer?" Leigh asked. "Or shall I just pay you the expected compliments about your generosity and your lavish hospitality? You have been more than kind to all of us," she added.

"I didn't ask you here," he said, indicating the room in which they sat, "to hear words that you would say if we were in a crowd."

Leigh nodded. "I think that you throw a splendid party," she replied, "although it's a little rough for my own tastes."

The prince shrugged delicately. "Go on."

"I think your Shadow Court is not all that different from any other Shadow Court that might exist. I fail to get the point behind all this posturing and constant carousing."

"I was afraid you wouldn't understand," Yrtalien said slowly. "There is a deeper meaning behind the revelry and the rowdiness. I am changing minds within these walls. Once you agreed with me that traditions should be broken as soon as they outlive their usefulness. I believe that it is time we ceased our zealous hoarding of Glamour. I want to impress my courtiers with the fact that Glamour is theirs to be squandered. We are Kithain. Glamour is our birthright."

"All I can see is that you're encouraging your courtiers—as you call them—to abuse mortals and to waste their Glamour on useless pastimes. You have had three chimera hunts, just since I've been here. I've seen you and Lady Glynnis and Lord Devlin and the others toss cantrips back and forth like they were powered by an inexhaustible commodity." She lowered her voice. "I've also walked through the streets of Hilo and seen the closed signs on a number of artisan's shops—not the tourist traps—places where people brought their dreams to life. That was your doing, wasn't it? You ripped the creativity from the souls of those mortals to give you enough Glamour to indulge your fantasies."

Leigh bit her lip, fearful that she had said too much. The prince's handsome face confirmed her suspicion.

"Your stint among the unwashed masses has changed you, Eleighanara," Yrtalien said quietly. "In another time, you would not have cared so deeply for the pathetic hopes of a few mortals with overactive imaginations. Their lack of creativity—as well as any depressive moods they might suffer—are only temporary. If they are truly inspired, their dreams will eventually return. That is the beauty of ravaging."

"I once accused Valmont of ravaging," Leigh responded bitterly. "I didn't know the meaning of the word until now."

"Of course not," Yrtalian said, his voice caustic. "You can't expect an eshu to master the finer details of such a complex process."

Leigh stood up. "I think we have very little to say to each other," she said, her voice as soft and cold as the prince's. Before she could move, Yrtalien was on his feet. He put his hands on her shoulders and pushed her, not ungently, back into her seat.

"Please," he murmured. "Don't be so hasty in your judgment of me. You have not seen the real truth behind all this elaborate display."

Leigh closed her eyes. Despite her resentment at being forcefully thwarted in her attempt to escape an increasingly uncomfortable confrontation, she remained seated and nodded her head.

"I'm listening," she said, opening her eyes and looking up at the prince.

Yrtalien touched the pouch at his throat. "This

stone," he said, "and the emerald you have are the keys to a power neither of us can begin to imagine."

I can imagine it, Leigh thought. *It is the purpose of our quest.* She forced herself to remain silent, sensing that the prince had not finished speaking.

"With your stone and mine," he continued, "we can transform this world into a place where the children of Arcadia can once again ascend to the glory they deserve. The Shadowstone has the ability to defeat the corrosiveness of Banality, to neutralize its effects upon our natures. Your stone, the Keystone, can unlock virtually anything—even gateways that have been denied us since the Sundering."

Yrtalien reached behind him and pulled the ottoman closer to Leigh. He seated himself on it once again, this time folding his arms on her knees. "I used to sit with you, like this," he said gently, "in your father's house. We would talk for hours about our dreams and about the possibility of spending an immortal future together."

Leigh shook her head. "I'm sorry," she murmured, "I don't remember."

"I have memories enough for both of us," Yrtalien said. "I had nothing to do in my prison but remember. They were merciful enough to leave me that much." His voice betrayed a pain that Leigh could not believe was feigned.

"What do you know of Silver's Gate?" Yrtalien asked abruptly.

"Not much," Leigh said, suddenly on her guard. "Just that it was the last of the gates to close at the time of the Shattering." As soon as she heard the lie escape her, she felt the need to qualify her words. "At least that is all I know for certain."

"You thought you had found it when you opened the gate that allowed my release," Yrtalien said.

Leigh nodded glumly. "We should have known better than to think that finding it would be that easy," she said.

"But that is the quest with which you are charged, is it not?" the prince asked. "To find the five gems that will allow the gate to be opened from the mortal realm?"

"Four," Leigh corrected him. Too late, she saw the look of satisfaction cross his face. *He was guessing at the number of gems*, she realized. *And I have just told him something he did not already know.* Her heart sank.

Yrtalien nodded. "Four," he repeated. "And you and I together have two of those gems. We need only find the others and we can reunite this world with that of the Dreaming. Together we can establish a kingdom of the fae that will surpass anything that existed before the dividing of the worlds."

"I have no desire for power of that sort," Leigh said adamantly.

"What you desire and what your destiny holds are often quite different," Yrtalien retorted. "You came here to take the Shadowstone away from me, did you not?" the prince asked, his voice as cold as iron.

"I have a duty to my liege," Leigh said. "I will not break my oath to him."

Yrtalien laughed. "You need not break your oath," he said. "By joining yourself to me, you will be keeping both the oath you swore to your duke and the oath you swore to me in the halls of your father's royal house."

"If this freehold is a sample of your dream," she said, "I cannot ally myself with what you hope to achieve."

"Then you will be forsworn, like me," Yrtalien replied. "Does that shame mean nothing to you? Do you take your oaths so lightly that you break them at the slightest inconvenience?"

Suddenly Leigh remembered. "The oath I swore to you was one of love," she said, so softly she could hardly hear her own voice. "If I must seem to break that oath in order to keep it, then you may call me what you will."

"So you still love me, Eleighanara," the prince said just as softly.

"Yes." The word was wrenched from Leigh's lips. "But it no longer gives me any pleasure."

Yrtalien stood up and kicked the ottoman aside.

"We appear to have reached an impasse," the prince said coldly. He extended a hand to Leigh, clearly indicating his desire for her to stand. Leigh ignored his gesture and rose from her chair without his assistance.

"So it would seem," Leigh answered.

"I had hoped that we would not have to battle each other for the gems we possess," Yrtalien said. He smiled and shook his head as Leigh's hand strayed unconsciously toward the sword she wore at her waist. "Not that sort of battle," he said. "At least I do not wish for it to come to that."

"When words fail, what else is there?" Leigh asked, assessing the prince with a warrior's eye and wondering if she could defeat him in single combat. "You wish to gain control of the stone I bear. I, in turn, am charged with recovering the Shadowstone from your possession. If you will not turn it over to me and if I will not surrender my stone to you—"

"Then we have the makings of a game worthy of our royal houses," the prince said. "My freehold is still open to you," he said. "After all, you cannot afford to leave without that for which you came. I have tried to be open with you about my desires," Yrtalien continued as he and Leigh walked slowly toward the door. "Now it seems that openness has failed and our business must be conducted, appropriately enough, in the shadows. And in that arena, the advantage falls to me."

Yrtalien held the door open for Leigh to pass through before him. "Tomorrow, at the winter solstice

the hill

ceremony, I shall formally ascend to my position, and I will secure my power with an offering of Glamour, the likes of which have not been seen in this realm since before the Sundering," he said. "By that time, I hope we shall have resolved our disagreement."

Leigh managed to refrain from a hasty reply as she left Yrtalien's presence. As soon as he was out of sight, she shed her dignified mien and ran up the spiral staircase two stairs at a time. Reaching the sanctuary of her chambers, she threw herself upon her bed and let her tears flow freely until she had cried herself out. After a time, she attempted to pull herself together and set herself to decide upon a course of action.

She repeated the prince's words in her mind: *Tomorrow is the winter solstice ceremony.* Valmont's allegation that Yrtalien planned to sacrifice Kanani in some sort of ritual at the peak of the solstice no longer sounded so ludicrous. She had agreed, after hearing Valmont express his concern for the menehune's safety, that the eshu had been wise not to include either of the childlings in his confidence. That was because she had refused to believe that Valmont had correctly interpreted Kanani's words. Wiping the tears from her face, she went in search of the eshu.

"He's with the prince," Lady Siva, the satyr recently ennobled by Yrtalien as a gesture of his egalitarian rule, told her. "They went in there." The satyr pointed to the library where Leigh had so recently learned a bitter truth.

Though he was nervous to be alone with Yrtalien, Valmont could not keep from examining the collection of books that lined the library's walls.

"Do you see anything that interests you?" Yrtalien asked. The prince had seated himself in the rattan chair earlier occupied by Leigh, his feet resting on the black ottoman.

"I am always drawn to anything that will increase my knowledge," Valmont replied.

"In that, at least, we are alike," Yrtalien said. "Actually," he continued, waving a hand in an airy gesture that encompassed the shelves of books, "most of these books have been acquired only recently. As you well know, I arrived in this world with little in the way of personal belongings."

Side-stepping the small talk, Valmont asked, "Why did you send for me?"

Yrtalien regarded the eshu with amusement.

"I find your direct approach refreshing," he said. "I understand from my own sources that you and I have more in common than a simple desire to expand our knowledge."

Valmont arched an eyebrow inquisitively.

"What could a lord of the sidhe have in common with a mere eshu?" he asked, not bothering to hide the sarcasm in his voice.

"The Shadow Court," Yrtalien said. "You occupied a position of some standing among the Unseelie of Pacifica, so I have been told."

Valmont laughed. "Your sources are sadly mis-informed," he replied. "I once served as prince of the Shadow Court during the Samhain revels, but that position has no real power or influence behind it."

"That was not always the case," Yrtalien said softly. "Once, long ago, the Shadow Court was a force to be reckoned with."

"Those days are gone," Valmont replied. "I am, above all, a realist—if that word can be said to apply to children of the Dreaming. The Shadow Court is only as powerful as the Seelie rulers allow it to be. I foresee no great changes in the current pecking order."

"But I do." There was an almost palpable vehemence in Yrtalien's voice. Valmont took an involuntary step backward. The eshu stood silently, waiting for the prince to continue. *I'm not sure where this is going,* he thought, *and I'm not sure I want to know.*

Yrtalien laughed softly, breaking the sudden tension.

"Forgive me," he said. "I did not intend to be so abrupt. I wanted to speak with you because you—and others like you—represent a great, untapped force for change and growth." The prince shook his head. "I am the first of the offenders," he said ruefully. "I feel that I have been remiss in seeking you out."

"You were otherwise occupied," Valmont said. "I understand that you and Leigh are old friends."

"We knew each other in Arcadia," Yrtalien replied. "I'm afraid I succumbed to the desire to renew our old acquaintance." The prince smiled. "I have noticed that you have found your own source of amusement in my freehold," he said.

"Oh?" Valmont tried to sound casual.

Yrtalien reached for a small object resting on a table near his chair. He held it out to Valmont.

"Kanani asked me to give this to you," he said. "That was the other reason I wanted to see you privately."

Valmont accepted the proffered gift, a circular onyx brooch. "This is from Kanani?" he asked.

"She did not feel it was proper to give it to you herself," Yrtalien explained. "Among her people, courtship is generally conducted through mediaries."

"I spent some time with the menehune," Valmont said, pinning the brooch to his vest, "but I admit I did not think to ask them about their courtship rituals."

"She is quite fond of you," the prince added. "She

will be pleased to know that her feelings are returned. Of course, this gift does not signify a lasting commitment, but it does indicate that she welcomes your attention."

Valmont nodded. "I wish I had something to give her in return," he said. "Should I thank her directly?"

Yrtalien shook his head. "I will convey your thanks," he replied, "but a gift from you at this point would be precipitous."

Valmont laughed. "I think I understand. I need to make it seem as if I have given the matter a great deal of thought, although I already know how I feel." His handsome face grew somber. "I do care for Kanani," he said.

"I know," Yrtalien responded. "Your attentions to her have not gone unnoticed."

"Have we been that obvious?" Valmont asked.

Yrtalien nodded gravely, but his dark eyes shone with mischief. Valmont felt himself warming to the prince. *I must remember that he is still new to this world*, the eshu told himself. *In many ways, he is like a child learning unfamiliar customs.*

"Now that I have discharged my duty as matchmaker," Yrtalien said, "perhaps we can speak of other pressing matters." He shifted in his seat, removing his feet from atop the ottoman and gesturing for Valmont to sit.

"To put it plainly," the prince said, "I would like to enlist your expertise as a member of my Shadow Court."

"I'm listening," Valmont said.

Leigh waited for more than an hour before the door opened and Valmont left the library alone. Catching the eshu by the arm, Leigh dragged him into an

t h ε   h i l l

unoccupied parlor a few doors down and asked him again about his suspicions.

Valmont gave Leigh a puzzled look. "I said that?" he asked her mildly. "I must have been mistaken. The prince has no designs on Kanani whatsoever," he said. "I, however, have an appointment with the maiden for a walk in the gardens in just a few minutes." The eshu smiled at Leigh. "If you'll excuse me," he mumured as he left her and hurried toward the rear doorway of the palace.

In his room, Edmund admired his new chimerical armor in the mirror. He did his best imitation of a knightly posture, his shoulder blades thrown back so hard they hurt, and his sword hand held across his body, the fingers just touching the blade of his short sword.

"Whaddya think, Mr. Dumpy?" he asked the chimerical clown that perched on the foot of Edmund's pirate-ship shaped bed. "Is this cool or what?"

Mr. Dumpy smiled approvingly at the diminutive redcap knight.

Edmund marched around the room, listening to his boot heels clink softly on the polished wooden floor.

"I dunno why everyone thinks the prince is such a bad guy," Edmund said. "He gave me this way cool armor and he even promised me a horse if we stay here long enough. Do you think we should stay, or not?"

Mr. Dumpy shrugged.

"Y'know, I think the prince is sweet on Leigh," the redcap confided. "Personally, I think Glynnis is much more of a babe than Leigh, but there's no accounting for taste, I guess."

The clown nodded his head sympathetically.

"The prince told me that if he and Leigh can get it together, we'll all be rolling in Glamour from now until the Long Winter."

Mr. Dumpy looked impressed. "The prince says he'll knight me just as soon as I do something that will give him an excuse to do so. I think it would be way cool to be a knight. Leigh's a knight and she's only a girl and everybody thinks she's hot shit."

Edmund got tired of patrolling his room and sat down on the bed next to his chimerical friend.

"Yrtalien asked me to do something that he said would guarantee that Leigh will decide to stay with him. I dunno whether I should do it or not."

Mr. Dumpy regarded Edmund thoughtfully.

"Help me out here," the redcap said. "I gotta decide before it all comes down tomorrow night."

Mr. Dumpy patted Edmund on the shoulder.

"Yeah, I know it's my own decision," he said. "But I'm stuck."

Edmund jumped down from the bed and rummaged around in a pile of discarded clothing until he unearthed a handful of marbles. He returned to his seat beside the clown and munched on the crunchy taws and agates, his eyes screwed shut in contemplation.

Finally, as he swallowed the last marble, he came to a decision. "I gotta do the right thing for all of us," he said officiously. "That's what a real knight does."

Mr. Dumpy smiled happily.

Edmund decided he felt like going outside for some sword practice.

"You gotta get back in my pouch," he told Mr. Dumpy. "We'll talk again later on tonight, okay?" The chimera obediently allowed itself to shrink back to its physical form so that the redcap could stow it carefully in its pouch.

t h e   h i l l

I wonder what color horse it will be? Edmund wondered as he left his room and tried running down the stairs in his gleaming blue-black armor.

Late that night, when the rest of the freehold either slept or lay in a comatose stupor from the day's overindulgences, Ryder woke screaming from the pain that turned his hand to molten fire.

For a few minutes, he lay bathed in his own sweat, half expecting either Diana or Signe to come bursting into his room to find out what had caused his sudden outburst. When neither one arrived, he realized that his outcry had not traveled beyond the walls of his room.

He struggled to sit up, fighting the waves of pain that washed through him. *One more day and I can leave this place,* he thought. *One more night and I will have kept my bargain with that spawn of darkness and the Kithain I have been seeking will be mine.*

He stood up, intending to spend the rest of the evening pacing around his room to stave off the agony in his palm, but an attack of dizziness drove him back onto the bed. He panted as his chest muscles tightened, threatening to cut off his breath. He tried massaging his hand, but that only increased his torment. It was as if the stone had a mind of its own and was willing the pain to multiply exponentially. *Maybe it's not the stone,* he thought, as a bone-chilling cold swept through him, sending him into uncontrollable shivers.

This has got to stop, he told himself, but he realized that there was only one way to bring an end to this particularly vicious bout of suffering. Clutching his hand to his chest and grabbing the bedpost for support, he clambered to his feet and launched himself in the direction of the door.

Haltingly, using the walls for support, he left his chambers and made his way down the length of the palace to the prince's rooms. He fell against the door, the thud of his body serving in place of a knock. The door opened almost immediately.

Yrtalien was waiting for him when he staggered through the open doorway.

"I thought you'd be here," the prince said, a beatific smile on his face.

"Please," Ryder heard himself say. Helplessly he held his hand out to the prince.

Yrtalien looked at it and shrugged. He closed the door and paced in a circle around the haggard, pain-wracked Dauntain. Stopping in front of Ryder, he pointed to the floor. Inwardly cursing himself, Ryder sank to his knees, still holding his hand outstretched toward the prince.

Yrtalien laughed. "Since you insist," he said softly, the Shadowstone already in his hand.

"By the way," he informed the Dauntain. "I've changed my mind. You can have Eleighanara as well."

Ryder closed his eyes and waited for his release.

t h e   h i l l

chapter

twelve

The gargantuan beast slumbered deep within the mountain's rocky heart. Born in eons past from the dreams of the world itself, her spirit had learned early to clothe itself in flesh. Hers was the flesh of earth and rock, adorned with perpetual leis of roots and leaves and ferns and flowers. In the ages when the tales spun by human Dreamers still possessed the power to make substance out of shadow and give names to that which had heretofore been nameless, she sometimes stirred her massive bulk in answer to the name accorded her: Pele, goddess of the fire, spirit of the volcano.

Along with all the other deep spirits of the earth, she felt the first tremors of disbelief as the cold winds of the Sundering began to whisper their icy message of Banality across the face of the world. Fearing the destruction of her soul, she sought refuge in her mortal body's molten core, protected from the cold instruments of science and the colder hearts of the scientists and explorers who named her volcano, and who defined her body in alien terms: caldera, lava flow, steam vent, crater.

Shrouded in enchantments, her raw dream-flesh armored by molten rock and crusted stone, she grew weary of waiting for the danger to pass. She slept. Occasionally, she moved within her sleep, disturbed by some vague troubling in the depths of her rocky bed. Then, she belched forth flame and smoke, her hot breath spiced with the sulfurous fumes of molten rock. At other times, her body would ooze forth tears and blood, and flaming gouts of sluggish lava or sudden bursts of steam erupted from her restless form, breaking past her barricade of rock and piercing the surface of the earth.

Mortal eyes gazed upon her, and their stunted senses saw only the volcanic mountain. It was only through the eyes of the Dreaming, through the faerie sight that penetrated the Mists and saw behind the layers of cold rationality, that she could be seen for what she really was—a creature of raw and brutal splendor, a Dreamchild born from the oldest of dreams. Occasionally, just before she shifted in her sleep, she would dream, and in her dream a small part of her would assume a form patterned after the creatures who now walked the earth. In her dream-shape, she, too, would walk the surface of her own body, treading on the blanket of soil that covered her sleeping form. From these manifestations grew the legends that told how Pele wandered over the land, giving warning that the earth around her would soon erupt in flame.

She was so old that her true form had many shapes and many names, depending on the imaginings of those who were so lucky—or so foolish—to see her undisguised splendor. One of those names was dragon.

On the morning of the winter solstice, Yrtalien's guests awoke to view with astonishment the blanket of chimerical snow covering the grounds of the palace. In the downstairs rooms, crackling fires that gave off light without heat from fireplaces that had not been there the night before. Winter greenery garlanded the walls and hung from the chandeliers. The enticing aroma of mulled cider and cinnamon filled the palace.

"Snowball fight!" cried Edmund, barreling out of his room and nearly colliding with Morgan, who was bundled up in layers of chimerical finery suitable for winter's chill.

"You look like a stuffed panda," the redcap said,

eyeing Morgan's long black coat lined with puffy white fur.

"I'm going to build a snow castle," Morgan informed Edmund. "Want to help?"

Edmund looked at the sidhe childling suspiciously.

"I don't do heavy labor," he said.

Morgan shrugged. "Then you can be the captain of the guard," she said, shoving her mittened hands into her white fur muff and starting down the stairs.

"That's cool," Edmund said, running past Morgan to be the first of the pair to savor the icy wonderland outside.

Positioning himself squarely in front of the door to the palace, the redcap scooped up a handful of snow in his bare hands and formed it into a solid ball. As Morgan walked sedately out the door, he drew back his arm and launched his missile. The snowball struck Morgan on the shoulder, bursting in a powdery shower of white flakes.

"Gotcha!" Edmund chortled. Then he looked thoughtfully at his hand. "Hey!" he said. "It's not cold!"

Morgan squealed as the snowball splattered on her coat. She pulled her hands out of her muff and bent down to gather up her own supply of snow. A second snowball smacked her in the cheek.

"That's not fair!" she cried, reaching up to brush the snow off her face. Like Edmund, she paused in her activity and looked puzzled. "It's *not* cold," she said, echoing Edmund's observation.

"Well, duh," the redcap said. "Maybe it's 'cause we're in Hawaii. Maybe the snow doesn't get cold here."

"This is the tropics," Morgan reminded him. She started to say, "I saw a program on the Nature Channel..." but a gentle pressure on her shoulder interrupted her. She turned to find Rasputin standing behind her.

"Don't let me interrupt you," the pooka drawled. "I think it would be a wonderful idea if you exposed this enchanted landscape to scientific explanations of weather and climate."

Morgan's eyes widened and she covered her mouth with a mittened hand. "Oops," she mumbled indistinctly.

"Salvo!" Edmund cried. The redcap had taken advantage of the exchange between Morgan and Rasputin to amass a pile of hastily packed snowballs. Morgan ducked behind Rasputin as Edmund launched his onslaught of missiles. The pooka caught several of them in mid-air and sent a return volley toward the redcap. Kneeling in the snow behind Rasputin, Morgan busied herself making more snowballs and feeding them to her protector. Edmund changed tactics, darting about in the snow to find an angle where Morgan's body was exposed.

Soon the three Kithain were covered in powdery snow.

"My arms are tired!" Edmund called out.

"Truce!" Morgan said. "So are mine!"

"I could keep this up all day," Rasputin admitted, rubbing his forearms vigorously. "Leigh told me she didn't want to see either of you right away."

"Why?" Morgan asked. "Is something wrong?"

Rasputin shook his head. "Nothing at all," he said, holding out a hand for Morgan to take as he turned and headed back inside the palace. Edmund grabbed a last handful of snow and shoved it into his pocket. *If it's chimerical, maybe it won't melt,* he thought.

"So that was snow," the redcap muttered as he followed the others into the palace.

t h e   h i l l

Leigh and Tor were waiting upstairs in the sitting room of Leigh's suite as Rasputin entered with the two childlings in tow.

"Where's Valmont?" Leigh asked.

"I didn't look for him," Rasputin said. "Everybody I asked said they had seen him."

Leigh nodded, her face grim. "We'll have to catch up with him later," she said.

Morgan wrinkled her brows at Leigh's brusque tone. "What's the matter?" she asked.

"I've been a fool," Leigh said bitterly.

"We all have," Tor responded.

"That's not true," Rasputin said.

"What is this, a twelve-step support group?" Edmund sneered. He flopped down on the sofa not far from the door and propped his legs up on the polished teak table.

Leigh shook her head. "Hardly," she said. She drew a deep breath. "Last night, Yrtalien tried to get me to join his cause."

"Tell it to them like you told it to me and Rasputin," Tor said.

"I'll try," said Leigh. Haltingly, Leigh informed the others of her conversation with Yrtalien and of its disturbing end. "We practically declared war on each other before I left him," she said. "He wants the Keystone."

Morgan's eyes grew large.

"Lady Glynnis tried to get me to borrow the Keystone from you so she could teach me how to use it to make Glamour work better," she said in a breathy voice. "She even hinted that I should steal it from you—only temporarily—if you didn't want to let me borrow it."

"What a surprise," Rasputin muttered from his place near the sitting room window.

"Were any of the rest of you approached about

acquiring the stone?" Leigh asked, looking around at her oathmates.

"Nah," Tor rumbled. "I spent most of my time trying to get Lord Devlin off my back."

Morgan giggled. "I think he's funny," she said. "He always seems so proud of himself." She tossed back an imaginary mane of silver hair as she spoke.

Leigh found herself smiling despite her troubled heart.

Tor grunted. "You wouldn't think he was so funny if you saw him out ravaging the crafters in town," the troll snarled. "He tried to talk me into doing it, too."

"You didn't, did you, Grandpa?" Morgan asked, suddenly concerned.

Tor shook his head. "He gave me a shot of second-hand Glamour he'd collected, though. I'm still not certain how he did it," the troll mumbled.

"This whole place has been very deceptive," Leigh said. "From the beginning, they've tried to divide and conquer." She waved an arm in front of her, indicating her lavishly decorated set of rooms. "Separate suites for all of us, individual temptations, no time to get together and compare our experiences. It seems to me that even the party was calculated, providing a constant background of distractions that would make it hard for us to keep track of each other."

"I guess we didn't do a very good job of pretending to be Unseelie," Morgan said doubtfully. "Otherwise they wouldn't have had to try so hard to win us over."

"Oh, I never thought that we'd convince them we were anything other than what we are," Leigh said.

"What *did* you think?" Morgan asked.

Leigh's eyes softened and a wistful smile played at the corners of her mouth. "I guess I thought that somehow we could win them—him—over. That's what I mean about being a fool," she said.

Morgan got up from her seat on the overstuffed footstool in front of the armchair her grandfather occupied. She walked over to Leigh and hugged her.

Edmund rolled his eyes. "Sheesh," he muttered to himself.

"You've been exceptionally talkative and disruptive," Rasputin said to the redcap. "Are you feeling well?"

Edmund brushed his dreadlocks away from his face and folded his arms across his chest.

"You're always telling me to shut up," he said. "I just thought I'd save you the trouble this time."

Leigh returned Morgan's hug. Keeping one arm around the childling, she cleared her throat to get the attention of the others.

"There's something else," she said. "A few nights ago, Valmont had a talk with me and Tor and Rasputin."

"I know," said Morgan. "I wondered why you left me and Edmund out of it."

"Valmont didn't want to get you upset about something he only thought might be happening."

"What was that?" Morgan asked.

"You remember that Chief Makani asked us to make sure Kanani was safe?" Leigh watched as the others nodded their heads. "Something she said to Valmont made him believe that Yrtalien has been preparing her to be a sacrificial victim of some kind."

Morgan sucked in her breath sharply. "But she's Kithain! It's against all the laws of the Dreaming for one Kithain to kill another."

"It would be just as wrong if she were mortal," Leigh said sharply.

"What made Valmont think the prince is planning to sacrifice her?" the childling asked.

"According to Valmont," Leigh said, "some ancient societies used to select a beautiful maiden or young man from among their population. They would spend a period of time showering every sort of honor and luxury on that person, even according them the status of a god or a great ruler. Then they would hold a festival and offer the life of that person to whatever deity they worshipped."

"Like the Aztecs?" Morgan offered.

Leigh nodded.

"Let's not mention the rumors about the druids," Rasputin added. "And especially let's not talk about the *tiend*."

"The what?" Morgan asked, screwing up her face at the unfamiliar word.

"I thought you knew all about faeries," Leigh said, chidingly. "The word means tithe or offering. Human legends about the faeries talk about the tithe to hell paid every seven years by the high king or queen."

"That's disgusting!" Morgan said.

Leigh nodded her agreement. "I don't think the legends were accurate," she continued. She looked around. "I wish Valmont were here," she said. "He's better at storytelling than I."

"Well, he's not," Tor said, "so just tell it as best you can. Remember, Rasputin and I have already heard it once."

"I'll try," Leigh said. "Valmont says that one of the stories his kith have preserved in their wanderings hints that the real offering wasn't to hell, but to the world of the dead, and that it was the price the faeries paid for immortality. Every seven years, on Samhain Eve—"

"—Halloween!" Morgan offered helpfully.

"Yes," Leigh said. "On the night when the borders between the living and the dead became thin enough for spirits to walk the earth, the faeries would send their chosen offering—usually one of their own—to the Underworld. In later times, when the faeries noticed that Glamour was beginning to fade, some of them tried to cheat by taking mortals to live among them and using *them* as their offering. My father used to sing an old Scottish ballad about a human knight who was kidnapped by the queen of the faeries and rescued by his lover before he could be used to pay the *tiend*."

"We studied about Orpheus in school," Morgan said. "He didn't die, though. He just walked right through the gates of Hades or something like that."

"But it's not Halloween," Edmund muttered from the sofa.

"I know," said Leigh. "But it is the winter solstice, and the longest night of the year. It is, in fact, the highpoint of the Unseelie half of the year, which used to begin on Samhain Eve."

"So what makes you think that Yrtalien is going to do something to Kanani tonight?" Morgan asked.

"I didn't think so at first," Leigh admitted. "That was Valmont's idea. Tor and Rasputin and I didn't think his theory held water. Something Yrtalien said to me last night made me change my mind." Leigh closed her eyes, trying to recall the prince's exact phrasing. "He called it the winter solstice *ceremony*, for one thing." Leigh opened her eyes to watch the faces of her companions for their reactions to her words. "To me, that implies some sort of ritual."

Tor nodded encouragement.

"He also said that he would secure his power with an offering of Glamour *the like of which has not been seen since before the Sundering*. The last part was what made me think that he was planning to sacrifice one of the fae. That was what made me recall Valmont's fears about Kanani."

Morgan's expression became determined. "Then we'll just have to find Kanani and take her back to her father's village," she said. "Where is she?"

Leigh shook her head. "That's part of the problem," she replied. "None of us have seen her today."

"Maybe Valmont's gone to look for her," Morgan said. "If he believes—"

"—that's the other part of the problem," Leigh interrupted. "I wasn't the only one who had a conversation with the prince. Yrtalien talked to Valmont last night as well, and now Valmont is insisting that he was mistaken about Kanani."

There was a knock on Leigh's door. Tor rose to answer. Opening the door a fraction of an inch, he glanced into the hallway, and then held the door open to admit Valmont. He looked as if he had just got out of bed.

"Lady Siva said you've been looking for me," he said as he entered the room and took a seat beside Edmund on the sofa.

"Where have you been?" asked Tor.

"I was in bed," he replied.

"I sent Rasputin to look in your rooms," said Leigh. "He said—I mean he gave us to understand that you weren't there."

Valmont smiled and shrugged. "I didn't say I was in *my* bed," he replied blandly.

Leigh raised an eyebrow.

"Where'd you get the pin?" Morgan asked, looking closely at Valmont.

"What, this?" Valmont pointed to a small onyx circle he wore on the lapel of his long crimson vest. "It was a gift from the prince," The eshu said. "He gave it to me last night as a token of—"

"Take it off!" Leigh commanded.

Valmont's brows furrowed. "Why?" he asked.

"Just do it, or I'll come over and remove it myself," she said, her voice stern.

Valmont shrugged and lifted his hand to comply. His

fingers paused inches away from the pin. A puzzled look came over the eshu's face.

"I can't seem to reach it," he said quietly.

Tor strode over to the eshu and tore the pin away, ripping the cloth of the vest as he did so. Holding it in his hand, he looked at Leigh questioningly. She got up and opened the window, and Tor threw the pin as hard as he could to the ground two stories below.

Leigh walked across the room and stood in front of Valmont.

"Now do you still believe that Yrtalien intends no harm to Kanani?" she asked him.

Valmont closed his eyes and lowered his head to hide the expression of horror on his face.

"That bastard," he muttered softly. "He told me Kanani had asked him to give the pin to me. He said that he was acting on her behalf—"

"And you believed him," Leigh said, her voice accusing.

The eshu nodded, his shoulders slumped in shame. "I was a fool," he said. "I let him ensorcel me through one of the oldest cons of all."

"Thank goodness you were the only one," Rasputin said brightly.

"What's done is done," Tor said. "Let's decide what we're going to do."

Valmont raised his head. Avoiding Leigh's eyes, he sent the troll a look of gratitude.

"What have I missed?" he asked, a rare note of humility in his voice.

Taking a deep breath, Leigh repeated her story for the third time that morning.

By the time she was finished, it was already early afternoon.

"I still think we need to find Kanani," Morgan said. "If the prince has hidden her away somewhere, we can rescue her and then get the Shadowstone away from him."

"That's a good idea," Leigh said. "How do you suggest we do it?"

Morgan assumed her favorite innocent expression. "I thought you could take care of the planning part," she said to Leigh.

"Morgan is on the right track," Valmont said, some semblance of confidence returning to his voice. "The first thing we need to do is locate Kanani. Have you checked the garden?"

Leigh nodded. "We've looked everywhere." She hesitated, then gave Valmont a curious glance. "I thought you said that you spent the night—"

"In Lady Siva's room," Valmont said, giving his companions an embarrassed smile. "I'm not really sure how that happened—"

"The prince's ensorcelment couldn't have had anything to do with that," Rasputin observed.

"It's not important," Leigh said, although her voice sounded less convincing than her words. "So you haven't seen Kanani since yesterday either? You told me last night you had an appointment with her."

"I did," Valmont said. "At least I believe I did. Now I'm not sure. I remember meeting her in the garden and walking with her, but I don't remember anything we said."

"It's a big garden," Morgan announced. "Maybe you just weren't looking in the right place at the right time."

Leigh nodded. "We have to start somewhere," she said. The companions rose to begin their search, but Leigh called them to a stop.

"Now what?" Edmund groaned.

"There was one other thing," Leigh said. "The prince knows about Silver's Gate and he knows that four stones are needed to open it."

"How did he discover that bit of information?" Valmont asked.

Leigh sighed heavily. "I told him," she said simply. This time, it was she who avoided the eshu's gaze.

As early as he could, Ryder slipped away from the prince's freehold and walked across town to the Seacrest Hotel, where Vargas was waiting for him in his room.

"I got your last message," the wiry Latino said after greeting his companion. "Everything is ready." Vargas motioned to the small pile of leather satchels and the long, flat pouch that had traveled with the Dauntain from San Francisco.

"Good," Ryder said. "I spoke with Signe and Diana this morning, and they know what they are supposed to do." Ryder repeated the instructions he had given his other companions. Vargas listened intently, his gaze concentrated on Ryder's face.

"You look different, somehow," he said, when Ryder had finished speaking. "It is as if years have dropped away from you." He raised an eyebrow in sudden comprehension. "You are no longer in pain," he said.

Ryder nodded.

"Do you wish to tell me about this?" Vargas asked, his voice carefully neutral.

Ryder closed his eyes and sat heavily on the bed. As briefly as he could, without sparing the details of his humiliation, he told Vargas of his discovery by Yrtalien and of the bargain he had been forced to make. His eyes, when he finally opened them, were full of pleading.

Vargas was silent for a moment. Then he nodded at Ryder in solemn understanding.

"I cannot say that I condone your compromise," he began, "but in the service of our sacred duty, hard choices must sometimes be made."

Ryder looked relieved.

"I had to make sure that our targets did not discover our presence in the palace," he said.

"And this *prince* has assured you that he will deliver the ones we seek into our hands?"

Ryder nodded. "He has made certain that they will not find out where he has taken his sacrificial victim until after we have placed ourselves in a position where we can take them by surprise. We will have to leave now to make sure that we have the time we need."

"I do not like the idea that we will be assisting this servant of madness in achieving the goal of his sacrifice," Vargas said, his voice heavy with disapproval. "That he would stoop to such a deed only proves the depths of his darkness."

"I don't like the thought of human sacrifice either," Ryder said. "Even if the girl is one of them, her body and soul are still human. I have sworn that I will do nothing to interfere with Yrtalien's schemes in return for the opportunity to capture our targets. However, I made no promises that are binding where your actions are concerned."

A slow smile spread over Vargas' face. He nodded his understanding. "You and the others concentrate on the Kithain we originally came here to find," he said. "I will deal with the prince."

"It is my intention to take as many of them alive as possible," Ryder said. "Some of them may be worth saving."

Vargas nodded again.

"What you do with Yrtalien," the Dauntain leader went on to say, "is no concern of mine."

The garden was empty. As the companions broadened their search to include the rest of the palace grounds and, finally, the palace itself, they discovered that nearly all the Kithain who had so lately ranged throughout the freehold had apparently departed. Only the human servants and a cluster of nockers recovering from the night before remained within the palace.

"Where is everybody?" Morgan asked one groggy nocker female who sat in the kitchen of the palace, hanging her head over a cup of steaming cider. The bleary-eyed Kithain looked up at the childling and hiccupped before answering.

"They've gone to the volcano," she said. "The prince is going to wake the sleeping dragon at midnight."

"Which volcano?" Valmont demanded.

"Dragon?" Edmund repeated, his interest piqued.

The nocker blew the steam from her mug and took a long slurp.

"Kilauea," she replied. "Home of Pele and the dragon."

"We'll never get there in time!" Morgan wailed as she and the companions rushed back to their rooms to get their things. "It's nearly dark already."

"Morgan's right," Leigh said, her voice despairing. "It's over twenty miles from here and it's a big volcano."

Valmont looked thoughtful for a moment. Then his expression brightened.

"I can take us there," the eshu said.

"Last time, you got us lost," Edmund reminded him.

"No he didn't," Morgan said, her voice soft. Her eyes were closed and there was a small smile on her face.

"He was just ahead of himself."

"There's still the problem of getting us there in time," Leigh said.

Valmont shook his head. "No, there isn't," he said. "My kith are masters of the journey. I have once been to a place close to where we need to be. With the luck that seems to favor you," he looked at Morgan and smiled as the sidhe childling nodded her head, "I should be able to return us to that spot."

"How does it work?" asked Tor.

"I need a map of the island," said Valmont. Leigh quickly rummaged in her backpack and retrieved the guidebook she had bought her first day in Hilo. She handed it triumphantly to Valmont. The eshu flipped through the book until he found the page he wanted, then tore it out and placed it on the floor.

"Now I need a pen," he said. He grimaced when Morgan handed him her pink ballpoint, but murmured his thanks. He drew a bright pink circle on the map labeled Hawaii Volcanoes National Park.

"This is approximately where we were when we met the old woman," the eshu said.

"You mean Pele?" Morgan asked.

Valmont nodded. He stood up and motioned the others to circle around the map. "Do we have everything we are going to need?" he asked. "I doubt we'll be returning here later."

When everyone was ready, Valmont thrust his arms, one hand atop the other, into the center of the circle, directly over the map.

"Grasp my hands," he said, "and close your eyes."

"This is like when we swore our oath," Morgan whispered, remembering an afternoon three months earlier, when the companions had gathered in the Toybox to begin their quest with a binding oath of loyalty and fellowship.

t h e   h i l l

"Isn't this a little risky?" Leigh asked, looking at Valmont through eyes that were partly shut.

The eshu nodded. "If it weren't," he said, "I wouldn't be as good at it. Now close your eyes!"

Leigh did as he requested.

"Help me with this, Morgan," Valmont said. Her eyes still closed, Morgan nodded her head and began to imagine herself and her companions sitting by their cookfire while the white-haired crone sucked on a piece of fresh pineapple. She could feel the bright tingle of Glamour welling up inside her and she clicked her heels together to send its power from her body into the center of the circle.

"Whoaaa!" Edmund whooped as the ground seemed to drop out from under him. He felt the grip of his companions' hands tighten and knew that they were all experiencing the same sensation. A hot flush swept through his body and his stomach lurched. Then he was standing once more on solid ground.

"We're here," Valmont announced.

One by one, the oathmates opened their eyes and looked around them in the growing darkness.

"This is the spot, all right," rumbled Tor, pointing to the dark shape formed by a jagged rock that thrust itself out of the ground. "That looks familiar."

Rasputin clapped his hands together over his head. Reaching behind his left ear, he drew out a slender tubular rod of soft blue chimerical light.

"I thought we might want to stumble all over ourselves," he said. Leigh nodded her approval.

"That was an incredible display," she said to the eshu. "I'm impressed."

"So am I," Valmont admitted. "I've never done it successfully before."

"Now which way do we go?" she asked.

"Why don't we head for that bright red glow over

there?" Morgan suggested, pointing to a place in the distance where an eerie incandescence lit up the sky.

"I was just about to suggest that direction myself," said Valmont. Guided by the light of Pele's fires, their passage eased by the pale blue glow from Rasputin's chimerical wand, the oathmates began their trek across a landscape that grew more and more alien with each step.

Yrtalien and Glynnis stood as near as they dared to the satellite crater known as Pu'u O'o, an active volcanic rift on the eastern edge of Kilauea. Behind the prince, Argo held the comatose form of Kanani in his sturdy arms. Farther down the slope of the volcano, unwilling to draw any closer to the trail of flowing lava that slowly trickled from the fissures in the ground, a group of nervous courtiers stirred restlessly, eager to be gone from a place of such obvious danger yet fascinated by the lure of the spectacle they were about to behold. Holding a scented handkerchief to his nose to counteract the smoky fumes that thickened the air around him, Lord Devlin stood with the spectators, content for once to be just one among the crowd.

Glynnis started as a roiling bubble of liquid magma gurgled out of the ground a little too close for her comfort. She breathed a sigh of relief as it disappeared back into the blackened earth.

"It will resurface farther down the slope," said Yrtalien, calmly. "We are well within the limits of acceptable risk where we are."

"I do not believe the crowd will wait until midnight, my lord," Glynnis said, trying to keep her voice from betraying her own desire to leave the area.

The prince looked about him and shrugged.

"You may be right," he said. "I keep forgetting that they are still too cowed by their own mortal frailty to enjoy the thrill of placing their lives in peril. Very well," he announced. "Let's be done with this."

Raising his hands high in the air, aware of the smoky reddish glow that served as a distant backlight for his form, Yrtalien turned around and took a step toward the waiting crowd.

"Children of the Long Winter that precedes the Return of the Dreaming," he began. "We stand in one of the few places in this mortal world where the earth is still alive to the presence of the Dreaming. We live in a time of change, a time when old traditions should be broken and new traditions formed—a time when even older traditions cry out to be reawakened. It is my purpose in coming here to reenact a tradition that has been ignored for too long.

"Gone is the age in which we could stand high above the lip of the volcano and cast our finest treasures into its seething cauldron. Too much of the earth lies dormant, numbed by the lack of belief in its living, breathing spirit. This," he made a sweeping gesture with his hand toward the smoking rift behind him in the distance, "is what is left of the pulsing heartbeat of a once proud and noble creature of the realm of dreams. Beneath this mountain, a dragon sleeps, no longer honored, no longer feared, no longer part of the world that denies her existence.

"Tonight, we will offer her a prize for which she has hungered for years beyond counting. Tonight, we offer her one of our own, a child of the Dreaming who has lived among us and received our care and our affections. Here, within the fiery cauldron of rebirth, her Glamour will merge with the spirit of the dragon. Her sacrifice will mark the resurgence of the true

Court of Shadows, whose other name is the Court of Constant Changes."

"There they are!" Morgan whispered loudly as she caught sight, still in the distance, of the figure of the Forsworn Prince silhouetted against the smoky red sky. "Hurry!" she begged, stepping up her pace over the cracked and rocky ground.

"It's not midnight," Edmund called loudly from the rear of the group.

"Hush," Tor whispered fiercely. "It might be hard to see out here, but that doesn't mean we can't be heard."

"Sorry," Edmund muttered, his voice still well above his normal conversational tone.

"Maybe they don't know what time it is," Rasputin offered in a muted voice.

Valmont saw the shape of one of Yrtalien's troll bodyguards begin walking toward a stream of sluggishly flowing lava, its blackened crust occasionally punctured by a flare of molten red liquid.

"I'm going in!" the eshu announced. "It's now or never for Kanani!" Drawing his scimitar, Valmont let out a bloodcurdling scream and dashed forward, boosting his speed with a sudden outpouring of his personal Glamour.

From his place of concealment, Ryder and his companions watched the line of Kithain move past him. As Valmont signaled his charge, Ryder gave his own signal to Vargas and the others.

t h e   h i l l

"Now!" an unfamiliar voice cried out from somewhere behind the oathmates. Morgan shrieked as a shadowy form rushed toward her in the darkness, nearly colliding with her as she attempted to thrust herself out of her attacker's path. She stumbled on the uneven surface of ropy volcanic rock and lost her balance.

Tor's battle-trained ears heard a hollow thunking sound.

"Flare!" he called out, and drew his battle ax, trying to spot Morgan as the darkness exploded suddenly in a brilliant flash of man-made daylight. He saw a figure in gleaming black armor raise a glowing chimerical sword above the fallen childling.

"His hand!" Morgan screamed. "He's got one of the eyestones in his hand. It's glowing!"

As he raised his own weapon to deflect the blow meant for Morgan, Tor had time to see the brilliant blue sapphire embedded in the strange knight's left palm.

"You'll have to kill me before you so much as touch her," Tor snarled, stepping over Morgan to engage her attacker.

"Done," the knight replied and took a step back up the slope to allow Tor to square off against him.

Leigh turned around at the sound of Morgan's cry. Warned by Tor, she shut her eyes just as the flare lit up the night. When she opened them again, her sword at the ready, she saw that her way to the sidhe childling was blocked by a brawny female troll. She recognized her as the Kithain called Diana, one of the prince's guests. Now Diana was wearing dull, blackened leather armor and she carried a heavy club capped with iron.

She'll be slow, Leigh thought, *but as strong as she looks, I don't know if I can afford to take even one of her blows.* She thrust her chimerical sword above her head at an angle which she hoped would block the club as far from its iron tip as possible. A chilling thought crossed her mind. *If her iron hits my sword, I'll have to use my hands and feet.* She breathed a sigh of relief as her aim was true, meeting the force of Diana's weapon halfway down its length. Leigh's sword arm ached from the jarring impact. She felt a sting as something hard slammed into the back of her neck. *A snowball?* Her concentration momentarily broken, she barely had time to dodge the troll's next blow.

"Oops! I'm coming!" she heard Edmund call out and caught a glimpse from the corner of her eye of the redcap's racing figure. Edmund held his sword almost straight out in front of him, swinging it wildly about as he let loose with a volley of nearly unintelligible epithets.

"Duck!" he yelled, a fraction of a second too late as his sword slashed perilously close to Leigh's side. She felt something at her belt give way and realized that the redcap's erratically aimed blow had severed the string which held the leather pouch containing the eyestone.

"I got it!" Edmund cried, bending over to snatch up the pouch in his free hand. On impulse, the redcap scooped up a small piece of volcanic rock that lay near the red leather pouch. "Don't worry about it," he assured Leigh.

She nodded, concentrating on her opponent's next move and stepping quickly out of the way of the descending club. "Sorry," she heard the redcap mutter. She thrust her own weapon upward, aiming for the troll's midsection, and smiled grimly as she felt it connect with Diana's lower ribs. As the troll grunted and stepped back to absorb the blow, Leigh glanced down at her side where Edmund had so recently been. He was gone. Out of the corner of her eye, she saw him heading toward a spot farther up the slope, where Tor battled a dark-armored knight whose palm was wreathed in a sapphire-blue radiance.

Valmont reached the edge of the lava flow at nearly the same moment as Yrtalien's bodyguard. Even as he lowered his head for a full body rush, the only maneuver that stood a chance of bearing the troll away from the deadly river of molten sludge, he heard footsteps behind him and felt the rush of air that marked the sound of a weapon poised to strike.

"No!" he screamed. "Not now! Help me save the girl! We can fight later!"

"That's a bargain," a female voice answered him and Valmont saw a slender eshu armed with an iron pipe move to his side. "My name is Signe," she said, her words coming out in a breathless rush. "You aim for his gut, I'll go for his legs."

Yrtalien stood above the battle, his expression a mixture of excitement and annoyance.

"They were supposed to wait until after the sacrifice," he complained to Glynnis. "Damn those fools."

"It is you who are damned," a male voice with a slight accent called out from the darkness. Stepping forward, Vargas braced himself and let go a blast from the rifle he held pointed at the prince.

At the sound of the gun's report, Devlin panicked.

"Run!" he screamed to the Kithain standing around him. Not waiting to see if they had heard him, the silver-haired sidhe sprinted blindly down the uneven, rocky slope.

Rasputin saw his chance and raced for Morgan's prone figure. Scooping the childling up in his arms, the pooka carried her out of the immediate arena of battle.

"My ankle hurts," Morgan whimpered. "I can't stand up."

"That's good," Rasputin said. "Don't worry, I'm going to abandon you." He placed his shoulder bag on the ground next to Morgan and, opening it, began to arm himself with a handful of wooden juggling clubs.

"Here," Morgan said, drawing her own chimerical dagger from her belt-sheath and holding it up to Rasputin. The pooka took it and looked at it skeptically, then jammed it firmly between his teeth.

Leigh's arms were beginning to ache; she was holding her sword above her head, slanted at a sharp angle to fend off another resounding blow from Diana's iron-tipped club.

"Don't you ever give up?" the troll bellowed, staggering a little as their weapons came together.

"Not until I'm down," Leigh said. Seeing that her opponent was off balance, she ducked under the troll's arm and swiveled around for a clear cut at Diana's upper thigh. Too late, Leigh realized that she had been misled. The club caught her on the side of the head and she crumpled to the ground.

I can't lose consciousness, she told herself. *I have to remember what I am.*

Struggling to keep hold of the Glamour that still connected her to her faerie nature, Leigh let herself go limp, feigning unconsciousness. She had to clench her jaws to keep from crying out as the troll pulled her arms behind her and slapped a pair of iron manacles on her wrists. The touch of the unworked metal sent a wave of nausea through her.

"One down," she heard the troll call out as she fought to keep the mists of forgetfulness from clouding her mind.

Tor and Ryder's battle had taken them dangerously close to the edge of the lava flow. The Dauntain, for the troll was certain that his opponent was the same hunter whom Edmund had encountered in San Francisco three months earlier, was nearly as powerful as Tor. The two combatants had fallen quickly into a steady rhythm of clashing weapons and measured pacing. Only the troll's advantage of height and weight controlled the Dauntain knight's direction, as Tor deliberately forced his opponent into a position from which he could not retreat.

Valmont barreled into Argo's body, willing himself to keep moving, with the hope that the impetus of his forward charge would drive the troll back away from the burning river. As he crashed into the troll, he saw Signe leave his side and move quickly behind their opponent. Her iron pipe flashed sideways, catching the troll behind one knee. With an agonizing groan, Argo lurched back, his leg giving way beneath him.

"I'm right beside you, Tor!" Edmund cried, coming up to stand just a little behind the troll.

"Outta my way!" Tor bellowed. Edmund backed up a step.

"That's real lava!" the redcap muttered, momentarily fascinated by the black and red glowing river only a few feet away from him.

Vargas' bullet caught Yrtalien in the shoulder. Beside him, Glynnis dropped to the ground, a cry of fear escaping from her throat. Yrtalien screamed in pain and clutched his arm. He saw the gunman lift his weapon for a second shot. Bringing his wounded hand up to his throat, he grasped the pouch containing the Shadowstone.

"Take hold of me if you're coming along," he snapped at Glynnis. He concentrated on the gem, willing his thoughts in the direction of a patch of shadowy twisted trees further down the slope. He felt Glynnis catch hold of his shirt and then his senses were swept up in darkness and the rush of displaced air.

Vargas swore as he saw his target disappear before his very eyes. He turned, bitter with defeat, and made his way back toward the other battle.

From his hiding place well below the sounds of the battle, Yrtalien raged at his betrayal. The prince still clutched the Shadowstone in his hand as Glynnis tore a strip of cloth from the edge of her cloak and wrapped it tightly around his arm to help staunch the flow of blood.

"All bargains are off," he muttered, as he concentrated on the stone and loosed its power once again, this time in the direction of his former Dauntain ally. "You thought last night's agony was unbearable," he whispered. "That was nothing compared to this."

As Argo went down with a thud, Valmont recovered his balance and snatched Kanani from the arms of the fallen troll. He walked a few paces away from the lava flow and then stood, uncertain as to his next course of action.

"Give her to me," a cackling voice said from the darkness in front of him. As he stared into the smoky blackness, he saw a familiar, white-haired old woman hobble into his view. She held out her arms.

"She is not part of your world, however much you might care for her," the old woman said. "In all the centuries since they came to this land, the islanders have never presumed to offer this sort of sacrifice to me. I do not accept it. I will return her to her village if you will place her in my keeping."

"Madame Pele," Valmont said, his voice filled with respect and awe, "you asked for our trust once before and you did not lead us astray. I can only place my trust in you again." With a bow, he laid Kanani's barely breathing form in the old woman's arms. "Aloha," he said softly, kissing the maiden's forehead. The fire-goddess carried the maiden as if she weighed no more than the leis that hung from her slender neck.

"Aloha, child of the Dreaming," the old woman whispered and stepped back into the night.

"That's done," Valmont heard Signe's voice behind him. He turned, and caught the full force of her iron pipe across his throat.

Rasputin heard the soft click of a weapon being cocked.

"I have no desire to kill you or the child," he heard an unfamiliar voice announce quietly. "But if either of you moves, I will put a bullet through the little girl's head."

"Don't," Rasputin said calmly. "Shoot."

"He's trying to surrender," Morgan said quickly.

"I heard both of you," Vargas said, stepping into view and, with one hand, tossing two pairs of iron manacles onto the ground near the pair of Kithain.

"Put those on each other," he said. "Or I will pick one of you for an object lesson."

Rasputin's ears drooped sadly as he bent over to pick up both pairs of manacles. His fingers trembled when they touched the sickening iron. Smiling sadly, he held one of the pairs out to Morgan.

"Don't worry," he said, "they won't bother you at all."

Morgan braced herself for the nausea she knew she would feel as she took the cold iron chains in her hands.

Ryder screamed as his hand erupted with a fire that burned like the molten liquid behind him. The light

s h a d o w s   o n

in his hand blossomed into a brilliant band of dark blue light that pulsed as if it had a life of its own.

Tor aborted his attack when he saw the Dauntain drop his sword and stagger to one knee, clutching his hand. He waited for his enemy to regain control. Instead the Dauntain's cry of pain only intensified.

Ryder had only one thought on his mind, and that was to rip the gem from his hand. He dug his nails into his palm and tried to gouge the flesh that surrounded the glowing stone. He felt his hand grow slick with blood, but the sapphire remained firmly set in place. *This time it will never go away*, he thought, and the certain knowledge of that fact filled him with despair.

Tor watched helplessly as his erstwhile enemy now turned his killing rage against his own flesh.

"Oh God, oh God, oh God, please stop the pain!"

Private Tor Larssen held the bleeding soldier's head in his lap. The young man's body ended just past his hips, where a mangled bloody mass of flesh and splintered bones were all that remained of his legs. The battle was over, their attackers had finally all been killed or driven back into the jungle. Now only the groans of the wounded filled the tropical night.

Tor smoothed the soldier's forehead with his massive palm. The boy was dying, and he knew he was dying, but he wasn't dying fast enough. His screams had subsided into incoherent, pleading moans. With his free hand, Tor eased his pistol out of its holster at his side. With an expert's eye, he placed the barrel at the juncture between the jaw and the ear. Just before he pulled the trigger, he thought he heard the dying soldier murmur a word of thanks.

Tor blinked as the memory faded back into the smoky darkness of the present. Only the look in the eyes of

the hill

the agonized knight reminded him of that other war in that other jungle.

"Hold out your hand," Tor said.

Ryder wrenched his gaze upward and saw the troll looming above him, his double bladed ax held in an executioner's grip. With a sob that held within it both desolation and the promise of relief, Ryder laid his throbbing, burning hand flat against the ground. Without giving himself a chance to think, Tor brought the ax down quickly, barely feeling the impact of the keen steel blade against bone and flesh.

Ryder felt the pain vanish as the troll's ax severed his hand from his arm. A part of him knew that the old pain would soon be replaced with a new agony, but the sudden trauma to his nerves gave him a few moments of blissful numbness.

Tor bent down to grasp the Dauntain under his good arm, and pulled him to his feet. He intended to hoist his mutilated enemy onto his shoulders and carry him away from the burning river. The knight shook his head and stepped away from Tor.

"It's over," he said, his voice dull and hoarse from screaming. "I don't have to stay here anymore." He looked over his shoulder at the slow-moving flow of burning lava.

"No!" Tor thundered, trying to grab for the Dauntain.

Ryder gave the troll a weary smile and let himself fall backward into the molten stream.

"Got it!" Tor heard Edmund's voice nearby, but paid no attention as the redcap snatched up the severed hand and disappeared into the darkness.

Sick with sorrow, Tor watched the Dauntain's body explode into flame and slowly sink beneath the surface of the lava. For a brief moment, the troll thought he could see a gigantic, dragonlike form begin to emerge from the molten stream, engulfing his enemy's remains.

Tor blinked, and the vision was gone.

"I swear to God if you so much as try to fight me, I'll kill you for what you've done," Tor heard a woman call out from right behind him. He recognized the voice.

"I didn't kill him, Diana," Tor said, his voice cracked with pain. Without turning around, Tor dropped his ax.

"I don't care. He's dead, and I'm just waiting for an excuse to see to it that you join him."

"Morgan—" Tor began, remembering that he had taken on the Dauntain knight in order to protect his granddaughter.

"I'm all right, Grandpa," Morgan called from somewhere nearby. "Rasputin and I have surrendered. So have the others." Her voice was faint and trembly.

Tor let his hands fall to his sides and slowly turned around. "Don't move," Diana barked harshly. He felt the painful clank of an iron manacle close about his wrist.

"Put your other hand behind your back," Diana said.

Only when his hands were secured behind him did Diana order Tor to turn around to face her. She grabbed him by the collar of his tunic and pulled him toward the others.

Morgan tried to run to her grandfather, but Vargas put a hand on her shoulder and held her back. Instead, she smiled up at the troll, with tears in her eyes. "It's okay," she whispered. "Really, I'm all right." Tor nodded. Then, puzzled, he looked around, seeing Valmont, Rasputin, and Leigh seated on the ground around a dark-complexioned woman.

"This is Signe," Valmont said, looking up at his captor.

"Where's Edmund?" Tor asked suddenly.

"I thought he was with you," Leigh replied, her words coming slowly through a haze of pain.

"He was, but then he left just after—"

the hill

"Just after you pushed Ryder into the lava flow," Diana finished for him.

"I didn't kill him!" Tor insisted. "He wanted to die!"

"My grandfather doesn't lie!" Morgan told her hotly.

"Shut up, all of you," Vargas snapped. "The little brat got away like all the others."

The companions were herded down the slope of Kilauea to where a van was parked in the closest place accessible by vehicle. Diana held the back of the van open while Vargas nudged the five Kithain inside. Signe climbed into the van with the prisoners, while Diana shut the door, locking them in.

A few minutes later, the companions felt a lurch as the van started down the bumpy road.

"Where are we going?" Leigh asked, looking at Signe, who sat, cross-legged on the floor, her back against the van's double doors, a pistol across her lap.

"To a place where no one can find you," the Dauntain replied. "To a place where we will bring you to your senses, if we can."

"And kill us if you can't?" Valmont asked in a low, insistent voice.

"I didn't say that," Signe replied.

"My name is Eleighanara, and I am a sidhe of House Fiona," said Leigh. She looked at Morgan.

"I am Baroness Morgania of House Eiluned and I too am a sidhe," the childling said, her voice high and firm.

"Stop that," Signe said. "I know what you're doing."

One by one, they continued in turn.

"I am a child of the Dreaming, one of the wandering kith. I am called Valmont, but I have many names."

"I'm Tor, and I'm a troll."

"I was never called Rasputin in all my life. I am not a pooka, and I had a lovely childhood where no one ever hurt me before I became what I am today." He focused his large, soft eyes on Signe's delicate face.

"Stop it," she repeated, a note of pleading in her voice.

Valmont looked at her and smiled. Despite the jolting of the van, which slammed the chained Kithain into one another as the vehicle bumped its way down the narrow road, the eshu managed to look poised, as if this were his natural mode of travel.

"Thank you for helping me save Kanani," he said to Signe.

"Then you did get to her in time," Morgan said. "I was afraid we were too late."

Signe nodded. "I don't believe in killing," she said simply.

"Then how can you kill our faerie souls?" Morgan asked her.

"We're saving your sanity," the Dauntain replied.

"Yes," said Rasputin. "She's going to restore us to the joy of the life we knew before we became what we have always been," the pooka replied.

"No," Signe said. She closed her eyes and the image of Rasputin's face, haunted and terrified, filled her mind. She tried to suppress it, but her will was not strong enough.

"Do you know who we met after we defeated the troll together?" Valmont asked her.

Signe remembered the strange old lady. She also remembered the legends she had heard about Hawaii.

She nodded. "I know the legend of the goddess of the volcano," she said. "But that's only a myth."

"Then you came face to face with a myth," Valmont said, "and that myth was real, and that myth saved the life of a young girl who would have been consumed in the fires of the volcano without the help of both of us."

"Do you know what you're condemning us to?" Leigh wanted to know.

"Of course she doesn't," Rasputin said softly.

Slumping against her grandfather, Morgan started to cry.

Softly, Signe whispered, "His mortal name was Cyprian Ryder, but he was known to the Dreaming as Chevalier."

After a minute, Valmont looked up at her and smiled.

"I will remember," he said.

For awhile, no one else spoke. Rasputin leaned back against the side of the van and shut his eyes.

Signe watched the captives. *Ryder's dead*, she thought, *and he was the only thing that held me to this loathsome job of witchhunting. I did it for him.*

Once, Rasputin screamed, and then the sound was reduced to a soft whimpering. Signe thought she could make out the words "Papa, don't stop beating me!" between the frantic little cries.

It's not worth it, she thought. *He's better off inside his madness.* Her decision made, she reached into her pocket for the keys to the manacles.

The van pulled to a stop. Both Diana and Vargas got out to open the back door of the vehicle.

"It's time to switch guards," Diana began, and then stopped as Signe stepped out of the van, her pistol pointed at her heart.

"We made a mistake," Signe said. "It cost Ryder

his life. Now move away from the van before it costs us another."

"You won't shoot me," Diana said.

"Maybe not, but *I* will if I have to," Leigh replied, stepping out from behind Signe and placing her unchained hands carefully around the eshu's. "Now move aside."

Hesitant, Diana stepped back. Vargas belatedly raised his rifle. Leigh shoved herself and Signe out from in front of the door as Tor launched himself from the van to tackle him.

Vargas hit the ground hard, the breath knocked out of him. His rifle clattered to the dirt beside him. Valmont darted out and seized the weapon, hurling it as far away from him as he could manage.

Finally, Rasputin and Morgan stepped out from the van. Rasputin handed Signe the keys to the chains.

"He wants to say thank you," said Morgan, "but he can't."

Signe nodded. "The keys to the van are probably still in the ignition," she said. "Get out of here before I change my mind."

"Ryder said one of us might turn traitor," Diana said caustically. "I could have guessed it would be you."

"What are you going to do?" Morgan asked Signe. "You can't go back with them, can you?"

Signe looked first at Diana, then at the prone figure of Vargas, whom Valmont had secured with his own chains.

"I'll go somewhere," she said.

"Why don't you come with us?" Morgan offered.

Signe shook her head. "I'll find my own way," she said. "After all, I am one of the traveling Kithain."

Tor moved behind Diana.

"I'll help you get a head start," he said, and slammed his massive fist into the troll's lower jaw.

Diana dropped to the ground. "Sorry," Tor mumbled, looking a little ashamed.

"Let's go," said Valmont as he climbed into the van and turned the key. Leigh sat in the front seat beside him, while the rest of the companions piled into the back.

Signe watched them drive off before she, too, turned away and began walking in the opposite direction. Searching within herself, she found a trace of Glamour deep inside her. *An eshu knows how to get where she needs to be*, she reminded herself as she followed the pull of her destiny.

The companions at last drove into Hilo. They took a pair of adjoining rooms in the first hotel they could find with a vacancy, on the other side of the city from the Seacrest. It was a tourist trap that displayed a garish pair of neon palm trees above a sign that read *Twin Palms Motor Court*.

Exhaustion and hunger finally drove them into deep slumber.

Tor woke just before dawn. He rose from the bed of blankets and pillows he had made for himself on the floor and looked at the pair of strange men who occupied the twin beds in the seedy motel room. Puzzled, he checked his wallet, and found that he still had a few dollars left. There were some other things in the wallet as well, but hunger was the main thing on his mind.

I hate being homeless, he thought as he quietly left the room to wander the streets of Hilo until he found an open diner.

360

Morgan burst into tears when Valmont broke the news that Tor was missing.

"How could you let him just walk away?" she sobbed.

The eshu looked helplessly at Leigh, who knelt down and took the childling in her arms.

"We'll find him," she said. "Somehow, we'll find him. How hard can it be to locate a troll?"

"But that's just it," Morgan wailed. "He doesn't remember he's a troll. I should have stayed with him last night," she said. "I should have known that he wouldn't have enough Glamour left and that it would desert him in the night and that he'd not know where he was and—" she paused for breath and then gave way to a new flood of wordless tears.

Rasputin stood glumly in the doorway. He opened his mouth to say something, then thought better of it and simply shrugged.

"What do you think we should do?" Valmont asked. "You know that the gems are gone as well—the Keystone, the Shadowstone, and the blue one that Chevalier had."

"It's called the Waystone," Morgan sobbed. Her tears stopped abruptly. "That's its name," she whispered. Leigh stroked the childling's hair.

"The quest is over," she whispered. "I don't know where to go from here."

Morgan pulled away from Leigh and stood by herself in the center of the shabby room.

"It's not over," she said fiercely. "It's just been changed. We have a new quest—to find my grandfather and bring him back to the Dreaming."

"And then we'll all go home," Rasputin said.

the hill

Valmont took Morgan by the hand. "We need to eat," he said. "And we need to make some plans."

As they headed for the van, Morgan stopped suddenly. "It was Edmund who betrayed us," she said. "I had a dream way back when we were staying with the selkies, only I couldn't remember the traitor's name. It was Edmund."

Rasputin shook his head. "It wasn't us that he betrayed," he said.

"So when do I get my horse?" Edmund asked Yrtalien as the black swan ship pulled out of its hidden harbor north of Hilo and headed out toward the open sea. "And which gem do I get to keep?"

The prince looked at the redcap and tapped the neckpouch that now bulged with three of the four eyestones.

"I told you that I would keep my promise to you when you had demonstrated to me your worth," he said. "Glynnis can tell you that I am the one who decides when that occurs." He turned away from Edmund and Glynnis and walked toward the prow of the ship.

"Where's he taking us?" the redcap asked Glynnis. "Now that he's shut down his freehold, what claim has he got on being a prince, anyway?"

Glynnis flashed him a look of warning.

"Be careful what you say around him," she said. "More than any of us, he is a true son of Arcadia."

"What does that mean?" Edmund looked confused.

"It means that although he appears in mortal flesh, he is anything but human. He is wholly and

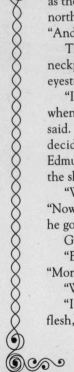

utterly of the fae."

"Bummer," Edmund said. He glanced about him cautiously to make sure that the prince was occupied with staring at the distant horizon. He shoved a hand into his pocket and felt for the pouch containing Mr. Dumpy. *Why didn't you warn me about him?* he thought fiercely. His fingers brushed against the small piece of lava he had impulsively retrieved from the edge of the battle on the slopes of the volcano.

"I went through a lot to get those stones for him," he muttered to Glynnis. "He hasn't even said thank you. I feel used." He lowered his head as he felt the unfamiliar sting of tears welling up in his eyes. He blinked hard to push them back.

Glynnis moved to pat him on the head. "Welcome to the club," she replied.

the hill

biography

A native of Appalachia, Jackie Cassada has spent most of her life (with the exception of a ten-year sojourn in Boston) in the Blue Ridge Mountains. An avid reader, in college she majored in English with a specialty in Victorian literature. Her discovery of role-playing games in 1978 resulted in rediscovering a talent for "let's pretend" and an appreciation for the art of oral storytelling.

She has been the science fiction columnist for *Library Journal* since 1984. In 1993, she began working as a freelance writer for White Wolf's **Wraith: The Oblivion** and other games in the **Storyteller** ™ system, and her short stories have appeared in White Wolf's fiction collections **Death and Damnation, Truth Until Paradox, City of Darkness: Unseen,** and **The Splendour Falls.**

Besides writing, she has played in several rock, folk rock and traditional folk bands, worked as a "techie" for local college and community theatres, and collaborated on the musical score for an adaptation of *Pinocchio* for children's theatre. She currently works as a member of the administrative support staff for the Asheville-Buncombe Library System.

She shares a house in Asheville, North Carolina with a long-time companion and five demanding cats. **Shadows on the Hill** is her second novel.

a **trilogy** of **novels**	a series of corresponding sourcebooks

for the storytelling game
changeling: the dreaming

immortal eyes: shadows on the hill,
a sourcebook for **changeling: the
dreaming,** details the people and places of
this novel. Live the adventure as the
characters begin to discover the full scope
of the unseelie conspiracy.

- Features three mini-stories that mesh with
  the **immortal eyes chronicle.**
- Describes the Hawaiian freeholds
  and inhabitants.
- Includes crossover information for
  **vampire: the masquerade,
  werewolf: the apocalypse,**
  and **mage: the ascension.**